# CHILDREN OF GEBELAWI

# Children of Gebelawi

## NAGUIB MAHFOUZ

### Translated by Philip Stewart

**HEINEMANN**
LONDON

Heinemann Educational Books Ltd
22 Bedford Square, London WC1B 3HH

IBADAN NAIROBI
EDINBURGH MELBOURNE AUCKLAND
HONG KONG SINGAPORE KUALA LUMPUR NEW DELHI
KINGSTON PORT OF SPAIN

ISBN 0 435 90225 3 (AWS)
ISBN 0 435 99415 8 (AA)

Published in the United States of America 1981
by Three Continents Press
4201 Cathedral Avenue, N.W.
Washington, D.C.
ISBN 0 89410 213 3

Set in 9pt Times
Set printed and bound in Great Britain by
Cox & Wyman Ltd Reading

# CONTENTS

# *Translator's Introduction*

It is not often that preachers lead their flocks into the streets to shout for the banning of a novel hailed by many as a masterpiece, nor that the editor of a great newspaper has to rely on his friendship with the Head of State to ensure that a serial is published uncut to the end. But this is what happened in Nasser's Egypt in 1959 when the semi-official *Al-Ahram* printed 'Children of Gebelawi' by Naguib Mahfouz. So great was the uproar that no Egyptian publisher dared bring it out in book form, and for years it passed from hand to hand in the newspaper version. It was only in 1967, and in Lebanon, that it was at last made available, slightly expurgated, by Dar-al-Adab.

The reason for these strong reactions was that Naguib Mahfouz had boldly taken up the issues that most deeply divide Egypt and, perhaps, the world. The successive heroes of his imaginary Cairo alley relive unawares the lives of Adam, Moses, Jesus and Mohammed; and their aged ancestor, Gebelawi, represents God, or rather 'not God, but a certain idea of God that men have made', as Mahfouz put it in the course of discussion with me, so that his fate takes on a dreadful significance. Most readers became so passionately involved that they could see in the novel only their own ideology, or that of their most hated opponents, though a closer study would have shown them that the book has many dimensions and that its interpretation is no simple task.

Mahfouz confounded friends and foes alike by his choice of subject. He had earned a reputation for himself as 'the Galsworthy of Egypt', particularly with his *Trilogy*, which he completed in 1952 and for which he shared the State Prize for Literature in 1957. Why now did this chronicler of social history turn to a religious theme? A second look at his earlier work shows that his spiritual preoccupations were by no means new. Even in *Midaq Alley* (available in English as number 2 of Heinemann's Arab Authors series), first published in 1947 and often superficially described as 'Dickensian' – though Mahfouz admits to never having managed to read more than half a Dickens novel – the two key figures are Radwan Hussainy, 'who stepped lightly over the sorrows of the world, his heart soaring towards heaven as he embraced all men in his love', and Sheikh Darwish, 'who had abandoned family, friends and acquaintances, and had wandered off into the world of God'. Similarly, in the works published since 1959 Mahfouz has returned again and again to the subjects of illusion and reality, hallucination and mystic enlightenment, most notably in *Zaabalawi* (translated in volume 3 of Arab Authors) which is the author's gloss on Gebelawi.

Naguib Mahfouz was born in 1911 in Gemalia and lived there till the age of six. Its sights and sounds and smells were to provide him with the setting for all the works written between the pharaonic novels of 1939 to 1944 and the 'post-revolutionary' writings of 1960 onwards. He did a degree in philosophy, but turned aside from a university career feeling that it would take him away from his vocation of writer. All his books have been produced in the spare time left to him by his jobs: in the University Secretariat (1936–39), in the Ministry of Religious Affairs (1939–54) and in the Ministry of Culture (from 1954; the year in which he also married and moved from his mother's home).

With the Revolution of 1952, occurring just after he had finished writing the *Trilogy*, he felt 'that the world I had made it my mission to describe had disappeared', as he told me. For five years he wrote nothing; then, in 1957, seized by a new and original literary plan, whose genesis he is unable to explain, he set to work on *Children of Gebelawi*. In it he was to take the reader one last time into his vanished world. Now, though, it was no longer the Gemalia of recent history, assailed by wireless and Marxism and British soldiers, but a half imaginary society, cut off from outside events and influences, a distillation of the old Cairo, depicted with a wealth of detail.

Gebelawi Alley is situated on the frontier between real districts of Cairo and a fictitious 'Mukattam Desert' (which is occupied in fact by the endless cities of the dead, in which the 'houses' are family tombs). On the eastern horizon looms a real mountain, Gebel Mukattam, whose brooding presence gives animist undertones to the name of Gebelawi, which means 'Mountain Dweller'. Over it all hangs the sky, ever changing and rarely forgotten despite the fact that so much of the action takes place in dark rooms, cramped courtyards and narrow alleys. This attention to the heavens, like so many other details, is by no means incidental but points to the deeper meaning of the book.

## Notes on the translation

The language of daily life in Cairo is the dialect of Lower Egypt – a colourful variety of Arabic, which people take pleasure in using with wit and imagination. Mahfouz writes in literary Arabic, a modern version of the classical language, which is altogether more deliberate, not to say solemn. In this novel, he comes nearer than ever before to combining the virtues of both. Much of the dialogue would need only changes of syntax to be turned into spoken Egyptian, and there are many songs, rhymes and proverbs that are given in straight colloquial Arabic. This translation aims to produce a similar effect in the English dialogue, while in the narrative passages an attempt is made to transmit the local colour without resorting to footnotes and the transliteration of Arabic words. The spelling of proper names is intended to convey as nearly as possible the Cairo pronunciation, though without the glottal stop. The names Gebel, Gebelawi and Gebel Mukattam are of particular importance for their symbolism, and the spelling chosen is intended to allow either the Cairo pronunciation with g as in 'get' or the standard Arabic with g as in 'gem', and to recall both the jebels and djebels familiar in Arab place names and the corresponding gebels of the Old Testament. The Arabic vowel, however, is closer to that of 'jab'.

## Acknowledgements

I owe special thanks to Naguib Mahfouz for his friendship and encouragement, to Professor A. F. L. Beeston for help unstintingly given all along the road, and to Professor Fatma Moussa-Mahmoud for many useful suggestions. Thanks are also due to Mrs Nihad Salem who explained many obscure points, to Mrs Iskander of the American University in Cairo library for helping in countless ways and to Mr A. H. Hourani of St Antony's College, Oxford for his valuable criticism. Mention must also be made of Professor Marsden Jones, my academic supervisor while I worked on the translation in Cairo in 1962. Finally, it was my wife Lucile who saved my typescript from oblivion, teased me into revising it and patiently typed the new version.

PHILIP STEWART
St. Cross College
Oxford

# *Prologue*

This is the story of our alley, or these are its stories. I myself have lived only through the most recent events, but I have written down everything as it is told by our many professional storytellers who learnt them in the cafés or from their fathers.

The tales are told on a thousand and one occasions. Whenever people are wronged or injured they point to the Big House at the top of the alley, where it meets the desert, and say sadly: 'There is our ancestor's house. We are all his children and we all have a right to his estate; why should we be hungry and wretched?' Then they tell the stories of the great heroes of our alley: Adham and Gebel, Rifaa and Kassem . . .

Our ancestor lived so long, far longer than any normal man, that he became proverbial. He had withdrawn to his house long ago, and after that no one saw him at all. The story of his age and his isolation is almost unbelievable, and imagination or wishful thinking no doubt helped the legend to grow. However that may be, his name was Gebelawi – Mountain Man – and our alley is named after him. He was the owner of all the property held in trust for it, the master of all that stood on its soil and of all the surrounding desert.

I once heard a man say of him: 'From him came our alley, from which came Cairo, mother of the world. He lived here alone when it was desert and mastered it by the strength of his arm and by forcing the respect of the Governor. Time will not bring another man like him. He was a chief so tough that wild animals cringe at the mention of him.' I heard someone else say of him: 'He was a true chief, not like others. He never extorted protection money from anyone, nor did he strut about the world proudly, and he was merciful to the weak.'

Then came a time when a few people spoke of him in a tone which did not befit his power and importance; such is the way of the world. I myself have always found conversation about him fascinating, never for

1

a moment dull. Many a time it made me go and walk round the Big House in the hope of catching a glimpse of him, but always in vain. I have often stood in front of the huge gate, gazing at the stuffed crocodile mounted over it, or sat in the desert of Mukattam, not far from the great wall, able to see only the tops of the mulberry and fig and palm trees that hide the house, and a few shuttered windows without any sign of life. Was it not sad to have such a forebear without our ever seeing him, nor he us? Was it not strange that he should be hidden away in this great, locked house, while we lived outside in the dust? If you are curious to know how all this came about, listen now to the stories of Adham and Gebel and Rifaa and Kassem. They will bring you no comfort.

As I said, no one saw our ancestor after his withdrawal, but that did not matter at all to most people. From the beginning they were only interested in his estate and in the famous ten conditions attached to it. This is the source of the conflict that has been raging ever since I was born and has grown more dangerous with every generation. But I do not want any sarcastic comment when I point out that our people have always been one family, into which no outsider has ever married. Everyone knows everyone, both men and women, yet no alley has known such savage feuds as ours. For every one man who tries to do good you will find ten chiefs brandishing their cudgels and looking for a fight, so people are accustomed to buying security with protection money and with submission and servility. They are severely punished for the slightest wrong word or deed, or even for looking as if they think the wrong thoughts.

The remarkable thing is that people in neighbouring parts, such as Otouf and Kafr el Zeghari and Derrasa and Husseinia, envy us and talk of our inexhaustable estate and our unbeatable chiefs. This is all true, but they do not realize that we are as poor as beggars, that we live amidst filth and flies and lice, that we have to be content with crumbs, and that we go about half-naked. They see these chiefs of ours swaggering along and are overcome with admiration, forgetting how they trample on us. Our only consolation is to look at the Big House and say, 'There lives Gebelawi, the owner of our estate. He is our ancestor; we are all his children.'

I have witnessed the latest period of our history and lived through the events brought about by Arafa, a worthy son of the alley. It is thanks to one of Arafa's friends that I am writing our story. He said to me one day: 'You are one of the few who can write. Why not set down the story of the alley? Until now it has been told in any old order and each storyteller twists it his own way. It would be worth a great deal if you could put it all together in one trustworthy book for our convenience. I shall help you with secret information.'

2

So I got busy carrying out the idea, partly because I was satisfied that it was a good one and partly out of friendship for the man who suggested it. I am the first in the alley to have made a profession of writing, although it earned me a great deal of scorn and sarcasm. My job is to write down the complaints of those who are oppressed or in need. Although many unfortunate people come to me, I have been unable to raise myself above the general level of our beggars; but I have gained a heart-breaking knowledge of many people's secret sorrows. However, I am not writing about myself and my troubles, which are nothing compared with those of the alley.

Amazing little alley with your amazing events; how did it all begin? What was it all about? Who were these heroes of yours?

# Adham

✳ ✳ ✳ ✳ ✳ ✳ ✳ ✳ ✳ ✳ ✳ ✳ ✳ ✳ ✳ ✳ ✳ ✳ ✳ ✳

In the beginning the site of our alley was part of the desert at the foot of the mountain Gebel Mukattam. Nothing stood in this desert save the Big House that Gebelawi had built in defiance of fear and barbarism and banditry. Its towering wall enclosed a garden to the west and the house with its three storeys to the east.

One day the master of the house summoned his sons to the downstairs drawing-room, which opened on the terrace. All his sons came, Idris, Abbas, Radwaan, Gelil and Adham, wearing silk smocks. They stood in front of him, with such respect that they hardly dared look at him directly. He told them to be seated, and they sat down on the chairs arranged round him. For a while he searched them with his piercing eyes; then he stood up and went over to the great door on to the terrace and gazed out at the huge garden, crowded with mulberry and fig and palm trees, up which climbed henna and jasmine and whose branches thronged with singing birds. The garden was full of life and song, but in the room there was silence. It seemed to the brothers that the chief of the desert had forgotten them. With his great height and breadth he seemed superhuman, a being from another world. They looked at each other wondering what it could be; he used to be like this when he made an important decision. They were worried, because he was as despotic at home as he was outside, and in his presence they were nothing. He turned towards them without moving from the spot where he stood and his voice boomed, filling the whole room though its walls were hung with tapestries and rugs:

'I think it will be best for someone else to manage the estate instead of me.'

He examined their faces again, but their expressions betrayed nothing. Managing the estate was not a prospect to please young men who liked leisure and amusement. However that might be, Idris, the eldest son, was the obvious choice; none of them thought twice about that. Idris said to himself: 'What a nuisance, all those holdings and those beastly tenants!'

Gebelawi went on:

'I have chosen your brother Adham to manage the estate under my supervision.'

Their faces changed at this sudden shock, and they exchanged furtive glances of consternation, except for Adham who looked at the floor in shame and confusion. Gebelawi turned his back on them and said impassively:

'That is why I sent for you.'

Idris was very angry and was carried away with hatred. His brothers looked at him unhappily, and silently resented the rebuff to Idris which was moreover a blow to their own honour. Idris said, in a voice so calm that it might have been someone else's:

'But father . . .'

His father turned quickly round to face them.

'But?'

They all looked down, in case he should read their thoughts, except Idris who said with determination:

'But I am the eldest.'

Gebelawi said angrily:

'I'm aware of that; I am your father.'

'The eldest has rights that can't be set aside without good reason.'

Gebelawi gave him a long look, as if to leave him a chance to change his mind, then said:

'I assure you I have made my choice for everybody's good.'

Idris's patience was at an end. He knew that opposition enraged his father and that he must expect worse things if he persisted, but he was so furious that he did not give a thought to the consequences. He strode across to Adham till he was almost on top of him, puffed himself up like a cock in full display, to show them how much bigger and better and more splendid he was than his brother, and shouted:

'I and my full brothers are sons of a fine lady, an aristocrat, but this fellow is the son of a black maid.'

Adham's brown face paled, but he sat quite still. Gebelawi shook his fist and said menacingly:

'Behave yourself, Idris.'

But Idris was wild with fury. He roared:

'He's the youngest of us, too; give me one reason why you should prefer him to me. Is this the age of servants and slaves?'

'Hold your tongue, you idiot, for your own sake.'

'I would rather you cut my hand off than humiliate me.'

Radwaan looked up and said very gently:

'We are your sons, and we're right to be upset if we lose your favour. But you have the last word; all we want is to know the reason ...'

Gebelawi turned to Radwaan, keeping calm for some reason, and said:

'Adham knows the tenants and most of their names. He also knows how to write and do sums.'

Idris and his brothers were amazed by their father's statement. Since when had knowing the masses been a distinction by which a man won preferment? And going to school, was that a distinction too? Would Adham's mother have sent him to school unless she had despaired of his succeeding in the world of chiefs? Idris said bitterly:

'Is that a reason for humiliating me?'

Gebelawi waved this aside angrily:

'It is my will, all you need do is accept it. What do you others say?'

Abbas could not bear his father's look; he said heavily:

'I obey you.'

Gelil looked at the floor and did not hesitate.

'You have spoken, father.'

Radwaan swallowed hard.

'Anything you say.'

Idris laughed angrily and his face was horribly twisted. He shouted:

'Cowards! I knew you would just surrender. Because you have no guts this son of a black slave will push you around.'

Gebelawi thundered:

'Idris!'

But Idris was out of his mind and shouted:

'What sort of a father are you? A bullying chief, that's all you are! You deal with us, your sons, the same way as with your other victims.'

Gebelawi took two pondeorus steps forward and said quietly:

'Hold your tongue!'

But Idris went on:

'You're not going to frighten me; you know I can't be frightened. And if you want to raise that son of a slave above me, you can't expect any sweet nonsense about obedience from me.'

'Don't you know what impudence leads to, you damned idiot?'

'The real damned idiot is that son of a slave.'

Gebelawi bellowed:

'She's my wife, you fool. Now behave yourself or I'll wipe the floor with you.'

The other brothers were terrified, Adham as much as any of them, for they knew the tyrant's violence. But Idris thought no more of danger. He shouted:

'You hate me. I didn't realize, but there's no doubt you hate me. Perhaps it was that slave-girl who made you hate us; you are lord of the wilderness, owner of the estate, the dreaded Chief, but a slave-girl can play with you. Tomorrow people will be saying all sorts of interesting things about you, lord of the desert!'

'I told you to hold your tongue, damn you!'

'Don't insult me for Adham's sake; even the rocks will protest against that. Your crazy decision is going to make us the laughing-stock of all the neighbourhood.'

Gebelawi shouted in a voice so loud that it was heard all over the garden and in the women's quarters:

'Get out of my sight!'

'This is my home and my mother's home, and she is its true mistress.'

'You will never be seen here again, never.'

His great face darkened and he trembled and clenched his granite fists. They all knew the end had come for Idris. It would be just one more of the tragedies that the house had witnessed silently. So many fine ladies had been turned by a single word into miserable beggars. So many men had reeled out after long service, carrying on their bare backs the marks of leaded whips, bleeding at nose and mouth. The respect which protects everyone when all is well is of no avail to anyone, however important, when tempers are lost. And so they all knew the end had come for Idris – Idris of all people, the eldest, his father's equal in strength and good looks! Gebelawi took two steps towards him, and said:

'You are not my son and I am not your father. This is not your home, and you have here no mother, no brothers and no servants. In front of you is the world. Go, with my anger and my curse. Time will teach you your true importance as you wander aimlessly, stripped of my love and my care.'

Idris stamped his foot on the Persian carpet:

'This is my home, and I am not going to leave it.'

His father was upon him before he could defend himself and seized his shoulder in a tight grip. He forced Idris backwards, stumbling, through the door on to the terrace and down the steps, then hustled him down the path, roofed over with roses and henna and jasmine, to the great gate. He thrust him out, locked the gate and shouted in a voice that was heard by everyone in the house:

'Death to any man who helps him or allows him to come back!'

He raised his eyes to the shuttered windows of the women's quarters.

'Immediate divorce for any woman who helps him!'

From that sad day on, Adham went every morning to work in the estate office in the garden house beside the Big House. He worked hard, collecting the rents for the holdings, giving out shares to beneficiaries and presenting the accounts to his father. In his dealings with the tenants he showed discretion and tact, and they liked him, though they were known for their rudeness and aggression.

The conditions according to which the estate was run were a secret known only to his father. By choosing Adham to manage it Gebelawi aroused the fear that he was preparing to prefer him in his will. In fact he had never before shown any favouritism between his sons. The brothers had lived in peace and harmony thanks to their father's fairness and their respect for him. Even Idris, in spite of his occasional excesses, had never been unpleasant to any of his brothers before that day. He was a generous, good-tempered boy, lovable and easy to admire. The four older brothers may perhaps have had a secret sense of the distance between themselves and Adham, the half brother, but none of them showed it, and there had never been any hint of insulting words or behaviour on their part. Adham may have felt this distance more than they, and may have compared his dark skin with their fair ones, his weakness with their strength, or his lowly mother with their noble one. He may have suffered on account of this some sorrow, some inward pain. But the atmosphere of the house, sweetened by aromatic herbs, submissive to the fathers' power and wisdom, had not allowed him to have any persistent feeling of unhappiness, and he had grown up pure in heart and mind.

Adham said to his mother before he first went to the estate office:

'Give me your blessing, mother. This work is just a test for you and me.'

She replied humbly:

'May success go with you, my child; you are a good son, and good people succeed in the end.'

So Adham went to the garden house, followed by many pairs of eyes in the drawing room, in the garden and at the windows. He sat down on the manager's seat and began his work. His was the most responsible position held by anyone in that desert area between Mount Mukattam in the east and Old Cairo in the west. Adham made reliability his motto, and wrote down every piastre in the ledger for the first time in the estate's history. He used to give his brothers their allowances with a tact that made them forget their resentment. Then he would take his father the money he had collected.

One day his father asked him:

'Adham, how do you find the work?'

'As long as you give it to me, it will remain the most important thing in my life.'

A smile spread across his father's broad face, for in spite of his harsh nature, he was softened by flattery. Adham used to love being with him, and would sit looking up at him admiringly. He used to enjoy it when his father told him and his brothers of the old days and of his youthful adventures as a chief: how he had gone round in these parts, brandishing his terrible cudgel and mastering every spot he trod on.

After Idris was driven out, Abbas, Radwaan and Gelil kept up their old practice of meeting on the roof of the house, eating and drinking and gambling. But Adham only liked sitting in the garden, and playing on his pipe. He continued this after he took over the affairs of the estate, although it no longer took up most of his time. After he had finished the day's work he used to spread out a rug beside a stream, lean his back against the trunk of a palm or fig tree or lie down beneath a canopy of jasmine, and rest, watching all the doves and the song birds. Then he would play his pipe, imitating their trilling and cooing, or he would gaze up through the branches at the sky.

His brother Radwaan once came upon him when he was lying there like this. He eyed him scornfully and said:

'What a waste of time, all those hours you have to worry about managing the estate!'

Adham smiled.

'If I wasn't afraid of annoying father I might complain.'

'Thank God for leisure.'

'I hope you enjoy it.'

Radwaan smiled to hide his annoyance and said:

'Wouldn't you love to be like us again?'

'I perfer being in the garden with my reed pipe.'

Radwaan said bitterly:

'Idris would have loved to work.'

Adham looked down:

'Idris never had any time for work; it was for other reasons that he went berserk. But real happiness, now; you will find that here in the garden.'

When Radwaan had gone Adham said to himself: 'The garden, with its song birds and its water and the evening casting its spell on me – that's the real life. But it's as if I was looking for something. What can it be? The pipe almost tells me sometimes; but I still don't know the answer. If only the birds spoke my language, they would surely tell me. And the stars too must have something to say. As for collecting the rent, it clashes with the music.'

Adham stood one day looking at his shadow on the path beside the roses when suddenly another shadow grew out of the side of his own, announcing that someone had come round the corner behind him. He turned and saw a dark girl about to retreat on discovering him. He signalled her to stop, and she did so. He took a good look at her, then asked her gently:

'Who are you?'

'Om . . . Om . . . Omayma.'

He remembered the name; she was a servant, a relative of his mother, who must have been just like this before she married. He felt like talking to her and asked:

'What has brought you to the garden?'

Her eyelids dropped as she replied:

'I thought it was empty.'

'But you women are not allowed here.'

Her voice was almost inaudible.

'I have done wrong, sir.'

She retreated round the corner. Then he heard her running away. He murmured, deeply moved: 'You lovely girl!' He felt that he had never been more one of the creatures of the garden than he was now, and that the roses, the jasmine and the carnations, the song birds, the doves and he himself were part of one great melody. He said to himself: 'Omayma is lovely – even her thick lips. All my brothers are married, except proud Idris. How like me she is in colour, and how beautiful it was to see her shadow grow out of mine, as if she was part of my body with its confusion of desires. My father will not disapprove of my choice, or how could he have married my mother?'

## 3 * * * * * * * * * * * * * * * * * *

Adham returned to his work enraptured. He tried hard to concentrate on the day's accounts, but all he could see was the image of the brown girl. It was not surprising that he had not seen her before, as the women's quarters in this house were like a man's heart, of whose existence he knows and by virtue of which he lives but which he never sees. Adham gave himself over completely to rosy daydreams, until he was wrenched out of them by a thunderous voice so loud that it seemed to be coming from the garden house itself.

'Here I am in the desert, Gebelawi, cursing you all. A curse on the heads of your men and your women! I defy anyone to disagree with me. Do you hear me, Gebelawi?'

Adham shouted 'Idris!' and went out of the garden house into the garden. He saw Radwaan coming towards him. Radwaan said before he could speak:

'Idris is drunk. I saw him from the window, staggering about. What further scandals can fate have in store for our family?'

Adham closed his eyes with pain:

'My brother, it breaks my heart.'

'What's to be done? This could bring disaster.'

'Don't you think we should talk to father about it?'

'Father never goes back on his word. Idris's present state would only anger him even more.'

Adham groaned:

'What can make up for all this?'

'The women are crying in their quarters. Abbas and Gelil are so upset that they've shut themselves in their rooms. Father is alone in his room and no one dares go near him.'

Adham asked anxiously:

'Don't you think we should do something?'

'Of course, we all want peace, but the surest way to lose it is to want it at any price. I'm risking nothing, not even if the heavens fall. As for the family's good name, Idris is already dragging it in the dust.'

'Then why did you come to me?' All of a sudden Adham felt as much out of place as an owl amongst ravens. He said:

'I am innocent in all this. But life won't seem any good to me if I say nothing.'

Radwaan said as he was about to go:

'There are plenty of reasons why *you* should do something.'

He went off and Adham was left on his own with the phrase echoing in his ears: 'There are plenty of reasons . . .'

Yes. The blame fell on him though he was innocent. Whenever anyone was sorry for Idris, he cursed Adham. Adham went to the gate, opened it quietly, and slipped out. He saw Idris not far off, reeling round in circles and rolling his eyes. His hair was tangled, and the front of his smock was open showing his hairy chest. When his eyes fell upon Adham he sprang to the attack, like a cat that has sighted a mouse; but drink had fuddled him and he fell to the ground. He filled his hand with soil and threw it at Adham, hitting him on the chest and dirtying his coat. Adham called gently to him:

'Brother!'

Idris raved as he swayed:

'Shut up you dog, you son of a bitch! You are not my brother, and your father is not my father, and I am going to bring down this house over your heads.'

Adham said with true affection:

'You are the finest and noblest son of this house.'

Idris laughed a hollow laugh and shouted:

'Why did you come out, son of a slave-girl? Run back to mummy and take her down to the servants' quarters.'

Adham said as warmly as ever:

'Don't get carried away by anger, and don't close the door to your friends.'

Idris shook his fist and said:

'Damned house! Only cowards can be happy in it – people who accept scraps humbly and love being crushed. I will never return to a house in which you are master. Tell your father I am living in the desert he came from, and that I have become a bandit like he was, and a bad, quarrelsome criminal like he is. Wherever I go, smashing things up, people point to me and say "Gebelawi's son". And so I shall drag you through the mud, you who think you're lords when you're really robbers.'

'Snap out of it, brother, don't say things you'll be sorry for. The way is not closed to you. I swear things will go back to what they were.'

Idris came one step towards him, as slowly as if he were walking against a gale:

'What will you swear by, son of a slave?'

Adham looked at him carefully.

'By brotherhood!'

'Brotherhood! I stuffed that down the first lavatory I came across.'

'Before now I have only heard good from you.'

'Your father's tyranny has taught me to speak the truth.'

'I hope nobody sees you in this state.'

Idris let out a drunken laugh.

'They will see me in a worse state every day. Shame and evil and scandal will haunt you because of me. Your father chased me out shamelessly and he must bear the consequences.'

He flung himself at Adham, who side-stepped so that Idris almost fell to the ground, but he managed to hold himself up against the wall. He stood there choking with rage and searching the ground for stones. Adham retreated quietly to the gate and went in. His eyes swam with tears. Idris's shouts still went on. Adham turned reluctantly towards the terrace, and saw his father through the door, crossing the drawing-room. He walked up to his father – who did not see him coming – too sad to be afraid. Gebelawi looked at him with expressionless eyes. He was standing, tall and broad-shouldered, in front of a picture painted in an alcove on the far wall of the room. Adham said with a slight bow:

'Good morning!'

Gebelawi probed him deeply with his look, and then said, in a voice that pierced him to the heart:

'Explain why you have come.'

Adham almost whispered:

'Father, my brother Idris . . .'

His father cut him short with a voice like iron on flint:

'Don't ever mention his name in front of me! Get back to your work.'

4 ✳ ✳ ✳ ✳ ✳ ✳ ✳ ✳ ✳ ✳ ✳ ✳ ✳ ✳ ✳ ✳ ✳ ✳ ✳ ✳

The days and nights passed in the desert, and Idris fell deeper and deeper into disgrace, adding some new antics to his record every day. He would prowl round the house, hurling the foulest insults at it; or he would sit near the gate, as naked as the day he was born, pretending to sunbathe and singing the lewdest songs; or he would wander about the near-by districts, swaggering along, provoking the passers-by with offensive stares, and picking a quarrel with anyone who got in his way. People whispered to one another, 'Gebelawi's son'. He had no worries about meals; he would simply grab the food where he found it, in a restaurant or on a cart, eat till he was full, then go off without payment or thanks. When he felt like revelling he would go into the first tavern he came across, and keep ordering liquor until he was drunk. Then his tongue would be loosened and he would pour forth his family's secrets, its peculiar habits and its cowardliness, winding up to his rebellion against his father, the greatest tyrant in all these parts. Then he would start joking to lose himself in laughter, and perhaps singing and dancing. His happiness was complete if the night's entertainment ended with a fight. Then off he would go, shouting greetings at everyone.

He became well known everywhere for this way of life, and people avoided him if they could, but they accepted him like a natural disaster. The family was deeply pained by all this. Sorrow overcame Idris's mother and she sickened and lay dying. Gebelawi came to take leave of her, and she pointed at him an accusing hand, which showed no sign of disease. She died of grief and resentment, and sorrow entangled the family in its net. The brothers' evenings on the roof came to an end, and Adham's pipe was silent in the garden.

One day their father burst out again. The victim this time was a woman. He raised his great voice to curse a maid called Nargis and chased her out of the house. He had learnt that the girl was pregnant and he interrogated her till she confessed that Idris had seduced her before his expulsion. So Nargis left the house, wailing and beating her cheeks, and wandered about all day long until Idris came across her. He took her in tow without either welcome or rebuff, treating her like an object that might come in useful later.

But there comes a day when every misfortune, however grave, is accepted. So life began to return to normal in the Big House, just as people return to the homes that an earthquake forces them to leave. Radwaan and Abbas and Gelil went back to their parties on the roof, while Adham started to spend his evenings in the garden again, whispering through his flute. He found that Omayma lit up his thoughts and warmed his feelings, and the picture of her shadow embracing his was firmly printed on his imagination. He went to see his mother in her room, where she was making a shawl, and he confided in her.

'It's Omayma, mother, your relative.'

His mother smiled a pale smile which showed that her happiness at the news could not overcome the pain of her illness.

'Yes, Adham, she is a good girl; she will be as good for you as you will be for her. She will make you happy, please God.'

When she saw the blush of pleasure on his cheeks, she went on:

'You mustn't court her yet, my child, or you'll spoil everything. I shall speak to your father about it. Perhaps I shall have the joy of seeing your children before I die.'

When Gebelawi summoned him into his presence, Adham found him smiling so sweetly that he said to himself, 'The only thing equal to father's sternness is his kindness.' Then his father said:

'So you're looking for a wife, Adham; how time flies! This house despises the poor; but you are honouring your mother by choosing Omayma. Perhaps you will produce some good children; Idris is lost, and Abbas and Gelil are childless, and none of Radwaan's children has lived so far, and all that any of them has inherited from me is my pride. So fill the house with your children; otherwise my life will have been in vain.'

The district had never seen anything like the bridegroom's procession of Adham. Even today, the memory of it is still proverbial in the alley. That night, lamps were hung from the branches of the trees and from the walls, so that the house was an oasis of light in the darkness. A pavilion was erected on the roof for the musicians and dancers. Food and drink were set out in the drawing-room and the garden and outside by the entrance gate.

The procession started out from the far end of Gemalia soon after midnight. It was joined by everyone who loved or feared Gebelawi, till it included the whole district. Adham strode along in a silk smock and a brocaded scarf, between Abbas and Gelil, with Radwaan in front. To the right and left people carried candles and flowers. In front went a great troop of singers and dancers. The singing rang out, accompanied by the sounds of the band, by the greetings shouted out by the admirers of Gebelawi and Adham, and by the women's youyous, awakening the whole district. The procession wound its way from Gemalia through Otouf and Kafr el Zaghari and Mabyada. Even the girls came out to join in the welcome. Many people did the stick dance and other dances, and the taverns handed out free drink, so that even the servants got drunk. The pipe was handed round free to the guests at all the hashish dens, and the air was thick with hashish smoke.

Suddenly Idris appeared at the end of the road, like a demon emerging from the darkness. At the corner leading to the desert he was lit up by the torches at the head of the procession. The torchbearers stopped dead and Idris's name was whispered around. The singers caught sight of him, and fear stopped up their throats. The dancers saw him and froze in their tracks. At once the drums fell silent, the pipes died away, and the laughter ceased. Many people wondered what to do; if they yielded to him they would not be safe, but if they attacked him they would be attacking the son of Gebelawi. Idris brandished his cudgel and shouted:

'Whose is this procession, you cowardly scum?'

There was a deathly hush, and all necks were craned towards Adham and his brothers. Idris asked again:

'When did you make friends with the slave-girl's son and with his father?'

At that Radwaan came forward a few steps and cried out:

'Brother, you would be wise to let the procession pass.'

Idris scowled:

'You should be the last to speak, Radwaan, you traitor, you son of a coward, you weakling; you sold your honour and your brother for an easy life.'

'There's no need to quarrel in front of everybody. People aren't interested in our disagreements.'

Idris roared with laughter.

'Everybody knows what villains you are; if they weren't such thorough cowards, you wouldn't have found a single musician or singer for your procession.'

Radwaan said with determination:

'Your father has entrusted your brother to us; we must defend him.'

Idris laughed again, and asked.

'Do you think you can defend yourself, let alone the slave-girl's son?'

'Where is your commonsense, brother? You will get back to the house only by being wise.'

'You're a liar, and you know it.'

'I shan't blame you as far as I'm concerned, but now let the procession pass in peace.'

Idris's answer was to hurl himself on the procession like a mad bull. His cudgel began to rise and fall, smashing torches, bursting drums, scattering flowers. The people panicked and fled like chaff before the wind. Radwaan, Abbas and Gelil stood shoulder to shoulder in front of Adham and warded off the wrath of Idris.

'Cowards, you defend the man you hate for fear of losing your food and drink.'

He rushed upon them, and they retreated, taking his blows on their sticks without trying to retaliate. Suddenly he threw himself between them, forcing his way to where Adham stood. The clamour from the windows rose to a peak, and Adham, getting ready to defend himself, shouted:

'Idris! I'm not your enemy. Come to your senses.'

Idris raised his cudgel. At that moment someone yelled 'Gebelawi!', and Radwaan shouted to Idris:

'Your father is coming . . .'

Idris leapt to the side of the road and turned to see Gebelawi coming surrounded by a ring of servants carrying torches. Idris gnashed his teeth and shouted as he made off:

'Soon I shall present you with a bastard grandson to gladden your eyes.'

And off he went towards Gemalia, into the darkness, while the people drew back to make way for him. Gebelawi reached the spot where the brothers stood, and he pretended to be calm under the stare of thousands of eyes. Then he said in a commanding voice:

'Proceed as before!'

The torchbearers returned to their places, the drums sounded, the pipes started up, the singers sang, the dancers danced, and the procession resumed its course.

The Big House was awake till morning with singing and drinking and merry-making. When Adham entered his room, overlooking the desert of Mukattam he found Omayma by the looking-glass, her face still veiled in white. He was drunk, hardly able to stand up. He moved towards her, exerting a great effort to control his limbs, and lifted the veil from her face, which looked up at him with exquisite loveliness. He bent his head to kiss her firm lips, then said in a drunken voice:

'All's well that ends well.'

Then he went to the bed, staggering a little, and flung himself across it, still wearing his scarf and red shoes. Omayma looked at his reflection and smiled with anxious yearning.

Adham found with Omayma a happiness he had never known before. Because of his openness, he showed this happiness in his words and his behaviour, so that his brothers made fun of him. At the end of his prayers he would stretch out his hands and cry out: 'Praise be to the Lord of grace. I praise him for my father's pleasure; I praise him for my wife's love; I praise him for garden and song and flute.' The women of the house all said Omayma was a loving wife, tending her husband like a son. She got on well with her mother-in-law and loved serving her and even her family. She cared for her home as though it were part of her body. Adham was a husband full of love and consideration. His work on the estate had already taken up part of the time he had previously spent on innocent pleasure in the garden, and now love took up the remainder of the day, and he lost himself in it completely.

The first exciting days passed, lasting too long for the scornful brothers Radwaan, Abbas and Gelil, and then gave way to an even tranquility, just as a rushing stream flows down into a smooth-flowing river. Adham's mind turned to reflection and he felt that time was no longer flying by, and that night was following day. He saw that the duet lost all meaning if it went on like this indefinitely, and that the garden had been a good friend which deserved better than to be deserted. He did not feel that any of these things meant that his heart was turning away from Omayma; she was still at the centre of it; but life goes on in stages, and a man becomes aware of them only gradually. He returned one day to his old haunt by the stream, and his gaze wandered over the flowers and birds, gratefully and almost apologetically. Suddenly, there was Omayma, looking very pretty. She sat down beside him and said:

'I peeped out of the window to see what was keeping you; why didn't you ask me to join you?'

He replied, smiling:

'I was afraid of boring you.'

'Boring me? I have long loved this garden. Don't you remember our first meeting here?'

He took her hand in his and rested his head against the trunk of a tree, looking up at the branches and the sky between them. She assured him again of her love for the garden, and the more silent he grew, the more eagerly she did so, for she hated silence as much as she loved the garden. She spoke brightly of their life together and then saw fit to chatter on about recent events in the house, especially relations between the wives of Radwaan, Abbas and Gelil. Then she said reproachfully:

'You are very far away from me, Adham.'

**18**

'How can that be when you fill my heart?'

'But you aren't listening to me.'

This was true. But although he had not welcomed her arrival, neither did he resent it. And if she had tried to go away again, he would have stopped her quite sincerely. The truth was, he felt her to be part of himself. He said almost apologetically:

'I love this garden; nothing in my past life was sweeter to me than sitting in it. Its tall trees and its twittering birds and its silver streams know me almost as well as I know them. I want you to share my love for it. Have you seen how the sky looks through the branches?'

She raised her eyes for a moment, then looked at him with a smile.

'It is indeed beautiful, worthy to be the dearest thing in your life.'

He detected the hidden reproach in her words and hastened to say:

'That's how it was before I knew you . . .'

'And now?'

He squeezed her hand lovingly.

'Its beauty is incomplete without you.'

She raised her eyes to his.

'One good thing about it is that it doesn't mind when you desert it for me.'

Adham laughed and drew her to him and kissed her on the cheek, then asked her:

'Don't these flowers deserve better than talk about our sisters-in-law?'

Omayma said with concern:

'The flowers are more beautiful; but your sisters-in-law never stop talking about you and the management of the estate, always the management of the estate, and your father's faith in you, over and over again.'

Adham frowned, forgetting the garden and said bitterly:

'They don't miss anything.'

'I'm really afraid you'll get the evil eye.'

Adham cried out angrily:

'Damn the estate! It has weighed me down and turned people against me and robbed me of my peace of mind; to hell with it!'

She put her finger on his lips.

'Don't be ungrateful, Adham; managing the estate is important and it may bring benefits we haven't thought of.'

'Up till now all it's brought is trouble. The sufferings of Idris are bad enough . . .'

She smiled wanly, but her eyes showed that she was seriously worried.

'Look at our future as hard as you look at the sky and the birds.'

After that Omayma regularly shared Adham's sessions in the garden, and was hardly ever silent. But he got used to her, and learned to listen with only half an ear, or not to listen at all. When he felt like it he would

**19**

take out his pipe and make music. He could really say with complete satisfaction that everything was good. He got used even to Idris's sufferings. But his mother's illness was getting worse, and she was racked by new pains. His heart grieved for her. She used to call for him often, and prayed countless prayers for him. One day she entreated him. 'Pray to God constantly to protect you from evil and to lead you on the right path.' She would not let him leave, but went on moaning to herself and speaking to him and mentioning her last wishes, until she died in his arms. Adham and Omayma wept for her, and Gebelawi came and looked upon her face, then shrouded her reverently, his keen eyes filled with anguish.

Hardly had Adham's life returned to normal than a sudden change came over Omayma, for which he could see no reason. It started with her giving up her visits to the garden, which did not please him as he had sometimes thought it would. He asked her why she had stopped coming and she made various excuses such as work or tiredness. He noticed that she did not rush to welcome him with the old ardour, and that when he made love to her, she met him without real passion, as though she were humouring him reluctantly. He wondered what could be the matter. He had already been through something like this himself, but his love had sustained him and conquered it. He could have been harsh with her, and wanted to very much at times, but her fragility and paleness and her politeness to him held him back. Sometimes she seemed depressed and sometimes confused. One time he caught a look of repulsion on her face, and he was both angry and sad, and said to himself: 'I will be patient a while; either she will improve, or to hell with her!'

He went to his father's study one day to present the month's accounts to him. Gebelawi studied them without much interest and then asked him what was wrong. Adham looked up at him in astonishment.

'Nothing, father.'

His eyes narrowed and he said quietly:

'Tell me about Omayma.'

Adham looked down under his father's piercing glance.

'She is well. Everything is fine.'

Gebelawi said impatiently:

'Tell me what is wrong.'

For a time Adham was silent, almost believing that his father was omniscient. Then he confessed:

'She has changed very much and seems unfriendly.'

A strange look came into his father's eyes:

'Have you quarrelled?'

'Never.'

Gebelawi said with a deeply contented smile:

'Be gentle with her, you ignorant fellow, and don't make love to her until she asks you to. Soon you will be a father.'

6 ✳ ✳ ✳ ✳ ✳ ✳ ✳ ✳ ✳ ✳ ✳ ✳ ✳ ✳ ✳ ✳ ✳ ✳ ✳

Adham sat in the estate office receiving the new tenants, one by one. They were standing in a queue, the first in front of him, the last at the back of the big garden house. When the last tenant came, Adham asked brusquely without lifting his head from the ledger:

'Your name?'

A voice replied:

'Idris Gebelawi.'

Adham looked up fearfully and saw his brother standing before him. He leapt up to defend himself, watching him warily. But Idris's appearance was new and unaccustomed. He was dishevelled and seemed gentle and self-effacing, contrite and trustworthy. The sight of him drew out of Adham's heart any remaining anger, though he did not feel completely at ease.

'Idris!'

Idris nodded and said very gently:

'Don't be afraid. I am simply your guest in this house, if your generosity can stretch to that.'

Could these friendly words really come from Idris? Had suffering tamed him? His meekness was just as disconcerting as his former rudeness. Was he not asking for Adham's hospitality as a way to spite his father? He had come uninvited, but Adham found himself asking Idris to sit down. They sat looking at each other strangely, until Idris said:

'I mingled with that crowd of tenants so as to be able to speak to you alone.'

'Did anyone see you?'

'No one from the house saw me, you can be sure of that. I haven't come to spoil your happiness; I am simply throwing myself on your mercy.'

Adham looked away, deeply moved. The blood rushed to his face. Idris went on:

'Perhaps you are amazed at the change in me, and are wondering what has happened to my pride. I want you to know that I have suffered more than a man can bear, and yet I have not behaved like this with anyone but you. A man like me can only forget his pride in the presence of someone gentle.'

'May God lighten your burden and ours! How your fate has spoilt and saddened my life!'

'I ought to have known this from the beginning, but I was mad with rage. Then drink robbed me of my honour, and the life of an aimless parasite extinguished the last spark of humanity in me. Did you ever know such behaviour in your brother?'

'Never. You were the best of brothers and the noblest of men.'

Idris said in an agonized voice:

'Oh for those days! Now I know nothing but misery. I wander about the desert dragging a pregnant woman after me, spreading chaos wherever I go and paying for my food by doing harm and making enemies.'

'You break my heart, brother.'

'Forgive me, Adham. That's you as I've always known you. Didn't I hold you in my arms when you were little? Didn't I watch you as a child and as a youth, seeing your fine, noble character?'

'Curse anger!'

'Yes, indeed!'

Idris sighed and said as if to himself:

'For the wrong I have done you, I deserve worse than what has happened to me.'

'May God lighten your burden. You know I never gave up hope of you returning. Even when Father was at his most furious, I risked talking to him about your situation.'

Idris smiled, showing teeth that had become dirty and yellow:

'That's what I felt; I said to myself, if there was any hope of father relenting, it wouldn't happen without your help.'

Adham's eyes shone as he said:

'I feel your generosity has come out on top; don't you think the time has come to speak to father about it?'

Idris shook his head hopelessly.

'I am much older and more experienced than you. I know that father will forgive anything except being made a laughing-stock. He will never forgive me after what has happened. I have no hope of coming back to the Big House.'

There was no doubt that Idris was right, and this depressed Adham. He murmured wretchedly:

'What can I do to help you?'

Idris smiled again:

'Don't bother to think about helping me with money. I'm sure you're an honest manager of the estate, and I know that if you helped me in that way, it would be out of your own pocket, which I could not accept. You're already a husband and soon you'll be a father. No, I have come to you not because poverty compelled me, but in order to tell you how I regret the harm I have done you, and to win back your friendship, and also because I have a favour to ask.'

Adham looked at him with concern and asked:

'Tell me the favour.'

Idris brought his head close to his brother's, as if afraid lest the walls should overhear.

'I want to be sure of my future, now that I have ruined the present. I too am going to be a father; and what is to become of my children?'

'You'll find me ready to do anything I can.'

Idris put his hand affectionately on Adham's shoulder.

'I want to know whether father has cut me out of his will.'

'How could I know anything about that? But if you want my opinion . . .'

Idris cut him short impatiently:

'I'm not asking you for *your* opinion; I want father's.'

'But you know perfectly well that he tells nobody what he has in mind.'

'But he will certainly have written it into the book which contains everything about the estate.'

Adham shook his head and said nothing. Idris repeated:

'Everything is in the book.'

'I know nothing about it. You know that no one in the house knows anything about it. My job as manager is completely under my father's direction.'

Idris gave him a melancholy look.

'It's a fat book. I once saw it when I was a boy, and asked father what it contained. At that time I was his favourite, and he told me it included everything about us. He wouldn't go on with the conversation about its contents. My fate is fixed in it now for certain.'

'Only God can know!'

'It is in a secret chamber in father's bedroom. You must have seen the little door at the far end of the left hand wall; it is always locked, but its key is kept in a tiny silver box in the drawer of the bedside table. The book itself is on a table in the secret chamber.'

Adham raised his eyebrows in confusion and muttered:

'What are you after?'

Idris said with a sigh:

'If there is any peace of mind left to me in this world, it depends on my knowing what is written about me in that book.'

Adham, relieved, replied:

'The simplest thing will be for me to ask him straight out what is in the ten conditions.'

'He wouldn't tell you; he'd be annoyed. Probably his opinion of you would suffer. Or he would guess the real reason for your question and lose his temper. How I should hate you to lose your father's confidence as a reward for your kindness to me. He certainly does not mean to reveal his ten conditions or he would have told us all what they are. No! The only way to the book is the one I have described to you. It will be very easy at daybreak, when your father walks in the garden.'

Adham's face grew pale.

'I shall do nothing so wicked as what you suggest, brother.'

Idris masked his disappointment with a faint smile.

'It is not a crime for a son to find out the things that affect him in his father's book.'

'But you want to steal a secret that he is anxious to keep.'

Idris sighed heavily.

'When I decided to seek your help, I said to myself: "It will be very difficult persuading Adham to undertake something against his father's will." But I had hopes and thought: "Perhaps he'll agree when he realizes how much I need his help." It would be no crime and it would be easy to succeed, and you would save someone from torment without losing anything yourself.'

'God keep us from doing wrong!'

'Amen! But I beg you to put me out of my agony.'

Adham stood up, troubled and confused. Idris stood up too. He smiled a smile of complete hopelessness and said:

'I have upset you, Adham: one thing about my unhappy state is that whenever I meet someone, he suffers in some way or other. Idris is still a wandering curse.'

'How it torments me not being able to help. Nothing could be worse.'

Idris came close to him and put his hand gently on his shoulder, kissed him on the forehead and said:

'It's all my fault that I'm in a mess; why should I burden you with more than you can do? Let me leave you in peace. May God's will be done!'

And with those words Idris went off.


7 ✳ ✳ ✳ ✳ ✳ ✳ ✳ ✳ ✳ ✳ ✳ ✳ ✳ ✳ ✳ ✳ ✳ ✳ ✳ ✳

Omayma's face came alive for the first time in weeks and she asked Adham anxiously:

'Didn't your father ever tell you about the book?'

Adham was sitting cross-legged on the divan looking out through the window at the wilderness plunged in darkness.

24

'He never spoke to anyone about it.'

'Not even to you?'

'I am just one of several sons.'

She smiled gently.

'But he picked you to manage the estate.'

'I told you; he never spoke about it to anyone.'

She smiled again and said cunningly:

'Don't let it bother you; Idris isn't worth that; his nastiness to you can never be forgotten.'

Adham turned his head towards the window.

'The Idris who came to me today is not the Idris who did me wrong. I'm haunted by his look of sadness and regret.'

She said triumphantly:

'That's what strikes me most about what you say, and it is what really worries me. But you seem depressed, which is unusual for you.'

He was looking out into the thick darkness, and said:

'Worrying won't get us anywhere.'

'But your repentant brother asks your sympathy.'

'I can see that, but what can I do?'

'You must patch things up with him, and with his brothers. Otherwise you're going to find yourself alone against them one day.'

'You are more worried about yourself than about Idris.'

She shook her head vigorously.

'I am quite right to worry about myself, which means also about you and our unborn child.'

'What did the woman want? How thick this darkness was; it even swallowed up Gebel Mukattam. He held his peace and was silent, but she went on:

'Do you remember ever going into the secret chamber?'

He ended his short silence:

'Never. I used to want to as a child, but father prevented me, and mother wouldn't let me go near it.'

All the time he talked to her about the question, he was expecting her to draw him back, not to egg him on. He badly needed someone to reassure him that his attitude to his brother was right. But he was like a traveller calling in the dark for a guide and attracting a bandit instead. Omayma asked again:

'Do you know the drawer with the tiny silver box?'

'Everyone who has been into the room knows it. Why do you ask?'

She left her seat on the divan and came close to him, and said temptingly:

'My God! Don't you *want* to see the book?'

'Heavens, no! Why should I want to?'

'Who can resist the desire to know the future?'

'You mean your own future?'

'My future and your future, and Idris's future which worries you so much in spite of what he has done to you.'

The woman had given voice to his thoughts, which annoyed him. He turned his head further towards the window and said:

'What father doesn't want, I don't want.'

She raised her pencilled eyebrows.

'Why should he hide this thing?'

'That's his business. What a lot of questions you're asking tonight!'

She said, talking to herself:

'The future! We should know the future, and we should at least be able to help poor Idris that much. And all it needs is to read a page, without anyone knowing. Could anyone, either a friend or an enemy, accuse us of bad intentions, or say that it affected your dear father even slightly?'

Adham was gazing at a brilliant star which outshone all the others. He pretended to ignore her words.

'What a wonderful sky! If the night wasn't so damp, I should have sat in the garden looking at it through the branches.'

'He must certainly have favoured some people in the conditions.'

Adham shouted:

'I am not interested in favours that bring nothing but trouble.'

She sighed:

'If I knew how to read I should go myself to the silver box.'

He wished it could happen that way. He grew still more annoyed with her and with himself. He felt as though he had already done the forbidden thing and was thinking about it as a past event. He turned to her, frowning, and in the light of the lamp which swung in the breeze that wafted through the window his face looked bothered and weak in spite of its scowl:

'Damn me for telling you about it at all!'

'I don't mean you any harm, and I love your father as much as you do.'

'Let's give up this tiresome conversation. This is a time of day when you usually rest.'

'It seems my mind will not rest until we have decided to do this simple thing.'

He whispered:

'God, bring her back to her senses!'

'Did you disobey your father by seeing Idris in the annexe?'

His eyes opened wide with surprise.

'I found him there in front of me; I couldn't avoid seeing him.'

26

'Did you tell your father about his visit?'

'How persistent you are tonight, Omayma!'

She said triumphantly:

'If it's all right for you to disobey him in something which may harm you, why can't you disobey him in something which will help you and your brother and will harm nobody?'

He could very well have broken off the conversation, had he wanted to, but temptation was too strong. The truth was that he had let her run on only because something in him needed her support. He asked petulantly:

'What do you mean?'

'I mean you should stay awake till dawn, or until the way is clear for us.'

'I thought pregnancy had just stopped you being passionate; now I see that it stops you being sensible too.'

'You agree with what I say, by God. But you are afraid – and that doesn't suit you.'

Over his face came a darkness quite out of keeping with the compliance he felt within. He said:

'We shall remember this as the night of our first quarrel.'

She said with great gentleness:

'Adham, let's think about it seriously.'

'It won't make any difference.'

'That's what you say; but you'll see.'

He felt the heat of the fire that was fast approaching, and he said to himself: 'If you get scorched, tears won't quench it.' He turned his head to the window, and imagined that the inhabitants of that bright star must be glad to be so far away from this house. He murmured feebly:

'Nobody loves his father as much as I do.'

'You would never do anything that would harm him.'

'Omayma, you needn't lose any more sleep.'

'It's you who're keeping me awake.'

'I hoped to hear the voice of reason from you.'

'That's the only thing you did hear.'

He wondered to himself in a whisper:

'Won't it destroy me?'

She stroked his hand which rested on the edge of the divan and said reproachfully:

'We share our fate, if you love me.'

He said, with a resignation which showed that he had already made his decision:

'Even that star doesn't know my fate.'

No longer cautious, she said:

'You will read my fate in the book.'

His gaze went out to the unsleeping stars, and to the shreds of cloud lit up by their calm light. He imagined that they had heard his conversation, and he murmured, 'What a lovely sky!' Then he heard Omayma saying playfully:

'You taught me to love the garden, let me return the favour.'

8 * * * * * * * * * * * * * * * * * * *

At dawn Gebelawi left his room for the garden. Adham was watching from the end of the corridor, and Omayma stood behind him in the darkness with her hand on his shoulder. They listened to the heavy, even tread, but could not make out its direction in the dark. It was Gebelawi's custom to walk about at this hour with neither light nor companion. The noise died away, and Adham turned to whisper to his wife:

'Don't you think it would be best to go back now?'

She urged him on, whispering in his ear:

'Perish the thought that you can mean anyone any harm!'

He took a few steps forward, confused and unhappy, his hand clutching the little candle in his pocket. He felt his way along the wall till his hand touched the door. Omayma whispered:

'I shall stay here on guard. Go on, and good luck!'

She stretched out her hand and pushed the door open, then drew back. Adham tiptoed warily into the room, and was met by a strong smell of musk. He closed the door behind him and stood peering into the darkness until he could make out the windows, overlooking the desert, that let in the first light of day. Adham felt that the wrong – if wrong there was – had already been done with the entry into the room, and that he must now go through with it. He followed the left-hand wall, falling over chairs once or twice, passing the door to the secret chamber on the way, until he reached the end of it. Then he followed the end wall, and soon fumbled his way to the desk, opened the drawer and felt among its contents till he found the box. After pausing to regain control of himself, he returned to the door of the chamber, groped for the keyhole, put the key in and turned it. He opened the door, and there he was slipping into the secret place that no one but his father had ever before entered. He closed the door, took out his candle and lit it. He saw a square room with a high ceiling and no opening other than the door. A small carpet covered the floor. To the right was an ornate table and on it rested the thick volume, fastened to the wall with an iron chain. His mouth was dry, and when he swallowed it was as painful as if he had a sudden sore throat. He clenched his teeth as if to crush the fear that travelled through his trembling limbs to the candle in his hand. He went over to the table, gazing at the cover of the book, which was decorated with gold-inlaid lettering. Then he stretched out his hand and opened it. He composed his thoughts and overcame his confusion with difficulty, then began to read in the Persian script: 'In the Name of God . . .'

But suddenly he heard the door open. His head was jerked round violently towards the sound, without his volition, as though the door pulled him towards itself as it opened. In the candlelight he saw Gebelawi, blocking the doorway with his great bulk, looking at him with a cold, cruel stare. Adham looked into his father's eyes, silent and motionless. The power to speak or think or move deserted him. Gebelawi commanded him:

'Out!'

But Adham was unable to move. Utterly hopeless, he stayed where he was, like a lifeless object. His father shouted:

'Out!'

Terror aroused him from his trance. His father moved from the doorway, and Adham left the secret chamber, with the candle still flickering in his hand. He saw Omayma standing speechless in the middle of the room, tears streaming down her face. His father motioned to him to stand beside her, then addressed him coldly:

'You will answer my questions truthfully.'

Adham's expression conveyed his willingness. Gebelawi asked:

'Who told you about the book?'

Adham answered without hesitation, like a broken vessel pouring out its contents:

'Idris.'

'When?'

'Yesterday morning.'

'How did you meet?'

'He came with the new tenants and waited till we were alone.'

'Why didn't you throw him out?'

'I couldn't bring myself to throw him out, father.'

Gebelawi said sharply:

'Don't call me "Father".'

Adham gathered all his strength and said:

'You are still my father in spite of your anger and my stupidity.'

'Was it he who egged you on to do this?'

Omayma answered, although he had not addressed the question to her:

'Yes, sir.'

Gebelawi shouted:

'Quiet, vermin!' then to Adham: 'Answer me!'

'He was desperately unhappy and repentant, and he wanted to feel secure about his children's future.'

29

'And you agreed to do this for him!'

'On the contrary . . . I apologized and told him I couldn't.'

'What made you change your mind?'

Adham sighed in despair, and muttered:

'The Devil.'

Gebelawi asked him cruelly:

'Did you tell your wife what had passed between you?'

At this point Omayma began to wail. Gebelawi silenced her, then motioned Adham to answer:

'Yes.'

'And what did she say to you?'

Adham kept quiet and swallowed hard. His father shouted:

'Answer me, you wretch!'

'She was very keen to find out your will, and thought it would harm nobody.'

Gebelawi glared at him with utter contempt:

'And that is how you consented to betray the one who preferred you to your betters?'

Adham said with a groan:

'It's no use my making excuses for my crime; but your mercy is greater than any crime or any excuses.'

'So you plot against me with Idris whom I expelled for your sake?'

'I did not plot with Idris. I have done wrong, and my only hope is your mercy.'

Omayma implored him:

'Sir . . .'

'Quiet, vermin!'

He looked from one to the other, frowning, then said in a terrible voice:

'Get out of the house!'

Adham cried out:

'Father!'

'In a brutal voice Gebelawi said:

'Get out of the house before I throw you out.'

# 9

The great gate opened again, this time to see the enforced departure of Adham and Omayma. Adham carried a bundle of clothes, and Omayma followed with a few pots and pans and a little food. They left, crushed and hopeless. When they heard the gate close behind them their voices rose to a wail, and Omayma said between her sobs:

'I deserve worse than death.'

Adham said in a faltering voice:

'For once you are telling the truth; but I too deserve worse than death.'

They had gone hardly any distance from the house when a drunken laugh rang out. They looked in that direction, and there they saw Idris, in front of the hut he had built of tins and sticks. Nargis, his wife, was sitting there quietly, spinning, and Idris was laughing spitefully, enjoying their misery. Adham and Omayma were astonished and stood staring at him. Idris began dancing about snapping his fingers till Nargis got annoyed and went into the hut. Adham watched, his eyes hot with tears of anger. He saw at once the trick Idris had played, and felt the true foulness of the crime. He realized too his own colossal ignorance and stupidity, on account of which the villain was dancing with malicious joy. This was the real Idris, the incarnation of evil. Adham's blood boiled and his mind was darkened. He picked up a handful of earth and threw it at him, shouting, in a voice choked with rage:

'Filthy beast! You make even the scorpions look harmless.'

Idris's answer was to dance still more vigorously, wagging his head from side to side and jerking his eyebrows up and down, still snapping his fingers. Adham's fury was redoubled and he shouted:

'Bloody, lousy, mean . . . liar . . . twister!'

Idris began wriggling his blody as cleverly as he was wagging his head, sniggering silently. Adham shouted, taking no notice of Omayma who was trying to get him to go:

'You even try the prostitutes' tricks, you filthy bastard!'

Idris started wiggling his behind, spinning round slowly and provocatively. Adham was blind with fury. He threw down his bundle, pushed away Omayma who tried to hold him back, rushed at him and seized his neck with all his strength. Idris showed no signs of feeling the attack, and went on dancing skilfully and slowly. Adham, by now quite mad, rained blows on him, but Idris only made more fun of him, and began chanting:

'Tinker, tailor, soldier, sailor . . .'

Then he stopped, raving and cursing, and gave Adham a mighty push in the chest which sent him staggering back. He lost his balance and fell on his back. Omayma hurried over to him and helped him up and began brushing the dust off his clothes, saying:

'Why should you bother with this savage? Let's get right away.'

He picked up the bundle without saying a word, and she took her baggage, and they went round to the other side of the Big House.

Adham was already tired and he threw down the bundle and sat on it, saying he wanted a rest. His wife sat down facing him, crying. They heard

Idris's voice again. He stood looking defiantly at the house, thundering:

'For the sake of your most despicable child you threw me out, and you see how he treated you? And now you have thrown him out. Tit for tat! And the one who started it is the loser. This is so that you know that Idris can't be beaten. Now you can stay alone with your useless, spineless sons. You won't have any grandsons except the ones who will run about in the dirt and rubbish. Tomorrow they will be peddling sweet potatoes and melon seeds. Tomorrow they will be at the mercy of the chiefs in Otouf and Kafr el Zaghari. Soon your seed will be mixed with that of the lowest of men. You will sit alone in your room, changing things in your book in anger and frustration. You will grow old alone in the shadows and, when your end comes, no one will mourn for you . . .'

Then he turned to Adham and continued his crazy shouting:

'And you, you weakling, how are you going to face life on your own? You have no power to help you, no strength to draw on. In this desert what's the use of your arithmetic and writing? Ha!'

Omayma went on weeping till it got on Adham's nerves and he said listlessly:

'Stop crying!'

She dried her eyes.

'I can't help it, Adham; I'm to blame for all this.'

'I'm just as much to blame as you. If I hadn't been so weak and cowardly it wouldn't have happened.'

'It's all my fault.'

'You're blaming yourself to prevent me from blaming you.'

She lost a little of her zeal for self-reproach and sat for a long time with bent head. Then she went on in a faint voice:

'I never thought he could be so harsh.'

'I know him; I have no excuse.'

She hesitated awhile, then said:

'How can I live here when I am pregnant?'

'After being in the Big House we must now live in this desert. If only tears were some use! But we must build a hut.'

'Where?'

He looked around, and his glance fell for a second on Idris's hut.

'We can't go too far from the Big House, even if it means living near to Idris. Otherwise we should perish, all alone in this desert.'

Omayma pondered for a while.

'Yes, and we should stay within view of your father in case he softens towards us.'

Adham sighed.

'I shall die of grief. If you weren't here with me I'd think this was a nightmare. Have I lost his affection for ever? But I shan't fight him back like Idris. Oh no, no! I am not like Idris in any way; and am I to get the same treatment?'

Omayma said bitterly:

'These parts have never known a father like yours.'

'When will you curb your tongue?'

'For goodness' sake, I haven't committed a crime. Tell anyone you like what I have done and what I got as my reward; I bet you anything he will be shocked. My God! There's never been a father like yours.'

'The world has never seen so fine a man. This mountain, this desert, and the sky itself bear witness to that. Anyone else would have shrunk back from the challenge.'

'With his tyranny soon none of his sons will be left in the house.'

'We were the first to go, and we were the worst.'

She denied it angrily:

'I'm not — we're not.'

'The truth comes out only at times of trial.'

They took refuge in silence. In the desert there was no living thing to be seen, except a few people moving about far away at the foot of the mountain. The sun beat down cruelly from a cloudless sky, drenching the vast expanse of sand, in which glinted a few stones or bits of glass. Nothing stood out to relieve the monotony, apart from the *gebel* on the horizon, a great rock that lay to the east like the head of a body buried in the sand, and Idris's pitiful hovel, planted defiantly at the eastern end of the Big House. The whole atmosphere was one of harshness, weariness and fear.

Omayma heaved a deep sigh and said:

'We are going to have a hard time of it, making life comfortable.'

Adham looked at the Big House and said:

'We'd have an even harder time getting back through that gate.'

10 ✳ ✳ ✳ ✳ ✳ ✳ ✳ ✳ ✳ ✳ ✳ ✳ ✳ ✳ ✳ ✳ ✳ ✳ ✳

Adham and Omayma set about putting up a hut for themselves, to the west of the Big House. They fetched the stones and slates from the foot of Gebel Mukattam, and picked up the timber around Otouf and Gemalia and Bab el Nasr. They soon realized that building a hut would take longer than they could manage. By then they had finished the supplies of cheese and eggs and molasses which Omayma had brought from the house. Adham made up his mind to go and work for his living. He decided to sell some of his fine clothes to buy a barrow for peddling sweet potatoes, melon seeds, cucumbers and whatever else was in season.

When he began collecting his clothes together, Omayma burst into tears, but he took no notice. He said, half angry half mocking:

'These clothes no longer suit me. Wouldn't it be a joke — me going to sell sweet potatoes in a brocaded camel hair coat!'

In no time he was pushing his barrow across the desert to Gemalia — Gemalia which still remembered his wedding procession. He felt oppressed and at first refrained from crying his wares. His eyes were almost blinded with tears, and he went towards the more distant neighbourhoods to try and escape. From morning till night he kept up his walking and shouting till his hands were tired and his shoes were worn out and his feet and all his joints ached. How he disliked the women's haggling, and being forced by weariness to lie on the ground beside a wall, and having to stop in a corner to relieve himself! And when he came back to Omayma in the early evening, he did not come back to peace and quiet, but had to get on with building the hut.

Life began to seem unreal, and the garden and managing the estate, and the room looking out over Gebel Mukattam began to seem like fairytales. He said to himself: 'Nothing in this world is real, neither the Big House, nor the unfinished hut, not the garden, nor the barrow, nor yesterday, today and tomorrow. Perhaps I have done well to live beside the Big House, so that I shall not lose the past as I have lost the present and the future. Would it be strange if I lost my memory as I have lost my father and lost my true self?'

Once he sat dozing at midday in Watawit Alley, when he was wakened by a movement and saw some boys about to make off with his barrow. He stood up threatening them, and one boy noticed him and warned his friends with a whistle, pushing the barrow over to distract him from giving chase. The cucumbers spilt all over the ground while the boys bounded away like locusts. Adham was furious and poured forth a torrent of the foulest curses. Then he bent down to gather up the cucumbers which were smothered in dirt. He found no outlet for his anger and it mounted till he said with passion: 'Why did your rage burn everything up? Why did you love your pride more than your own flesh and blood? How can you be happy with your life of ease and plenty, knowing that we are trampled on like insects. Mercy and sweetness and tolerance are all lacking in your great house, you tyrant.' He took hold of the shafts of the barrow and was about to push it far away from this wretched alley, when he heard a jeering voice:

'How much are those cucumbers, mister?'

He saw Idris standing with a mocking smile on his lips, resplendent in a brightly coloured smock and a white scarf. At the sight of his smirk his whole world went dark. He gave his cart a push, meaning to go, but Idris blocked his path and said:

'Doesn't a customer like me deserve better treatment?'

Adham raised his head nervously and said:

'Leave me alone.'

'Don't you like the way your big brother is talking to you?'

'Idris, aren't you satisfied with what you have already done to me? I have no wish to know you or for you to know me.'

'How can you say that when we are neighbours?'

'I did not want to live near you, but I decided to stay near the house, which . . .'

Idris interrupted him gleefully:

'Which you were thrown out of.'

Adham said nothing, but his discomfort was plain from his pale face. Idris persisted:

'The mind stays in the place it has been thrown out of, doesn't it?'

Adham kept silent, and his brother went on:

'You are hoping to get back into the house, you schemer; you may be weak, but you are full of crafty schemes. But let me tell you, I'm not letting you go back without me, not if the sky falls.'

Adham asked, his nostrils dilated with anger:

'Aren't you content with what you've done to me?'

'Aren't *you* content with what you've done to me? I was thrown out because of you, though I was the light of the house.'

'On the contrary, you were thrown out because of your arrogance.'

Idris roared with laughter.

'And *you* were thrown our because of your weakness. There is no room in the house for either strength or weakness. You see your father's tyranny; he allows no one besides himself to combine strength and weakness. He is so strong that he destroys his loved ones, and so weak that he marries a woman like your mother.

Adham frowned angrily and said in a voice that trembled:

'Let me go! And if you want to start a fight, pick someone your own size.'

'Your father is ready to start a fight with weak or strong.'

Adham said nothing, and frowned still more. Idris said mockingly:

'You don't want to be drawn into insulting him! That is a very clever trick, and a proof that you still dream of going back.'

He picked up a cucumber and looked at it with repulsion.

'How can you bring yourself to go around with these filthy cucumbers? Can't you find any better work?'

'I am content with it.'

'Or rather, necessity has driven you to it. And all the while your father enjoys the good life. Think about it a bit; wouldn't it be best for you to join up with me?'

Adham was annoyed:

'I was not made for your sort of life.'

Look at my smock. Its owner was strutting about in it only yesterday, and he had no right to it.'

'How did you get it?'

'The way strong people usually do these things.'

Had he stolen or killed?

'I can't believe that you are my brother, Idris.'

Idris replied, laughing:

'There's no need to be surprised as long as you remember I am Gebelawi's son.'

Adham shouted, his patience exhausted:

'Why don't you get out of my way?'

'As you wish, you idiot!'

Idris filled his pocket with cucumbers, threw a scornful glance at him, spat on the barrow and left.


Omayma stood up to meet him as he neared the hut. Darkness covered the desert, and in the entrance of the hut the stump of a candle was burning. In the sky the stars shone, and by their light the Big House was just a huge shape. Omayma realized from his silence that his mood made it best to avoid him. She brought him a jug of water to wash in and a clean smock. He washed his face and his feet and changed, then sat on the ground with legs outstretched. She approached him cautiously, sat down and said soothingly:

'If only I could bear some of your tiredness for you.'

It was as if she had scratched a wound. He shouted:

'Shut up! You're the one all the mischief and misery came from.'

She moved away until she was almost hidden from him, but he shouted after her:

'More than anyone else you remind me of my carelessness and stupidity. Damn the day I first saw you!'

He could hear her sobs in the darkness, but his temper grew worse, and he said:

'To hell with your tears! They're just your badness spilling out.'

He heard her tearful voice:

'Words can't tell you how I suffer.'

'Don't let me hear your voice again. Get right out of my sight.'

He screwed up his dirty clothes and threw them at her. She wailed: 'My tummy!' At once his anger cooled and he felt anxious about the consequences. She sensed a change of heart from his silence, and said:

'I shall go right away as you want me to.'

She stood up and walked away, until he shouted after her:

'Do you think this is a time for joking?'

He started to get up, shouting:

'Come back! I'm friends with you again.'

He peered into the darkness till he saw her shadowy figure returning. Then he propped his back against the wall of the house and looked up at the sky. He wished he could be reassured that she was not hurt, but his pride prevented him and he put it off for a while. He prepared the way by saying:

'Wash some cucumbers for supper.'


11 ✳ ✳ ✳ ✳ ✳ ✳ ✳ ✳ ✳ ✳ ✳ ✳ ✳ ✳ ✳ ✳ ✳ ✳ ✳

'The place has a sort of peace. No plants; no water; no birds, or branches for them to sing on. Only the bare, unfriendly desert, clothed at night in mystery, breeding ground for dreams. Above, the dome of the sky, sown with stars. The woman is in the hut. Loneliness speaks, and sorrow smoulders like coals buried in the ashes. The walls of the Big House repel the yearning heart. How can I make this terrible father hear my cry? Wisdom tells us to forget the past, but it is the only one we have. I hate my weakness and curse my vileness, and am content with hardship for a companion; and I shall father children for him. The smallest bird is better off than me, for no power can keep it out of the garden. My eyes long for the streams flowing between the rose bushes. Where is my reed pipe? You hard-hearted man; half a year has passed; will you never soften?'

From the distance came the sound of Idris singing in a hateful voice: 'Strange things, my God, strange things!' There he was, lighting a fire in front of his hut. It kept blazing up and dying down again. His wife came and went, bulgingly pregnant, bringing food and drink. In a fit of drunkenness he shouted at the Big House. 'This is the hour for cream of jute leaves and roast chicken, you lot; smother it with poison!' Then he started singing again.

Adham said to himself sadly: 'Whenever I am by myself in the dark that devil goes and lights his fire and gets rowdy and spoils my solitude.'

Omayma appeared at the door of the hut, and he realized that she was not asleep as he had supposed. She was weakened by her pregnancy and by hardship and poverty. She said with gentle concern:

'Aren't you coming to sleep?'

He replied crossly:

'Leave me alone in the one hour when life is good.'

'You will be going off with your barrow first thing in the morning; you badly need rest.'

'When I'm alone I become a gentleman again, or so it seems to me, contemplating the sky and remembering the old days.'

She sighed heavily.

'I should love to see your father coming out of the house or going in; I'd throw myself at his feet and beg his forgiveness.'

'I've told you over and over again to leave off those ideas. It's quite impossible for us to get back his favour that way.'

She was silent for a while then murmured:

'I'm thinking of the fate of my unborn child.'

'And that's my only concern too, although I've become an animal.'

She said in a low, sad voice:

'You're the best man in the whole world . . .'

Adham laughed bitterly and said:

'I'm no longer a human being; only an animal worries all the time about the next meal.'

'Don't be sad. Lots of men start off like you, then life gets easier till in the end they own shops and houses.'

'I think pregnancy has affected your head.'

She said with conviction:

'You'll be an important man, and our child will grow up in the lap of luxury.'

Adham was amazed at her and asked sarcastically:

'Am I to do this by drink or hashish?'

'By working, Adham.'

'Working for a living is a curse. I used to spend my life in the garden, with no work except looking at the sky and playing my pipe, but now I'm just an animal, pushing my barrow every day for the sake of a few scraps to eat in the evening and to crap in the morning. Working for a living is the worst curse of all. The real life is the life in the Big House, where there's no drudgery but only pleasure and beauty and song . . .'

And there was Idris's voice saying:

'Well said, Adham; work is a curse and a humiliation we are not used to. Didn't I suggest that we join forces?'

Adham turned towards the voice and saw the shape of Idris standing near to him. He used to slip across like this unnoticed in the darkness, and listen to the conversation as long as he wished, joining in when he felt like it. Adham stood there miserably and said:

'Get back to your shack.'

Idris said with feigned seriousness:

'Me too, I say work is a curse which doesn't fit man's dignity.'

'You are inviting me to be a crook, which is worse than a curse.'

'If work's a curse and crookery's worse, how's a man to live?'

Adham did not like the conversation and kept quiet. Idris waited for him to speak, but he didn't, so he went on:

'Perhaps you are hoping to get food without work! But that would be at the expense of other people.'

He laughed hatefully:

'It's a problem, son of a slave.'

Omayma shouted furiously:

'Go home! The devil has bitten you.'

His wife at that moment called him loudly, and he went the way he had come, singing 'Strange things, my God, strange things.'

Omayma implored her husband:

'Don't get tangled up with him at any price.'

'I keep finding him standing over me without knowing how he came.'

Silence reigned and they found in it a refuge from their anxiety. Then Omayma began speaking again, gently:

'My heart tells me I'll make this hut into a house like the one we've been thrown out of, including the garden and the nightingales, and our child will know ease and pleasure in it.'

Adham stood smiling a smile she could not see in the darkness, and said sarcastically, brushing the dust from his smock:

' "Fine gherkins! Sweet cucumbers!" The sweat pours from my body, and the boys bait me, and my feet kill me, and all for a few piastres.'

He went into the hut and she followed, saying:

'But the day of wealth and happiness will come.'

'If you suffered like me, you'd have no time for dreams.'

They both lay down on the straw-filled sackings, and she said:

'Isn't God able to turn our hut into a house like the Big House we've been thrown out of?'

Adham said, yawning:

'What I wish for is to go back to the Big House itself...' Then, yawning more: 'Work is a curse!'

She whispered:

'Maybe, but a curse you get rid of only by working!'


12 ✳ ✳ ✳ ✳ ✳ ✳ ✳ ✳ ✳ ✳ ✳ ✳ ✳ ✳ ✳ ✳ ✳ ✳ ✳

One night Adham woke to the sound of groaning. As he was half asleep, it was a little time before he made out Omayma's voice crying: 'Oh my back! Oh my tummy!' He sat up at once, peering at her, and said:

39

'You're always in this state these days, and then it turns out to be nothing. Light the candle.'

'Light it yourself! This time it's the real thing.'

He got up, feeling for the candle in its place among the pots and pans. He managed to find it and set it on the table. Omayma appeared in its feeble light, lying propped up on her arms, moaning and raising her head up to breathe with obvious difficulty. He said anxiously:

'That's what you say every time you feel pains.'

Her face crumpled up.

'No, no! I'm certain it's the real thing this time.'

He helped her to prop her back against the wall and said:

'It'll be soon anyway. Try to bear it while I go to Gemalia for the midwife.'

'Go safely. What time is it now?'

Adham went out of the hut and looked at the sky:

'Dawn is near. I'll be back as soon as possible.'

He hurried off towards Gemalia. When he made his way back through the darkness he was leading the old midwife by the hand. As they drew near to the shack, Omayma's cries for help came to him, shattering the stillness. His heart pounded and he strode out till the midwife complained. They went into the hut together and the woman took off her cloak and said to Omayma, laughing:

'The worst is over. There'll soon be peace after the suffering.'

Adham asked her:

'How are you?'

She groaned:

'Almost dead with pain. My body is falling apart . . . my bones breaking. Don't go . . .'

But the midwife said:

'He must wait quietly outside.'

Adham left the hut for the open air and caught sight of a figure standing near by. He knew him even before he could make him out clearly, and his breathing quickened; but Idris put on a polite tone and said:

'She's in labour? Poor girl. My wife went through this not long ago, as you know; but it's a misleading pain and soon goes. Then you'll meet whatever fate has alotted you, just as I met Hind – a charming baby, but she's always piddling or crying. Keep your chin up.'

Adham was suffering. He said:

'God is master of all things.'

Idris let out a harsh laugh and asked:

'Did you fetch the midwife from Gemalia to her?'

'Yes.'

'Dirty, greedy old woman! I fetched her too. She charged too much, so I chased her off, and she still curses me whenever she sees me go past her house.'

Adham hesitated, then said:

'You mustn't treat people like that.'

'You fine fellow! Your father taught me to be hard to people, and to have no scruples.'

Omayma's voice went up in a pitiful cry that echoed the rending in her womb. Adham clenched his teeth on what he was about to say and went anxiously towards the hut, crying out in a weak voice:

'Courage!'

Idris repeated his words in a loud voice:

'Courage, sister-in-law!'

Adham was concerned in case his wife heard Idris's voice. But he hid his annoyance, saying:

'It'd be best if we stayed right away from the hut.'

'Come to my place; I'll give you some tea and you can see Hind snoring.'

But Adham moved away from his hut without going towards Idris's cursing him secretly and hiding his anger. Idris followed him saying:

'You'll be a father before sunrise. It's an important change in your life. One advantage is that you'll experience the bond your father breaks with so little thought or difficulty.'

Adham breathed so hard.

'This talk is annoying me.'

'Maybe, but there's nothing else to interest us.'

Adham hesitated, then said:

'Idris, why do you follow me about, when you know there's no love between us?'

Idris laughed loudly:

'What a shameless child you are! Your wife's cries woke me from a delicious sleep, but I didn't let it annoy me. On the contrary, I've come to help you if you need any help. Your father must have heard her cries as clearly as I did, but he just went back to sleep, as if he had no heart.'

Adham said curtly:

'The fate he's laid on us is bad enough; can't you ignore me as I ignore you?'

'You hate me, Adham, not because I was the cause of your being thrown out, but because I remind you of your weakness. You hate your own rotten self in me. Now I no longer have any reason to hate you. On the contrary, today you're my comfort and consolation. Don't forget we're neighbours, the first people to live in this desert. Our children will crawl here side by side . . .'

'You enjoy tormenting me . . .'

41

Idris said nothing for a while, so that Adham hoped for release, but he went on, asking in a serious voice:

'Why can't we agree?'

Adham said with a sigh:

'Because I'm a barrow boy, as my circumstances require, and you go in for quarrels and fights.'

Omayma's cries became louder again, and Adham looked up at the sky imploringly. He noticed at once that the darkness was less thick and that day was breaking over the gebel. Adham shouted:

'Pain is a curse.'

Idris said laughing:

'How soft you are; you were made for managing the estate and playing your pipe . . .'

'Make fun of me as much as you like; I'm suffering.'

'Why? I thought it was your wife who was suffering.'

Adham shouted:

'Leave me alone!'

Idris asked with aggravating calmness:

'Are you hoping to become a father without paying for it?'

Adham kept quiet, breathing heavily, and Idris said sympathetically:

'You're a sensible man. I've come to propose a job by which you could bring happiness to your future children. The event you can hear is the first but not the last. Our desires will be satisfied only by building a mountain of screaming children. What do you say?'

'It's almost day. Go and finish your sleep.'

The cries came again, continuously, till Adham could no longer bear to stay where he was and returned to the hut from which the darkness was lifting. He reached it as Omayma let out a deep sigh like the end of a sad song. He went up to the door, asking:

'How are things with you?'

He heard the voice of the midwife saying 'Wait.' He prepared to relax, for the voice seemed to him to be triumphant. Very soon the woman appeared at the door, saying:

'You've been blessed with two sons.'

'May God provide for them!'

From behind him came Idris's ear-splitting laugh, and he heard him saying:

'Now Idris is father to a girl and uncle to two boys . . .'

And he went off to his hut singing:

> What's happened to fate and fortune?
> Tell me, time, the answer to that.

The midwife spoke again:

'Their mother wants to call them Kadri and Hammam.'

Adham, buoyant with happiness, began murmuring:

'Kadri and Hammam; Kadri . . . and Hammam . . .'

## 13 ✳ ✳ ✳ ✳ ✳ ✳ ✳ ✳ ✳ ✳ ✳ ✳ ✳ ✳ ✳ ✳ ✳ ✳ ✳

Kadri said, drying his face on the corner of his smock:

'Let's sit down and eat.'

Hammam stood looking at the setting sun.

'Yes, time has been flying.'

They sat down cross-legged in the sand at the foot of Gebel Mukat-tam. Hammam undid the knot in the striped red handkerchief, revealing bread, felafel and leeks. They fell to, glancing from time to time at their sheep, some of which wandered about while others stood chewing peace-fully. There was nothing in the twins' features or build to distinguish them, except that Kadri had a definite hunter's look in his eye, which gave him a distinctive sharpness of expression. Kadri spoke again, chew-ing a huge mouthful:

'If only this whole desert belonged to us alone, we could graze our sheep without any worries.'

Hammam said with a smile:

'But we share the place with shepherds from Otouf and Kafr el Zag-hari and Husseynia. The wisest thing is to be friendly with them.'

Kadri laughed scornfully, spitting out some crumbs as he did so, and said:

'These fellows have one answer for anyone who tries to be friends with them — punches!'

'But . . .'

'There's no but, brother; I only know one way; I grab the man by his smock and bang his head till he falls on his face — or his back for that matter.'

'And that's why we can hardly count our enemies.'

'Who asked you to count them?'

Hammam was serious and seemed very far away. He began to whistle to himself, then stopped and returned to a philosophical silence. He picked out a leek, stroked it with his fingers, put it in his mouth with relish and said:

'That's why we're alone and have to go a long time without talking.'

'Why do you need conversation? You sing all the time!'

Hammam looked at him trustingly and said:

'It seems to me that this loneliness gets you down sometimes.'

'I'll always find a reason to be gloomy, whether it's loneliness or something else.'

Silence fell, broken by the smacking of lips. Far away appeared a group going back from the gebel towards Otouf, singing a song, one leading and the others chanting the responses. Hammam said:

'This part of the desert is in our district. If we went off to the north or south, the chances are we'd never return . . .'

Kadri roared with laughter and said:

'You'd find plenty of people to the north and south who'd love to kill me, but you wouldn't find one who dared take me on.'

Hammam said, looking at the sheep:

'Nobody can say you're not brave; but don't forget that we live thanks to our grandfather's name and our uncle's frightful reputation, in spite of our quarrel with him.'

Kadri frowned his disagreement, but did not venture to deny it. His eye went to the Big House visible far off to the west, a great palace, its features indistinct.

'That house – I've never seen anything like it, with the desert on all sides, next to streets and alleys famous for quarrels and bullying, owned by a tyrant who won't be stood up to, this grandfather who's never seen his grandsons, though they live a stone's throw from him.'

Hammam looked towards the house and said:

'Our father never mentions him without respect and admiration.'

'And our uncle never mentions him without cursing him.'

Hammam said uneasily:

'He's our grandfather, anyway.'

'And what's the use of that, you baby? Father strains along behind his barrow, and mother slaves all day and half the night, and we go out with the sheep, barefoot and half naked. But he, he hides away behind those walls, completely heartless, enjoying whatever he wants.'

They finished their food. Hammam shook the handkerchief, folded it and put it in his pocket, then lay down on his back, pillowing his head on his arms, gazing up at the cloudless sky from which filtered the peacefulness of sunset, while the kites flew over the horizon. Kadri got up and went aside to urinate, and said:

'Father says grandfather used to go out a lot in the past, and used to pass them as he left or came back. But now nobody sees him; it's as if he was afraid . . .'

Hammam said dreamily:

'How I'd love to see him . . .'

'Don't dream of seeing anything exciting. You'd find him like father or uncle, or like both of them. I'm amazed at the way father always mentions him respectfully, in spite of the way he's been treated by him.'

'It's obvious that he's very much attached to him, or that he believes the punishment he had was justified . . .'

'Or that he still hopes for forgiveness.'

'You don't understand father; he's a loving man with a sweet nature.'

Kadri returned to his seat, saying:

'Well, he doesn't impress me and nor do you. I tell you, our grandfather is a queer old man and deserves no honour. If he had an atom of goodness, his own flesh and blood would not have suffered in this crazy way. I look on him, like uncle does, as one of fate's curses.'

Hammam said with a smile:

'Perhaps his least qualities are those very things you pride yourself on — strength and daring.'

'He got this land as a gift without any trouble, and then he became proud and tyrannical.'

'Don't deny what I realized a short time ago; that not even the Governor himself had it in him to live alone in such a desert.'

'Do you think the story we're told justifies his anger towards our parents?'

'You find much smaller things to justify your aggressiveness towards people.'

Kadri took the jug and drank his fill, belched and said:

'And what have his grandsons done wrong? He doesn't know what it is to be a goatherd, damn him. I wish I knew his will and what he's prepared for us.'

Hammam sighed and said dreamily:

'Riches that will rescue us from hardship so that life can pass in ease and pleasure.'

'You're talking like father. You suffer torment in the mud, and you dream of playing the pipe in a blooming garden. Really, I admire uncle more than father.'

Hammam sat and yawned, then got up and stretched, and said:

'Anyway, we've got somewhere; we have a big enough home, and enough food to keep us alive, and goats and sheep to graze. We sell their milk, and fatten them up to sell them too, and mother makes clothes from their wool.'

'And the pipe and the garden?'

He did not answer, but went towards the flock after picking up his stick from the ground at his feet. Kadri stood and shouted, addressing himself mockingly to the Big House:

'Do you allow us to be your heirs, or will you punish us in your death as you punish us in your life? . . . Answer, Gebelawi . . .'

The echo came back: 'Gebelawi!'

Far away they saw a figure coming towards them, its features as yet indistinct. It approached slowly until they could make it out, and Kadri drew himself up automatically, his eyes shining with joy. Hammam smiled at his brother, then looked at the sheep unconcernedly and announced quietly:

'Dusk is not far off.'

Kadri said scornfully:

'Let dawn come for all I care!'

He took a few steps forward, waving his arms to welcome the girl. She drew near to them, tired by the walk, partly because of the distance, and partly because the sand dragged at her slippers. She was looking at them with her green eyes, which were bold as well as enticing. She was wrapped in a shawl up to her shoulders, leaving her head and neck bare, and the wind played with her plaits. Kadri's voice rang out with a pleasure that wiped the signs of cruelty from his face:

'Hello, Hind!'

She replied in her gentle voice:

'Hello!' Then, to Hammam: 'Good evening, cousin.'

Hammam smiled.

'Good evening, cousin, how are you?'

Kadri took her hand and went with her towards the big rock which stood a few yards from where they were. They went round the rock to the side facing the gebel, cut off from the desert and its occupants. He drew her to him and enfolded her in his arms and gave her a long kiss on the lips till their teeth touched. For a moment the girl was carried away. Then she managed to free herself from his arms and stood breathing hard and straightening her shawl, meeting his eager look with a smile; but the smile faded, as if she had thought of something, and she pursed her lips in displeasure and said:

'I came after a struggle. Oh dear, what an unbearable life.'

Kadri understood what she meant and scowled.

'Don't take any notice. We are the children of fools. My good father is a fool, and your wicked father is just as foolish. All they want is for us to inherit their hatred for each other. What stupidity! But tell me how you managed to come?'

She puffed, and said:

'The day passed like every day, with a non-stop quarrel between mother and father. He hit her once or twice and she screamed curses at him and worked off her anger by breaking a jug, but her temper didn't get any worse than that today; she often grabs him by the collar and curses him, bearing his blows as best she can. But when wine's got into him, then you're only safe right out of his sight. So I often want to run away, and feel I hate life, and I comfort myself by crying till my eyes are sore; but it doesn't matter. I waited till he had dressed and gone out; then I took my shawl, and mother came at me and tried to stop me as usual, but I escaped from her and came out.'

Kadri took her hand in his and said:

'Didn't she guess where you were going?'

'I don't think so, but it doesn't worry me; she'd never dare tell father.'

Kadri laughed.

'What do you think he'd do if he knew?'

At a loss, she echoed his laugh.

'I'm not afraid of him in spite of his harshness, in fact I love him and he loves me in a simple way that's quite out of keeping with his harsh nature. But he doesn't bother to tell me I'm the most precious thing in his world, and perhaps that's the root of my troubles.'

Kadri sat down on the ground at the foot of the rock, and invited her to do so too by smoothing the ground at his side. She sat down, throwing off the heavy shawl. He leaned over and kissed her cheek and said:

'It seems to be easier to get the better of my father than of yours, and yet he gets very violent when your father is mentioned and refuses to admit that he has any good qualities.'

She laughed.

"Men! ... My father abuses yours just like that. Your father looks down on mine for his roughness, and mine on yours for his gentleness. The main point is that they'll never agree about anything.'

Kadri's head jerked up as if he were butting the air, and he said defiantly:

'But we shall do what we like.'

Hind said, looking at him with tender affection:

'My father is like that – able to do whatever he likes.'

'I'm able to do many things. What does this drunken old uncle have in mind for you?'

She laughed in spite of herself and said half seriously, half playfully:

'Speak politely about my father.' She tweaked his ear. 'I've often wondered what he has in mind for me. It sometimes seems to me that he doesn't want me to marry anyone.'

He stared at her, refusing to take her seriously. She went on:

'I once saw him looking furiously at the Big House and saying: "If you're pleased to do down your sons and grandsons, are you going to do down your granddaughter as well? No place is fit for Hind except your barred and bolted house." Another time he told mother a young man from Kafr el Zaghari wanted to marry me. Mother was delighted, and he shouted at her in a rage: "You wretched, small minded creature! Who is this boy from Kafr el Zaghari? The lowest servant in the Big House is better than him." Mother asked him: "Who do you think is worthy of her?" He shouted: "The answer to that is with that monster hidden away behind the walls of his house. She's his granddaughter, and no one in the world is good enough for her. I want a husband who is like me for her. Mother said in spite of herself: "Do you want her to be as unhappy as her mother?" He sprang at her like a wild animal and kicked her till she ran away from the hut.'

'That's madness.'

'He hates our grandfather, and curses him whenever he mentions him. But deep down he's proud to be his son.'

Kadri clenched his fist and started pounding it on his thigh saying:

'We could have been a lot happier if we had never had that man for a grandfather.'

She said bitterly:

'We could have been . . .'

He drew her to him with a force that matched the heat of his words and hugged her powerfully, keeping her tight in his arms while their minds turned from troubling questions to the promised passion. He said:

'Your lips . . .'

At that Hammam retreated from his position by the rock and tiptoed back to the flock, smiling sheepishly and sadly. The very air seemed to him to be drunk with love, and love seemed to mean disaster, but he said to himself: 'His face was pure and gentle. He only looks like that behind the rock. There's no power like love to take away our cares.

Meanwhile the sky was losing its colour and surrendering to the gathering darkness, and gentle winds were stirring from the west. A billy goat mounted a nanny goat. Hammam began talking to himself again: 'Mother will be happy when this goat gives birth to its kids; but the birth of a human being can spell tragedy. There's a curse on our heads before we are born. I'm amazed by this enmity between brothers; how long must we bear this hatred? If the past were forgotten, how happy the present would be! But we shall go on gazing at this house which is the source of all our strength and all our misery.' His eyes rested on the goat and he smiled and set off round the flock, whistling and waving his stick, and turning towards the great rock, which stood in seeming indifference to all that existed.

Omayma woke as usual when there was but one star left in the sky. She called Adham till he woke up moaning. He got up and left the room, heavy with sleep, to waken Kadri and Hammam in the outhouse where they slept. The hut had been extended and in its new form was like a small house. A wall surrounded it and enclosed a space at the back as a sheep pen. A tangle of creepers covered the wall and softened its rough look, showing that Omayma had not yet lost hope of realizing her old dream of beautifying her hut as far as possible on the lines of the Big House. The men gathered round a tub of water in the yard and washed their faces, then put on their work clothes. The breeze carried the smell of burning wood and the sound of the younger children crying from inside the hut. At last they sat round the table in front of the entrance, eating stewed beans from a big dish.

The autumn air was moist and slightly chilly at this early hour, but they had tough bodies well able to withstand its attacks. In the distance could be seen Idris's hut which had also been extended. As for the Big House, it stood silent and turned in on itself, as though no ties held it to the outside world . . .

Omayma carried a jug of fresh milk, put it on the table and sat down. Kadri asked her mockingly:

'Why don't you sell the milk to the house of our respected grandfather?'

Adham, now grey at the temples, turned to him and said:

'Shut up and eat! Silence is the best we can ever hope for from you.'

Omayma said, chewing a mouthful:

'The time has come to pickle lemons and olives and green peppers. Kadri, you used to enjoy the days when we made pickle and you helped with the lemons . . .'

Kadri said bitterly:

'We used to love it when we were small, for no good reason . . .'

Adham asked him, returning the jug to its place:

'What's the trouble with you today; who do you think you are?'

Kadri laughed and made no answer, but Hammam said:

'Market day is near; we must sort out the sheep.'

His mother nodded in agreement, but his father spoke to Kadri again:

'Kadri, don't be a brute. Whenever I meet anyone who knows you, he complains to me about you. I'm afraid you may repeat your uncle's way of life . . .'

'Or my grandfather's way of life!'

Adham's eyes blazed with anger.

'Don't speak badly of your grandfather; have you ever heard me talk that way? Besides, he's never done you wrong.'

Kadri protested vigorously:

'As long as he wrongs you he's wronging us.'

'Shut up! Give us the pleasure of your silence.'

'Because of him we're forced to lead this life, which is also the fate of our uncle's daughter.'

'What is she to us? Her father was the cause of the disaster.'

Kadri shouted:

'I mean it's not right for a woman of our blood to grow up out in this desert. Tell me who this poor girl is going to marry?'

'Let her marry the Devil himself. She's no business of ours. She must be a beast of prey like her father.'

He looked at his wife for support. Omayma said:

'Yes, like her father.'

Adham spat and said:

'Damn her and her father!'

Hamman said:

'Isn't this talk spoiling our breakfast?'

Omayma said gently:

'Don't exaggerate; the happiest times are the times when we're all together.'

At that moment they heard Idris roaring curses and insults at the top of his voice. Adham said in disgust:

'The dawn prayer has begun.'

He took a last mouthful and left the table. He went to his barrow and began pushing it along, crying: 'Look after yourselves.' They said good-bye, and off he went to Gemalia. Hammam got up and went down the path to the goat pen. Soon the goats and sheep were bleating, and their hooves pattered as they filled the path on their outward journey. Kadri got up too and picked up his stick. He waved good-bye to his mother and caught up with his brother. When they neared Idris's hut Idris stood in their path and asked sarcastically:

'How much a head, young man?'

Kadri studied him with curiosity while Hammam avoided looking at him, Idris asked again:

'Will neither of you sons of the cucumber merchant be good enough to answer me?'

Kadri answered sharply:

'If you want to buy, go to the market.'

Idris asked chuckling:

'And if I decided to take one by force?'

Hind's voice came from inside the hut:

'Father, we don't want any scenes . . .'

He answered her playfully:

'You mind your own business and leave the slave's sons to me.'

Hammam said:

'We haven't got in your way; don't get in ours.'

'Oh! The voice of Adham! You should be among the sheep, not behind them.'

Hammam said defiantly:

'Father ordered us not to answer your taunts.'

Idris guffawed loudly.

'May God reward him well! But for these orders of his you'd surely be done for. You live as respected men thanks to my name. God's curse on you all; get out of my sight!'

They went on their way, twirling their sticks from time to time. Hammam remained pale with emotion. He said to Kadri:

'The man is despicable. Even at this early hour his breath reeks of wine.'

'He talks a lot, but he doesn't lift a finger to harm us.'

Hammam denied this hotly:

'On the contrary, he has stolen sheep from us more than once.'

'He's a drunkard, but unfortunately he is our uncle; we just have to accept that.'

They were silent for a while as they made for the big rock. A few clouds floated in the sky and the sunshine drenched the endless sands. Hammam could no longer bear to hide what he wanted to say:

'You'd be making a great mistake if you joined his family.'

Kadri's eyes flashed with anger. He shouted:

'Don't you try to tell me what to do; father is bad enough.'

Hammam, who had not yet recovered from Idris's insults, said:

'Our life is full of troubles; don't add to them.'

Kadri shouted:

'I hope they'll destroy you – these troubles you create for yourselves; as for me, I shall do what I like.'

They had now reached the place where they grazed the sheep, and Hammam turned to his brother and said to him:

'I think you're running away from the consequences of what you're doing.'

Kadri seized him by the shoulder and shouted:

'You're just jealous, that's all.'

Hammam was flabbergasted. His brother's words had taken him by surprise. But on the other hand he was used to his sudden outbursts. He lifted his brother's hand off his shoulder, saying:

'God help us!'

Kadri folded his arms and shook his head scornfully. Hammam said:

'The best thing I can do is leave you to yourself until you're sorry: you won't own to your mistake – not until it's too late.'

He turned his back on him and made for the shady side of the rock. Kadri stood glowering in the hot sunshine.

# 16 ✳ ✳ ✳ ✳ ✳ ✳ ✳ ✳ ✳ ✳ ✳ ✳ ✳ ✳ ✳ ✳ ✳ ✳ ✳ ✳ ✳

Adham's family was sitting in front of the hut, eating supper by the faint light of the stars, when there happened something the like of which had not been seen in the desert since the expulsion of Adham. The gates of the Big House opened, and out came a figure bearing a lamp. All eyes were raised to the lamp in amazement, following it as it moved through the darkness like a will o' the wisp. When it was half-way to the hut, their eyes fixed on the figure, examining it by the light of the lamp, till Adham whispered: 'It's Amme Kerim, the gatekeeper.' Their astonishment grew when they realized for certain that he was making for them. They all became quite still, some with food in their hands and some with mouths full. The man reached them and stood with hand raised, saying:

'Good evening, Mr Adham sir.'

Adham trembled at the sound of the voice he had not heard for twenty years. It recalled from the depths of his memory his father's voice, the scent of jasmine and henna, longings and sorrows. The earth seemed to tremble with him. He said, fighting back his tears:

'Good evening, Amme Kerim!'

The man said with undisguised emotion:

'I hope you and your family are well.'

'Quite well, Amme Kerim, thank God.'

The man said kindly:

'I wish I could tell you all that is in my mind, but I have been charged only to inform you that my noble master summons your son Hammam to meet him at once.'

There was silence. They exchanged glances, and confusion overcame them. A voice asked:

'Only Hammam?'

They turned resentfully to see Idris listening near by. However, Amme Kerim did not answer him, but raised his hand in salute and went back towards the Big House leaving them all in the darkness. Idris was enraged at him and shouted after him:

'Are you going to leave me without an answer, you son of a bitch?'

Kadri awoke from his trance and asked furiously:

'Why only Hammam?'

And Idris asked again:

'Yes, why only Hammam?'

Adham said to him, finding perhaps an outlet for his emotion in speaking to him:

'Go home and leave us in peace.'

'Peace? I'll stand where I please.'

Hammam looked up at the Big House in silence, his heart beating so hard that he felt he could hear it's echo from Gebel Mukattam. His father said:

'Go to your grandfather, Hammam, go in safety.'

Kadri turned to his father and asked him defiantly:

'And me? Aren't I your son like him?'

'Don't talk like Idris, Kadri. You are certainly my son just as much as him. I'm not to blame; I didn't give the invitation.'

Idris contradicted him:

'But it's in your power to refuse this discrimination between two brothers.'

'That's not my business. Hammam, you must go. Kadri's turn will come, I'm sure of that.'

Idris said as he was about to go:

'You're an unjust father, like your own father; poor Kadri! Why should he be punished without having done wrong? But in our family, curses always fall on the best members first. God has indeed damned this crazy house.'

He went, and the darkness swallowed him up. At that Kadri cried out:

'You have done me wrong, father!'

'Don't talk like him. Come here, Kadri; and you, Hammam, go.'

'I wish my brother was coming with me.'

'He'll meet you afterwards.'

Kadri shouted furiously:

'What's this injustice? Why has he preferred him to me? He doesn't know him any more than he knows me; why should he pick him out to invite?'

Adham gave Hammam a push saying:

'Go!'

And Hammam left.

Omayma whispered:

'Take care of yourself.'

Weeping, she took Kadri in her arms, but he broke away from her and set off in his brother's footsteps. Adham shouted at him:

'Come back. Don't gamble with your future.'

Kadri said angrily:

'No power on earth will bring me back.'

Omayma's crying grew louder, and the younger children inside cried. Kadri strode out till he caught up with his brother. Nearby in the darkness he saw the figure of Idris drawing Hind along by the hand. When they reached the gates, Idris pushed Kadri to the left of Hammam and Hind to his right and withdrew a few paces, shouting:

'Open up, Amme Kerim. The grandchildren have come to meet their grandfather.'

The door opened and on the threshold appeared Amme Karim, lamp in hand. He said politely:

'Please come in, Mr Hammam, sir.'

Idris cried out:

'And this is his brother Kadri, and this is Hind, who is the image of my mother who died crying.'

Amme Kerim said politely:

'You know, Mr Idris, sir, that no one enters this house without his permission.'

He signalled to Hammam, who entered, and Kadri followed him taking Hind by the hand, but a voice that Idris knew came from beyond the garden, saying sternly:

'Go in your shame, you two.'

Their feet stayed as if nailed to the ground. The gate closed. Idris rushed on them and seized them by the shoulders and asked in a voice trembling with rage:

'What shame does he mean?'

Hind screamed with pain, while Kadri turned suddenly towards Idris and lifted his hands from himself and Hind. Hind turned tail and fled into the darkness. Idris darted back, then aimed a blow at Kadri. The boy stood up to it in spite of its force and punched him back even harder, and they let fly, exchanging punches and kicks with savage brutality under the walls of the Big House, Idris yelled:

'I'll kill you, you son of a bitch.'

Kadri shouted:

'I'll kill you before you can kill me.'

They exchanged blows till the blood flowed from Kadri's mouth and nose. Adham came, running like a madman, and shouted at the top of his voice:

'Leave my son alone, Idris!'

Idris yelled with hatred:

'I'll kill him for his crime.'

'I shan't let you kill him. And if you kill him I shan't let you go on living.'

Hind's mother came up wailing and shouted:

'Hind has run away, Idris, catch her before she disappears.'

Adham threw himself between Idris and Kadri and shouted at his brother:

'Come to your senses; you're fighting for no reason. Your daughter is pure and untouched, but you've terrified her and she's fled; catch her before she disappears.'

He drew Kadri to himself and led him back quickly, saying:

'Hurry! I left your mother unconscious.'

As for Idris, he went off into the darkness crying at the top of his voice: 'Hind! Hind!'


# 17 ✳ ✳ ✳ ✳ ✳ ✳ ✳ ✳ ✳ ✳ ✳ ✳ ✳ ✳ ✳ ✳ ✳ ✳ ✳

Hammam followed Amme Kerim, and they passed down the path under a canopy of jasmine, making for the terrace. In the garden night seemed to be something new, soft, full of the scent of flowers and fragrant herbs. Its loveliness flowed into his depths. He was overcome with feelings of wonder and love for the place, and knew that he was enjoying the most precious moments of his life. There was light behind the shutters of some of the windows, and from the door of the drawing-room a rectangle of light was cast on the ground in the garden. His heart pounded as he imagined the life in the great rooms behind the windows – who lived there and how. His heart beat still harder when he realized that he was descended from the children of this house, a drop of this life, and that he had come to meet it face to face, in his long blue smock and his white cap and with his bare feet. They climbed the steps to the terrace and went to a little door at the right-hand end which opened on to a staircase. They went up in a deathly silence, till they reached a long gallery lit by a lamp hanging from the carved ceiling. They made their way to a big closed door in the middle of the gallery, and Hammam said to himself with emotion: 'Somewhere in this gallery, perhaps on this very spot, my mother stood twenty years ago to guard the way. What a pathetic thought.'

Amme Kerim knocked on the great door, seeking permission for Hammam to go in, then he pushed him forward gently and stood to one side, motioning him to enter. The boy went in, sunk in thought, polite and afraid, and he did not hear the door close behind him. He felt only mystery in the light which shone on the ceiling and on the corners. His whole attention was drawn towards the focal point where the old man sat cross-legged on a divan. He had never seen his grandfather before, but he did not doubt for a moment the identity of the man sitting before him. Who could this giant be if not his grandfather of whom he had heard such amazing things? He approached his seat, meeting from his large eyes a look which drew out of his memory all that it contained, but which at the same time filled his heart with peace and calm. He bowed so low that his forehead almost touched the divan, and held out his hand. The old man gave him his hand, and he kissed it with deep devotion and said, with unexpected boldness:

'Good evening, grandfather!'

The answer came in a booming voice with a certain kindness in its tone:

'Welcome, my son; sit down!'

The boy went over to a chair to the right of the divan and sat on the edge of it. Gebelawi said:

'Sit back comfortably.'

Hammam slid deep into the chair, his heart overflowing with joy. His lips moved in a whisper of thanks, then there was silence. For a long time he stared at the pattern in the carpet at his feet, feeling the impact of the gaze that was fixed on him. His attention suddenly turned to the secret chamber on his right and he glanced at the door fearfully and sadly. The old man at once asked:

'What do you know of this door?'

His limbs trembled and he marvelled at his observation. He said boldly:

'I know it was the gateway to our sufferings.'

'And what did you think of your grandfather when you heard the story?'

He opened his mouth to speak, but the old man added:

'Tell me the truth.'

His tone had the effect of making Hammam say frankly:

'It seems to me that my parents' behaviour was quite wrong, but their punishment was terribly harsh.'

Gebelawi smiled and said:

'That is more or less how you feel. I hate lying and deception, and that is why I have expelled from my house everyone who disgraces himself.'

The tears came to Hammam's eyes. His grandfather went on:

'You seem to me to be a decent boy; that is why I sent for you.'

Hammam said in a voice dampened by tears:

'Thank you, sir.'

His grandfather said quietly:

'I've decided to give you a chance which has not been offered to anyone else from outside. It is that you should live in this house and marry in it and begin a new life here.'

Hammam's heart raced, drunk with joy, and he waited for more. After a pause, he said:

'Thank you for your kindness.'

56

'You deserve it.'

The boy looked from his grandfather to the carpet, then asked anxiously:

'And my family?'

Gebelawi said reproachfully:

'I said quite clearly what I meant.'

Hammam implored him:

'They deserve your mercy and forgiveness.'

Gebelawi asked rather icily:

'Didn't you hear what I said?'

'Yes indeed, but they are my mother and father and brothers. My father is a man who . . .'

'Didn't you hear what I said?'

There was anger in his voice. Silence fell. Then the old man announced the end of the conversation by saying:

'Come back when you've said good-bye to them.'

Hammam stood up and kissed his grandfather's hand and left. He found Amme Kerim waiting. The man moved off and Hammam followed him without a word. When they reached the terrace Hammam saw a girl in the patch of light at the near end of the garden, hurrying out of sight. He just saw the side of her face and her neck and her slender figure. His grandfather's voice echoed in his ears: 'Live in this house and marry in it' . . . marry a girl like this one – the life my father knew; how has fate been so cruel to him? Where has he found the courage to bear life after that, pushing about his barrow? This chance is like a dream – my father's dream for twenty years.

18 ✳ ✳ ✳ ✳ ✳ ✳ ✳ ✳ ✳ ✳ ✳ ✳ ✳ ✳ ✳ ✳ ✳ ✳ ✳ ✳

Hammam went back to the hut and found his family sitting up, looking out for his return. They swarmed round him full of questions. Adham asked anxiously:

'What happened, my son?'

Hammam noticed Kadri's swollen eye. He went and took a closer look. Adham said sadly:

'There has been a fight between your brother and that man.'

And he pointed towards Idris's hut which seemed to be drowned in darkness and silence. Kadri said angrily:

'All because of the foul, lying accusation thrown at me from inside the house . . .'

Hammam pointed at Idris's hut and asked anxiously:

'What is going on over there?'

Adham said sadly:

'That man and his wife are searching for their runaway daughter.'

Kadri shouted:

'Who is to blame if not that damned old monster?

Omayma implored him:

'Don't talk so loud.'

Kadri yelled furiously:

'What are you afraid of? Nothing, except that your hopes of returning should come to nothing. Believe me, you won't leave this hut until you die.'

Adham was enraged:

'Stop raving. You are mad. God! Didn't you want to marry that runaway girl?'

'I shall marry her.'

'Shut up! I'm sick of your stupidity.'

Omayma said miserably:

'I can't bear to live near Idris any longer.'

Adham turned to Hammam and said:

'I asked you what happened.'

Hammam said in a voice without a trace of happiness:

'Grandfather has asked me to live in the Big House.'

Adham waited for him to go on, but when the boy said nothing, he asked in despair:

'And us? What did he say about us?'

Hammam shook his head sadly and said:

'Nothing.'

Kadri laughed a bitter laugh and asked scornfully:

'And what has brought you here?'

'Yes indeed, what has brought me here? Only that happiness was not made for the likes of me. I didn't forget to remind him about you.'

Kadri said:

'Thank you, but what made him prefer you to us?'

Adham said with a sigh:

'Without any doubt you are the best of us all, Hammam.'

Kadri shouted bitterly:

'You're the one, father, who never mentions that man without some praise he doesn't deserve.'

Adham said:

'You don't understand anything.'

'That man is worse than his son Idris.'

Omayma said beseechingly:

'You have broken my heart, Kadri, and closed the doors of hope in my face.'

Kadri said contemptuously:

'There is no hope except in this desert. Realize that and relax. Forget about that damned house. I'm not afraid of the desert; I am not afraid even of Idris. I can pay back his blows many times over. Spit on that house and relax.'

Adham wondered to himself: 'Can life go on like this for ever? Why have you raised our hopes, father, without forgiving us? What can soften your heart if all this time has not softened it? What is the use of hope if all this suffering has not made us fit to be forgiven by the one we love?' He said in a heavy voice:

'Tell me what's troubling you, Hammam.'

'He said: "Come back when you've said good-bye to them." '

The darkness did not hide Omayma's attempt to smother her sobs. Kadri asked evilly:

'What's keeping you?'

Adham said firmly:

'Go Hammam, with our blessing, and take care of yourself.'

Kadri said with mock seriousness:

'Go, you fine man, and don't take any notice of anyone.'

Adham shouted:

'Don't insult your good brother.'

Kadri said laughing.

'He's the worst of us all.'

Hammam said:

'If I decide to stay it won't be for your sake.'

Adham said firmly:

'No; go without any hesitation.'

Omayma said between her tears:

'Yes, and take care of yourself.'

'No, mother, I'm not going.'

Adham cried out:

'Are you mad, Hammam?'

'Not at all, Father. The matter needs thinking over.'

'It doesn't need any such thing.'

Hammam said with determination, pointing to Idris's hut:

'I think things are going to happen . . .'

Kadri said:

'You're too weak to defend even yourself from harm, let alone other people.'

'The best thing for me is to ignore what you say.'

Adham spoke again hopefully:

'Go, Hammam.'

Hammam went towards the hut, saying:

'I shall stay with you.'


# 19 ✳ ✳ ✳ ✳ ✳ ✳ ✳ ✳ ✳ ✳ ✳ ✳ ✳ ✳ ✳ ✳ ✳ ✳ ✳

Only the afterglow of the sun remained. People were no longer about, and Kadri and Hammam were alone with their flock in the desert. In that whole day they had only exchanged such words as their work made necessary. Kadri had been away much of the time, and Hammam had guessed that he was sniffing out news of Hind. He had stayed alone near the goats in the shadow of the big rock.

Suddenly Kadri asked Hammam rather provocatively:

'Tell me what you mean to do about going to our grandfather; have you changed your mind?'

Hammam was annoyed:

'That's my business.'

Anger flared up in Kadri's heart, and his face darkened. He said:

'Why did you stay? When will you leave? When will you have the courage to say what you mean to do?'

'No; I stayed to take my share of the suffering which your behaviour has brought.'

Kadri laughed cruelly:

'You say that to cover up your jealousy.'

Hammam shook his head in amazement and said:

'You deserve my pity, not my jealousy.'

Kadri came closer to him, shaking with fury, and said in a half choked voice:

'How I hate you when you pretend to be wise.'

Hammam stared contemptuously at him but said nothing. Kadri went on:

'People like you are a disgrace to the world.'

Hammam did not lower his eyes under the look of hatred that was directed at him, but said firmly:

'You know, I'm not afraid of you.'

'Has that greatest of villains promised to protect you?'

'Your anger makes you very nasty.'

Suddenly Kadri hit him in the face. The blow did not catch him off his guard and he hit back even harder, shouting:

'Don't get any madder . . .'

Kadri bent down swiftly and picked up a stone and threw it with all his might at his brother. Hammam jumped to dodge it, but it hit him on the forehead. He let out a cry and stood rooted to the spot, anger still blazing in his eyes. Suddenly the anger in them was extinguished and they went quite blank, as though turned inwards; he staggered and fell on his face. Kadri's mood changed at once. His anger evaporated, leaving him like cold steel after the smelting, and fear gripped him. He wished desperately that the prostrate man would get up or move, but he did not. He bent over him and stretched out his hand to shake him gently, but he did not respond. He turned him on his back to lift his nose and mouth out of the sand, but he lay there motionless, his eyes in a fixed stare. Kadri knelt beside him and began shaking him and rubbing his chest and hands, looking in terror at the blood pouring from the wound. He called his name hopefully, but he didn't answer. His silence was as heavy and deep as if it were part of him. This stillness was different from the stillness of a living creature or of non-living matter – no feeling, no stirring, no concern with anything; like something from another world, nothing to do with this world.

Kadri instinctively knew death. He began tearing at his hair in despair. He looked round fearfully, but nothing stirred save the sheep and insects, which took no interest in him. Soon night would fall, and the darkness would deepen. He stood up resolutely, took his stick, and went to a place between the rock and the gebel. He began digging, scooping the earth up with his hands, working obstinately, with the sweat dripping from him and his limbs trembling. Then he hurried back to his brother, shook him and called him for the last time, without hoping for any response, and dragged him off by the ankles to the grave. He looked at him, groaning, hesitated a while, then heaped the soil over him. He stood wiping the sweat from his face with the sleeve of his smock, then covered the patches of blood with sand.

He threw himself down exhausted, feeling all force had gone out of him. He wanted to cry, but the tears would not come. He thought: 'Death has defeated me.' He had not invited it, nor intended it, but it had come as it pleased. If he could have turned into a goat he would gladly have disappeared amongst the flock. If he could have become a grain of sand he would gladly have been buried in the ground. 'I can't claim any strength, for I can't give back the life I have taken. That sight will never leave my memory. What I buried was neither living nor lifeless, but something else that my hand has made.'

Kadri came home driving the goats. Adham's barrow was not in its place. His mother's voice called from indoors:

'Why are you two late?'

He shooed the flock into the path leading to their pen saying:

'I fell asleep. Is Hammam not back yet?'

Omayma raised her voice above the noise of the children:

'No. Wasn't he with you?'

He swallowed hard and said:

'He left me at midday without telling me where he was going. I thought he had come back here.'

Adham, who had just arrived and was pushing the barrow into the yard, asked:

'Did you quarrel?'

'Never.'

'I think you must have been the cause of his going off, but where can he be?'

Omayma had come out into the yard, while Kadri had shut the gate of the pen and was washing his hands and face in a basin under the barrel. He had to face up to the situation. The world had changed, but despair is a powerful force. He joined his parents in the darkness, drying his face on a corner of his smock. Omayma asked:

'Which way did Hammam go? He's never been off like this before.'

Adham agreed with her, saying:

'Yes; tell us how he went, and why.'

Kadri's heart pounded at the picture that sprang to his memory, but he said:

'I was sitting in the shade of the rock. I happened to turn and I saw him going towards our place. I thought of calling him but didn't.'

Omayma said, much upset:

'If only you had called him instead of letting your anger get the better of you.'

Adham looked anxiously into the surrounding darkness. He saw a feeble light in the window of Idris's hut, which showed that life was stirring there again, but he paid no attention to it. His gaze fastened on the Big House, and he asked:

'Do you think he has gone to his grandfather?'

Omayma said:

'He wouldn't do that without telling us.'

Kadri said in a faint voice:

'Perhaps shame prevented him.'

Adham gave him a questioning look, alarmed by the lack of scorn or enmity in his voice.

'We pressed him to go but he wouldn't.'

Kadri said weakly:

'He was embarrassed to accept in front of us.'

'That wouldn't be like him. What's the matter; you look sick?'

'I had to do all the work by myself.'

Adham cried out wretchedly:

'I'm really worried.'

Omayma said in a hoarse voice:

'I shall go to the Big House to ask about him.'

Adham shrugged his shoulders hopelessly and said:

'No one will answer you. But I assure you he didn't go there.'

Omayma sighed heavily and said:

'O God! I've never been so upset before. Do something, man . . .'

Adham groaned and said:

'Well, then, let's look everywhere for him.'

Kadri said:

'Perhaps he is on his way here.'

Omayma cried out:

'We mustn't lose any time.' Then, overcome with grief, looking at Idris's hut: 'Can Idris have waylaid him?'

Adham said gruffly:

'Idris's enemy is Kadri, not Hammam.'

'He wouldn't hesitate to kill any one of us. I am going to see him.'

Adham prevented her from going, saying:

'Don't make matters any more complicated. I promise you I shall go to Idris, and to the Big House, if we don't find him . . .'

He gave Kadri a worried look. What was he thinking so quietly? Didn't he know more than he had said? Where could Hammam be? Omayma made to leave the yard and Adham hurried to her and took her by the shoulder. Just then the gate of the Big House opened. They looked at it and in a few moments Amme Kerim's form appeared, coming towards them. Adham went out to meet him, saying: 'Welcome Amme Kerim.' The man greeted him and said:

'My noble master asks what is keeping Hammam.'

Omayma said wretchedly:

'We don't know where he is. We even thought he might be with you.'

'My master asks what is keeping him.'

Omayma cried out:

'God forbid what I suspect.'

Amme Kerim went away. Omayma began rolling her head about as if she were going to have a fit. Adham led her to their room inside, where the younger children were crying. He shouted roughly:

'Don't leave this room. I shall come back with him, but mind you don't leave this room.'

He returned to the yard and stumbled upon Kadri sitting on the ground. He bent over him and hissed:

'Tell me what you know about your brother.'

He raised his head quickly, but something prevented him from speaking. His father asked again:

'Kadri, tell me what you have done to your brother.'

The boy said in a voice that could scarcely be heard:

'Nothing.'

Adham went back inside and returned with a lamp which he lit and put on his barrow. Its light fell on Kadri's face, and he examined him for a while and said:

'There is pain in your face.'

Omayma's voice came from inside but was almost inaudible above the noise of the children. Adham shouted:

'Keep quiet woman. Die if you like, but die quietly!'

He examined his son again. Suddenly his hands trembled. He took hold of the hem of Kadri's sleeve and said in terror:

'Blood? What's this? Your brother's blood?'

Kadri stared at his sleeve and shuddered without meaning to, then hung his head in despair. By this movement he acknowledge the truth. Adham pulled him to his feet and pushed him out into the open with a violence he had not known before. A darkness blacker than night covered his eyes.

# 21 ✷ ✷ ✷ ✷ ✷ ✷ ✷ ✷ ✷ ✷ ✷ ✷ ✷ ✷ ✷ ✷ ✷ ✷ ✷ ✷

Adham pushed Kadri out into the desert, saying:

'We will make for the Derrasa desert, so as not to pass Idris's hut.'

They went deep into the darkness, Kadri staggering slightly under his father's heavy grip. Adham hurrying along, asked in an old man's voice:

'Tell me, did you hit him? What did you hit him with? What state did you leave him in?'

Kadri did not answer. His father's grip was very tight, but he hardly felt the pain. He wished the sun would never rise. Adham went on:

'Have pity on me and speak – but you don't know the meaning of pity. I condemned myself to suffer the day I fathered you. Curses have followed me for twenty years, and here I am asking pity from someone who knows none.'

Kadri burst into tears, and his shoulder shook in Adham's heavy hand. He went on shaking with sobs, so that Adham was touched, but he said:

'Is that your answer? Why, Kadri, why? How could you? Confess now in the darkness, before you see yourself in the light of day.'

Kadri shouted:

'May day never come!'

'We are the children of darkness; day will never dawn for us. I used to think evil lived in Idris's hut; but here it is in our own flesh and blood. Idris gets drunk and laughs at us and misbehaves. But in our family one kills another. O God! Did you kill your brother?'

'No, no!'

'Then where is he?'

'I didn't mean to kill him.'

Adham shouted:

'But he's dead.'

Kadri started crying again and his father's grip tightened. 'If Hammam is dead — Hammam the flower of life, his grandfather's favourite — it's as though he had never been. But for this gnawing pain, I wouldn't have believed it.' They reached the big rock and Adham asked him in a harsh voice:

'Where did you leave him, you criminal?'

Kadri went to the grave he had dug for his brother and stood by it, between the rock and the gebel. Adham asked:

'Where is your brother? I see nothing.'

Kadri said almost inaudibly:

'I buried him here.'

Adham shouted:

'You buried him?'

He took a box of matches from his pocket, lit one and examined the ground by its light, till he saw a patch that had been disturbed and the trail left by the corpse leading up to it. Adham groaned with pain and began scraping the sand away with his trembling hands. He worked on, in despair, until his fingers touched Hammam's head. He pushed his hands through to the sides of the corpse and lifted it gently. He fell on his knees beside it, placing his hands on its head, his eyes closed in hopeless misery, moaning from the depth of his being. He murmured:

'My forty years of life seem like a long illness as I kneel beside your body, my son.'

Kadri was standing on the other side of the corpse. Suddenly Adham stood up looking at him with blind hatred and said in a savage voice:

65

'Hammam will go home again on your shoulders.'

Kadri was horrified and began to retreat, but Adham rushed round the corpse and caught him by the shoulder and yelled:

'Carry your brother!'

Kadri groaned:

'I can't.'

'You were able to kill him . . .'

'I can't, father.'

'Don't call me father; a man who kills his brother has no father, no mother, no brothers.'

'I can't.'

He tightened his grip on him and said:

'A murderer must bear the burden of his victim.'

Kadri tried to escape from Adham's grip, but he would not let him. In his nervous state, Adham rained blows on his face, but he neither dodged the blows nor groaned with pain. Adham stopped, then said:

'Don't lose any time; your mother is waiting.'

Kadri shuddered at the mention of his mother and said hopefully:

'Let me disappear.'

Adham pulled him towards the corpse saying:

'Come, let us carry him together.'

Adham turned to the corpse and placed his hands under Hammam's armpits while Kadri bent down and took his legs. They lifted the body together and went slowly into the desert of Derrasa. Adham was so deep in painful thoughts that he lost all sensations, but Kadri went on suffering from a trembling heart and limbs. His nose was full of a penetrating earthy smell, while the feel of the corpse crept up through his arms and deep down into him. The darkness around them was thick, while on the horizon glimmered the lights of the unsleeping town. Kadri was in utter despair. He stopped and said:

'I'll carry the body by myself.'

He put one arm under its back and one under its thighs, and went along with Adham following.

22 ✳ ✳ ✳ ✳ ✳ ✳ ✳ ✳ ✳ ✳ ✳ ✳ ✳ ✳ ✳ ✳ ✳ ✳

When they neared the hut, Omayma's voice came to them asking anxiously:

'Have you found him?'

Adham shouted in a commanding voice:

'Go inside and wait for me, woman.'

He went in front of Kadri to the hut so as to hide him. At the door Kadri stopped still. His father motioned him to go in but he refused, saying in a whisper:

'I can't face her.'

His father whispered angrily:

'You were able to do something much worse.'

But Kadri stayed where he was.

'No, this is worse.'

Adham pushed him firmly in front of him so that he was forced to move, till they reached the back room. Then Adham rushed at Omayma and stifled the scream that was about to escape from her lips. He said harshly:

'Don't scream, woman. We mustn't attract any attention until we have straightened things out. Let us bear our fate in silence and suffer patiently. The evil was born of your womb and my loins. The curse lies on us all.'

He held her mouth tight. She tried to free herself from his hand, in vain. She attempted to bite him, but could not. Her breathing became irregular, her strength left her and she fainted. Kadri stood holding the body, silent and ashamed, staring at the lamp to avoid looking at her. Adham turned to him and helped him to lay the body on the bed, then covered it tenderly. Kadri looked at his brother's corpse lying under its sheet on the bed they had shared all their lives and felt that there was no longer any place for him in the house. Omayma moved her head and opened her eyes. Adham hurried over to her, saying firmly:

'Mind you don't scream.'

She made to get up and he helped her, warning her not to make any noise. She tried to throw herself on the bed, but he prevented her. She stood, defeated. Then she began relieving her feelings by tearing out her hair, handful after handful. Adham did not care what she did, but said brutally:

'Do what you like, but do it silently.'

She said hoarsely:

'My son! My son!'

Adham said quietly:

'This is his body. Your son, my son has not come back. Here is his murderer; kill him if you like.'

Omayma beat her cheeks and said to Kadri savagely:

'The vilest animal doesn't do what you have done.'

Kadri hung his head in silence, and Adham said:

'Has he died in vain? You don't deserve to live – that would be justice.'

Omayma cried out:

'Yesterday hope dawned. We told him to go but he wouldn't. If only he had gone! If only he hadn't been noble and kind he would have gone; is this murder his reward? How could you do it, you stone-hearted brute? You are no longer my son nor I your mother.'

Kadri uttered not a word, but he said to himself, 'I killed him once but he is killing me every second. I'm not alive. Who says I'm alive?'

Adham asked him roughly:

'What shall I do with you?'

Kadri said calmly:

'You said I must not live.'

Omayma cried:

'How could you bring yourself to kill him?'

Kadri said hopelessly:

'It's no use being sorry. I'm ready to be punished. Death is the least thing I can suffer.'

Adham said angrily:

'But you have made our life worse than death too.'

Omayma shouted, beating her cheeks:

'I hate this life. Bury me with my son. Why don't you let me wail?'

Adham said with bitterness and scorn:

'Its not your throat I'm worried about; I'm afraid that devil might hear us.'

Kadri said:

'Let him hear as much as he likes; I don't care for life any more.'

At that moment Idris's voice came from near the front door:

'Brother Adham! Come here you poor thing.'

They all shuddered, but Adham shouted:

'Go home, and beware of arousing me.'

Idris replied in a loud voice:

'What a dreadful business! Your trouble has saved you from my anger. But let's not talk like this. We're both hurt; you've lost your dear son, and my only daughter has disappeared. Our children were our comfort in our exile, and they've gone. Come, poor brother, let's comfort one another.'

So the secret was out! How? For the first time Omayma was afraid for Kadri. Adham said:

'Your gloating doesn't worry me. It's a small thing beside my pain.'

Idris protested:

'Gloating! Don't you know I cried when I saw you pull the body out of the grave Kadri had dug for it?'

Adham shouted furiously:

'Lousy spy!'

'I cried not only for the victim but also for the murderer, and said to myself "Poor poor Adham; you have lost two sons in one night." [1]

Omayma began to wail, taking no notice of anyone. And Kadri rushed suddenly out of the hut. Then Adham ran after him, and Omayma screamed:

'I don't want to lose both.'

Kadri tried to attack Idris, but Adham pushed him right away then faced his brother defiantly and said:

'Don't provoke us!'

Idris said calmly:

'You're a fool, Adham; you can't tell a friend from an enemy. You attack your brother to defend your sons murderer.'

'Go away from me.'

Idris laughed:

'As you wish. Accept my condolences; and good-bye!'

Idris went off into the darkness. Adham turned to where Kadri had been and found Omayma there asking where he was. Adham was horrified and went off searching the darkness and calling at the top of his voice:

'Kadri! Kadri! Where are you?'

He heard Idris shouting loudly:

'Kadri! Kadri! Where are you?'

# 23 ✳ ✳ ✳ ✳ ✳ ✳ ✳ ✳ ✳ ✳ ✳ ✳ ✳ ✳ ✳ ✳ ✳ ✳ ✳

Hammam was buried in a graveyard belonging to the estate at Bab el Nasr. His funeral was attended by many people, acquaintances of Adham, most of them fellow traders, a few of them customers who liked his gentle character and straight dealing. Idris took it upon himself to be present at the funeral – more than that: he stood receiving condolences as uncle of the deceased. Adham disapproved silently. The funeral procession included many chiefs and layabouts, thieves and bandits. At the burial, Idris stood by the grave, heartening Adham with words of comfort which he endured patiently, making no answer, the tears rolling down his cheeks. Omayma eased her grief by wailing and beating herself and rolling in the dust.

When the people had gone, Adham turned to Idris and said angrily:

'Is there no limit to your cruelty?'

Idris pretended to be taken aback and asked:

'What are you talking about, my poor brother?'

Adham said sharply:

'I never thought you could be as cruel as this, although I didn't think much of you. Death is the end for each of us; how can it give you pleasure?'

Idris said in astonishment:

'Grief has made you forget your manners, but I'll make allowances for you.'

'When will you realize that we are no longer joined by any tie?'

'Merciful heavens! Aren't you my brother? That's a tie that can't be broken.'

'Idris! You've tormented me enough.'

'Grief is ugly, but we've both been hit; you've lost Hammam and Kadri, and I've lost Hind. Gebelawi's got a whoring granddaughter and a killer grandson. Anyway, you're better off than me; you have other children to make up for what's happened.'

Adham asked miserably:

'Are you still jealous of me?'

Idris said in astonishment:

'Idris jealous of Adham?!'

Adham roared:

'If your punishment is not as bad as your deeds, let the world turn to dust.'

'Dust ... dust ...'

Painful days passed, full of sorrows. Grief overcame Omayma and her health worsened and she wasted away. In a few years Adham had aged more than most men do in a long life. The couple constantly suffered from frailty and sickness. One day they both felt very ill and retired to bed, Omayma in the back room with her two youngest children, and Adham in the front room that had belonged to Hammam and Kadri. The day passed and night fell, but they lit no lamp. Adham was content with the moonlight coming in from the yard. He began dozing for short spells and waking into semi-consciousness. He heard Idris's voice outside asking sarcastically:

'Do you need any help?'

He was upset and did not answer. He used to dread the hour when Idris left his hut for his nights out. He heard the voice again saying:

'Let every one witness my devotion and his obstinacy!'

Idris went off singing:

> Three of us climbed the gebel to hunt;
> Passion killed one and love took another.

Adham's eyes filled with tears. 'This evil which never stops teasing, fighting, killing, tossing aside all respect, acting harshly and tyrannically, mocking at the consequences, and laughing till the horizons echo ... it torments the weak, enjoys funerals, sings over tombstones . . . I am near to death and still he mocks me with his laughter. The murderer and his victim under the ground have gone, and in my hut we cry for them both. Time has turned the laughter of childhood in the garden to frowns and tears. What's left of my body is filled with pain. Why all this suffering? Where is the happiness of dreams . . . where?'

Adham imagined he heard footsteps, slow and heavy. Submerged memories flooded back – a penetrating fragrance beyond description. He turned his head towards the door of the hut and saw it open. Then the doorway seemed to be filled by a huge person. He gazed in astonishment and with a mixture of hope and despair. He sighed deeply and murmured:

'Father?!'

It seemed that he heard the old voice saying:

'Good evening, Adham.'

His eyes swam with tears and he tried to stand up but could not. He felt a joy he had not known for over twenty years. He said in a quavering voice:

'Let me believe . . .'

'You cry, but you are the one who has done wrong.'

Adham said in a tearful voice:

'It was a great wrong but a great punishment. But even insects don't lose hope of finding shelter.'

'And so you teach me wisdom!?'

'Forgive me! Forgive me! I am crushed by sorrow and illness. Even my sheep are threatened with destruction.'

'How good you are to be afraid for your sheep.'

Adham asked hopefully:

'Have you forgiven me?'

He answered after a pause:

'Yes.'

Adham shouted, his whole body trembling:

'Thank God! A little while ago I was at the bottom of hell.'

'And now you've found the way out?'

'Yes, like a clear sky after a nightmare.'

'Because of that you're a good son.'

Adham sighed and said:

'I'm the father of a murderer and his victim.'

'The dead can't come back. What do you want?'

Adham groaned and said:

'I used to long for the music in the garden, but today nothing would seem good to me.'

'The estate will belong to your descendants.'

'Thank God!'
'Don't tire yourself; try to sleep.'


Within a short time of one another Adham and Omayma and then Idris departed this life. The children grew up, and after a long absence Kadri returned with Hind and several children. They grew up side by side and married and increased their numbers. The settlement grew, thanks to the money from the estate, and our alley came into existence. From these ancestors are descended all its people.

# Gebel

\* \* \* \* \* \* \* \* \* \* \* \* \* \* \* \* \* \*

The houses built with the revenue of the estate stand on either side of our alley, which is the longest in the neighbourhood. It starts next to where the Big House stands alone in the desert and runs in the direction of Genalia. Most of the better houses are built round courtyards, as in Hamdaan's quarter, but there are plenty of hovels, especially in the half nearer Gemalia. To complete the picture we must mention the Trustee's house at the top of the right-hand row, and the Chief's house facing it at the top of the left-hand row.

The gates of the Big House were closed on its master and his trusted servants. Gebelawi's sons died young, and the only surviving descendant of those who had lived and died in the Big House was Effendi, Trustee of the estate at that time. The people of the alley included peddlers and barrow-boys, owners of shops or cafés and a good many beggars. There was a general trade in drugs, especially hashish, opium and 'gunshot', in which anyone who was able took part. Then, as now, the alley was crowded and noisy, with barefoot children, almost naked, playing in every corner, filling the air with their squeals and covering the ground with their filth. The doorways were surrounded by women, chopping jute leaves, peeling onions, lighting charcoal, gossiping and joking, cursing and swearing. There was ceaseless laughing and crying, the beat of the exorcist's drum, barrows hurrying about, battles of words or fists breaking out here and there, cats miaowing, dogs growling and often fighting over the heaps of rubbish, rats and mice running about the yards and along the walls, people teaming up to kill a snake or scorpion, flies, equalled in numbers only by the lice, sharing every plate and every mug, playing round people's eyes, buzzing into their mouths, seeming to be everybody's friends.

If a young man happened to be bold or muscular, in no time he was attacking decent people and bullying peaceful citizens and making himself the chief of one of the quarters of the alley, extorting protection money from the hard working, living for trouble. Such men were Kidra and Laythi, Abu Saria, Barakat and Hamouda. One of them, Zoklot, got into fights with one after another, until he had beaten them all and become chief of the whole alley, making all the others pay him protection money. Effendi, the Trustee, saw that he needed a man like this to carry out his orders and to ward off any danger that threatened. He took him into his confidence and gave him a large salary out of the revenues of the estate. Zoklot lived in his house opposite the Trustee's and had consolidated his power. The battles between chiefs became rare because their chief could not abide contests that led to one of them gaining strength and thus threatening his own position. And so they could find no outlet for their bottled-up malice, save in the poor, peaceable people.

How had our alley come to this pass?

Gebelawi had promised Adham that the estate would be used for the good of his descendants. The houses were built, the benefits were shared out, and the people enjoyed a period of happiness. When the old man finally closed his doors and cut himself off from the world, the Trustee followed his good example for a while. Then greed got the better of him, and soon he was taking the income of the estate for himself. He began cooking the accounts and whittling away the allowances; then he stopped paying out anything at all, confident of the protection of the chief whose allegiance he had bought, and the people found no way to avoid the meanest kinds of work. Their numbers grew and their poverty increased and they were plunged in misery and filth. The stronger took to bullying, the weaker to begging and all of them to drugs. A man would slave and suffer to earn a few morsels which he then had to share with a chief, not in return for thanks, but for cuffs and insults and curses. The chiefs alone lived in ease and plenty, with their chief over them and the Trustee over everybody, while the ordinary people were trodden underfoot. If some poor man could not pay his protection money, a chief would take his revenge on the whole quarter, and if the victim complained to the Chief or to the Trustee, it would just mean that they beat him too.

I myself have seen this wretched state of affairs in our own day – a faithful image of what people tell us about past times. As for the storytellers in the cafés scattered about the alley, they only tell of the heroic times, avoiding anything that would hurt the mighty, and singing of the virtues of the Trustee and the chiefs; of a justice we do not enjoy, of a mercy we do not meet, of a nobility, a restraint and a fairness that we never see. I ask myself what kept our forefathers, what keeps us, in this accursed alley. The answer is easy: in the other ones we would only find a worse life than that which we endure here, if their chiefs did not destroy us in revenge for the treatment they have had from ours. The

74

worst of it is that we are envied. The people of the neighbourhood say 'What a lucky alley; they have their unique estate and their chiefs whose very mention makes your flesh creep!' But we get nothing from our estate except trouble, and from our chiefs nothing but pain and humiliation. Yet we stay, in spite of all that, and bear the sorrow, looking towards a future which will come no one knows when. We point at the Big House, saying: 'There is the ancestor of us all,' and we point at the chiefs saying: 'And these are our men. All things are in the hand of God.'

25 ✳ ✳ ✳ ✳ ✳ ✳ ✳ ✳ ✳ ✳ ✳ ✳ ✳ ✳ ✳ ✳ ✳ ✳ ✳ ✳

The patience of Hamdaan's people gave out and waves of rebelliousness swept their quarter. They lived at the top of the alley, next to the houses of Effendi and Zoklot, around the place where Adham had built his hut. Their head was Amme Hamdaan, the owner of a café, the best in the whole alley, which was in the middle of the quarter.

Hamdaan was sitting to the right of the entrance of his café, wearing a grey cloak and with an embroidered turban round his head. He kept an eye on Abdoun, the waiter, who hurried about all the time, and he chatted with some of the customers. The café was narrow, but ran back a long way to the storyteller's bench at the far end, under a painting of Adham on his death bed looking at Gebelawi who stood at the door of the hut. Hamdaan signalled to the storyteller who took up his fiddle and prepared to chant. To the accompaniment of its music he began with a salute to Effendi, 'the man dearest to Gebelawi', and Zoklot, 'the finest of men'; then he related an episode of Gebelawi's life a little before the birth of Adham. There were sounds of the drinking of coffee and tea and cinnamon, and smoke rose from the hashish pipes and collected round the lamp in thin clouds. All eyes were on the storyteller and the men nodded their heads at the beauty of the telling or the goodness of the moral. The time of romance passed pleasantly for the eager listeners, and ended. People shouted their appreciation. At that, the rebelliousness that had overtaken Hamdaan's people stirred, and Atris el Aamash said from his seat in the middle of the café, following on from the story about Gebelawi which they had heard:

'There was some good in the world; even Adham was never hungry, not even for a day.'

Old Tamarind appeared at the door, lowering the basket of oranges from her head. Then, addressing Atris el Aamash, she said:

'Bless you, Atris; your words are as sweet as my oranges.'

Hamdaan scolded her:

'Go away woman, and spare us your blabber.'

But Tamarind sat down on the ground in the doorway of the café.

'How nice it is to sit beside you! I've been tramping around and shouting my wares all day and half the night, and all for a few piastres.'

Hamdaan was about to answer her when he saw Dolma coming up with a scowl on his dust-covered face. He watched him coming till he stood in front of him in the doorway of the café and shouted:

'Damn the tyrant! Kidra! Kidra's the biggest tyrant. I asked him to let me put off payment for a day, and he knelt on my chest till I couldn't breathe.'

From the back of the café came the voice of Daabas:

'Come and sit beside me, Dolma. Damn the bastards. We're the rightful masters of this alley, yet we are beaten like dogs. Dolma can't find the money for Kidra, and Tamarind goes about selling oranges, though she can't see an arm's length in front of her; where's your courage, Hamdaan, son of Adham?'

Dolma looked towards the doorway, and Tamarind echoed:

'Where is your courage, son of Adham?'

Hamdaan shouted:

'Be off, Tamarind. You're fifty years too old for marriage: why are you so keen on talking to us men?'

'What men?'

Hamdaan frowned, but Tamarind spoke again before he could, and said apologetically:

'Let me hear the storyteller, sir.'

Daabas said bitterly to the storyteller:

'Tell her how Hamdaan's people were trampled on in this alley.'

The storyteller smiled and said:

'Careful, Mr Daabas; careful, master!'

Daabas protested:

'Who is the master round here? the master beats people, bullies people, murders people; you know who the master is!

The storyteller said anxiously:

'And what if we suddenly find Kidra or another of those devils standing amongst us?'

Daabas said sharply:

'They are all the children of Idris.'

The storyteller said in a hushed voice:

'Careful, Mr Daabas, or we'll find the café tumbling about our ears.'

Daabas rose from his seat, strode across the café and sat down to the right of Hamdaan on his bench. He tried to speak but his voice was drowned by the shouts of some boys who had descended like locusts outside the café, swearing at one another. Daabas yelled at them:

'You little devils! Don't you have any holes to bolt to at night?'

But they did not care what he yelled, and he leapt up as if he had been stung by a scorpion and hurled himself at them. They ran off down the alley shouting: 'What's this?' More than one woman's voice came from the windows of the house opposite the café: 'For Gods sake, Daabas, you've frightened the children, man.' He shook his fist furiously and went back to his seat, saying:

'A man gets desperate; no peace from the brats, no peace from the chiefs, no peace from the Trustee!'

Everyone agreed with his words; Hamdaan's people had lost their rightful share of the estate. They were dragged ever deeper in filth and misery. They were in the power of a chief who was not even one of them but came from the meanest quarter, Kidra, who stalked about proudly among them, beating up anyone he wished and getting protection money as he pleased. And so the patience of Hamdaan's people was at an end.

Daabas turned to Hamdaan and said:

'We'll agree, Hamdaan. We are your people, and there are lots of us; our origin is well known, and our right to the estate is as good as that of the Trustee himself.'

The storyteller moaned:

'O God, let this night pass without evil.'

Hamdaan drew the cloak round himself and raised his thick eyebrows.

'We've said again and again, something must happen; I smell something in the air now.'

Ali Fawanis entered the café, calling out his greetings, gathering up his smock, with his grey cap tilted over his forehead. In a moment he was saying:

'Everyone is ready; and if the business needs money everyone will pay, even the beggars.'

He squeezed in between Daabas and Hamdaan, calling for tea without sugar. The storyteller called his attention with a cough. Ali Fawanis smiled, slipped his hand into the breast of his smock, pulled out a purse, opened it, and took out a package which he threw to the storyteller. Then he placed a questioning hand on Hamdaan's thigh, and Hamdaan said:

'We're heading for a trial.'

Tamarind said:

'We're doing the best thing.'

But the storyteller said, unwrapping the package:

'Think of the consequences.'

Ali Fawanis said sharply:

'Nothing could be worse than our present state, and there are plenty of

**77**

us to pay the price. Effendi knows where we come from and how closely related we are to him and to the owner of the estate.'

The storyteller said, giving Hamdaan a meaningful look:

'There's no shortage of solutions.'

Hamdaan said, as if to answer him:

'I have a daring idea: we should appeal to the Trustee.'

Abdoun said, bringing the tea for Fawanis:

'A great move! And after that there will be graves to dig.'

Tamarind laughed and said:

'Your children are telling you your future!'

But Hamdaan insisted:

'We must go; let's all go together.'

26 ✳ ✳ ✳ ✳ ✳ ✳ ✳ ✳ ✳ ✳ ✳ ✳ ✳ ✳ ✳ ✳ ✳ ✳ ✳

A great crowd of Hamdaan's people, men and women, collected in front of the Trustee's house, headed by Hamdaan, Daabas and Atris el Aamash, Dolma, Ali Fawanis and Radwaan the storyteller. Radwaan thought Hamdaan should go alone, to avoid any appearance of rebellion and to guard against its consequences; but Hamdaan said to him simply: 'To kill me would be easy, but to kill all the children of Hamdaan is something they cannot do.'

The whole alley turned out to see the crowd, especially their neighbours and relatives. The women poked their heads out of the windows. People carrying baskets, men behind their barrows stared at them, and young and old crowded round, asking each other what Hamdaan's people were after.

Hamdaan took hold of the brass knocker and knocked on the gate. After a little while it was opened by the gatekeeper with his gloomy face, and the scent of jasmine wafted out. The gatekeeper looked uneasily at the crowd and asked.

'What do you want?'

Hamdaan felt stronger for having his people behind him. He said:

'We wish to meet his honour the Trustee.'

'All of you?'

'None of us is more worthy to meet him than the others.'

'Wait while I ask if you may come in.'

He tried to close the gate, but Daabas forced his way in, saying:

'It will be more dignified to wait inside.'

The rest flocked in after him, Hamdaan going along with them in spite of his annoyance at Daabas's initiative. The demonstrators moved along the covered path through the garden to the drawing-room. The gate-keeper shouted:

'You must get out!'

Hamdaan said:

'A guest can't be turned out. Go and tell your master.'

The man glared and his lips moved in a silent protest, then he turned and hurried to the drawing-room. They followed him with their eyes until he disappeared behind the curtain over the doorway. Then some kept their eyes fixed on the curtain while others let their gaze wander round the garden, taking in the fountain ringed with palms, the trellises of vines, the jasmine climbing up the walls. They looked around, but with uneasy feelings, and their eyes soon returned to the curtain over the doorway of the drawing-room.

The curtain was thrown back, and out stalked Effendi himself, scowl-ing horribly. He came with short angry steps till he stood at the top of the steps. All that could be seen of him outside his bulky cloak was his furious face, his camel-hide slippers and the long rosary in his right hand. He cast a contemptuous look at the demonstrators, then fixed his eye on Hamdaan, who said with great politeness:

'A very good morning to you, your honour.'

He acknowledged the greeting with a wave of his hand and asked:

'Who are these people?'

'Hamdaan's people.'

'Who gave them leave to enter my house?

Hamdaan said cunningly:

'Its their Trustee's house, so it's their house as they're under his pro-tection.'

Effendi's expression did not soften, and he said:

'Are you trying to make excuses for your bad behaviour?'

Daabas was annoyed by Hamdaan's politeness and said:

'We're one family, we're all children of Adham and Omayma . . .'

Effendi said angrily:

'That's ancient history. Thank God some people know their proper place.'

Hamdaan said:

'We suffer terribly from poverty and ill treatment. We've all agreed that we should appeal to you to alleviate our sufferings.'

At this Tamarind said:

'Upon my word, what we live on would disgust a cockroach.'

Daabas added in a voice that grew steadily louder:

'Most of us are beggars, our children are starving, our faces smart from the blows of the chiefs; is that fit treatment for the children of Gebelawi who have a right to his estate?'

Effendi's hand tightened on the rosary and he shouted:

'What estate is this?'

Hamdaan tried to prevent Daabas from speaking, but he poured the words out as if he were drunk:

'The great estate – don't get angry your honour – the great estate that belongs to everyone in our alley from the highest to the lowest, that includes every holding in the desert round about: Gebelawi's estate, your honour.'

Anger burned in Effendi's eyes, and he shouted:

'This is my father's estate and my grandfather's; you have no claim on it. You pass round your fairy stories and believe them, but you have not a shred of proof.'

Several voices, including those of Daabas and Tamarind spoke up clearly:

'But everyone knows . . .'

'Everyone? What does that mean? If you all told each other that my house belonged to one of you, would that be enough to take my house from me, you fools? A real alley of drug smokers! Tell me when one of you ever had a piastre of the estate's revenue.'

Silence reigned for a while, then Hamdaan said:

'Our fathers used to receive . . .'

'Can you prove it?

'They told us, and we believe them.'

Effendi shouted:

'Lies upon lies! Kindly leave, before I throw you out.'

Daabas said firmly:

'Tell us the ten conditions.'

Effendi shouted:

'And why should I tell you them? Who are you? What have they to do with you?'

'We should be beneficiaries of the estate.'

At this point the voice of Lady Hoda, the Trustee's wife, came from behind the door:

'Leave them and come in; don't make yourself hoarse arguing with them.'

Tamarind said:

'Use your good influence, Madam.'

Lady Hoda said in a voice trembling with rage:

'You aren't going to get away with daylight robbery.'

Tamarind said angrily:

'God forgive you, madam; the truth is with our ancestor who has locked the gates on himself.'

Daabas threw his head back and shouted thunderously:

'Gebelawi, come and see the state we're in; you've left us at the mercy of the merciless.'

His voice echoed powerfully, so that some of them thought it must have reached the old man in his house, but Effendi cried in a voice choking with fury:

'Get out! Get out at once!'

Hamdaan said sadly:

'Come on then.'

He turned and went towards the door and they followed him silently, even Daabas; but he lifted his head and shouted again with all his force:

'Gebelawi!'


27 \* \* \* \* \* \* \* \* \* \* \* \* \* \* \* \* \* \* \*

Effendi went into the hall livid with rage. He found his wife standing there scowling, and she said:

'A strange business, and it'll lead to other things. It'll be the talk of the whole alley. If we take it lightly we shan't know much peace.'

Effendi said with disgust:

'Scum and children of scum; and they want the estate! Who can know his origin in an alley like a rabbit warren?'

'Have a showdown. Call Zoklot and arrange things. Zoklot shares the revenue of the estate without doing anything; let him earn the money he has robbed us of.'

Effendi gave her a long look, then asked:

'And Gebel?'

She said confidently:

'Gebel! He's our foster son – my son. He knows nothing of the world except our house. As for the children of Hamdaan, he doesn't know them, and they don't know him. And if they counted him as one of them, that would only make him more attached to us; I'm sure of that as far as he's concerned. He'll soon come back from his round of the tenants and will be at the meeting.'

Zoklot came at the Trustee's request. He was of middle height, stocky, well built, with brutal features, and scars on his neck and chin. They sat down together and Zoklot said:

'I've heard bad news.'

Hoda said angrily:

'Bad news travels fast.'

Effendi looked craftily at Zoklot.

'We're as worried as you are.'

Zoklot bellowed:

'Some time has passed since we used our cudgels or shed any blood.'

Hoda smiled and said:

'What an arrogant lot, these people of Hamdaan! They haven't produced a single chief and yet the lowest of them thinks he's lord of the alley.

Zoklot said, with disgust:

'Pedlars and beggars! A spineless people will never produce a chief.'

Effendi asked:

'And what's to be done, Zoklot?'

'I'll crush them like cockroaches.'

Gebel heard Zoklot's words as he entered the hall. He was red in the face after his walk in the desert. Youthful energy pulsed in his tall, powerful body and his face with its strongly marked features, especially his straight nose and his wide, intelligent eyes. He greeted the company politely and began talking about the holdings that he had dealt with that day, but Lady Hoda cut him short, saying:

'Sit down, Gebel, we've been waiting for you because of an important matter.'

Gebel sat down, his eyes mirroring the uneasiness that could be seen in Hoda's eyes. She said:

'I think you can guess what's worrying us.'

He said quietly:

'Everyone outside is talking about it.'

She looked at her husband.

'You hear that? Everyone is waiting for our answer.'

Zoklot's face grew still uglier.

'A fire that can be put out with a handful of sand! I want to get on with the job.'

Hoda turned to Gebel.

'Have you anything to say, Gebel?'

He looked at the ground to hide his anguish.

'It's your problem.'

'I'm anxious to know what you say.'

He thought for a long time, conscious of Effendi's hard stare and Zoklot's angry gaze, then he said:

'I'm your foster son, but I don't know what to say: I'm one of Hamdaan's people, just that!'

Hoda said sharply:

'Why do you mention Hamdaan when you have neither a father nor a mother nor relations among them?'

Effendi let out a grunt of scorn like a stifled laugh, but said nothing.

Gebel's face showed that he was suffering real pain, but he answered:

'My father and mother belonged to them; you can't deny it.'

Hoda said:

'How vain were my hopes of my son.'

'God forbid! Mukattam itself couldn't change my devotion to you. But denying the truth doesn't change it.'

Effendi stood up, at the end of his patience, and said to Zoklot:

'Don't waste your time listening to this rubbish.'

Zoklot got up, smiling, and Hoda said to him, glancing secretly at Gebel:

'Don't be unreasonable, Mr Zoklot; we want them disciplined, not destroyed.'

Zoklot left the hall, and Effendi gave Gebel a reproachful look and asked sarcastically:

'So you're one of Hamdaan's people, Gebel?'

Gebel was silent, and Hoda had pity on him and said:

'In his heart he's with us, but it was too hard for him to deny his origin in front of Zoklot.'

Gebel said:

'They are wretched, although they have the noblest origin of anyone in the alley.'

Effendi shouted:

'An alley without any origins!'

Gebel said earnestly:

'We are the children of Adham; and our ancestor, God preserve him, is still living.'

Effendi asked:

'Who can be sure that he's the son of his father? It does no harm to say things like that from time to time, but a man must not use them as an excuse to rob others of their wealth.'

Hoda said:

'We shan't want to harm them as long as they don't have designs on our property.'

Effendi wanted to end the conversation, and said to Gebel:

'Go to your work, and don't think about anything else.'

Gebel left the drawing-room and went to the estate office in the garden house. He had to record in the ledgers the number of tenancies and to check the totals for the month. But grief distracted him. It was a fact that Hamdaan's people did not like him. He knew this, and remembered how coldly he had been received in Hamdaan's café the few times he had gone there. He was upset moreover by the trouble that was being prepared for them; he would have loved to fend off the harm from them, if he had not feared the displeasure of the house that had adopted him, sheltered him and brought him up. What would have happened if Lady Hoda had not given him her love? Twenty years before, she had seen a naked child splashing about in a pool of rainwater, and she had been charmed by the sight, and, being childless, had been strongly drawn to him. She had sent someone to bring him to her, and he had come, crying and afraid.

She had inquired about him and learnt that he was an orphan looked after by a woman who sold chickens. Hoda had sent for this woman and asked her to hand the child over to her, and she had welcomed the opportunity. Thus Gebel had grown up in the Trustee's house, and under his protection he had been better cared for than any other child in the alley. He had gone to school and learnt to read and write, and when he reached manhood, Effendi had put him in charge of the estate. Wherever there was estate property they called him 'Mr Manager, Sir', and looks of respect and admiration followed him wherever he went. Life had seemed friendly and full of promise of happiness until Hamdaan's people rebelled. Now Gebel found he was not one person, as he had always supposed, but two people, one of them loyal to his mother, the other asking in dismay: 'And what about Hamdaan's people?'

28 ✳ ✳ ✳ ✳ ✳ ✳ ✳ ✳ ✳ ✳ ✳ ✳ ✳ ✳ ✳ ✳ ✳ ✳ ✳ ✳

The fiddle began to play for the story of Hammam's death at the hand of Kadri. All eyes turned to Radwaan the storyteller with a mixture of interest and anxiety. Tonight was not like other nights; it brought to an end a day of revolt, and many of Hamdaan's people were asking themselves: 'Will it end in peace?' Darkness enfolded the alley; even the stars were hidden behind autumn clouds, and no light showed except the glow from shuttered windows and from the lamps on barrows here and there. The corners resounded with the noise of the boys who clustered like moths round the lamps on the barrows. Tamarind spread a sack on the ground in front of one of the houses in Hamdaan's quarter and began singing. Cats wailed as they scrapped over food or females. The storyteller's voice grew louder as he chanted: 'Adham shouted in Kadri's face: "What have you done to your brother?" . . .'

At that moment Zoklot appeared in the circle of light cast by the lamp of the café, suddenly, as though the darkness had been torn open to reveal him. He looked hateful; his eyes were full of malice and he gripped his cudgel in his fist. He looked down at the people sitting in the café as if they were insects. The storyteller fell silent, Dolma and Atris came out of their intoxication, Daabas and Ali Fawanis stopped whispering and Abdoun ceased running to and fro. Hamdaan himself bit the mouthpiece of the hubble-bubble more tightly. There was a deathly hush.

There followed a flurry of movement. The clients who were not Hamdaan's people left hastily. The chiefs of the various quarters came – Kidra and Laythi, Abu Saria, Barakat and Hamouda – and lined up behind Zoklot. The news spread quickly, as if a house had collapsed. Windows were flung open, children came running, and people were torn between anxiety and sadistic pleasure. Hamdaan was the first to break the silence. He stood up to receive them.

'Welcome Mr Zoklot, Chief of our alley; please sit down.'

But Zoklot ignored him as though he neither heard him nor saw him, but went on glancing cruelly around; then he asked roughly:

'Who's the chief of this quarter?'

Hamdaan answered, though the question was not addressed to him:

'Kidra.'

Zoklot turned to Kidra and asked sarcastically:

'Are you the protector of Hamdaan's people?'

Kidra came one step forward – a short, squat man with a boxer's face.

'I protect them against everyone except you, Chief.'

Zoklot smiled grimly.

'Couldn't you find anything better than the women's quarter to protect?'

He shouted into the café:

'You women, you bastards; don't you realize that the alley has a chief?'

Hamdaan, his face pale, said:

'Mr Zoklot, there is no quarrel between us.'

Zoklot yelled:

'Shut up, you scabby old fool! Now you're going to pay for your attack on your masters.'

Hamdaan said in an agonized voice:

'There was no attack at all; it was a complaint that we brought to his honour the Trustee.'

Zoklot shouted:

'You hear what the bastard says? Hamdaan, you stink. Have you forgotten what your mother used to do? By God, not one of you will walk safely in this alley until he has said at the top of his voice: "I'm a woman."'

He lifted his cudgel quickly and brought it down hard on the table and sent flying cups, mugs, plates, boxes of coffee, tea, sugar, cinnamon, ginger, coffeepots. Abdoun sprang back, bumped into a table and fell over with it. Zoklot aimed a sudden blow at Hamdaan's face; the man lost his balance and fell sideways on to the hubble-bubble which broke. Zoklot lifted his cudgel again, shouting:

'There's no crime without punishment, you bastards!'

Daabas took a chair and hurled it at the lamp which smashed and plunged the café into darkness. The cudgel fell on the old woman behind the table; Tamr Henna screamed and the women of Hamdaan echoed her scream from their windows and doorways. Zoklot went berserk and let fly in every direction, hitting people, walls, chairs. Screams, groans, shouts for help followed, wave upon wave. Bodies floundered in every direction, falling over one another. Zoklot shouted thunderously:

'Everyone will stay in his house!'

They all hurried to carry out the order, whether they were of Hamdaan's people or not. There was a stampede. Laythi brought a lamp, and its light showed Zoklot with the chiefs around him in the deserted alley, in which all that could be heard were the screams of women. Barakat said, laying on the flattery:

'Save yourself for more important things, Chief; we must deal with these beetles.'

Abu Saria said:

'If you wanted, we'd make Hamdaan's people into dust for your horse to trample on.'

Kidra, the chief of Hamdaan's quarter, said:

'If you ask me to beat them up you'll be granting my wish; all I want is to work for you, Chief.'

Tamarind's voice came from behind a door:

'Damn the monster!'

Zoklot yelled at her:

'Tamarind, I challenge any man of Hamdaan to count the number of men you've slept with.'

Tamarind shouted:

'God is our witness: Hamdaan's people are lords of the . . .'

Her last words were stifled by a hand over her mouth. Zoklot spoke to the chiefs in a voice that was meant to be heard by Hamdaan's people:

'If any man of Hamdaan leaves his house he's to be beaten up.'

Kidra shouted:

'Anyone who calls himself a man come out.'

Hamouda asked:

'And the women, Chief?'

'Zoklot deals with men, not women.'


Day broke, and not a man of Hamdaan left his house. Each of the chiefs sat in front of the café in his own quarter watching the road. Zoklot patrolled the alley every few hours and people vied with one another in greeting him and praising and flattering him: 'My God, the Chief of our alley is a lion,' 'Well done; you're a great man, you've made Hamdaan wear a yashmak,' 'Thank God you've brought down the stuck-up people of Hamdaan, Zoklot.' And no one was upset at all.

# 29 ✳ ✳ ✳ ✳ ✳ ✳ ✳ ✳ ✳ ✳ ✳ ✳ ✳ ✳ ✳ ✳ ✳ ✳ ✳

'Do you like this tyranny, Gebelawi?' asked Gebel lying on the ground at the foot of the rock where the stories say Kadri lay with Hind and where Hammam was killed. He looked at the sunset, but with eyes that could only see imperfection everywhere. He was not one of those who seek solitude because of their many worries, but lately he had been feeling an overwhelming desire to be alone, for the fate of Hamdaan's people had filled him with turmoil; perhaps in the desert the voices that tormented him would be silent, voices that shouted from the windows as he passed: 'Filthy traitor to Hamdaan!' and voices that cried from the depths of his own being: 'Life at the expense of others cannot be happy.' Hamdaan's people were his people; his father and mother had been born among them and buried in their tomb. They were oppressed, horribly oppressed, and cheated of their property; and by whom? By his generous patron, the man whose wife had picked him out of the mud and raised him to the level of the Big House.

Everything in the alley is run by bullying, so it is not surprising that its lords should be imprisoned in their houses. Our alley never knew a single day of justice or peace; its fate was sealed when Adham and Omayma were driven out of the Big House. Don't you know that, Gebelawi? It is plain that the darkness will get thicker the longer you are silent. How long will you say nothing, Gebelawi? The men are prisoners in their houses, and the women expose themselves to mockery when they go into the street; and I swallow the humiliation without a word. How strange that the people of our alley should laugh! What are they laughing at? They think the world of whoever happens to be victorious, and rejoice in whoever is powerful, and they worship cudgels; and so they hide the terror that is in their hearts. We eat degradation with every mouthful in this alley. No one knows when his turn will come for the cudgel to crack down on his skull.

He lifted his head to the sky and found it still and calm, clouds visible on the horizon, the last kites flying away. People had stopped going about, and the hour had come for insects to settle. Suddenly Gebel heard a rough voice shouting near by 'Stop, you bastard!' He was roused from his thoughts and got up, trying to remember where he had heard that voice. He went round Hind's rock to the south side and saw one man running frantically and another chasing him. He looked hard and recognized the man in flight as Daabas and his pursuer as Kidra, chief of Hamdaan's quarter. He understood at once, and watched anxiously as the chase drew nearer to him. In a moment or two Kidra overtook Daabas and grabbed him by the shoulder. They stopped running, both out of breath, and Kidra shouted with what wind he had:

'How dare you leave your hole, you viper? You shan't go back in one piece.'

Daabas yelled, covering his head with his arms:

'Leave me alone, Kidra, you're the chief of our quarter and you're supposed to defend us.'

Kidra shook him till the turban fell from his head and shouted:

'You know, you son of a bitch, that I'll defend you against anyone except Zoklot.'

Daabas caught sight of Gebel and recognized him.

'Help me, Gebel, help me; you're one of us, not one of them.'

Kidra said with brutal defiance:

'No one can help you against me.'

Gebel found himself walking towards them till he stood by them. He said calmly:

'Be gentle with the man, Mr Kidra.'

'I know what I have to do.'

'Maybe it was necessary for him to leave his house.'

'It was his fate that made him leave it.'

He squeezed Daabas's shoulder till he moaned loudly, and Gebel said sharply:

'Be gentle with him; can't you see he's older and weaker than you?'

Kidra punched Daabas with a force that doubled him up, then hit him in the back with his knee so that he fell on his face. In a moment he was kneeling on him, raining blows on him and saying in a voice full of hatred:

'Didn't you hear what Zoklot said?'

Anger set fire to Gebel's blood and he shouted:

'Damn you – and Zoklot! Let him go you shameless beast!'

Kidra stopped hitting Daabas and raised an astonished face to Gebel.

'Do you say that, Gebel? Didn't you hear his honour the Trustee order Zoklot to punish Hamdaan?'

Gebel shouted still more furiously:

'Let him go you shameless beast!'

Kidra's voice quivered with rage.

'Don't get the idea your work in the Trustee's house will protect you against me if you want your reckoning.'

Gebel sprang at him as if he were out of his mind, and kicked him in the side, shouting:

'Go back to your mother before she misses you.'

Kidra leapt up, picking his cudgel up from the ground, then raised it quickly, but Gebel was too quick for him and punched him hard in the stomach. He staggered about in agony, and Gebel seized this chance to snatch the cudgel out of his hand and stood watching him carefully. Kidra drew back two places, then bent down swiftly and grabbed a stone; but before he could throw it, the cudgel cracked down on his head. He screamed and spun round, then fell on his face, the blood flowing from his forehead. Night was falling, and Gebel looked round and saw nobody except Daabas, who stood brushing his smock and feeling the places that hurt him. Then he came over to Gebel and said gratefully:

'You're a real brother, Gebel.'

Gebel did not answer him, but bent over Kidra and turned him on his back and murmured:

'He's fainted.'

Daabas bent over him too, then spat on his face. Gebel pushed him right away, then bent over him again and began shaking him gently but he showed no signs of coming to.

'What's wrong with him?'

Daabas bent over him again and put his ear to his chest, then peered into his face and lit a match. Then he stood up and whispered:

'He's dead.'

Gebel's flesh crept and he said:

'You're lying.'

'Dead as dead, upon your life.'

'How dreadful!'

Daabas made light of the matter:

'Think of all the people he's beaten up or killed! Let him go to Hell!'

Gebel said sorrowfully, as though talking to himself:

'But I've never beaten or killed anyone.'

'It was in self defence.'

'But I didn't mean to kill him; I didn't want to.'

Daabas said anxiously:

'You're tough, Gebel, you needn't be afraid of them; why, you could be a chief if you wanted.'

Gebel struck his forehead with his hand and cried out:

'Good grief! Have I become a murderer with the first blow I struck?'

'Come to your senses. Let's bury him now, otherwise there'll be trouble.'

'There'll be trouble whether we bury him or not.'

'I'm not sorry. Now we must fix the other chiefs. Help me to bury this brute.'

Daabas took the cudgel and began digging in the ground not far from the spot where Kadri had once dug. Soon Gebel joined him with a heavy heart. The work went on without a word until Daabas said, to lighten the weight of Gebel's feelings:

'Don't be sad; killing in our alley is as easy as eating palm nuts.'

Gebel sighed:

'I didn't want to become a murderer ever. O God! I didn't think I had such a temper.'

When they had finished digging, Daabas stood wiping his forehead with the sleeve of his smock and blowing his nose to get rid of the earthy smell that filled it. He said:

'This grave is big enough for that bastard and the other chiefs too.'

Gebel said resentfully:

'Respect the dead man; we all die.'

'When they respect us alive we shall respect them dead.'

They lifted the corpse into the grave and Gebel put the cudgel by its side and then heaped the earth over it. When Gebel looked up he found that night had covered the world, and he sighed, holding back his tears.

30 \* \* \* \* \* \* \* \* \* \* \* \* \* \* \* \* \* \* \*

'Where's Kidra?' wondered Zoklot and the other chiefs. Their colleague was no more to be seen in the alley than were the men of Hamdaan. Kidra had lived in the quarter next to that of Hamdaan. He was a bachelor and used to spend the nights out, only returning home at dawn or later. He was often away for a night or two, but he had never been missing for a whole week without anyone knowing where he was. It was specially strange during this blockade which demanded of him great watchfulness. Suspicion fell on Hamdaan's people and a search of their houses was decided on. The chiefs, led by Zoklot, burst into their houses and searched them thoroughly from cellar to roof, digging up their yards from end to end. The men of Hamdaan met with every kind of humiliation, and not one escaped being kicked or punched or spat upon. But the searchers found nothing suspicious. They went off into the varous parts of the desert asking for information, but no one could tell them anything of any value.

Kidra remained the topic of conversation as the pipe went round at Zoklot's hashish den under the vine trellis in his garden. Darkness covered the garden, but for the faint light of a small lamp standing a couple of feet from the brazier to give Barakat some light as he cut up and flattened the hashish and crumbled the charcoal. The lamp light danced in the breeze on the gloomy faces of Zoklot and Hamouda, Laythi and Abou Saria, with their drooping eyelids and their crafty eyes. The croaking of the frogs came like muffled cries for help in the stillness of the night. Laythi said, taking the pipe from Barakat and passing it to Zoklot:

'Where's the man gone? The earth seems to have swallowed him up.'

Zoklot inhaled deeply, tapping the stem of the pipe, then breathed out a thick cloud of smoke and said:

'The earth has swallowed Kidra, and he's slept in its bowels for a week.'

They all looked up anxiously at him, except Barakat who was absorbed in his work. Zoklot went on:

'A chief doesn't disappear without a reason; and I know the smell of death.'

Abou Saria said, after a cough that bent his back as a strong wind bends a reed:

'And who killed him?'

'Amazing! Who else if not a man of Hamdaan?'

'But they haven't left their houses. We've searched them.'

Zoklot struck the side of his cushion with his fist and said:

'What do the other people in the alley say?'

Hamouda said:

'The people in my quarter claim that Hamdaan had a hand in Kidra's disappearance.'

'Can't you understand, you drunkards; as long as people say Kidra's murderer was from Hamdaan, we must assume that's how it is.'

'Even if the killer was from Otouf?'

'Even if the killer was from Kafr el Zaghari. It's less important to punish the right man than to deter others.'

Abou Saria cried out in admiration:

'Great God!'

Laythi said as he shook the ash out in the brazier and passed the pipe back to Barakat:

'God help you, Hamdaan!'

Their harsh laughter blended with the croaking of the frogs and they wagged their heads threateningly. A gust of wind rustled the dry leaves. Hamouda clapped his hands together and said:

'The matter is no longer a dispute between Hamdaan and the Trustee; it is a question of the honour of the chiefs.'

Zoklot thumped the end of his cushion with his fist again and said:

'No chief was ever killed by his quarter before.'

His face grew so fierce with anger that his companions were afraid of him and avoided any word or movement that might draw his fury upon them. Silence fell and was disturbed only by the gurgle of the pipe and an occasional cough. Then Barakat asked:

'And if Kidra comes back in spite of our suspicions?'

Zoklot said angrily:

'I'll shave my moustache off, you drunkard.'

Barakat was the first to laugh; then they were silent again. They pictured to themselves the carnage – the sticks cracking down, the blood staining the ground, the screams from windows and roofs, the dead and the dying – and they lusted for the chase and looked at each other cruelly. They did not care about Kidra himself, indeed they had not even liked him; none of them liked the others at all, only they shared a desire to intimidate and to prevent rebellion. Laythi asked Zoklot:

'And now?'

'I'll go back to the Trustee as we agreed.'


31 ✳ ✳ ✳ ✳ ✳ ✳ ✳ ✳ ✳ ✳ ✳ ✳ ✳ ✳ ✳ ✳ ✳ ✳ ✳ ✳ ✳

Zoklot said:

'Hamdaan's people have killed their chief, Kidra, your honour.'

He fixed his eye on the Trustee, and at the same time he could see Lady Hoda to his right and Gebel to the right of her. The news did not seem to surprise Effendi for he said:

'I've heard reports of his disappearance, but have you really given up hope of finding him?'

The afternoon light through the door of the hall threw Zoklot's ugliness into relief.

'He hasn't been found, and I know all about these tricks.'

Hoda said nervously, looking at the face of Gebel who was staring at the far wall:

'If it's true that he's been killed, that's dangerous.'

Zoklot clasped his hands still more tightly together.

'And it calls for a terrible punishment, or it's good-bye to us all.'

Effendi toyed with the beads of his rosary.

'He stands for our prestige.'

Zoklot said:

'He stands for the whole estate.'

Gebel broke his silence:

'Perhaps it's a frame-up.'

92

Zoklot was furious at this, and he said:

'There's no need for us to waste time talking.'

'Prove that he's been murdered.'

Effendi said in a voice that he made forceful to hide his doubts:

'No one in our alley would disappear in this way unless he'd been murdered.'

The mild autumn breezes could not sweeten the ugly atmosphere. Zoklot shouted:

'The crime calls us to act, and its voice is heard in the neighbouring alleys. Talking is just a waste of time.'

But Gebel said:

'The men of Hamdaan are prisoners in their houses!'

Zoklot laughed, but only with his voice, and said scornfully:

'A pretty puzzle!'

Then he settled back in his chair and challenged him with a piercing look:

'All you care about is clearing your people.'

Gebel made an effort to control his temper, but his voice was angry as he said:

'I care for the truth. You attack people for the slightest reason, often for no reason at all. All you want now is permission to plunge peaceful people into a blood bath.'

Zoklot's eyes blazed with fury:

'Your people are criminals. They killed Kidra while he was defending the estate.'

Gebel turned to Effendi and said:

'Sir, don't let this man slake his thirst for blood.'

Effendi said:

'If we lose our prestige we shall lose our lives.'

Hoda asked Gebel:

'Do you want us to be buried alive in our own alley?'

Zoklot said in disgust:

'You remember the criminals and forget the people who've been so good to you.'

Gebel's anger mounted till he could no longer control it. He shouted at the top of his voice:

'They are not criminals. But our alley is bursting with criminals!'

Hoda's hand gripped the end of her blue shawl. Effendi's nostrils opened wide and his face went white. Zoklot took courage from these signs and said with hatred and scorn:

'You have an excuse for defending the criminals if you're one of them.'

'Your attack on the "criminals" is fantastic when you're the chief criminal in our alley.'

Zoklot leapt to his feet, his face terrible to see.

'If it wasn't for your place in this household, I'd tear you to pieces where you sit!'

Gebel said with a fearful calm that betrayed the emotion within:

'You're raving, Zoklot!'

Effendi shouted:

'How dare you both in front of me!'

Zoklot said evilly:

'I am struggling with him in defence of your prestige.'

Effendi's fingers almost burst the rosary. He said to Gebel:

'I will not allow you to defend Hamdaan.'

'This man is telling lies about them for his own ends.'

'Leave me to judge that.'

There was silence for a little while. From the garden came the chirping of the birds and from the alley a great hubbub in which filthy insults could be heard. Zoklot smiled and said:

'Do I have your honour's permission to punish the culprits?'

Gebel was sure the fateful hour had come, and he turned to Hoda and said despairingly:

'I find myself forced to join my people in their imprisonment and to share their fate.'

Hoda cried out:

'Oh, how my hopes are disappointed!'

Gebel hung his head in confusion but he had a feeling he should look at Zoklot and he saw him smiling a hateful smile. His lips tightened in anger and he said:

'I have no choice, but I shan't ever forget your goodness to me as long as I live.'

Effendi looked at him coldly and said:

'I must know whether you are for us or against us.'

Gebel said sadly, well aware that he was making the final break with his present life:

'I owe everything to your generosity; it's impossible for me to be against you; but it'd be shameful for me to leave my people to be destroyed while I live comfortably under your protection.'

Hoda was thoroughly upset by this crisis that threatened her as a mother and said:

'Mr Zoklot, let's put off the discussion till another time.'

Zoklot scowled horribly. His eyes went to and fro between Effendi and his wife, then he muttered:

'I don't know what will happen tomorrow in the alley.'

Effendi gave Hoda a sidelong glance and asked:

'Answer me, Gebel, are you for us or against us?' Then, in burst of fury without waiting for an answer: 'Either you stay with us as one of us or you go to your people.'

Gebel was aroused, noticing especially the effect of these words on Zoklot's face. He said with determination:

'You're driving me out. I'm going.'

Hoda cried out:

'Gebel!'

Zoklot shouted:

'Before you stands the man as his mother bore him.'

Gebel could no longer bear it. He stood up, then walked straight over to the door of the drawing room. Hoda got up but Effendi held her back. In a moment Gebel was gone. Outside a wind was blowing, making curtains flap and shutters bang. The atmosphere in the room was tense and oppressive. Zoklot said quietly:

'We must get to work.'

But Hoda protested, with nervous firmness:

'No, no! The blockade is enough for now. Be careful that Gebel does not meet with any harm.'

Zoklot was not annoyed, for nothing could upset him after the victory he had won. He looked up at the Trustee questioningly. Effendi said, looking as though he were chewing a lemon:

'We'll talk about it another time.'


32 ✳ ✳ ✳ ✳ ✳ ✳ ✳ ✳ ✳ ✳ ✳ ✳ ✳ ✳ ✳ ✳ ✳ ✳ ✳

Gebel gave a parting look at the garden and the garden house and remembered the tragedy of Adham which was recited to the music of the fiddle every evening. He went to the gate, and the gatekeeper stood up for him:

'Are you going out again, sir?'

'I am going away for good, Amme Hassanayn.'

The man gaped at him, then mumbled:

'Because of Hamdaan's people?'

Gebel hung his head in silence; the gatekeeper went on:

'Would you believe it! How can her ladyship allow it? Good Heavens! How will you live, son?'

Gebel crossed the threshold, looking towards the alley crowded with people and animals and rubbish, and said:

'Like the people of our alley.'

'You weren't made for that.'

Gebel smiled faintly.

'It was sheer chance that I was taken away from it.'

He left the house, followed by the gatekeeper's gloomy warnings not to expose himself to the anger of the chiefs. The alley stretched before his eyes with its bare earth, its donkeys and cats, its children and its hovels. He realized how great was the change in his life, what hardships awaited him and what comfort he had lost. But anger masked his suffering, and he seemed not to care about the flowers and the birds and the mother-love.

He passed a chief, Hamouda, who said sarcastically:

'If only you'd lend us a hand to punish Hamdaan's people.'

He paid no attention, but made for a big house in Hamdaan's quarter and knocked on its door. Hamouda joined him and said:

'What do you want?'

'I am going back to my people.'

Amazement filled Hamouda's narrow eyes and he seemed not to believe his ears. Zoklot saw them as he was leaving the Trustee's house for his own, and he shouted to Hamouda:

'Let him go in. And if he comes out again, bury him alive.'

Hamouda's surprise left him, and he smiled a stupid smile of satisfaction. Gebel went on knocking until the windows of the house and of the neighbouring ones opened, and many heads appeared – Hamdaan and Atris, Dolma and Ali Fawanis, Abdoun, Radwaan the storyteller and Tamarind. Dolma asked scornfully:

'What do you want, sir?'

Hamdaan asked:

'Are you for us or against us?'

Hamouda shouted:

'They've thrown him out and he's sinking back to the level he came from.'

Hamdaan asked eagerly:

'Have they really thrown you out?'

'Open the door, Mr Hamdaan.'

Tamarind shrieked with joy and shouted:

'Your father was a good man, and your mother was a fine woman.'

Hamouda laughed and said:

'Congratulations on the old tart's evidence!'

Tamarind shouted angrily:

'What about your mother and her merry nights at Hammam al Sultan?'

She hurriedly closed the shutters and the stone that flew from Hamouda's hand struck them with a noise which made the little boys squeal on every corner. The door opened and Gebel went into the steamy atmosphere with its strange smell. The people welcomed him with embraces

96

and there was a confusion of kind words. But the welcome was cut short by the noise of quarrelling at the back of the yard. Gebel saw Dabaas arguing heatedly with a man called Kaabelha. He went over and pushed himself between them, saying sternly:

'Can you two quarrel while they imprison us in our houses?'

Daabas said pointing:

'He stole a sweet potato from a basin by my window.'

Kaabelha shouted:

'Did you catch me stealing? Shame on you, Daabas.'

Gebel shouted angrily:

'Let's have pity on each other so that God in heaven will have pity on us.'

But Dabaas said:

'My sweet potato is inside him, and I'm going to shake it out.'

Kaabelha said, putting his cap back on his head:

'God! I haven't tasted sweet potatoes for a week.'

'You're the only thief in this house.'

Gebel said:

'Don't condemn without proof, as Zoklot does.'

Daabas shouted:

'This son of a pickpocket must be punished.'

Kaabelha yelled:

'Daabas, you son of a radish seller!'

Daabas leapt at Kaabelha and punched him. Kaabelha staggered, and the blood ran from his forehead, but Daabas went on hitting him, ignoring the reproaches of the bystanders, till Gebel was enraged and jumped in to grab him by the neck. Try as he would, Daabas could not free himself from Gebel's grip, and he said in a choked voice:

'Do you want to kill me as you killed Kidra?'

Gebel pushed him away hard, so that he was thrown against the wall, and stared at him furiously. The others looked from one man to the other, wondering whether it was really Gebel who had killed Kidra. Dolma embraced him and Atris shouted:

'Bless you; you're the best of Hamdaan's people.'

Gebel said to Daabas resentfully:

'I only killed him to defend you.'

Daabas said quietly:

'But you enjoyed killing.'

Dolma shouted:

'What ingratitude, Daabas; you ought to be ashamed of yourself.' Then, taking Gebel by the arm: 'You can be my guest. Come, leader of Hamdaan's people.'

Gebel allowed Dolma to lead him, but he felt that the abyss that had opened before him that day was bottomless. He whispered a question in his ear as they went along together:

'Is there any way to escape?'

'Are you afraid someone will betray you to our enemies?'

'Daabas is a fool.'

'Yes, but he's not a traitor.'

'I'm afraid they may suspect you more because of me.'

Dolma said:

'I'll show you the way to escape if you want, but where will you make for?'

'The desert is wider than you think!'

33 \* \* \* \* \* \* \* \* \* \* \* \* \* \* \* \* \* \* \* \*

It was only possible for Gebel to escape towards the end of the night. He crossed from roof to roof in the stillness, till he found himself in Gemalia. He walked through the pitch darkness towards Derrasa, then into the desert, making for the rock of Hind and Kadri. When he reached it by the feeble starlight he could no longer fight off sleep, for he had been awake all night and was very tired. He threw himself down on the sand, wrapped in his cloak, and fell asleep. He opened his eyes as the first rays of dawn struck the top of the rock.

He got up at once, so as to reach the gebel before anyone started moving about in the desert. But before he set off his eyes were drawn to the spot where he had buried Kidra. His limbs trembled and he gazed at it until his mouth was dry; then he fled, feeling very unhappy. He had only killed a criminal, but he was like a hunted man as he fled from the grave. He said to himself: 'We were not made for killing, even if they kill more of us than we can count.' He was amazed that the place he had chosen to sleep in was the very spot where he had buried his victim. He felt his desire to escape redoubled; he felt he must part for ever both from those he loved and those he hated; his mother, Hamdaan, the chiefs. He reached the foot of Gebel Mukattam, overcome with grief and loneliness. Nevertheless he went on southwards till he reached Souk Mukattam at mid morning. He gave the desert behind him a long look and said with some relief: 'Now I am far away from them!' He began examining the souk which lay before him, the little market place hemmed in by narrow alleys, resounding with the hubbub of men talking and donkeys braying.

There were signs that a saint's day was being celebrated; the market place was crowded with passers-by and pedlars, idiots, dervishes and clowns, although the real commotion of the festival would not begin before sunset. His eye wandered over the sea of jostling people, and at the edge of the desert he saw a hut made of tins, round which were placed wooden chairs. It seemed in spite of its poverty to be the best café in the souk and to have the most customers, and he made for an empty chair and sat down, badly needing rest. The patron came over to him, taking a great interest in his appearance, which marked him off from the other customers – his fine cloak, his large turban and his expensive red slippers. Gebel ordered tea and began to enjoy looking at the people.

It was not long before his ear was caught by the row that was raging round a public pump. He saw the people crowding round it to fill their water jars. The turmoil was like a battle, with much violence and many victims. The noise grew louder and curses flew. Piercing shrieks came from two girls swamped in the middle of the crowd. They retreated to save themselves, and escaped from the battlefield with empty cans. They wore brightly coloured dresses that hung down to their ankles so that only their youthful faces could be seen. His gaze passed quickly over the shorter of the two then fixed on the other, who had dark eyes. They came over to an empty space near to where he sat and he noticed a family likeness between their faces, though the one who attracted him had a greater share of beauty. Gebel said to himself excitedly: 'What wonderful beauty; I never saw anyone like her in our alley.' They stood tidying their hair which had been disarranged, and putting their head scarves on again. Then they put down their cans upside down and sat on them. The short one said plaintively:

'How can we fill our cans in this crowd?'

The beauty said:

'The festival is terrible. Now father'll be getting impatient.'

Gebel entered the conversation without self consciousness:

'Why didn't he come himself to fill the cans?'

They turned towards him resentfully, but his distinguished appearance had a reassuring effect, and the beauty contented herself with saying:

'What's that to do with you? We didn't complain to you!'

Gebel was very happy to be spoken to by her and said apologetically:

'I meant, a man would be more able to push through the crowds.'

'This is our work; he has a hard enough job of his own.'

He smiled:

'What does your father do?'

'It's none of your business.'

Gebel rose, not caring about the eyes that stared at him. He stood in front of them and said politely:

'I'll fill the cans for you.'

The one who attracted him turned her face away:

'We don't need any help from you.'

But the short one said:

'Thank you very much, please do.'

She got up, pulling the other girl to her feet, and Gebel took the cans, one in each hand, and forced his way through the crowd with his powerful body, pushing the people aside and meeting a lot of resistance, till he reached the pump, behind which the water seller sat in his wooden kiosk. He paid him a couple of millièmes, filled the cans and brought them back to where the girls stood. He was upset to find them involved in a slanging match with some youths who had been pestering them. He put down the cans on the ground and turned to the youths threateningly. One of them came at him, but Gebel knocked him down with a punch in the chest. They got together to hit back, cursing and swearing at him, but a strange voice shouted:

'Get away, you wretches!'

All eyes turned to see an elderly man, short and stocky, with flashing eyes and a belt round his smock. The youths shouted in confusion 'Mr Balkiti!' and scattered fast, giving Gebel angry looks. The girls turned to the man, and the shorter one said:

'It is difficult today because of the festival, and these louts . . .'

Balkiti answered, studying Gebel:

'I remembered the festival because you were late and so I came, and just in time!' Then, to Gebel: 'And you are a gentleman, there are not many these days.'

'It was just a small service. It doesn't deserve any thanks.'

Meanwhile the girls had picked up their cans and set off silently. Gebel longed to feast his eyes on the beauty, but he did not dare look away from Balkiti's sharp eyes. He imagined this man could see deep down into him, and he was afraid he would read his secret desires, but the man said:

'You drove those villains off. Men like you are really good. Those youths, how dare they pester Balkiti's daughters! It's the booze! Did you notice they were drunk?'

Gebel shook his head, the other man went on:

'I have a nose like a genie. Never mind! Do you know me?'

'No, sir; I have not had the honour.'

'So you are not from this neighbourhood?'

'No, no!'

'I am Balkiti, the snake charmer and conjurer.'

Gebel's face lit up with sudden recollection.

'I'm honoured. Many people in our alley know you.'

'Which is it?'

'Gebelawi Alley.'

Balkiti raised his thin white eyebrows and said in a musical voice:

'I'm pleased and honoured. Who hasn't heard of Gebelawi, the owner of the estate, or of your chief, Zoklot? Have you come for the festival, Mr . . .?'

'Gebel.' Then, shrewdly: 'I've come to look for a new home.'

'You've left your alley?'

'Yes.'

Balkiti studied him still more closely, then said:

'As long as there are chiefs there will have to be outcasts! But tell me, did you kill a man or a woman?'

Gebel's heart pounded, and he said firmly:

'That's a bad joke to come from a good man!'

Balkiti laughed a toothless laugh, and said:

'You aren't one of the rabble the chiefs play with, and you aren't a thief. A man like you only leaves his alley because of murder.'

'I told you . . .'

'My dear sir, it doesn't worry me specially that you're a murderer, now that you've proved you're a gentleman. There isn't a man here who hasn't stolen or plundered or killed. So that you'll believe me, I invite you to have a cup of coffee and a puff or two in my house.'

They went along side by side, making their way through the souk towards an alley at the top. When they had left the crowds behind, Balkiti said:

'Was there anyone in particular you were aiming to see around here?'

'I don't know anyone.'

'And you have nowhere to go?'

'Nowhere.'

'Be my guest, if you like, until you find somewhere.'

Gebel's heart danced with joy and he said:

'How kind you are, Mr Balkiti!'

The man laughed and said:

'Don't be too impressed; my house has room for plenty of snakes, how could it not have room for a man? Are you alarmed by what I say? I'm a conjuror and snake charmer. You'll learn from me how to get on with snakes.'

They went up the alley and out into the desert.

On the edge of the desert Gebel saw a little house, a long way from the alley. Its walls were of bare stone, but it looked new compared to the dilapidated houses of the alley. Balkiti pointed to it and said proudly:

'The house of Balkiti the snake charmer.'

When they reached the house, Balkiti said:

'I chose this isolated place for my house because people think a snake charmer is just a great big snake.'

They went together into a long hall with a closed door at the end and a room on either side, both also closed. Balkiti went on, pointing to the end door:

'In that room are the tools of my trade, both living and non-living. Don't be afraid: the door is securely locked. I assure you snakes are safer to mix with than many people, the ones you've run away from for example!' He laughed a long toothless laugh and went on: 'People are afraid of snakes; even the chiefs are afraid of them, but I owe them my living and thanks to them I built this house.' He pointed to the room on the right. 'My daughters sleep here. Their mother died a while back, leaving me too old to marry again.' He pointed to the left. 'We shall sleep in here.'

The shorter girl's voice came from some steps at the side, which led up to the roof:

'Shafika, help me with the washing and don't stand there like a block of stone.'

Balkiti shouted:

'Saiyida, you'll wake the snakes; and you, Shafika, don't stand there like a block of stone.'

So her name was Shafika! What a lovely girl! Her rebuff had not been meant hurtfully, unspoken thanks had been in her dark eyes. Who would tell her that he had only accepted this dangerous hospitality for the sake of her eyes?

Balkiti opened the left-hand door and stepped aside for Gebel to enter, then followed him in and closed the door. He led Gebel by the hand to the divan which stretched the whole length of the right-hand wall of the little room, and they sat down together. Gebel took in the whole room with one look. He saw a bed with a grey bedspread on the other side, and, on the floor between bed and divan, decorated rush matting, in the middle of which lay a brass tray stained by long use. On it stood a brazier with a pyramid of ash, a pipe resting on its side, tongs, a spatula and some honeyed tobacco. There was one window, which was open, and from it he could see only the desert and the pale sky and one of the great black cliffs of Gebel Mukattam in the distance. Through it came the cry of a shepherd girl in the terrible silence, and a breeze laden with the heat of the sun.

Balkiti was examining him to an annoying extent, and he thought of distracting him with conversation. But the ceiling shook under the feet that walked on the roof, and Gebel at once pictured her feet, and his heart was full of a longing that happiness might come to this house, even if the snakes were let loose. He said to himself: 'Perhaps this man will murder me and bury me in the desert as I buried Kidra, without my girl knowing that I am her victim . . .' Balkiti's voice aroused him:

'Do you have a job?'

He answered, remembering the last of his money in his pocket:

'I shall find a job, any job.'

'Are you perhaps in no great hurry?'

The question alarmed him and he said:

'Oh yes; I'd better look for a job today rather than tomorrow.'

'You have the body of a chief.'

'But I hate quarrelling.'

Balkiti laughed and said:

'What work did you do in your alley?'

He hesitated a little, then said:

'I worked in the estate office.'

'Bad news! Why did you leave such a good position?'

'Fate!'

'Did you fix your eyes on some fine lady?'

'God forbid!'

'You're very cagey, but you'll soon get used to me and tell me all your secrets.'

'Perhaps so.'

'Have you any money?'

He was alarmed again but did not show it.

'I have a little, but it will not save me from working.'

Balkiti said with a wink:

'You're a clever devil; don't you think you'd make a good snake charmer? Perhaps we could work together. Don't be surprised; I'm an old man in need of an assistant.'

Gebel didn't take him seriously, but he had a deep desire to strengthen the bond between them and he was about to speak when Balkiti got in first:

'We can be thinking about that. And now . . .'

The man got up, bent over the brazier, lifted it and carried it out to light it.

Early in the afternoon the two men set out together, and Balkiti went on his rounds while Gebel made for the souk to look round and do some shopping. In the evening he returned to the desert and found his way to the lonely house by following the glimmer of light which came from a window. When he reached the house he heard voices raised in argument and he could not help listening. He heard Saiyida's voice.

'If what you say is true, father, he has committed some crime, and we can't handle the alley's chiefs.'

Shafika said:

'He doesn't seem to be a criminal.'

Balkiti said scornfully:

'Do you already know him that well, you little snake?'

Saiyida said:

'Why should he run away from a comfortable life?'

Shafika said:

'There's nothing strange about a man running away from an alley that is famous for the number of its chiefs.'

Saiyida asked:

'Where did you get this power of knowing what is hidden?'

Balkiti sighed:

'Keeping the company of snakes has made me father two vipers.'

'Are you going to put him up without knowing anything about him, father?'

'I know several things about him, and I shall soon know everything. I have a pair of eyes that can be relied on when need be. And I've invited him to stay, for I'm impressed by his character. I'm not going back on my opinion. He'd have thought twice about running away in any other circumstances. Hasn't he left his comfortable home without hesitation? But he'll obey the power that's brought him to this house.'

Gebel was overjoyed to hear this voice defending him, this kind voice that dispelled the loneliness of night in the desert and made the pale new moon look like a smile in the darkness. He stayed a while peering into the night, then coughed, went up to the door and knocked. The door opened to show Balkiti's face lit by the lamp he held in his hand. The two men went to their room. Gebel sat down after putting a package on the brass table. Balkiti looked at the package questioningly, and Gebel said:

'Dates and cheese and sesame cakes and hot felafel.'

Balkiti smiled and, pointing at the package and the pipe, said:

'The best evenings are spent with these things, aren't they, son of Gebelawi?'

His heart leapt, in spite of himself, and he saw in his mind's eye the lady who had adopted him and the garden with its music and its trellises of jasmine, its song birds and its running streams; peace and dreamy

104

stillness; the pleasant world that had vanished. Life seemed for a moment to have gone bad; then his memories were swept away by the thought of this lovely girl, and of the magical power that had brought him to a house with a snakes' nest. In a sudden burst of enthusiasm he said.

'Life is good here with you.'

35 ✳ ✳ ✳ ✳ ✳ ✳ ✳ ✳ ✳ ✳ ✳ ✳ ✳ ✳ ✳ ✳ ✳ ✳ ✳ ✳

He could not get to sleep till a little before dawn, for he was full of fears. Her image haunted him in terrifying fantasies that bred in the darkness of the strange house. He said to himself: 'You are just a stranger in this house of snakes, pursued by a crime and tormented by love.' All he wanted was peace, and he did not fear the snakes as much as he feared treachery from that man who was snoring in his bed. But how could he tell that the snoring was genuine? Nothing and no one seemed genuine any longer. Daabas himself, who owed him his life, would give away the secret in his stupidity; Zoklot would be furious, his mother would be miserable, and trouble would blaze up in the wretched alley. And the love that had brought him to this house and to the room of the snake charmer; how could he know he would live to divulge his secret feelings? And so he did not get to sleep till a little before dawn, after a night of anxiety.

He opened his tired eyes when the light of day streamed through the shutters. He saw Balkiti sitting up in bed, bending forward to rub his legs through the sheet with his withered hands. Gebel smiled with relief although his head ached from lack of sleep. He cursed the fantasies that had teemed in the dark and had fled like bats in the light. Yet were they not fantasies fit for a murderer's bad conscience? Yes, crime had been in the blood of his 'glorious' family for a long time. He heard Balkiti yawn long and loud, then sit up and cough so long and so hard that Gebel imagined his eyes would drop out. When he had finished he heaved a deep sigh and Gebel said:

'Good morning!'

He sat up on the divan, and Balkiti turned towards him, his face still red from coughing.

'Good morning, Mr Gebel; so you hardly slept all night!'

'Does my face show it?'

'No; I remember how you tossed about in the dark, and kept turning your head towards me as if you were afraid.'

The old snake! Let him be a harmless snake for the sake of her dark eyes.

'The fact is I was kept awake by the strangeness of the place.'

Balkiti laughed and said:

'You lay awake for one reason: you were afraid of me. You thought: "He'll kill me and steal my money and bury me in the desert just as I did with the man I killed." '

'You . . .?'

'Listen, Gebel, fear does a lot of harm, and a snake bites only when afraid.'

Gebel said, inwardly defeated:

'You read more than is in men's minds.'

'You know I haven't gone beyond the truth, you who managed the estate.'

A voice inside the house called 'Get up, Saiyida.' He became full of joy and anticipation, this dove in a nest of adders, who had judged him innocent and given him hope! Balkiti said, as if taking up Shafika's call:

'We get busy early in this house. The girls go off to fetch water and stewed beans to feed their old father. Then they send him off with his bag of snakes to earn a living for himself and for them.'

His mind was set at rest, and he felt he was a member of this family. Affection filled him, and he opened up and surrendered to his fate spontaneously:

'I'm going to tell you my true story.'

Balkiti laughed and started rubbing his legs again. Gebel went on:

'I am a murderer as you say, but there is a story behind it . . .'

And he told him his story. When he had finished Balkiti said:

'What tyrants! And you are a fine man, I was not wrong about you.' Then sitting more comfortably: 'It's only right now for me to answer frankness with frankness. Well, I come from Gebelawi Alley myself originally.'

'You!'

'Yes! I ran away from it in my early youth because I couldn't bear the chiefs.'

Gebel said, still recovering from his surprise:

'They are the curse of our alley.'

'Yes! But we can't forget it in spite of them. And that's why I took to you when I knew where you came from.'

'Which quarter are you from?'

'From Hamdaan, like you.'

'How amazing!'

'You shouldn't be amazed at anything in this world. But that is all ancient history, and nobody there knows me now, not even Tamarind who is my relative.'

'I know that brave old woman. But which chief were you up against, Zoklot?'

'In those days he was only the petty chief of one quarter.'

'They really are the scourge of our alley.'

'I spit on the past and everything in it. From now on concern yourself with your future. I tell you, you have what it takes to be a good snake charmer. We have a profitable area to work in south of here, far away from our alley. Anyway your chiefs and their hangers-on can't show up round here.'

Naturally Gebel knew nothing about snake charming, but he welcomed this offer, as a means of becoming attached to the family. He said in a voice that betrayed his eagerness:

'Do you really think I have what it takes?'

The man jumped acrobatically to the floor and stood before him, short and broad, the neck of his smock open to show thick white hair. He said:

'You'll do all right, and I've never been wrong about anything like that.'

They shook hands, then Balkiti said:

'I must confess, I like you better than any of my snakes.'

Gebel laughed, as excited as a child, and took hold of the man's hand to prevent him from going, so that he stood there wondering what was coming. Then Gebel said, with an impetuousness he could not control:

'Gebel wants to be your son-in-law, sir.'

Balkiti's bloodshot eyes smiled, and he asked:

'Really?'

'Yes, by Heaven!'

Balkiti laughed for a moment and said:

'I was wondering when you would be ready to bring up that subject. Yes, Gebel, I'm no fool. But you're the man I'd gladly give my daughter to. It's fortunate that Saiyida is an exceptional girl, like her mother was.'

Gebel's smile of delight wilted visibly; he was afraid his love would be snatched from him before he could take hold of her.

'But . . .'

Balkiti laughed and said:

'But you want Shafika: I know that, young man. I learnt that from your eyes and the girl's talk and my knowledge of snakes. Don't blame me, this is the way snake charmers make agreements.'

Gebel sighed from the bottom of his heart. He felt peaceful and contented, and full of strength and energy and freedom. He no longer cared even about his former luxurious home nor the lost prestige; and he was no longer afraid of the toil and hardship that awaited him. Let a curtain of darkness hang over the past and let forgetfulness swallow up its sorrows and pains and his yearning for the lost mother-love!

That morning Saiyida youyoued with joy, and the happy news ran round the neighbouring alleys.

Then Souk Mukattam witnessed the bridegroom's procession of Gebel.


## 36 ✳ ✳ ✳ ✳ ✳ ✳ ✳ ✳ ✳ ✳ ✳ ✳ ✳ ✳ ✳ ✳ ✳ ✳ ✳ ✳

Balkiti said scornfully:

'It's not good for a man to live like a rabbit or a chicken; but look at you; you haven't learnt a thing and your money's almost all gone.'

They were sitting on a skin in front of the house and Gebel had his legs stretched out on the sun-scorched sand, his eyes full of happiness. He turned to his father-in-law and said smiling:

'Our forefather Adham lived and died longing for the innocent life of the garden.'

Balkiti laughed heartily, then called at the top of his voice:

'Shafika; come to your husband before he dies of laziness.'

Shafika appeared at the door, cleaning lentils on a plate in her hand. She was wearing a purple head scarf, which brought out the freshness of her face. She said, without looking up from the plate:

'What's wrong with him, father?'

'He only enjoys two things; pleasing you and lazing about.'

She laughed.

'How can he please me and starve me to death at the same time?'

Gebel said:

'That is a conjuror's secret.'

Balkiti punched him playfully in the ribs and said:

'Don't make fun of the hardest of jobs. How do you hide an egg in the pocket of one of your audience and take it out of the pocket of another on the opposite side of the crowd? How do you turn a marble into a chicken? How do you make a snake dance?'

Shafika was delighted.

'Teach him, father. The only life he knows is sitting on a comfortable chair in the estate office.'

Balkiti stood up.

'It's time to work.'

Then he went into the house. Gebel gazed at his wife admiringly and said:

'Zoklot's wife is a thousand times less beautiful than you, yet she spends the day on a comfortable couch and the evening in the garden, breathing the scent of jasmine and playing with the stream.'

Shafika said, half scornful, half bitter:

108

'That's the life of those who rob the people of their living.'

Gebel scratched his head thoughtfully and said:

'But that is a way to perfect happiness.'

'Don't dream. You weren't dreaming when you got up to help me in the souk. You weren't dreaming when you chased away those human flies from me. And for that my heart opened to you.'

He felt like kissing her. He was sure he knew better than she, but that did not make him value her words any less. He said:

'And I – I loved you without any reason.'

'Round here only madmen dream.'

'What do you want from me, my darling?'

'I want you to be like my father.'

He said playfully:

'Where does your sweetness come from?'

Her lips parted in a smile, and her fingers moved faster amongst the lentils. He went on:

'When I ran away from my alley I was the unhappiest of men; yet if I had not run away I should not have married you.'

She laughed.

'We owe our happiness to the chiefs of your alley, just as my father owes his livelihood to snakes.'

Gebel sighed.

'And yet the best man our alley has known believed there was a way to give people a living while they sat in gardens and sang.'

'That again! Look, here comes father with his bag. Up you get! Good-bye!'

Balkiti came with his bag and Gebel got up, and the two went off by their usual path. Balkiti began speaking:

'Learn with your eyes as you learn with your brain. Watch what I do and don't ask questions in front of anyone. Be patient until I can explain what you don't understand.'


Gebel found the job really difficult, but from the beginning he took it seriously, and he gradually taught himself to do it well, though it cost him much effort. The fact was that no other job was open to him, unless he were content to be a pedlar or chief, a robber or thief. Nothing about the alleys of his new district marked them off from his own, except that they had no estate nor the stories that had grown up around it. He had forgotten any remaining regrets for the dreams of the past, any thoughts of his former prestige, any of the hopes for which Hamdaan had been punished as Adham had been punished before him. He was determined to forget the past by throwing himself into his new life, and seeking comfort from his wife whenever he was afflicted by sadness or home-sickness. He learnt so well that even Balkiti was surprised, practising constantly in the desert and working day and night. Days, weeks, months passed, and he did not tire or lose his determination.

By now he knew his way round the alleys and was familiar with the ways of snakes. He performed for thousands of children and tasted the sweetness of success and of earning. He heard the good news that he was to be a father. When he was free he would lie on his back looking at the stars or would spend his evenings sharing the pipe with Balkiti and telling the stories which were recited to the accompaniment of the fiddle in Hamdaan's café. Sometimes he would wonder about Gebelawi and would call his name out, and when Shafika worried in case the past should spoil the present, he would exclaim that his heart ached for Hamdaan's people, his people, and that Effendi was the head thief and Zoklot the head bully; how could life be good as long as such men lived?

One day he was performing his tricks in Zeinhom, surrounded by a crowd of children. He happened to turn, and there in front of him he saw Daabas, who had made his way to the front row and was staring at him in astonishment. Gebel was confused and looked away from him, but he was unable to go on with his show and brought it to an end in spite of the children's protests. He picked up his bag and went. Daabas soon caught up with him, shouting:

'Gebel! Is it really you, Gebel!'

He stopped and turned to him and said:

'Yes; what has brought you, Daabas?'

Daabas could not get over his surprise and kept saying:

'Gebel a snake charmer? When did you learn? And where?'

'It's not the strangest thing that's happened in this world.'

Gebel walked to the foot of the mountain, followed by the other man, and there they sat down in the shade of a hillock. The place was empty but for some goats grazing and a goatherd sitting naked, picking the lice out of his smock. Daabas studied his companion's face and said:

'Why did you run away, Gebel? How could you think I'd give you away? God! I'd never give away anyone of Hamdaan, not even Ka-abelha. For whose sake would I do that? Effendi's? Zoklot's? Damn them all! They've asked about you so often; it made me sweat whenever I heard them.'

'Don't you risk trouble by leaving your house?'

Daabas waved the question aside.

'The ban was lifted long ago. No one asks any more questions about Kidra or who killed him. People say it was Lady Hoda who saved us from being starved to death. But they've condemned us to permanent disgrace; we have no café, no honour. We go about our jobs far away from the alley, and when we get back we hide behind our walls, and if a chief comes across one of us he amuses himself by punching him or spitting on him. They think we are worse than dirt, Gebel. How lucky you are in exile.'

Gebel said impatiently:

'Never mind about how lucky I am. Tell me, has anyone been hurt?'

Daabas picked up a stone and hit the ground with it.

'Ten of us were killed during the blockade.'

'Good God!'

'They took them as hostages for Kidra, that wretched son of a wretch; but they weren't friends of ours.'

Gebel said angrily:

'Weren't they of Hamdaan, Daabas?'

Daabas blinked with shame and his lips moved in an inaudible excuse. Gebel spoke again:

'The others got off lightly with being punched and spat on.'

He felt responsible for the poor creatures who had died, and sorrow gripped him. He regretted bitterly every moment of peace he had enjoyed since he ran away. Daabas shocked him by saying:

'You are probably the only happy man today among all Hamdaan's people.'

He shouted:

'I shan't be able to pass a day without thinking of them.'

'But you are far away from trouble and sorrow.'

'I haven't escaped from the past at all.'

'Don't spoil your peace of mind for nothing. We've lost all hope.'

Gebel repeated his last words, but in mysterious tone:

'We have lost all hope.'

Daabas looked at him with anxious curiosity but said nothing, out of respect for the look of grief on his face. He looked at the ground and saw a scarab beetle scuttling under a pile of stone. The goatherd was shaking out his smock ready to cover his sun-scorched body. Gebel spoke again:

'Really, I only seemed to be happy.'

Daabas said comfortingly:

'You deserve to be happy.'

'I have married and taken a new job, as you see, but there was always an inner voice disturbing my sleep.'

'Bless you! Where do you live?'

He did not answer. He seemed to be talking to himself. Then he said:

'Life won't seem good as long as such brutes live.'

'You're right; but how do we get rid of them?'

The goatherd lifted up his voice, calling the flock, and he set off

111

towards them, his long staff under his arm. Then they heard him singing.

Daabas asked:

'How can I find you?'

'Ask for the house of Balkiti the snake charmer at Souk Mukattam. But keep quiet about me till then.'

Daabas got up and squeezed his hand and went. Gebel followed him with sad eyes.

37 * * * * * * * * * * * * * * * * *

It was nearly midnight; Gebelawi Alley was plunged in darkness but for the faint lights escaping from the doors of the cafés, which were half closed to keep out the cold. Not a star was to be seen in the winter sky. The boys were indoors, and even the dogs and cats had taken refuge in the yards. Through the silence came the drone of a fiddle accompanying the old stories. Hamdaan's quarter was wrapped in soundless darkness.

Two shapes came out of the desert. They went along under the walls of the Big House, then passed in front of Effendi's house, making for Hamdaan's quarter. They stopped in front of the middle house and one of them knocked. The knock boomed in the silence like a drumroll. The door opened on the face of Hamdaan himself, who looked white in the light of the lamp in his hand. He lifted up the lamp to see who had knocked and a moment later cried out in amazement: 'Gebel!' He stepped aside and Gebel entered, carrying a big bundle and sack. His wife followed, carrying another bundle. The two men embraced, and Hamdaan took a quick look at the woman, who was plainly pregnant, and said:

'Your wife?! Welcome to you both! Follow me, and don't hurry.'

They went down the long passage to the wide courtyard, which was open to the sky. Then they crossed to the narrow stairs and climbed them to Hamdaan's lodgings. Shafika went to the women's quarters, and Hamdaan took Gebel to a big room with a balcony overlooking the courtyard. The news of Gebel's return spread in no time, and many of the men of Hamdaan came along, led by Daabas and Atris, Dolma and Fawanis, Radwaan the storyteller and Abdoun. They shook hands warmly with Gebel and sat down on the cushions, gazing up at the homecomer with curiosity. The questions came one after the other, and Gebel told them something of his recent life. They looked at one another sadly. Gebel saw that their spirits had slackened in their wasted bodies, and that they were languishing. They told him of the humiliations they had met with, and Daabas said:

'I told you all that at our meeting a month ago. I wonder what can have brought you here. Perhaps you have come to invite us to move to your new place!'

Gebel said sharply:

'We have no other place than this.'

A certain note of power in his voice forced their attention. Curiosity shone in Hamdaan's eyes and he said:

'If they were snakes, it would not be difficult for you to control them.'

Tamarind came in with cups of tea and greeted Gebel warmly. She praised his wife and announced that he would have a son, but she added:

'Still, there's no longer any difference between our men and our women.'

Hamdaan cursed her as she left the room, but the men's eyes reflected a feeble acquiescence in what she said. The cloud of gloom over the gathering thickened, and no one even tasted the tea. Radwaan the storyteller asked:

'Why have you come back, Gebel, when you're not used to being pushed around?'

Hamdaan said triumphantly:

'I've told you so many times that it's better to bear our troubles than to wander among strangers who would hate us.'

Gebel said forcefully:

'Things are not as you think they are.'

Hamdaan shook his head but said nothing, and a heavy silence fell. Then Daabas said:

'Let's all leave him to rest.'

But he motioned them to stay and said:

'I didn't come to rest but to talk to you about an important matter, more important than you imagine.'

They looked at him in surprise, and Radwaan muttered that he hoped he was about to hear something good. Gebel moved his steady eyes from face to face for a while, then said:

'I could have stayed my whole life with my new family without ever thinking of coming back here. But some days ago I felt the urge to go walking alone, in spite of the cold and the dark. I went out into the desert, and I found my feet taking me to a point overlooking our alley. I hadn't been near it since I left.'

Their eyes were full of interest. He continued:

'I went on wandering in the pitch darkness. Even the stars were hidden. Before I knew what was happening, I had almost bumped into a huge person. At first I thought it was one of the chiefs, but he seemed unlike anyone from our alley, or any human being at all, tall and broad like a mountain. I was filled with terror and tried to retreat, but a strange

113

voice said "Stop, Gebel." I stayed where I was in a cold sweat, and asked "Who . . . Who are you?" '

Gebel paused in his story, and they leant forward fascinated. Dolma said:

'From our alley?'

But Atris quickly corrected him:

'He said no one in our alley was like him, nor any human being.'

But Gebel said:

'Yes, he was from our alley.'

They all demanded to know who it was, and Gebel said:

'He told me in his strange voice: "Don't be afraid; I am your grand-father, Gebelawi." '

They all exclaimed and looked at him in disbelief. Hamdaan said:

'You are joking of course.'

'No, I'm telling you the truth, no more, no less.'

Fawanis suggested:

'Perhaps you were drunk?'

Gebel protested:

'I've never been drunk.'

Atris said:

'He drinks nothing but the very best.'

Gebel's face clouded over with anger and he shouted:

'I heard him with my own ears saying "Don't be afraid; I am your grandfather, Gebelawi." '

Hamdaan said gently:

'But he hasn't left his house for many years, and no one has seen him.'

'Perhaps he goes out every night without anyone knowing.'

Hamdaan went on cautiously:

'But no one else has ever met him.'

'I met him.'

'Don't be angry, Gebel; I don't mean to doubt your truthfulness. But our imagination plays tricks. Tell me, by God, if the man can go out of his house, why hasn't he let anyone see him except you? And why does he let them play with the rights of his children?'

Gebel frowned.

'That is his secret; he knows best.'

'It's easier to believe what is said about him retiring because of his age and feebleness.'

Daabas said:

'We're getting lost in words. Let's hear the story, if there is any more.'

Gebel said:

'I said to him. "I never dreamt of meeting you in this life," and he said "Here I am." I peered up into the darkness to see his face, but he said to me: "You will not be able to see my face while it is dark." I was amazed that he had seen me trying to look at him and I said: "But *you* can see *me* in the dark." He said: "I've been able to see in the dark since it became my custom to walk in it before the alley existed." I said in admiration: "Thank God you still enjoy good health." He said: "You, Gebel, are a man who is much relied on, yet you have left your comfortable life out of indignation at the way your people are oppressed. But your people are my people, and they have rights in my estate which they must take. Their honour must be defended, and their life must be good." I was full of enthusiasm, and I said: "What is the way to do this?" He said: "By force you will destroy injustice, you will take your rights, you will live a good life." I let out a great cry: "We shall be strong!" And he said: "Success will go with you." '

Gebel's voice left behind it a dreamy stillness, in which they all seemed to be under a spell. They pondered and exchanged glances, then looked at Hamdaan until he broke his silence saying:

'Let us turn this story over in our minds and in our hearts.'

Daabas said:

'It doesn't sound like a drunken fantasy, and everything in it is right.'

Dolma said with conviction:

'It would only be a fantasy if our rights were a fantasy.'

Hamdaan asked hesitantly:

'Didn't you ask him what stops him from establishing justice himself, or what made him give the trusteeship to men who don't respect the people's rights?'

Gebel was annoyed:

'I didn't ask him. I couldn't have asked him. You haven't met him in the desert in the dark. If you had, you wouldn't have thought of disagreeing with him; you wouldn't have doubted his authority.'

Hamdaan nodded, seeming to give in.

'These words were certainly worthy of Gebelawi, but it would be better for him to see to the matter himself.'

Daabas shouted:

'Wait till you die in your degradation.'

Radwaan cleared his throat, studying their faces carefully.

'Fine words! But think what it will lead to.'

Abdoun the waiter exclaimed:

'What are we afraid of? Nothing could be worse than the state we're in now.'

Hamdaan tried to make excuses:

'I'm not afraid for myself but for you.'

Gebel said contemptuously:

'I shall go to the Trustee's house alone.'

Daabas moved nearer to his seat:

'We shall go with you. Don't forget, you people, that Gebelawi promised him success.'

Gebel said:

'I shall go alone when I decide to go; but I shall want to be sure that you are solidly behind me, ready to withstand hardship.'

Abdoun shouted:

'Behind you until death!'

The boy's enthusiasm spread to Daabas, Atris, Dolma and Fawanis. Radwaan the storyteller asked rather cunningly whether Gebel's wife knew why he had come. Gebel told them how he had told his secret to Balkiti and how Balkiti had advised him to weigh the consequences, and how he had decided to return to the alley, and how his wife had chosen to go with him to the end. At that Hamdaan said in a voice that showed that he was with the others:

'And when will you go to the Trustee?'

'When my plans are ready.'

Hamdaan got up.

'I'll prepare a place for you in my home. You're my dearest son, and tonight is the beginning of great things; the fiddle will perhaps tell of it tomorrow, along with the story of Adham. Come, let's make a covenant for better for worse.'

At that moment the voice of Hamouda reached them, singing in a shaky, drunken voice:

> Drink, sweet boy and be merry,
> Stagger down the road and stumble.
> See how generous you can be,
> Eat a plate of shrimps with me.

They were only distracted by his voice for a moment, then they stretched out their hands to make the covenant with fervent hope.

38 ✳ ✳ ✳ ✳ ✳ ✳ ✳ ✳ ✳ ✳ ✳ ✳ ✳ ✳ ✳ ✳ ✳ ✳

The alley learnt of Gebel's return. They saw him walking along with his bag, and they saw his wife going off to Gemalia to do her shopping. They talked about his new job, which no one in the alley had ever taken up before, although he only put on his conjuring show in the neighbouring alleys and not in his own. He did not use the snakes in his performances, and nobody guessed that he knew how to handle them. He passed the Trustee's house several times, and it was as if he had never been there in his life, but he suffered a deep longing for his mother. The chiefs, Hamouda, Laythi, Barakat and Abou Saria, saw him, but they did not knock him about as they did with the rest of Hamdaan, only forcing him to the side of the road and making fun of his bag.

One time Zoklot met him. He looked at Gebel cruelly, then blocked his path and said:

'Where've you been?'

'In the wide world.'

'I'm your chief and I have a right to ask you anything; you must answer.'

'I answered you as best I could.'

'And what has brought you back?'

'Whatever it is that brings a man back to his own alley.'

'I wouldn't have come back if I'd been you.'

He lunged at Gebel suddenly, and would have caught him if he had not jumped aside, controlling his temper. At that moment the gatekeeper of the Trustee's house called him. Gebel turned towards him in surprise, then walked over to him. They met in front of the house and shook hands warmly. The man began asking him how things were with him, then told him the lady wanted to see him. Gebel had been expecting this invitation ever since he first showed himself in the alley: his heart had told him it was sure to come. It would have been impossible for him just to call at the house, because of the way in which he had left it. Quite apart from that, he had decided not to seek a meeting, so that neither the Trustee nor the chiefs could suspect anything in advance.

Scarcely had he entered the gate than the news was all over the alley. As he walked to the drawing-room he glanced quickly at the garden with its tall mulberry and fig trees, with its rose bushes and flowering shrubs in every corner. The familiar scents had disappeared with winter. A soft, still light, like twilight, filtered down from the ceiling of white cloud. He climbed the steps, fighting back a hundred memories. He went into the drawing-room and saw seated at the end of it Hoda and her husband, waiting for him. He looked at his mother and their eyes met. She stood up to meet him. He bent over her hands and kissed them, and she kissed him tenderly on the forehead, bringing pangs to his heart. He turned to the Trustee and saw him sitting there in his cloak, eyeing them both coldly. He offered him his hand and Effendi half stood up to shake it, then hastily sat down again. Hoda ran her eyes over Gebel with mixed surprise and concern as he stood there, looking thin and wearing a shoddy smock with a thick belt and worn-out shoes, and with a dirty cap over his tousled hair. Her eyes spoke her grief at his appearance and at the life he had contented himself with; her great hopes seemed to have come to nothing. She motioned him to sit down, and he sat on a chair

117

near to her. She herself sank into a chair as if exhausted. He understood what she felt and spoke to her in a strong voice about his life in Souk Mukattam, his work and his marriage. He spoke with satisfaction of that life, in spite of its harshness. She was annoyed by what he said.

'Live as you please. But why didn't you make my house the first you came to when you returned to the alley?'

He almost told her that his real goal in returning was her house, but he put off saying so because the moment was not suitable and because he had not yet recovered from the emotion of the meeting. He answered:

'I wanted to come to your house, but I didn't have the courage to enter it after what happened.'

Effendi asked him coldly:

'Why did you come back if life elsewhere was so good?'

Hoda gave her husband a reproachful look, which he ignored. Gebel said with a smile:

'Perhaps I came back, sir, because I wanted to see *you*.'

Hoda said:

'And you didn't come and see us until we sent for you, you ungrateful creature.'

Gebel looked down.

'Believe me, I never thought of the circumstances which drove me to leave this house without cursing them from the bottom of my heart.'

Effendi looked at him suspiciously and was about to ask him what he meant, but Hoda spoke before he could:

'You learnt, of course, that we had pardoned Hamdaan for your sake?'

Gebel realized that it was time for this well-bred pleasantness to end as it had been fated to from the beginning, and for the struggle to begin. He said:

'The truth is that they're suffering a degradation worse than death, and several of them have been killed.'

Effendi gripped his rosary and shouted:

'They're criminals and they got what they deserved.'

Hoda waved her hand hopefully and said:

'Let's forget the past.'

Effendi persisted:

'Kidra's blood couldn't be shed with impunity.'

Gebel said stubbornly:

'The real criminals are the chiefs.'

Effendi stood up nervously and addressed his wife:

'You see what happens when I give way to you about asking him to the house?'

Gebel said with determination:

118

'It was my intention to come to you in any case, sir; perhaps it's because I realize how much I owe this house that I waited till I was invited.'

The Trustee looked at him with fear and suspicion.

'What do you want out of coming here?'

Gebel faced Effendi boldly, knowing full well that he was opening the door through which a furious storm would burst, but his experience in the desert had given him courage.

'I've come to demand the rights of Hamdaan to the estate and to a secure life.'

Effendi's face darkened with rage, and Hoda's mouth hung open in despair. The Trustee glared as he said:

'Do you really dare to talk like that again? Have you forgotten how the disasters fell on your people one after the other after your stupid old head dared to come with these fantastic demands. I swear you're mad, and I don't waste my time on madmen.'

Hoda said tearfully:

'Gebel, I was going to ask you and your wife to come and live with us.'

But Gebel said in a powerful voice:

'I've simply passed on to you the wishes of one whose wishes can't be refused, your ancestor and ours, Gebelawi.'

Effendi studied Gebel carefully, bewildered. Hoda stood up anxiously and put her hand on Gebel's shoulder, saying:

'Gebel, what's come over you?'

Gebel said smiling:

'I'm well, thank you.'

'Well? You're well? What's come over you?'

Gebel said calmly:

'Listen to my story and judge for yourself.'

And he told them what he had told Hamdaan's people. When he had finished his story, Effendi said, peering suspiciously into his face:

'The owner of the estate hasn't left his house since he withdrew from the world.'

Gebel said:

'But I met him in the desert.'

He asked mockingly:

'And why didn't he tell *me* of his wishes?'

'That's his secret; he knows best.'

Effendi laughed bitterly.

'Conjuring is the right job for you; but you're not content with conjuring tricks, you want to juggle with the whole estate.'

Gebel said, still calm:

'God knows I've spoken nothing but the truth. Let's ask Gebelawi himself, if you can see him, or consult the ten conditions.'

Effendi's rage burst forth. He glowered, and his limbs trembled, and he shouted:

'You cunning thief, you shan't escape your horrible fate, not even if you hide on top of the gebel.'

Hoda wailed:

'Oh misery! I never expected you to bring me all this sorrow, Gebel.'

Gebel asked in amazement:

'All this just because I demanded my people's lawful rights?'

Effendi screamed at the top of his voice:

'Quiet! Cunning devil! Hashish addict! Alley of hashish addicts! Sons of bitches! Get out of my house! And if you come back with your drivel, you'll condemn yourself and your people to be slaughtered like lambs.'

Gebel scowled furiously and shouted:

'Mind the anger of Gebelawi doesn't catch up with you.'

Effendi sprang at Gebel and punched him in his broad chest with all his might, but Gebel stood the blow stoutly, then turned to Hoda and said:

'I only respect him out of respect for you.'

And he turned his back on her and went.


# 39 ✳ ✳ ✳ ✳ ✳ ✳ ✳ ✳ ✳ ✳ ✳ ✳ ✳ ✳ ✳ ✳ ✳ ✳

Hamdaan's people expected the very worst. Tamarind disagreed with the general view and thought that, as long as Gebel was head of Hamdaan's people, Lady Hoda would not allow them to be destroyed. However, Gebel himself did not share Tamarind's view, but maintained that, if the estate was threatened, no one counted, neither Gebel nor anyone else, however closely related to Effendi. Gebel reminded them of their ancestor's wish that they should be strong and put up with hardships. Daabas began saying Gebel had been rolling in luxury and had thrown it aside of his own free will for their sakes; it would not be right for anyone to let him down. If they used force and it did not succeed, it could not make things any worse for them than they already were.

The fact was, Hamdaan's people were afraid and their nerves were on edge, but in their despair they found a strength and purpose. They kept repeating the proverb 'May as well hang for a wolf as a sheep.' Radwaan the storyteller alone kept saying sadly: 'If the Founder wished, he would proclaim the truth and would find in our favour, and we'd escape the destruction that is obviously coming.' When Gebel heard him he was angry and went over to him scowling. He seized him by the shoulders and shook him till he almost pulled him out of his seat. He roared:

'Is this how the storytellers are, Radwaan? You recite the stories of the heroes and sing to the music of the fiddle, but when things get nasty you bolt to your holes and spread doubt and gloom. Damned cowards!' Then, turning towards those seated around: 'Gebelawi has not honoured any other quarter as he has honoured you. If he hadn't thought of you as being his family in a special way, he wouldn't have met me and spoken to me. He shines his light on our path; he has promised to back us up; I am going to fight, by God, even if I fight alone!'

But it seemed he was not alone; they all supported him, both men and women. They all expected an ordeal and it was as if they did not care about the consequences. Gebel had taken over the leadership of his quarter unprompted, as the result of events, without intending it or arranging it. Hamdaan himself had not tried to stop him but was happy to give up a position that would become the target for savage attacks.

Gebel did not stay in the house, but went out, against Hamdaan's advice, to walk about, as was his custom. He expected trouble at every step, but not one of the chiefs molested him. He was quite amazed at this and could only think of the explanation that Effendi had kept quiet about their meeting in the hope that Gebel in turn would say no more about his demands, and that it would be as though nothing had happened. Behind this policy he saw Hoda's sad face and her faithful mother-love. He was afraid that if her love lasted it would hurt him more than her husband's harshness. He thought for a long time about what must be done to rake the ashes from the fire.

Strange things began to happen in the alley. One day a woman's cries for help were heard from a cellar. It turned out that a snake had crawled between her feet and slithered towards the road. Some men volunteered to search for it and went into her home with their sticks. They hunted it down and killed it with a hail of blows. They threw it out into the road and the boys snatched it up and began playing with it noisily. This was not a strange event in the alley, but hardly an hour had gone by before another scream for help was heard from a house at the end nearest to Gemalia. No sooner had night fallen than there was uproar in a house in Hamdaan's quarter when somebody saw a snake; but it disappeared before anyone could catch it and all efforts to find it came to nothing. Then Gebel himself offered to fetch it out, with the help of the knowledge he had gained from Balkiti. Hamdaan's people talked for many years of the way Gebel stood naked in the courtyard and spoke to the snake in a secret language until it came obediently.

These events would almost have been forgotten by the next morning if they had not been repeated in the houses of some important people.

Everyone soon heard that a snake had bitten Hamouda as he was crossing the entrance passage of the house where he lived. The man had screamed in spite of himself until his friends came and helped him. At this point the events began to be talked about. People spoke about nothing but the snakes, but their strange activity did not stop. One of the men in Barakat's hashish den saw a snake appear between the rafters for half a second and then vanish. They jumped up in a panic and fled.

The news of the snakes eclipsed the tales of the storytellers in the cafés. They seemed to have gone beyond the bounds of decency when a big snake appeared in his honour the Trustee's house. The many servants of the house spread out and searched in every corner for the vanished snake, but they could find no trace of it. Fear gripped the Trustee and his wife, till she seriously thought of leaving the house until she could be quite sure that it was rid of snakes. While the house was turned upside down, screams and commotion were heard from the house of Zoklot. The gatekeeper went to find out about it and brought his master the news that a snake had bitten a son of Zoklot's and then disappeared. Panic reigned. Screams for help came from one house after another. Hoda decided finally to leave the alley.

Then Amme Hassanayn, the gatekeeper, said Gebel was a conjurer, and conjurers knew ways of catching snakes; Gebel had hunted out a snake from one of the houses of Hamdaan. Effendi turned pale and said not a word, but Lady Hoda quickly told the gatekeeper to fetch Gebel. The man looked at his master for his assent, and Effendi muttered a few angry words without making himself clear. Hoda told him to choose between sending for Gebel and leaving the house, and he gave the gatekeeper leave to go, trembling with rage. A crowd had gathered between the Trustee's house and the Chief's; the important people had come as a deputation to the Trustee's house, led by Zoklot, Hamouda, Barakat, Lathi and Abu Saria.

The assembled people could talk of nothing but the snakes. Abu Saria said:

'Something in the gebel must've driven the snakes into our houses.'

Zoklot, who seemed to be fighting with himself as he could find no one else to fight with shouted:

'All our lives we have been neighbours of the gebel and it has caused us no harm.'

Zoklot was furious over what had happened to his son, and Hamouda had still not recovered from the bite on his foot. Fear gripped them all. They said their houses were not safe to live in; the inhabitants had all gathered in the road.

Gebel came carrying his empty bag, and greeted everyone, then stood before the Trustee and his wife, polite and confident. Effendi could not bring himself to look at him, but Hoda said:

122

'They tell us, Gebel, that you would be able to drive the snakes out of our houses.'

Gebel said calmly:

'That was amongst the things I learnt.'

'I have sent for you to rid the house of snakes.'

Gebel looked at Effendi:

'Does your honour permit?'

Hiding his annoyance, the Trustee muttered:

'Yes.'

At this point Laythi came forward with a suggestion Zoklot had not thought of.

'And *our* houses and everyone else's?'

'My knowledge is at the service of everyone.'

Voices were raised in thanks; and Gebel let his large eyes rove round their faces for a while, then said:

'But perhaps I don't need to remind you that everything has its price, as usual in our alley.'

The chiefs looked at him in surprise. He went on:

'What are you surprised about? You guard the quarters in return for protection money, and his honour the Trustee manages the estate in return for control over its revenues.'

The situation was obviously delicate, and people could not reveal with their eyes what they felt in their hearts, but Zoklot said:

'How much do you want for your work?'

He answered calmly:

'I'm not asking for money. I want your word of honour, to respect the dignity of Hamdaan's people and their right to the estate.'

Silence fell. The very air seemed charged with hidden anger. Hoda's anxiety redoubled when the Trustee looked down at the ground. Gebel spoke again:

'Don't think I'm defying you. The fact is I'm simply reminding you of what justice dictates for your downtrodden brothers. The fear that has driven you out of your homes is only a taste of the bitterness your brothers drink every day of their wretched lives.'

Angry looks flashed in their eyes and were swiftly hidden, but Abu Saria shouted:

'I can send for a snake charmer, even it if means staying out of our houses for two or three days till he comes from his village.'

Hoda protested:

'How can a whole alley stay outside for two or three days?'

Effendi was thinking furiously, controlling his anger and hatred as best he could. Then he said to Gebel:

'I give you the word of honour you demand; begin your work.'

The chiefs were horrified, but the situation did not allow them to express their feelings. Their hearts were filled with murderous thoughts. Gebel however told them to go right away to the bottom of the garden, so that he had the whole place to himself. Then he stripped off his clothes and stood naked as the day when Hoda had lifted him out of the puddle. He went from place to place and room to room, now whistling softly, now muttering obscure words. Zoklot came up to the Trustee and said to him:

'It was *he* who sent the snakes into our houses.'

Effendi motioned him to be silent and murmured:

'Let him take his snakes away.'

A snake hidden in a light shaft obeyed Gebel, and he coaxed another out from the estate office. They twined round his arms, and he appeared with them in front of the drawing-room, where he popped them in his bag. Then he put on his clothes and stood waiting till everyone came. He said to them:

'Let's go to your houses so that I can clean them out.'

He turned to Hoda and said softly:

'But for my people's misery, I should never have made any conditions for serving you.'

Then he went over to the Trustee and said boldly:

'A free man's promise is binding.'

And he went out, everyone else following in silence.


40 ✳ ✳ ✳ ✳ ✳ ✳ ✳ ✳ ✳ ✳ ✳ ✳ ✳ ✳ ✳ ✳ ✳ ✳ ✳

Gebel succeeded in ridding the alley of snakes, under the eyes of all its people. Whenever one yielded to him shouts and cheers went up, till they filled the whole alley, from the Big House to Gemalia. When he had finished his work and went home, the young men and boys gathered round him singing to an accompaniment of claps:

> Gebel, helper of the paupers,
> Gebel, victor over vipers.

The singing and clapping went on even after he had gone in; but this had a strong effect on the minds of the chiefs. Soon Hamouda, Laythi, Barakat and Abu Saria went out to the demonstrators and let fly with curses and insults, kicks and blows, until they scattered for shelter to their houses. Only dogs and cats and flies stayed out of doors. The people wondered about the reason for this attack: how could they reward Gebel's work with an attack on those who were celebrating it? Would Effendi keep his promise to Gebel? Or was this attack the beginning of a

124

savage campaign of revenge? These questions went round in Gebel's head, and he called the men of Hamdaan to his place to plan things.

At the same time Zoklot was meeting the Trustee and his wife and was saying firmly:

'We shan't spare a single one of them.'

Effendi looked pleased, but Hoda said:

'And the word of honour which the Trustee gave?'

Zoklot scowled bestially and said:

'People are ruled by power, not honour.'

She said angrily:

'They will keep saying of us . . .'

'Let them say what they like as long as they keep quiet in front of us. They jabber away all night in the hashish dens, gossiping and joking about us; but when we go out into the road they jump to their feet, because they're afraid of the stick, not because they care about honour.'

Effendi looked at Hoda angrily:

'It was Gebel who hatched this plot with the snakes so that he could dictate his terms; everyone knows that. Who expects me to keep the word I gave to a low, cunning fraud?'

Zoklot said:

'Remember, madam, if Gebel succeeds in winning the rights of Hamdaan to the estate, no one in the alley will rest until he has obtained his rights too. So the estate will be lost and us with it.'

Effendi squeezed the rosary in his hand until its beads crunched and shouted:

'Don't spare any of them!'


The chiefs were summoned to Zoklot's house and were then joined by their most trusted men. The news spread that some dire fate was being prepared for Hamdaan's people. Women filled the windows, men crowded in the alley. Gebel had already laid his plans. The men of Hamdaan had assembled in the courtyard of the middle house, armed with sticks and baskets of stones, while the women were dispersed round the flats and on the roof. Each of them had his part to play, and any mistake or change of plan could only mean their destruction. Thus they took their places round Gebel, as tense and worried as could be. Gebel could not help seeing the state they were in and began reminding them of Gebelawi's support for him, and of his promise of success to the strong. He found them ready to believe him, some out of faith, some out of despair. Radwaan the storyteller leaned over and whispered in the ear of Hamdaan:

'I'm afraid our plan won't succeed. I think it'd be better to barricade the gate and to strike from the windows and the roof.'

Hamdaan shrugged his shoulders angrily and said:

'Then we'd condemn ourselves to be blockaded until we starved to death.'

Hamdaan went over to Gebel and asked him:

'Wouldn't it be best to leave the gate open?'

Gebel said:

'Leave it as it is, otherwise they'll be uncertain what to do.'

A cold fierce wind was howling and drove the clouds across the sky. They wondered whether it would rain. The noise of the crowd outside mounted until it drowned the miaowing of the cats and the barking of the dogs. Then Tamarind gave a warning cry: 'The devils have come!'

They had indeed come! Zoklot had left his house surrounded by the other chiefs and followed by their helpers, all carrying cudgels. They walked slowly past the gates of the Big House, then down to Hamdaan's quarter. The crowd greeted them with shouts and cheers. There were various motives for these cheers: a few people were delighted at the coming fight and wanted to see blood spilt; and some hated Hamdaan's people for priding themselves on a rank which no one else recognized; but most loathed the chiefs and their misdeeds and only hid their hatred and pretended to support them out of fear or as a good investment. Zoklot did not give a thought to any of them, but went straight on till he stood in front of Hamdaan's house and shouted:

'If there is a man among you let him come out to me!'

Tamarind's voice came from the window:

'Give us your word of honour that anyone who comes out will not be tricked.'

Zoklot was furious at her alluding to the 'word of honour'. He yelled:

'Is this old tart your only spokesman?'

Tamarind said:

'God forgive your mother, Zoklot!'

Zoklot screamed his command to attack the gate. Some of the men hurled themselves at it while others flung stones at the shutters, so that no one would dare to open them for a counter-attack. The attackers clustered round the gate, and started pushing powerfully against it with their shoulders. They kept on heaving away until it began to tremble. They grew still more determined, and it rocked and worked loose. Then they drew back and took a run and gave it one mighty blow, and it burst right open. Through it, at the end of the long passage, could be seen the courtyard, and in it Gebel and the men of Hamdaan, all with sticks poised. Zoklot made a crude gesture with his hand and laughed jeeringly, then charged down the passage with his men behind him.

No sooner were they half-way than the ground gaped open suddenly beneath them and the leaders tumbled to the bottom of a deep pit. Straight away the windows on either side of the passage were flung open, and from them water was poured out of jugs, pots, basins and water-skins. The men of Hamdaan at once rushed to the pit and threw in their baskets of stones. For the very first time the alley heard screams coming from its chiefs and saw the blood spurting from Zoklot's head and sticks battering the heads of Hamouda, Barakat, Laythi and Abu Saria as they floundered in the muddy water. Their followers saw what had happened to them and took to their heels, leaving the chiefs helpless before their fate. The hail of water and stones fell thicker and faster and the sticks cracked down without mercy. The people heard cries for help from throats which had only been used to uttering abuse and insults. Radwaan the storyteller was shouting at the top of his voice:

'Don't spare a single one of them.'

Hamouda was the first to die. Laythi and Abu Saria screamed loudly, but Zoklot gripped the side of the pit with his hands, trying to jump out. His eyes were full of hatred and he had begun to conquer his exhaustion and fear and to roar like a bull. The sticks rained down on him till he fell back, his hands slipping from the side of the pit, and dropped into the water, a lump of mud clutched in each hand. Silence fell. The men of Hamdaan stood and looked, panting. The crowd pressed round the entrance of the passage, staring in amazement into the pit. Radwaan shouted:

'This is the punishment of the tyrants.'

The news spread through the alley like wildfire. The crowds cried out that Gebel had destroyed the chiefs as he had destroyed the snakes. Everyone cheered him thunderously. They burned with enthusiasm, not caring about the cold wind, and called for him to be chief of Gebelawi Alley. They took the bodies and mutilated them. They started clapping, and some people began to dance. Gebel, however, did not for a moment lose his power to think clearly, and everything was worked out in his head. He shouted to his people:

'Come now to the Trustee's house.'

41 ✻ ✻ ✻ ✻ ✻ ✻ ✻ ✻ ✻ ✻ ✻ ✻ ✻ ✻ ✻ ✻ ✻ ✻

In the minutes that passed before Gebel and his people set out from the house everyone went wild with fury. The women came out of their houses to join the men, and they all fell upon the chiefs' houses, attacking their occupants with fists and feet, until they fled for their lives. The houses themselves were plundered of every piece of furniture, food and clothing, and everything else breakable was smashed, leaving a trail of splintered wood and glass.

The angry mob set off for the Trustee's house and gathered outside the locked gate shouting thunderously after their leader: 'Bring the Trustee! And if he won't come . . .'

Then they followed their shouts with mocking cheers. Some looked towards the Big House, calling upon their ancestor to come out of his isolation and set right what had gone wrong with their affairs and with those of the alley. Others began beating the Trustee's gate with their fists and pushing it with their shoulders, urging those who hung back fearfully to help batter it in. At that tense moment Gebel came up at the head of his people, both men and women, all walking purposefully because of the decisive victory they had won. The crowd made way for them and cheered and shrieked till Gebel signed to them to be quiet. Their voices trailed away little by little until there was silence, and they heard the howling of the wind again. Gebel looked at the faces gazing up at him and said:

'My greetings and my thanks to you all.'

They cheered again until he raised his hand for silence, then he said:

'Our work won't be done until we have broken up peacefully.'

From several throats came the cry:

'We want justice, master of the alley.'

He said in a voice that all could hear:

'Go now, quietly. The will of the Founder will indeed be done.'

There were cheers for the Founder, and for his son Gebel. Gebel's steady gaze urged the crowd to be gone. They would have liked to stay where they were, but under his stare they found there was nothing for it but to break up, and they went one after another, until none was left. Then Gebel went to the gate of the Trustee's house and knocked, shouting:

'Open up, Amme Hassanayin.'

The man's voice came, trembling:

'The people . . . the people . . .'

'There is no one here but us.'

He opened the gate and Gebel went in, followed by his people. They passed down the trellised path to the terrace, and there they saw Lady Hoda standing in resignation in front of the door of the drawing-room, while Effendi stood on the doorstep hanging his head, his face deathly pale. There was a murmur at the sight of him, and Hoda moaned:

'I'm in a dreadful state, Gebel.'

Gebel pointed contemptuously at Effendi and said:

128

'If the schemes of this shameless man had succeeded, we should all be mangled corpses now.'

Hoda's answer was a heavy sigh. Gebel turned a hard stare on the quailing Trustee and said:

'Now you see yourself with no strength, no power, no chiefs to protect you, no courage to support you, no manliness to plead for you. If I felt like leaving you to the mercy of the people of the alley, they would tear you to pieces and trample you underfoot.'

Effendi's heart pounded, and he seemed bent and shrunken, but Hoda took a step towards Gebel and said hopefully:

'I don't like to hear anything from you but the kind words I'm used to. We're in a dreadful state of nerves and deserve merciful treatment from a real man like you.'

Gebel frowned to hide his emotion and said:

'If it wasn't for my regard for you, things would go very differently.'

'I don't doubt it, Gebel. You're a man who doesn't disappoint hopes.'

Gebel said with regret:

'How much easier it would have been if justice had been done without spilling any blood!'

Effendi made a slight movement which showed how broken and exposed he was. Hoda said:

'What has been has been. You'll find us very ready to listen.'

The Trustee seemed to want to break his silence at any cost and said in a weak voice:

'This is a chance to make up for the wrongs of the past.'

They listened eagerly, anxious to know what state the tyrant was in now that his power had left him. They stared at him feeling at once appeased, disapproving and curious. The Trustee grew bolder, now that he had broken his silence. He said:

'You are worthy today to take the place of Zoklot.'

Gebel's face was grim and he said contemptuously:

'I have no desire to be the Chief. Find someone else to protect you; I only want the full rights of Hamdaan's people.'

'They are yours in full, and you can manage the estate if you like.'

Hoda added hopefully:

'As you used to before, Gebel.'

At this Daabas shouted from the middle of Hamdaan's people:

'And why shouldn't the whole estate belong to us?'

There was a buzz of excitement from Hamdaan's people, and the Trustee and his wife grew pale as death, but Gebel said angrily:

'The Founder told me to win back your rights, not to rob others of theirs.'

Daabas asked:

'And how do you know the others will get their rights?'

Gebel shouted:

'That's not my business. You seem only to hate oppression if it is turned against *you*.'

Hoda was deeply moved, and said:

'Gebel, what a fine, honest man you are. I hope so very much that you will come back to my house.'

Gebel said resolutely:

'I shall stay in Hamdaan's quarter.'

'It is not fitting for your position.'

'When we're rich, we'll make our houses as good as the Big House. That is the wish of our ancestor Gebelawi.'

The Trustee looked up hesitantly at Gebel's face and said:

'The way we saw the people of the alley behave today threatens our security, doesn't it?'

Gebel said scornfully:

'How you get on with them is nothing to do with me.'

Daabas said:

'If you respect your agreement with us, none of them will dare to defy you.'

The Trustee said eagerly:

'You rights shall be restored for all to see.'

Hoda said hopefully:

'You must have dinner with me tonight; that is a mother's wish.'

Gebel understood this declaration of friendship between himself and the Trustee's house, and he could not refuse her.

'Your wish is granted.'


42 ✳ ✳ ✳ ✳ ✳ ✳ ✳ ✳ ✳ ✳ ✳ ✳ ✳ ✳ ✳ ✳ ✳ ✳ ✳

The days that followed were bright with the rejoicings of Hamdaan's people, or Gebel's people, as they came to be called. Their café opened its doors again, and Radwaan the storyteller sat cross-legged on the bench, playing his fiddle. The drink flowed freely for several days, and the smoke of the hashish grew thick indoors. Tamarind danced till she was stiff. They no longer minded revealing who had killed Kidra, and Gebelawi's meeting with Gebel was described with a halo of imagined detail.

For Gebel and Shafika these were the best of days. One day he said to her:

'How lovely it would be to have Balkiti to stay!'

130

She, who was many months pregnant, said:

'Yes, so that he can greet his grandchild with a blessing.'

'You are the source of my happiness, Shafika. Saiyida will find a good husband amongst Hamdaan's people.'

'Say "Gebel's people" as everyone else does. You are the best man this quarter has known.

He said, smiling:

'No, Adham was the best of us all. How he longed for the happy life in which man would have only to sing and our dreams would come true.'

Daabas came into sight. He was drunk and was dancing with a group of Gebel's people. When he saw Gebel coming up he brandished his cudgel playfully and said:

'You don't want to be chief, so I'm going to be.'

Gebel shouted at him, so that everyone could hear:

'There's no chief among Hamdaan, but they must all be strong against anyone who means them harm.'

Daabas went into the café, and the rest followed him, staggering drunkenly. Gebel was happy and said to them:

'You are the dearest of the people of the alley to our ancestor, and you are its masters now. Love and justice and respect must rule between you. Let no crime ever be committed in your quarter.'

The sound of drums and singing came from the houses of Hamdaan, and the festive lights shone out, while the rest of the alley was sunk in its usual darkness. The children gathered at the edge of Hamdaan's quarter to watch from a distance. Then up came some men from down the road with gloomy faces. They went into the café and were received politely and invited to sit down, and tea was brought for them. Gebel guessed they had not come just for the pleasure. His guess proved right when Zenati, the oldest of them, said:

'Gebel, we're all sons of one alley and of one ancestor. Today you're the master of the alley and its most powerful man. It would be best for justice to rule in all the quarters and not only in Hamdaan's.'

Gebel said nothing, and his people looked indifferent. But the man went on with determination:

'It's in your power to bring justice to the whole alley.'

From the very first, Gebel had not cared about the rest of the alley, and none of his people cared. On the contrary, they had felt superior, even in their days of trial. Gebel said gently:

'Our ancestor charged me with my own people.'

'But he's everyone's ancestor, Gebel.'

Hamdaan said:

'There is room to disagree about that.'

**131**

He studied their faces to see the effect of his words, and he saw their gloom increase. He went on:

'As for *our* close connection with him, he himself confirmed that in the desert meeting.'

Zenati looked for a moment as though he wanted to say 'There is room to disagree about that.' But his spirit was broken. He asked Gebel:

'Are you pleased at our poverty and wretchedness?'

Gebel said earnestly:

'No, no! But that's not our business.'

The man persisted:

'How can it not be your business?'

Gebel wondered what right the man had to speak to him like this. Still he was not angry; he found part of himself sympathizing with him, but another part of him refused to go through fresh difficulties for the sake of the others. And who were these others? The answer came from the lips of Daabas, who shouted:

'Have you forgotten how you treated us during our time of trial?'

The man looked down for a while, then said:

'Who was able to speak his thoughts or show his true feelings in the days of the chiefs? Would they have forgiven anyone who treated people in a way that didn't please them?'

Daabas's lips tightened:

'You envied us our high position in the alley and you still do. Maybe you did so even before the days of the chiefs.'

Zenati hung his head in despair and said:

'God help you, Daabas!'

Daabas went on pitilessly:

'Thank our leader for deciding not to take vengeance on you.'

Gebel was filled with conflicting thoughts and retreated into silence. He was reluctant to offer a helping hand but he would not be happy if he rejected them outright. The men found themselves faced with open hostility from Daabas, cold looks from the others and an unencouraging silence from Gebel. They got up crestfallen, and went the way they had come. Daabas contained himself till they had disappeared, then shook his fist in disgust and shouted:

'To hell with you, you pigs.'

Gebel thundered:

'Gentlemen don't enjoy other people's suffering.'

43 ✳ ✳ ✳ ✳ ✳ ✳ ✳ ✳ ✳ ✳ ✳ ✳ ✳ ✳ ✳ ✳ ✳

A memorable day was the day that Gebel collected his people's share of the estate's revenues. He took his seat in the courtyard of the house where he had won his victory and summoned Hamdaan's people. He counted each family and shared out the money equally between them. He did not even single himself out for special treatment. Hamdaan did not seem altogether happy about this fairness, but he expressed his feelings indirectly, saying to Gebel:

'It isn't fair to stint yourself, Gebel.'

Gebel frowned and said:

'I have taken the share of two people, myself and Shafika.'

'But you are the head of this quarter.'

Gebel said, so that everyone heard:

'A leader must not rob his people.'

Daabas seemed to be awaiting the outcome of the dispute anxiously, then he said:

'Gebel is not Hamdaan, and Hamdaan is not Daabas, and Daabas is not Kaabelha.'

Gebel protested angrily:

'Do you want to divide one family into masters and servants?'

But Daabas clung to his opinion and said:

'We have café owners and pedlars amongst us; how can you treat them as equals? I was the first to go out during the blockade, getting myself chased by Kidra. I was the first to meet you in your exile, and later I was the first to agree with you completely when everyone else hung back.'

Gebel grew still angrier and bellowed:

'A man who praises himself is a liar. God! Men like you deserve whatever trouble you get.'

Daabas wanted to go on with the argument, but Gebel's eyes blazed with anger, and he withdrew and left the gathering without a word. That evening he went to the hashish den of Atris el Aamash and sat in the circle of guests, brooding. He sought comfort by inviting Kaabelha to gamble with him. They played Egyptian draughts on the ground using pebbles for pieces. Within half an hour Daabas had lost his share of the estate's revenue. Atris who was changing the water in the pipe, laughed:

'Bad luck Daabas! You're doomed to be poor, even against the wishes of the Founder.'

The loss had cleared Daabas' head and he growled:

'Riches are not lost so easily.'

Atris inhaled from the pipe to find out how much water there was in it, then said:

'But you've lost yours, brother.'

Kaabelha was arranging the notes carefully. Then he lifted his hand to put them in the breast of his smock, but Daabas stopped him with one hand and held out the other hand for the money. Kaabelha scowled and said:

'It isn't your money any more; you have no right to it.'

'Let go of the money, you scum.'

Atris looked at them anxiously, and said:

'Don't quarrel in my house.'

Daabas shouted, gripping Kaabelha's hand.

'You shan't rob me, you bastard.'

'Let go of my hand, Daabas, I'm not robbing you.'

'You mean you earned it?'

'Why did you gamble?'

Daabas hit him hard, and screeched:

'My money! Before I break your bones!'

Kaabelha snatched his hand away suddenly, and Daabas went mad with rage and poked Kaabelha in the eye. Kaabelha screamed loudly and leapt up, then covered his eye with both hands, letting the money fall into Daabas's lap. He staggered with pain then fell down groaning. The others gathered round him, while Daabas collected up the money and put it back in the breast of his smock. Atris came up to him and said, horrified:

'You've blinded him.'

Daabas sat for a short time, shocked, then got up suddenly and left the place.


Gebel stood in the courtyard of his victory with the assembled men of Hamdaan. Anger was in his eyes and in the set of his jaw. Kaabelha squatted in front of him, with a tight bandage over his eye, while Daabas stood, facing Gebel's wrath silent and alone. Hamdaan tried to calm Gebel's temper and said gently:

'Daabas will give back the money to Kaabelha.'

Gebel shouted at the top of his voice:

'Let him first give him back his eye.'

Kaabelha cried, and Radwaan the storyteller said with a sigh:

'If only it were possible to give that back.'

Gebel's face was dark. He said:

'But it is possible to take an eye for an eye.'

Daabas stared into Gebel's face fearfully. He gave the money to Hamdaan saying:

'I was out of my mind with rage; I didn't mean to injure him.'

Gebel studied his face angrily for a long time, then said:

'An eye for an eye; and the one who started it is the loser.'

They looked at one another helplessly. Gebel had never been seen angrier than today, and events had already proved the violence of his temper; the day he had left his luxurious home; the day he had killed

Kidra. He was indeed violent in his rages, and when he was angry no one could come between him and his goal. Hamdaan tried to speak, but Gebel got in before him:

'The owner of the estate did not prefer you so that some of you could attack others. Life must either be based on order, or on a chaos which will spare none of you; and for that reason, Daabas, I have decided that your eye shall be put out.'

Daabas was panic-stricken and shouted:

'Not a hand shall be laid on me, not if I have to fight the lot of you.'

Gebel sprang at him like a mad bull and punched him very hard in the face, knocking him out. He lifted up the unconscious man, holding him from behind in his arms, then turned to Kaabelha and said in a commanding voice:

'Get up and take your due.'

Kaabelha got up, but stood hesitating, while screams came from Daabas's house. Gebel looked grimly at Kaabelha and shouted:

'Come, before I bury you alive.'

Kaabelha went up to Daabas and put out his eye in full view of everyone. The screams from Daabas's house grew louder and some of his friends, Atris and Ali Fawanis, cried out. Gebel shouted at them:

'You wicked cowards! My God! You only hated bullying when you were its victims. No sooner does one of you find himself strong then he rushes to do wrong and attack his neighbour. The only thing for the devils hidden inside you is to beat them without pity, without mercy; either order or destruction!'

He left Daabas in the hands of his friends and went.

This event had an immense effect on people's minds ... Before it, Gebel had been a beloved leader and his people had thought him a chief who did not wish to take the name or the outward signs of his position. After it he was feared and dreaded. Some people whispered about his harshness and his tyranny, but they always found others to oppose them and mention the other side of his nature – his pity for the man who had been attacked and his sincere wish to establish an order that should guarantee justice and brotherhood among Hamdaan's people. The latter view found support every day in his words and deeds, until those who disliked him warmed towards him, those who feared him trusted him, and those who had shunned him turned towards him, and everyone wanted the order he stood for and nobody broke it. Uprightness and honesty reigned in his days. He remained among them as a symbol of justice and order, until he died without having swerved an inch from his path.

That is the story of Gebel.

He was the first to rebel against injustice in our alley and the first to have the honour of meeting Gebelawi after he withdrew from the world. He obtained such power that no one disputed it with him, and yet he refrained from bullying and crookery and from getting rich by taking protection money and trading in drugs. He remained a byword for justice and strength and order amongst his people. True, he did not worry about the others in the alley; perhaps he looked down on them or scorned them like the rest of his people. But he never acted unjustly to any of them nor did any of them any harm, and he was an example to everyone.

If our alley were not plagued with forgetfulness, good examples would not be wasted.

# Rifaa

✳ ✳ ✳ ✳ ✳ ✳ ✳ ✳ ✳ ✳ ✳ ✳ ✳ ✳ ✳ ✳ ✳ ✳ ✳ ✳ ✳

It was a little before daybreak. Every living thing in the alley had gone to sleep, even the chiefs and the cats and dogs. Darkness had settled in every corner as though it would never leave. Under cover of the stillness, the door of Victory House in Gebel's quarter was opened with the utmost caution, and out slipped two figures. They went silently towards the Big House, then followed its high walls round to the desert. They trod carefully and kept turning to look behind them, to be sure no one was following them. They walked on deep into the desert, guided by the light of the stars, until they made out Hind's Rock like a patch of deeper darkness in the dark.

They were a middle-aged man and a pregnant young woman, and both of them carried bulging bags. At the rock the woman sighed and said:

'Amme Shafey, I'm tired.'

The man stopped and said gruffly:

'Take a rest then, and damn those who caused your tiredness.'

The woman put down her bag and sat on it, spreading her legs for greater comfort. The man stood for a moment, peering about, then he too sat down on his bag. A moist dawn breeze stirred around them, but the woman did not forget the question that absorbed her:

'Where do you think I shall have my child?'

Shafey said crossly:

'Anywhere's better than our damned alley, Abda.'

He looked up at the outline of the gebel, which stretched from north to south, and he said:

'We shall go to Souk Mukattam. Gebel went there in his time of trial. I'll open a carpentry shop and do the work I did in the alley. I have a skilful pair of hands and a fair amount of money to make a start.'

The woman drew her shawl tighter over her head and shoulders and said sadly:

'We'll live in exile as if we had no people, we who belong to Gebel's people, the lords of the alley.'

The man spat angrily:

'Lords of the alley indeed! We are just miserable slaves, Abda. Gebel and his happy times have gone, and Zonfol has come, damn him, our chief who is against us and not for us, who gobbles up our earnings and destroys anyone who complains.'

Abda did not deny any of this. It was as though, having always known bitter days and sorrowful nights, she clung more tightly to her happy memories, now that distance made her secure from the hateful things in the alley. She said:

'There would be no alley like ours if it wasn't for its bad men. Where is there a house like our ancestor's, or neighbours like ours? Where else will you hear the stories of Adham and Gebel and Hind's Rock? Damn the villains!'

'The cudgels crack down for the slightest reason, and the mighty strut about among us like fate itself.'

He remembered the abominable Zonfol who had taken him by the collar and shaken him till his ribs almost rattled, and had then dragged him in the dust in front of the people, all because he had spoken once about the estate. He stamped his foot on the ground and went on:

'The damned crook kidnapped the baby of Seydhom, the head-meat butcher and after that nothing was ever heard of it again. He had no mercy on a month-old baby, and you ask where you're to have your child! You'll have it amongst people who do not murder children.'

Abda sighed and said gently:

'If only you could be content with the same as other people.'

He frowned in the darkness.

'What did I do wrong, Abda? Nothing. I just talked about what had become of Gebel and Gebel's time, and justice, and about what has brought Gebel's people back to poverty and wretchedness. He smashed my shop up and beat me, and would have killed me but for the neighbours. If we'd stayed in our house until you had your baby, he'd have pounced on it as he did with Seydhom's.'

She shook her head sadly:

'Oh if only you'd been patient, Shafey! Haven't you heard them say Gebelawi will certainly come back one day to save his children from oppression?'

Shafey puffed:

'So they say! I've been hearing that ever since I was a boy. But the fact is our ancestor has cut himself off in his house, and the Trustee of his estate has taken its money for himself, except what he gives to the chief to protect him; and Zonfol, chief of Gebel's people, takes his share and

138

buries it in his stomach, as if Gebel had never been, as if he hadn't taken the eye of his friend Daabas for the eye of poor Kaabelha.'

The woman was silent in the darkness. Morning would find her amongst a strange people. Her new neighbours would be strangers and their hands would receive her child. It would grow up in a strange land, like a cutting from a tree. She had been happy enough amongst Gebel's people, taking the food to her husband's shop, sitting at night by the window to hear the fiddle of Amme Gewaad the blind storyteller. How sweet was its music, and how lovely was the story of Gebel, the night he met Gebelawi in the darkness: 'And he said to him; "Don't be afraid." And he gave him his love and support until he should succeed, and he returned to his alley a changed man. And how sweet it is to come back from exile.'

Shafey was looking up at the sky, at the stars, and at the first signs of light over the gebel. He said in alarm:

'We must be on our way so as to get to the souk before sunrise.'

'I still need rest.'

Damn those who caused your tiredness.'

How beautiful life would be but for Zonfol; it was full of good things: the pure air, the starry sky, pleasant sensations. But there was also the Trustee Ihaab and the chiefs Bayumi, Jabir, Handusa, Khalid, Batikha and Zonfol. It would have been possible for every house to become like the Big House, for the moans to turn into songs; but the wretched people still yearned for the unattainable as Adham before them had yearned. And what was the state of these poor people? Their necks were red from beatings, their backs bruised with kicks. Flies clustered round their eyes, and lice nested in their hair.

'Why has Gebelawi forgotten us?'

The woman murmured:

'God knows how he is.'

Shafey shouted:

'Gebelawi!'

The echo threw back his voice. He stood up saying:

'We must trust in God.'

Abda stood up, taking him by the hand, and they went south towards Souk Mukattam.

45 ✳ ✳ ✳ ✳ ✳ ✳ ✳ ✳ ✳ ✳ ✳ ✳ ✳ ✳ ✳ ✳ ✳ ✳ ✳

Abda said, with joy in her eyes and on her lips:

'There is our alley! Here we are coming back to it as we longed to. Praise be to God, Lord of all worlds!'

Shafey smiled, wiping his forehead on the sleeve of his cloak, and said with composure:

'How wonderful to be back!'

Rifaa listened to his parents with a mixture of surprise and sadness on his handsome, open face. He protested:

'Will you forget Souk Mukattam and our neighbours there?'

His mother smiled, drawing the corner of her shawl over her greying hair. She understood that the boy felt as strongly for his birthplace as she did for hers. With his affectionate nature he could not forget friendships. She answered:

'Good things are never forgotten. But this is your real home. Your people are here, the lords of the alley. You'll love them and they'll love you. How wonderful Gebel's quarter will be after the death of Zonfol!'

Shafey said:

'Khonfis will be no better than Zonfol.'

'But Khonfis doesn't hate you.'

'Chiefs turn nasty as quickly as mud follows rain.'

Abda said hopefully:

'Don't think like that. We've come back to live in peace. You'll open a shop and make a living. And don't forget that you lived under a chief at Souk Mukattam. People everywhere have one over them.'

The family went on their way to the alley. Shafey in front carrying a sack, Abda and Rifaa following with a big bundle. Rifaa, with his height, his slim build and his open face, was an attractive young man, with an air of gentleness and friendliness. He seemed a stranger to the earth he walked on. He looked eagerly at the scene, till his eyes fell on the Big House which stood by itself at the head of the alley, the tops of the trees waving above its walls. He gazed at it for a long time, then said:

'Our ancestor's house?'

Abda said happily:

'Yes. You know what we told you about it; your ancestor lives there, the owner of all this land and everything that stands on it. If it wasn't for his withdrawal the alley would be filled with light.'

Shafey went on scornfully:

'And in his name Ihaab the Trustee robs us, and the chiefs attack us.'

They went towards the alley, past the south wall of the Big House, at which Rifaa continued to gaze. Then the Trustee's house came into sight with its gatekeeper sitting on the bench by the open gate. Opposite it stood the house of Bayumi, Chief of the alley, in front of which stood a donkey cart with baskets of rice and fruit. The servants were carrying them one after another into the house. The alley itself looked like a playground for barefoot children, and women sat on the ground or on rush matting in front of the houses, cleaning beans or mashing jute leaves and exchanging gossip and jokes and abuse. There was a great deal of laughing and shouting. Shafey and his family made for Gebel's quarter. An old blind man, feeling his way slowly with a stick, met them at the side of the road. Shafey put down the bag from his back and went up to him beaming. He stood in front of him and said:

'Mr Gewaad the storyteller! How are you?'

The man stopped, cocking an ear, then shook his head bewildered, saying:

'Hello! That's a voice I seem to know.'

'Have you forgotten your old friend Shafey the carpenter?'

The man's face lit up and he shouted:

'Mr Shafey; good heavens!'

He opened his arms and the two men embraced with such fervent affection that the by-standers stared at them, and two boys imitated their embrace playfully. Gewaad said, seizing his friend's hand:

'You left us twenty odd years ago, what an age! And how's your wife?'

Abda said:

'I'm well, Mr Gewaad. I hope you are too. And here's our son Rifaa. Come and kiss the storyteller's hand.'

Rifaa came up to the storyteller happily, took his hand and kissed it. The man put a hand on his shoulder and felt his head and his features. He said:

'Amazing! As handsome as Gebelawi!'

The praise lit up Abda's face, but Shafey laughed and said:

'If you could see how thin he is you wouldn't say that.'

'It's enough; there won't be another Gebelawi. What does the young man do?'

'His job is carpentry; but he's a spoilt, only child. He stays in my shop very little and wanders about in the desert and on the gebel most of the time.'

The storyteller smiled.

'A man doesn't settle down before he's married. And where have you been, Shafey?'

'In Souk Mukattam.'

The man laughed loudly.

'Like Gebel! But Gebel came back a snake charmer and you've come back a carpenter as you went. Anyway your enemy's dead. But the new lot are as bad as the old.'

Abda said quickly:

'They're all like that, but all we want is to live in peace.'

Several men recognized Shafey and hurried towards him. There were embraces all round and a babble of voices. Rifaa began looking about again with eager interest; his people were there around him, and this quelled much of the loneliness he had felt since he had left Souk Mukat-tam. His eyes roved around until they fell on a window in the first house, where a girl was gazing down into his face with interest. When their eyes met she looked away at the horizon. One of his parents' friends noticed this and whispered to him:

'Aysha, Khonfis' daughter; one look at her can start a massacre.'

Rifaa blushed and his mother said:

'He isn't that kind of boy; but this is the first time he has seen his alley.'

Out of the first house came a man as strong as an ox, strutting along in an ample smock, an aggressive moustache bristling on his scarred and pock-marked face. The people whispered 'Khonfis! Khonfis!' Gewaad took Shafey by the hand and led him forward, saying:

'A very good day to you, Chief of the Gebelites. Here is our brother, Mr Shafey the carpenter, who has come back to his alley after being away twenty years.'

Khonfis gave Shafey's face a piercing look, ignoring for a while his outstretched hand, then shook it without looking any friendlier and muttered coldly:

'Welcome.'

Rifaa looked at him angrily, and his mother whispered to him to go and greet him. Rifaa went reluctantly and offered him his hand. Shafey said:

'My son Rifaa.'

Khonfis gave Rifaa a look of dislike and contempt, interpreted by the onlookers as scorn at his gentleness, which was so unusual in the alley. He shook his hand limply, then turned to his father asking:

'Do you think you'll have forgotten the way we live here during your absence?'

Shafey understood the hint but hid his discomfort.

'We're at your service, sir, any time.'

Khonfis studied him doubtfully.

'Why did you leave?'

Shafey said nothing, searching for a suitable answer. Khonfis said:

'Running away from Zonfol?'

Gewaad the storyteller said hastily:

'It wasn't for any crime.'

Khonfis warned Shafey:

'You won't be able to escape from me when I'm angry.'

Abda said hopefully:

'You'll find us very good people, sir.'

Shafey and his family went in the midst of their friends to Victory House where they took over empty rooms that Gewaad showed them. At a window opening on to the entrance passage was a girl with a saucy kind of beauty. She stood combing her hair in front of the window pane. When she saw the people coming she asked flirtatiously:

'Who's this coming like a bridegroom in procession?'

Many people laughed and one man said:

'A new neighbour for you Jasmine. He'll live opposite you in the passage.'

She laughed:

'God grant us more men!'

Her eyes passed over Abda listlessly, but they rested on Rifaa with interest and admiration. Rifaa was even more struck by her look than by that of Aysha, Khonfis' daughter. He followed his parents to the door of the lodgings opposite Jasmine's, on the other side of the passage. Jasmine was singing: 'Oh mother, what a handsome son!'

# 46

Shafey opened his carpenter's shop by the gate of Victory House. In the morning Abda went shopping, and Shafey and his son Rifaa went to the shop and sat on its doorstep waiting for business. Shafey had enough money for a month or so and was not worried. He began looking at the passage, which was roofed over with lodgings, leading to the big courtyard. He said:

'This is the blessed passage where Gebel drowned his enemies.'

Rifaa looked at him with dreamy eyes and a smile on his lips. His father went on:

'And in this place Adham built his hut where so much happened; and here Gebelawi blessed his son and forgave him.'

Rifaa smiled still more, and his eyes were far away. Great memories were all born here, and, but for time, the footprints of Gebelawi and Adham would still be here, and their breath would be in the air. From here the water had been poured on the tyrants in the pit, from Jasmine's window it had fallen on the enemy; and today nothing fell from it but provocative glances. Time plays with everything, however great. Gebel himself had waited in the courtyard among weak men, and yet he had won.

'Gebel won, father, but what was the use of his victory?'

Shafey sighed and said:

'We agreed not to think about that: didn't you see Khonfis?'

A flirtatious voice called out:

'Mr Carpenter!'

Father and son exchanged disapproving looks. The father got up and turned his head and saw Jasmine looking down from the window, her two long plaits hanging down and swinging. He shouted:

'Yes!'

She said in a playfully soft, slow voice:

'Send your son up to fetch a table for mending.'

Shafey sat down again and said to his son:

'Go, and trust in God.'

Rifaa found the door of the lodgings ready open for him. He coughed, and she asked him to come in, and in he went. He found her in a brown gown with white trimmings round the neck and over the bosom, and her feet and legs were bare. She said nothing for a while, to test the effect of her appearance on him. When she saw that the innocence of his eyes did not change she pointed to a small table standing on three legs in the corner of the room and said:

'The fourth leg is under the divan; fix it on and varnish the table.'

'At your service, miss.'

'And the price?'

'I'll ask father.'

She exclaimed:

'And you? Don't you know the price?'

'He's the one who deals with all that.'

She studied his face hard and asked:

'And who will mend it?'

'Me; but with his help.'

She laughed heedlessly.

'The youngest of our chiefs, Batikha, is younger than you, but he can control a whole procession, and you can't put a leg on a table by yourself.'

Rifaa's tone showed he wanted to end the conversation:

'The important thing is that it comes back to you as good as new.'

He took the fourth leg from under the divan and carried the table on his shoulder towards the door saying:

'Good-bye.'

When he put the table down in the shop, his father said grumpily, examining it:

'I must say I really would have preferred our first job to come from somewhere cleaner.'

Rifaa said naïvely:

'There's nothing dirty about her, father, but she seems to be lonely.'

'Nothing's more dangerous than a lonely woman.'

'Perhaps she needs guidance.'

Shafey said scornfully:

144

'Our job's carpentry, not guidance. Bring me the glue.'

In the evening Shafey and Rifaa went to Gebel's café. Gewaad the storyteller was sitting on his bench, sipping his coffee. Shaldam, the owner of the café, sat near the door, while Khonfis was in the place of honour, surrounded by a circle of admirers. Shafey and his son went over to the chief to pay him their humble respects, then they took their seats next to Shaldam. Shafey ordered a pipe for himself and got his son a cup of cinnamon and hazel. The atmosphere of the café grew drowsy. A cloud of smoke gathered, and the still air was filled with the smells of tobacco and mint and cloves. The faces with their bushy moustaches and their heavy eyelids looked pale. There was a constant sound of coughing and jokes and coarse laughter. From the middle of the alley came the sound of some boys singing:

> Gebelawi's children, what news?
> Which of you are Christians, or Jews?
> What is it that you eat? Dates please.
> What is it that you drink? Coffees.

A cat crouched by the door, ready to spring; it pounced under a bench, and there was the sound of a scuffle; then it emerged and ran out carrying a mouse between its teeth. Rifaa put down his cup of cinnamon, upset by the sight. He looked up and saw Khonfis spitting. Khonfis shouted at Gewaad:

'When are you going to begin, you cunning old fox?'

Gewaad smiled and nodded, took up his fiddle and played some introductory tunes. Then he began with a salute to Ihaab, the Trustee, to Bayumi, chief of the alley, and to Khonfis, Gebel's successor, and went on to recite:

> Adham sat in the estate office receiving the new tenants. He was looking in his ledger when the last man announced his name: 'Idris Gebelawi'. Adham raised his head fearfully and saw his brother standing before him . . .

The storyteller carried on the story to an attentive audience. Rifaa followed him eagerly; this was a true reciter and these were the real stories. Many a time his mother had told him: 'Our alley is the alley of stories.' They were indeed good ones; perhaps they would console him for Souk Mukattam and his lone wanderings, and soothe his heart which burnt with a longing as mysterious as the big locked house – the Big House which showed no sign of life save the tops of the mulberry and fig and palm trees. What proof was there that he himself was descended from Gebelawi, apart from the likeness that Gewaad the storyteller imagined he felt with his hands?

Night was coming on and Shafey smoked his third pipe. The cries of pedlars and boys ceased in the alley, leaving only the music of the fiddle and the beating of a distant drum and the cries of a woman whose husband was beating her. In the story, Idris had by now brought about Adham's expulsion into the desert, followed by Omayma weeping .. ε 'Just as my mother left the alley, with me in her womb. Damn the chiefs, and the cats when the mice die in their mouths, and scornful looks and cold laughs! Damn any man who can welcome his home-coming brother with the words: "You won't be able to escape from me when I'm angry!" Bullies and hypocrites!'

By now Adham had nothing but the desert, and the storyteller was singing one of Idris's drunken songs. Rifaa leaned across and whispered in his father's ear:

'I want to visit the other cafés.'

Shafey said, amazed:

'But ours is the best in the alley.'

'What do the storytellers there say?'

'The same stories; but there they sound quite different.'

Shaldam heard their whispering and leaned towards Rifaa and said:

'There are no worse liars than the people of this alley, and the storytellers are the worst of all. You will hear in the next café that Gebel said he was a son of the alley when he only said, by God, that he was a son of Hamdaan.'

Shafey said:

'A storyteller wants to please his audience at any price.'

Shaldam whispered:

'Or rather he wants to please the chief.'

Father and son left the café in the middle of the night. The darkness was so thick they could almost feel it. Men's voices came out of the nothingness, and a cigarette glowed in an invisible hand. Shafey asked:

'Did you like the storytelling?'

'Yes! What good stories!'

The father laughed and said:

'Gewaad likes you; what did he say to you when he was resting?'

'He invited me to visit him in his house.'

'How quickly you make friends. But you learn slowly.'

'I have a whole lifetime for carpentry, but just now I'm anxious to visit all the cafés.'

They felt their way back to the passage and from Jasmine's lodgings they heard a drunken noise and a voice singing:

Who made your fine lace cap, my love?
My heart is caught. Please pity me.

146

Rifaa whispered to his father:

'She is not as lonely as I thought.'

His father sighed and said:

'What a lot of life you've missed, mooching about by yourself.'

They began climbing the stairs slowly and carefully and Rifaa said:

'Father, I'll go and see Gewaad the storyteller soon.'

47  ✳ ✳ ✳ ✳ ✳ ✳ ✳ ✳ ✳ ✳ ✳ ✳ ✳ ✳ ✳ ✳

Rifaa knocked on the door of Gewaad the storyteller in the third house in Gebel's quarter. From the courtyard came the violent abuse of some women who had gathered to do their washing and cooking He looked down over the railing of the balcony which ran round the courtyard. The cause of the trouble was a quarrel between two women, one of whom stood behind a washtub waving her soapy arms, while the other stood at the entrance of the passage with rolled up sleeves, answering back in still worse language. The other women had taken sides and the walls echoed their foul insults. Rifaa started at the sight and turned in disgust to the storyteller's door. 'Even the women, even the cats! Not to mention the chiefs! Claws on every hand, poison on every tongue, fear and hatred in every mouth. Clean air, that's only found in Mukattam Desert, or in the Big House where the Founder enjoys peace and solitude.' The door opened on the blind man's face. Rifaa greeted him, and he smiled and stepped aside for him.

'Welcome, my son.'

A smell of incense like a breath of heaven met Rifaa as soon as he went in. He followed Gewaad to a small square room, with decorated rush matting spread on the floor. The late afternoon light was dim behind the shuttered windows. The ceiling around the lamp was decorated with pictures of doves and other birds. The storyteller sat down cross-legged on a cushion and Rifaa sat down beside him. Gewaad said:

'We were just making coffee.'

He called his wife and she came carrying a coffee tray. He said:

'Come, Omme B'Khatirha: this is Rifaa, Mr Shafey's son.'

The woman sat down on the other side of her husband and began pouring out the coffee.

'Welcome, my son.'

She seemed to be in her middle sixties, strong and well built. She had a tattooed chin and penetrating eyes. Gewaad pointed towards his guest and said:

'He's a good listener, Omme B'Khatirha, he laps up stories. Such people are a storyteller's delight and inspiration. The others so quickly get drowsy from hashish.'

His wife said playfully:

'They are new stories for him, familiar ones for them.'

The storyteller said indignantly:

'That's the voice of one of your devils.' Then to Rifaa: 'She's an exorcist.'

Rifaa looked at her with interest, and their eyes met as she handed him his cup of coffee. How the beating of the exorcist's drums had attracted him at Souk Mukattam! His heart had danced to them. He used to stand in the road craning his neck towards the windows to see the smoke of incense and the wagging heads. The storyteller asked him:

'Didn't you know anything about the alley in your exile?'

'My father told me about it, and my mother too, but my heart was where I lived, and I didn't care much about the estate and its problems. I was amazed at the number of its victims, and I shared my mother's wish for peace and friendship.'

Gewaad said, shaking his head sadly:

'How is it possible for friendship and love to live alongside poverty and the cudgels of the chiefs?'

Rifaa did not answer, not because there was no answer but because his eyes had just come upon a strange picture at the top of the right-hand wall of the room, painted in oils on the wall like the pictures in the cafés. It represented a gigantic man, beside whom the houses of the alley looked like toys. Rifaa asked:

'Who is that a picture of?'

Omme B'Khatirha said:

Gebelawi.'

'Did someone see him?'

Gewaad said:

'No, no! None of our generation has seen him. Even Gebel couldn't make him out in the darkness of the desert. But the artist painted him as he's described in the stories.'

Rifaa said with a sigh:

'Why has he locked his doors against his children?'

'They say old age. Who can tell how time has dealt with him? My God! If he opened his doors none of the people of the alley would stay in their filthy hovels.'

'Couldn't you . . .'

Omme B'Khatirha cut him short:

'Don't think about him. When people start talking about the Founder they end up talking about the estate, and then all sorts of things happen.'

He shook his head in bewilderment:

'How can you not think about such a great ancestor?'

'Let's do as he does; he doesn't think about us.'

Rifaa looked up at the picture and said:

'But he met Gebel and spoke to him.'

'Yes, and when Gebel died, Zonfol and Khonfis came, and now it's as if nothing had ever happened.'

Gewaad laughed and said to his wife:

'The alley needs something to drive out its devils as you drive out evil spirits.'

Rifaa smiled:

'Mrs Gewaad, the real evil spirits are those people themselves; if only you'd seen how Khonfis received my father!'

'Those people are not my business; *my* kind of evil spirits obey me as the snakes obeyed Gebel. I have all the things they like: incense from Sudan, charms from Ethiopia and songs of power.'

Rifaa asked her eagerly:

'Where does your power over evil spirits come from?'

She looked at him cautiously.

'It's my job, as carpentry is your father's; it came to me from God who is the giver of all skills.'

Rifaa drained his cup and was about to speak, but his father's voice came from the alley shouting:

'Rifaa, you lazy-bones.'

Rifaa went to the window, looked out and caught his father's eye and shouted:

'Give me half an hour, father.'

Shafey shrugged his shoulders hopelessly and went back to his shop.

As he was shutting the window, Rifaa saw Aysha at her place, just as he had seen her the first time, gazing at him. It seemed to him that she smiled or spoke to him with her eyes. He hesitated a moment, but then he shut the window and went back to his seat. Gewaad was laughing.

'Your father wants you to be a carpenter, but what do you want?'

Rifaa thought for a while:

'Although I'm a carpenter like father, I love stories. These secrets about evil spirits, now tell me about them.'

She smiled and seemed ready to give him a little of her knowledge:

'Everybody has a ruling spirit, but not every spirit is evil and needs to be cast out.'

'How can we tell one from the other?'

'A man's behaviour shows it. You, for example, are a good boy, and your ruling spirit deserves good treatment. The spirits of Bayumi and Khonfis and Batikha are not like that.'

He said innocently:

149

'And Jasmine's spirit? Ought it to be cast out?'

Omme B'Khatirha said laughing:

'Your neighbour? But the men want her as she is.'

He said:

'I want to know about these things; don't grudge it to me.'

Gewaad said:

'Who could grudge anything to such a good fellow?'

Omme B'Khatirha said:

'It'd be good if you could join me whenever you have time, but on condition your father doesn't get angry. People will wonder what such a good boy has to do with evil spirits; but understand that all men's ills are spirits.'

Rifaa listened, gazing up at the picture of Gebelawi.

48 ✳ ✳ ✳ ✳ ✳ ✳ ✳ ✳ ✳ ✳ ✳ ✳ ✳ ✳ ✳ ✳ ✳ ✳ ✳

Carpentry was his job and his future: there seemed no escape from that. If he did not like it, what would he like? It was better than toiling along behind a barrow or carrying a basket of wares. As for other 'jobs' like being a scrounger or a chief, how hateful they were! Omme B'Khatirha stirred his imagination as nothing else had done, except of course the picture of the Founder on the wall of Gewaad's room. He urged his father one day to have one like it painted in the house or in the shop, but he said:

'We need the money it would cost; besides, it's a fantasy, and what's the use of a fantasy?'

'I wish I could see it here.'

'You see to your job. I shan't live for ever, and you must get ready for the day when you'll have to support your mother and your wife and children on your own.'

But Rifaa thought about hardly anything except what Omme B'Khatirha said or did. What she told him about evil spirits seemed to him of the utmost importance. It left his mind only at the times when he visited the cafés one after another. Even the old stories did not sink into him so deeply as Omme B'Khatirha's words, like: 'Everybody has a spirit that rules him, and a man is like his ruling spirit.' Many an evening he spent with the woman, following the beating of the drum and watching the evil spirits being brought under control. Some sufferers were led to the house, weak and apathetic. Others were carried in, bound and fettered because of their savageness. The appropriate incense would be burnt – for each condition had its incense – and the necessary rhythm would be beaten – for each spirit demanded a particular rhythm – and then wonderful things would happen. 'So we know the cure of each evil spirit; but what is the cure for the Trustee and his chiefs? They make fun of exorcism, but perhaps it was created just for them. Killing would only get rid of them, but evil spirits give in to pure scents and good drumming. Why should a wicked demon like something good? Our knowledge of spirits is wonderful.'

He told Omme B'Khatirha he wanted with all his heart to learn the secrets of exorcism. She asked him if he hoped to earn money and he replied that he wanted to clean the alley up and did not care about money. She laughed and said he was the first man to want that job; what drew him to it? He said with conviction: 'The wisdom of your work is that you overcome evil with good.' When she began telling him her secrets his heart was glad. To savour his joy, he used to go on to the roof of the house in the exhilaration of dawn and watch the light awakening, but the Big House took his mind off the stars and the stillness and the crowing of the cocks. He would gaze for a long time at the house sleeping amidst its trees and wonder 'Where are you, Gebelawi? Why don't you show yourself, even just for a moment? Why don't you come out, even just once? Don't you know that one word from you could change the alley completely? Or are you pleased at what goes on? How lovely the trees are round your house! I love them because you love them; look at them so that I can find your glances on them.'

Whenever he confided his thoughts to his father, he rebuked him and said: 'What about your work, lazy-bones? Boys like you are toiling about the streets after a living, or making the alley tremble with their cudgels.'

One day the family was sitting round after lunch and Abda said smiling:

'Tell him, Shafey.'

Rifaa looked at his father for explanation, but Shafey spoke to his wife:

'You tell him what you want to say first.'

Abda looked admiringly at her son and said:

'Good news, Rifaa: Mrs Zakia, wife of Khonfis our chief, has been to see me. I returned the visit naturally, and she gave me a warm welcome and presented her daughter Aysha to me, a girl as beautiful as the moon. Then she came to see me again, bringing Aysha.'

Shafey looked sidelong at his son who was lifting his cup of coffee to his lips, to see the effect of the story on him; then he shook his head over the difficult task that awaited him and said pompously:

'This is an honour that no other family in Gebel's quarter has enjoyed. Imagine it; the wife and daughter of Khonfis visiting this home of ours!'

Rifaa looked up at his mother in confusion. She said eagerly:

'Their home is so wonderful – comfortable chairs; a marvellous carpet, even curtains hanging over the windows and doors . . .'

Rifaa said angrily:

'All this finery out of the stolen wealth of Gebel's people.'

Shafey said, suppressing a smile:

'We agreed not to talk about that subject.'

Abda said anxiously:

'Let's just remember that Khonfis is the ruler of Gebel's people and that his family's friendship is an answer to prayer.'

Rifaa said:

'Congratulations on this friendship.'

Father and mother exchanged meaningful looks, and she said:

'Aysha's coming with her mother meant something.'

Rifaa felt apprehensive:

'What did it mean, mother?'

Shafey laughed, waving his hand hopelessly. He said to Abda:

'We ought to have told him how our marriage came about.'

Rifaa shouted:

'No, no! Oh no, father!'

'What do you mean? What's wrong with you, behaving like a girl?'

Abda tempted him hopefully:

'It's in your power to bring us into the trusteeship of Gebel's estate. They will welcome you, for his wife would not have gone this far if she wasn't sure of him. You'll be so important that the whole alley from end to end will envy you.'

His father said laughing:

'Who knows; we may see you the Trustee of Gebel's estate one day, or you may see one of your sons there.'

'Can *you* say that father? Have you forgotten why you left the alley twenty years ago?'

Shafey blinked in some confusion and said:

'Today we live like other people. We can't miss a chance like this.'

Rifaa murmured, as if he were talking to himself:

'How can I be son-in-law to a devil when all that matters to me is casting out devils?'

Shafey shouted:

'I never hoped to make more than a carpenter out of you, but now good fortune offers you a high place in our alley, and all you want is to be an exorcist! What a scandal! What evil eye has fallen on you? Say you'll marry her and stop joking.'

'I won't marry her, father.'

Shafey took no notice.

152

'I shall visit Khonfis to ask for her hand.'
Rifaa shouted heatedly:
'Don't do that, father.'
'Tell me what's wrong, boy.'
Abda pleaded with her husband:
'Don't be harsh with him; you know very well how he is.'
'Curse what I know! The whole alley will blame us for his softness.'
'Be gentle with him so that he'll think again.'
'Other boys his age are fathers, and people respect them.' He looked at him angrily and went on: 'Why do you go pale at the idea? You come from the loins of men.'
Rifaa sighed, almost on the point of tears, and thought: 'Anger destroys the ties of fatherhood, and home sometimes becomes a prison. What you seek is not in this place or among these people.' He said hoarsely:
'Don't torment me, father.'
'It's you who are tormenting me, as you have done since you were born.'
Rifaa bowed his head to hide his face from his parents. Shafey lowered his voice, controlling his temper as best he could, and asked:
'Are you afraid of marriage? Don't you want to marry? Explain to me what's in your mind. Or should I go to Omme B'Khatirha? Perhaps she knows things about you that we don't know.'
He shouted:
'No, never!'
And suddenly he got up and left the room.


49 ✳ ✳ ✳ ✳ ✳ ✳ ✳ ✳ ✳ ✳ ✳ ✳ ✳ ✳ ✳ ✳ ✳ ✳

Shafey went down to open the shop and did not find Rifaa there as he had expected. Still, he did not call him, but said to himself: 'It will be wisest to pretend not to mind about his absence!' The day passed slowly by, the sunlight disappeared bit by bit from the alley, and the sawdust piled up round Shafey's feet, but still Rifaa did not show up. Evening came and Shafey closed the shop, upset and angry. He went as usual to Shaldam's café and took his seat. When he saw Gewaad the storyteller coming alone he was overcome with amazement and asked:
'Where is Rifaa then?'
Gewaad answered, feeling his way towards his bench:
'I haven't seen him since yesterday.'
Shafey said anxiously:

'I haven't seen him since he left us after lunch.'

Gewaad raised his white eyebrows. He sat down cross-legged on the bench, putting the fiddle down beside him, and asked:

'Has there been any trouble between you?'

Shafey did not answer. He stood up suddenly and left the café. Shaldam was astonished at Shafey's anxiety and said scornfully:

'The alley hasn't seen such silliness since Idris set up his hut in the wilderness. When I was young I used to be away from the alley for days at a time and no one asked about me. When I got back, my father, God rest him, would shout: "What brings you back you son of a bitch!" '

Khonfis said from the place of honour:

'Because he wasn't sure you were his son.'

The café was rocked by laughter and people congratulated Khonfis on his joke.

Shafey went home and asked Abda if Rifaa had come back. She was filled with anxiety and said she had thought he was in the shop as usual. She grew still more worried when he told her that Rifaa had not been to Gewaad's house either. She kept asking:

'Where can he have gone, then?'

They heard Jasmine calling a fig seller. Abda looked questioningly at Shafey, and he shook his head wearily and let out a little laugh of scorn, but she said:

'A girl like her has a kind of power.'

Shafey went to Jasmine's house, driven by despair alone. He knocked at the door and Jasmine herself opened it. When she saw who it was she jerked her head back in a mixture of surprise and triumph. She said:

'You?! Every dreamer hides a schemer!'

He looked away from her flimsy blouse and said curtly:

'Is Rifaa with you?'

She was still more surprised:

'Rifaa! Why?'

He became embarrassed and she pointed inside and said:

'Come and look for yourself.'

But he turned to go, and she asked him scornfully:

'Has he grown up today?'

As he left he heard her speaking to someone inside:

'They're more worried about their boy than other people about a girl!'

Shafey found Abda waiting in the passage. She said to him:

'We'll go together to Souk Mukattam.'

He shouted angrily:

'Damn you! Is this my reward for a hard day's work?'

They took a donkey-cart to Souk Mukattam and asked their former neighbours and acquaintances about Rifaa but found no trace of him.

154

Of course, he used to go off for a few hours some afternoons to lonely places or to the gebel, but no one could imagine him staying in the desert till this hour of the night. His parents returned to the alley as they had left it, but still more worried.

Tongues wagged over his disappearance, especially after he had been away several days. He became a joke in the café and in Jasmine's place and all over Gebel's quarter. Everyone made fun of his parents' fears. Omme B'Khatirha and Gewaad were perhaps the only ones who shared the parents' sorrow. Gewaad said: 'Where's the boy gone? He's not that kind of boy; if he was, we wouldn't have worried.' Batikha shouted one time when he was drunk: 'Oyez, oyez! A child is lost; oyez!' Everyone laughed over this and the boys went about repeating it.

Abda grieved so much that she fell ill, and Shafey worked in his shop with his mind elsewhere and with eyes feverish from loss of sleep. Zakia, the wife of Khonfis, broke off her visits to Abda and cut her dead in the street.

One day Shafey was bending over, sawing a piece of wood, when Jasmine, on her way back from an outing, shouted:

'Mr Shafey . . . look!'

He found she was pointing at the end of the alley by the desert. He left the shop with the saw in his hand to see what she was pointing at, and he saw his son Rifaa, coming shamefaced towards the houses. Shafey dropped his saw in front of the shop and hurried towards his son, gazing at him in a daze. Then he took him by the arms and said:

'Rifaa! Where've you been? Don't you know what your absence has meant for us – for your poor mother who is almost dying of grief?'

The young man said nothing. His father saw how thin he was and asked:

'Have you been ill?'

'No, no! Let me see mother.'

Jasmine came up to them and asked Rifaa suspiciously:

'But where've you been?'

He did not look at her. Some boys collected round him, and his father took him home. They were soon followed by Gewaad and Omme B'Khatirha. When his mother saw him she leapt out of bed and hugged him to herself, saying in a weak voice:

'God forgive you! How could you think so little of your mother?'

He took her hand in his and sat her down on the bed, then sat beside her saying:

'I'm sorry.'

His father glowered, hiding the joy which danced within him. He said:

'We only wanted to make you happy.'

Abda's eyes brimmed with tears.

'Did you imagine we'd force you to marry?'

He said sadly:

'I'm tired.'

Several voices asked:

'Where have you been?'

He sighed and said:

'I couldn't bear life, and I went to the desert. I felt the need to be alone. I only left the desert to buy food.'

His father slapped himself on the forehead and shouted:

'Sensible people don't do that sort of thing.'

Omme B'Khatirha said anxiously:

'Leave him alone. I know all about these states. With a person like him it's wrong to force him to do anything he doesn't want.'

Abda said, clasping his hand:

'We wanted him to be happy, but fate has turned out differently. How thin you've got!'

Shafey asked angrily:

'When did anything like this ever happen in the alley?'

Omme B'Khatirha scolded him:

'There's nothing strange to me about his condition, believe me, Mr Shafey. He's just an unusual boy.'

'We've become the talk of the alley.'

Omme B'Khatirha said indignantly:

'There's no boy like him in the alley.'

Shafey said:

'This is a time for sorrow.'

Omme B'Khatirha shouted:

'For God's sake, man; you don't know what you're saying, and you don't understand what's said to you.'

50 ✳ ✳ ✳ ✳ ✳ ✳ ✳ ✳ ✳ ✳ ✳ ✳ ✳ ✳ ✳ ✳ ✳ ✳ ✳

The shop began to look busy and successful. Shafey stood at one end of the bench sawing wood, while at the other end Rifaa was hammering nails. Under the table the gluepot was half buried in the heap of sawdust. Window frames and doors leaned against the walls, with a pile of new boxes in the midst of them. Judging by the smooth finish of the pale wood, all it needed was varnish. The air was full of the smell of wood and the sounds of sawing and hammering and planing, and the gurgling of the pipe that four customers were smoking as they chatted, sitting by the door of the shop. Hejazi said to Shafey:

'I shall test your skill with this couch and, please God, the next job will be my daughter's trousseau.' Then, to his friends: 'I can't say it too often; if Gebel came back and saw these times we're living in, he'd go mad.'

They shook their heads sadly and went on smoking. Borhoom the gravedigger asked Shafey with a smile:

'Why don't you want to make a coffin? Everything has its price doesn't it?'

Shafey stopped sawing for a moment and said laughing:

'I wouldn't do it for anything! Having a coffin in the shop would scare away my customers.'

Ferhat said:

'Very true! Curse death and everything to do with it!'

Hejazi spoke again:

'The trouble with you is that you're more afraid of death than you ought to be. That's why Khonfis has such power over you, and why Bayumi rules, and why Ihaab has seized your livelihood.'

'Aren't you afraid of death like us?'

He spat and said:

'It's the fault of us all. Gebel was strong, and by strength he won us the rights that we've lost by cowardice.'

Rifaa stopped hammering, took the nails out of his mouth, and said:

'Gebel wanted to win our rights peacefully. He only used violence in self defence.'

Hejazi laughed mockingly and said:

'Tell me, my boy, can a nail be knocked in except by violence?'

'Men aren't wood, sir.'

His father gave him a look and went on with his work. Hejazi went on:

'The fact is, Gebel was a chief, one of the most powerful the alley has ever known, and he urged his people to be the same.'

Ferhat backed him up:

'He wanted us to be the chiefs of the whole alley, not just of Gebel's quarter.'

'And today we're just mice and rabbits.'

Shafey asked, wiping his nose on the back of his hand:

'Which colour would you prefer, Mr Hejazi?'

'Choose a colour that won't show the dirt.'

He went on with his conversation:

'The day Daabas put out Kaabelha's eye, Gebel put out Daabas's eye, and established justice by violence.'

Rifaa sighed deeply and said:

'Violence gets us nowhere. Every hour of the day and night we see people hitting or wounding or killing. Even the women draw blood with their nails. But where's the justice? How horrible all this is!'

157

They were all silent for a time; then Hanoura said, speaking for the first time:

'This young gentleman despises our alley. He's softer than he should be, and you're the cause, Mr Shafey.'

'Me?!'

'Yes! He's a spoilt child.'

Hejazi turned to Rifaa and said laughing:

'It would be best for you to find a wife.'

There was laughter. Shafey frowned and Rifaa blushed. Hejazi said:

'Violence . . . violence . . . without it there can be no justice.'

Rifaa said firmly, in spite of his father's looks:

'The fact is our alley needs mercy.'

Borhoom laughed and said:

'Do you want to ruin me?'

They roared with laughter which led in turn to fits of coughing. Hejazi said, with bloodshot eyes:

'In those old times Gebel went asking for mercy and justice, and Effendi sent Zoklot and his men after him, and but for the cudgels – not mercy – Gebel and his people would have perished.'

Shafey shouted:

'You fool! The walls have ears; if they hear you, you won't find anyone to put in a word for you.'

Hanoura said:

'The man's right; you're nothing but worthless hashish addicts. If Khonfis walked past now you'd fall at his feet.' Then, to Rifaa: 'Don't blame us, my boy; a hashish smoker has no inhibitions. Haven't you tried hashish, Rifaa?'

Shafey said laughing:

'He doesn't like hashish parties; if he takes more than two puffs he gasps for breath or falls asleep.'

Ferhat said:

'What a nice boy he is! Some say he's an exorcist because he sees so much of Omme B'Khatirha, and some think he must be a storyteller because of his liking for tales.'

Hejazi said with a snigger:

'And he hates hashish parties just as he hates marriage.'

Borhoom called for the boy from the café to take away the pipe. Then they got up and said good-bye and the session came to an end. Shafey put down his saw and glared at his son and said:

'Don't get yourself mixed up in the conversations of such people.'

Some boys came and played in front of the shop. Rifaa went round the table to his father and led him by the hand to a corner where no ears could hear them. He seemed deeply disturbed, but his mouth was set firmly. There was a strange light in his eyes and Shafey wondered what it meant. Rifaa said:

'I can't keep quiet any longer.'

His father was annoyed. What a nuisance he was, this darling son; wasting his precious time in Omme B'Khatirha's house and spending long hours alone at Hind's Rock. He couldn't pass an hour in the shop without bringing up some problem.

'Are you feeling tired?'

He said with a strange quietness:

'I can't hide from you what is in my mind.'

'What is it?'

He drew closer to him and said:

'Yesterday, after I had left the storyteller's house about midnight, I felt the urge to go off and I made for the desert. I walked through the darkness until I got tired, then I picked a spot under the wall of the Big House where it overlooks the desert and sat down with my back propped against the wall.'

Shafey's eyes were full of interest and urged him to go on.

'I heard a strange voice speaking, as if it was talking to itself in the dark. The feeling suddenly overwhelmed me that it was the voice of Gebelawi.'

Shafey gaped at his son's face and said in amazement:

'Gebelawi's voice! What gave you that idea?'

Rifaa said hotly:

'It's not an idea, father; you shall have proof. I stood up as soon as I heard the voice and turned towards the house, drawing back to be able to see it. But I saw only darkness.'

'Thank God!'

'Patience, father! I heard the voice saying that Gebel had done his job and given satisfaction, but things had become even worse than before.'

Shafey felt a burning in his chest and the sweat poured from his forehead. He said in a trembling voice:

'So many people have sat where you sat under the wall and have heard nothing.'

'But I did hear, father.'

'Perhaps it was someone talking in his sleep in the desert.'

He shook his head vigorously.

'No; the voice came from the house.'

'How do you know that?'

'I shouted, "Grandfather, Gebel is dead and others have taken his place. Stretch out your hand and help us." '

'I hope to God no one heard you.'

Rifaa's eyes shone.

'My grandfather heard me. His voice came again saying: "How wrong it is for a young man to ask his old grandfather to act: the beloved son is the one who acts." I asked: "What device can I who am weak use against those chiefs?" and he replied: "The true weakling is the fool who does not know his inner strength, and I do not like fools." '

Shafey was frightened.

'Do you really think these words passed between you and Gebelawi?'

'Yes, by heaven!'

Shafey moaned:

'Too much imagination can bring disasters.'

'Believe me, father. There's no doubt about what I say.'

'Don't take away my hope of finding some doubt.'

Rifaa said, his face radiant:

'And now I know what's wanted of me.'

Shafey shouted, slapping himself on the forehead:

'Is *anything* wanted of you?'

'Yes! I'm weak, but I'm not a fool, and the beloved son is the one who acts.'

Shafey shouted in agony:

'Your deeds will be dark. You'll be destroyed, and you'll drag us down to destruction.'

Rifaa smiled:

'They only kill those who have their eye on the estate.'

'And do you have your eye on anything but the estate?'

Rifaa's voice was full of confidence:

'Adham longed for a pure life of happiness. Gebel did so too, and he only wanted the estate as a way to that life; but he got the idea that it wouldn't be possible for anyone unless the estate was shared out equally so that each man received his due and enjoyed the use of it, released from toil and free to live the happy life. But the estate is such a petty thing; it is possible to attain true life without it and anyone who wants to can. It's in our power to be rich from this very hour.'

Shafey sighed, somewhat relieved:

'Did our ancestor say that to you?'

'He said he didn't like foolishness, and that the true fool is the man who doesn't know his inner strength. I'd be the last person to ask for a fight over the estate. The estate is nothing, father; the happiness of a contented life is everything. Only the demons hidden deep inside us come between us and happiness. It's not for nothing that I love the science of evil spirits and am perfecting it. Perhaps it's the will of God that has brought me to it.'

Shafey was relieved, but the anguish had left him weak. He leaned on

160

his saw, stretching out his legs and resting his back on a window frame that was waiting to be repaired. He asked his son sarcastically:

'How come we haven't attained the happy life when we had Omme B'Khatirha among us before you were born?'

Rifaa said confidently:

'Because she waits for well-to-do patients to come to her, and doesn't go to the poor.'

Shafey looked round the corners of his shop and said:

'Look how many jobs we're getting; what'll we get tomorrow thanks to you?'

'Everything good, father; healing the sick will upset only the evil spirits.'

Light filled the shop as a wardrobe by the door mirrored the rays of the setting sun.

31

There was anxiety that night in Shafey's house. When the story reached Abda it had dwindled somewhat, and all she knew was that Rifaa had heard their ancestor's voice and had decided to visit the poor and cast out evil spirits from them; and yet she was filled with anxiety and kept turning over in her mind the possible consequences. Rifaa was out. From the bottom of the alley, far away from Gebel's quarter, came the sound of a wedding feast, drums and pipes and the women's cries of joy. Abda tried to face up to the truth and said sadly:

Rifaa doesn't lie.'

'But his imagination has played tricks on him. It happens to all of us.'

'What do you think about what he heard?'

'How can I judge?'

'It's not impossible as long as our ancestor is alive.'

'God help us if the news gets out.'

She said hopefully:

'Let's keep the story secret and thank God that he's fixed his thoughts on people, not on the estate. As long as he harms no one, no one'll harm him.'

'Plenty of people are harmed in this alley without their harming anyone!'

The music of the wedding feast was drowned by an outburst of noise in the passage. They looked out of the window and saw the passage full of people. By the light of the lamp that one of them held, they made out the faces of Hejazi, Borhoom, Ferhat and Hanoura amongst others.

161

Everyone was talking or yelling and there was a babble of voices and general confusion. Someone shouted 'The honour of Gebel's people is in the balance. We shan't allow anyone to tarnish it!' Abda shivered. She whispered to her husband:

'Our son's secret is out.'

Shafey drew back from the window moaning:

'My heart has never lied to me.'

He rushed out of the house, not caring about the danger, and his wife followed close behind. He pushed his way through the crowd calling out loudly:

'Rifaa! Where are you, Rifaa?'

He could not see his son in the lamplight and could not hear his voice, but Hejazi came up to him and asked him above the din:

'Has your son got lost again?'

Ferhat shouted to him:

'Come and hear what people are saying, and see the latest game that's being played with the honour of Gebel's people.'

Abda shouted wretchedly:

'For God's sake, tolerance is a virtue.'

There were angry yells of 'The woman's mad!' 'She doesn't know what honour is.' Shafey was terrified and implored Hejazi to tell him:

'Where is the boy?'

Hejazi pushed his way to the gate and shouted at the top of his voice:

'Rifaa! Come here my boy and talk to Mr Shafey.'

The whole business was beyond Shafey. He had thought that his son was trapped in a corner of the passage; yet here he was, walking into the circle of lamplight. Shafey took hold of his arm and led him back to where Abda was standing.

A moment later Shaldam appeared, carrying a lamp, followed by Khonfis, who was scowling furiously. All eyes were fixed on the chief, and a hush fell. Khonfis growled:

'What's all this?'

Several voices answered at one:

'Jasmine has disgraced us!'

Khonfis said:

'One of you speak.'

Zaituna, a carter, came forward and stood in front of Khonfis. He said:

'A little while ago I saw her coming out of Bayumi's back door. I followed her back here and asked her what she'd been up to in the chief's house. I could see she was drunk. The whole passage reeked of wine. She got away from me and locked herself in. Now, I ask you, what could a drunken woman have been doing in the Chief's house?'

This relieved Shafey and Abda, but it worried Khonfis. He realized that his position was being severely tested. If he punished Jasmine lightly he would lose the respect of Gebel's people, and if he let the angry crowd deal with her, he would provoke Bayumi, chief of the alley. What was to be done? The men of Gebel were pouring out of their houses and gathering in the courtyard and in the road in front of Victory House. Khonfis's position grew more and more delicate. Voices shouted:

'Drive her out of Gebel's quarter.'

'She must be beaten before she's driven out.'

'Kill her.'

There was a scream from Jasmine who was listening in the dark behind her window. Everyone stared at Khonfis. They heard Rifaa saying to his father:

'Wouldn't it be better, father, if they directed their anger at Bayumi who seduced her?'

Many of them were annoyed, amongst others Zaituna, who answered him:

'She went to his house of her own accord.'

Another man shouted:

'If you've no sense of honour you'd better keep quiet.'

Rifaa went on, in spite of a look from his father:

'Bayumi only did what you do.'

Zaituna screamed:

'She's one of Gebel's people; she's not for other men.'

'The boy's stupid; he has no honour.'

Shafey kicked him to silence him, while Borhoom shouted:

'Let Mr Khonfis speak.'

Khonfis was almost choking with rage. Jasmine screamed for help. Murderous looks were directed at the girl's room. Jasmine's screams went on till Rifaa's heart was torn and he could bear it no longer. He slipped out of his father's grasp and pushed his way through to Jasmine's door shouting:

'Have pity on her weakness and terror.'

Zaituna shouted at him:

'You woman!'

Shafey called him entreatingly but he took no notice. He said to Zaituna:

'God forgive you.' Then, to the crowd: 'Have mercy on her. Do what you like to me. Don't her cries for help move your hearts?'

Zaituna shouted again:

'Don't bother with this shameless fool.' Then to Khonfis: 'It's for you to speak, Chief.'

Rifaa asked:

'Would it satisfy you if I married her?'

There were screams of anger and shouts of derision. Zaituna said:

'We're only interested in getting her punished.'

Rifaa persisted courageously:

'The punishment would be my business.'

'Not at all; it's everybody's business.'

Khonfis saw in Rifaa's suggestion an escape from his dilemma. He was not in his heart satisfied with it, but he had no better idea. He scowled still more to hide his weakness, and said:

'The boy has undertaken before us to marry her, let him have his wish.'

Zaituna was blind with fury. He shouted:

'Honour is lost because of cowardice.'

Khonfis punched him hard, and he staggered back howling, the blood streaming from his nose. They all understood that Khonfis would cover up his weak position by terrorizing anyone who opposed him. He looked at their frightened faces in the lamplight and not one of them showed any sympathy for Zaituna. On the contrary Ferhat reproached him: 'The trouble with you is your cheek.' and Borhoom said to Khonfis: 'Without you we couldn't have found a solution.' and Hanoura said to him: 'When you get angry, that's what counts most.'

The crowd began to drift away, until in the end there remained only Khonfis, Shaldam, Shafey, Abda and Rifaa. Shafey went up to Khonfis to greet him, and offered him his hand, but he flared up and hit Shafey's hand with his knuckles, and he drew back, catching his breath. His wife and his son hurried over to him, while Khonfis stormed out of the passageway, cursing Gebel's people and everyone else, and even Gebel himself.

The pain made Shafey forget his son's position. He put his hand in warm water and Abda rubbed it. She said:

'You see how Zakia has stirred up her husband against us?'

'The coward forgot that it was our stupid son who saved him from Bayumi's stick.'

52 ✳ ✳ ✳ ✳ ✳ ✳ ✳ ✳ ✳ ✳ ✳ ✳ ✳ ✳ ✳ ✳ ✳ ✳ ✳

Rifaa's parents had pinned all their hopes on him, and how great was their disappointment! By marrying Jasmine he would become a nobody, and his family was already the subject of gossip even before the marriage had taken place. Abda cried secretly till she was ill, and Shafey looked miserable, but in front of Rifaa they hid this. Jasmine perhaps made things better by the way she behaved after the scene; she hurried over to Shafey's house and knelt before him and his wife, poured out some of the gratitude that filled her heart, and told them of her regret for the past. It was impossible to back out of the marriage after Rifaa had undertaken it publicly in front of Gebel's people; and so Shafey and his wife surrendered to the idea and made up their minds to accept it. They had two conflicting wishes; one was to celebrate the marriage in the traditional way and have a bridegroom's procession, and the other was to have a quiet little ceremony in the house to avoid exposing it to the mockery of Gebel's people, who continued to criticize the match wherever they met.

Abda said with feeling:

'I have wanted for so long to see the bridegroom's procession of Rifaa, my only son, marching round the district.'

Shafey said angrily:

'Not one of Gebel's people would want to join in.'

Abda frowned.

'It'd be better to go back to Souk Mukattam than stay amongst people who don't like us.'

Rifaa stretched out his legs under the open window to catch the sun. He said:

'We shan't leave the alley, mother.'

Shafey cried out:

'If only we'd never come back.' Then, to his son: 'You were sad the day we got back, weren't you?'

Rifaa smiled.

'Today isn't yesterday. If we go away, who'll save Gebel's people from evil spirits?'

'Let the evil spirits possess them for ever.' Then after a pause: 'You come to our place bringing . . .'

'I shan't bring anyone to our place. I'll move to hers.'

His mother cried out:

'That's not what your father meant.'

'But that's what I mean, mother. My new home is not far away; we could shake hands out of the window every morning.'

Although Shafey was unhappy about it, he decided to have a wedding celebration, though in a very small way. He hung decorations in the passageway and over their doors, and he hired a singer and a cook. He invited all their friends and acquaintances, but the only ones to accept were Gewaad and Omme B'Khatirha, Hejazi and his family, and some poor people who came for the food. Rifaa was the first young man to marry without a procession. The family crossed the passageway to the bride's house. The musician sang without enthusiasm as the guests were so few. During the meal, Gewaad praised Rifaa for his fine character.

'He's an intelligent, wise, pure-minded young man, but he's in an alley which has no use for anything except bullying and cudgels.'

At that moment they heard some boys singing in the street:

> O Rifaa you louse-faced rat!
> Who told you to do like that?

They finished off with cheers and shouts. Rifaa looked at the ground and Shafey paled. Hejazi was angry and said:

'Sons of bitches!'

But Gewaad said:

'There's a lot of filth in our alley, but the good is never forgotten. How many chiefs have we had? Yet only Adham and Gebel are remembered.'

Then he asked the musician to sing so as to drown the noise. The party dragged on until everyone went, leaving Rifaa and Jasmine alone in the house. In her bridal dress she looked a picture of beauty. Beside her sat Rifaa in a fine silk smock with a brocaded turban on his head and bright yellow slippers on his feet. He sat down on a divan opposite the bed with its pink linen. In the wardrobe looking glass were reflected the pot and jug under the bed. She was obviously waiting for his initiative, or at least his preparations for the expected initiative, but he just went on looking up at the lamp and down at the matting. When the waiting grew too long she said gently:

'I shall never forget your kindness. I owe you my life.'

He looked at her affectionately and said in a tone that showed he did no want to return to this subject:

'We all owe our lives to other people.'

What a good man! On the night of the scandal he had refused to let her kiss his hands, and now he did not want to be reminded of his good deed. His goodness was only matched by his patience. But what could he be thinking of now? Was he annoyed that his goodness had forced him into marrying a girl like her?

'I'm not as wicked as people think. They loved me and despised me for the same thing.'

He comforted her:

'I know. What a lot of wickedness goes on in our alley!'

'They're always boasting about being descended from Adham, and at the same time they compete with one another in doing wrong.'

'As long as casting out evil spirits is easy, we're near to happiness.'

She did not see what he meant, but suddenly she felt how ludicrous her position was. She said laughing:

'What a strange conversation for a wedding night!'

She tossed her head back proudly and seemed to have forgotten her gratitude. She threw the shawl off her shoulders and eyed him seductively. He said:

'You'll be the first to find happiness.'

'Yes indeed. . . . I have some wine . . .'

'I drank a little at supper. It was enough.'

She thought for a while, bewildered, then said:

'I have some good hashish.'

'I tried it, and found I couldn't take it.'

'Your father is a real hashish addict. I once saw him coming out of a session at Shaldam's, and he couldn't tell night from day!'

He smiled and said nothing. She turned her eyes away in defeat. She got up and went to the door, bursting with anger, then came back and stood under the lamp. Her fine body was visible through her thin dress. She looked into his peaceful eyes until despair overcame her.

'Why did you save me?'

'I can't bear anyone to suffer.'

She was furious.

'Because of that you married me? Just because of that?'

'Don't get angry again.'

She bit her lip and said in a low voice:

'I thought you loved me.'

He said simply and sincerely:

'I do love you, Jasmine.'

Her eyes filled with amazement, and she murmured:

'Really?'

'There's no one in this alley that I don't love.'

She groaned and stared at him doubtfully.

'I understand. You will stay with me a few months and then divorce me.'

His eyes widened. He muttered:

'Don't go back to the old thoughts.'

'You bewilder me. What can you give me?'

'True happiness.'

She said resentfully:

'I sometimes enjoyed that before ever I saw you.'

'There's no happiness without honour.'

She laughed in spite of herself:

'It will take more than honour to make us happy.'

He said sadly:

'No one in our quarter knows real happiness.'

She took a few slow steps towards the bed and sat down listlessly on its edge. He looked at her affectionately:

'You're like all the people in our quarter; you only think of the lost estate.'

'God help me to understand your riddles.'

'They'll solve themselves when you are rid of your evil spirit.'

She shouted:

'I like myself as I am!'

'That's how Khonfis and the others speak.'

She puffed:

'Are you going to talk like this till morning?'

'Go to sleep. Sweet dreams!'

She lay back and looked from his eyes to the space beside her and back again. He said:

'Relax. I shall sleep on the divan.'

She had a fit of giggles, but not for long. She said sarcastically:

'I'm afraid your mother will come tomorrow to warn you against overdoing it!'

She looked at him to enjoy the revenge of seeing his embarrassment; but he looked at her with calm, pure eyes, and said:

'I should love to set you free from your evil spirit.'

She shouted:

'Leave women's work to women.'

And she turned her face to the wall, her heart burning with anger and dismay. Rifaa stood up, turned down the wick of the lamp and blew it out. Darkness fell.


53 ✳ ✳ ✳ ✳ ✳ ✳ ✳ ✳ ✳ ✳ ✳ ✳ ✳ ✳ ✳ ✳ ✳ ✳

The days that followed the wedding saw Rifaa's life full of ceaseless activity. He more or less stopped going to the shop, and but for his father's love and sympathy he would have had nothing to live on. He began calling on all the Gebelites he met to put their trust in him, so that he could deliver them from their evil spirits and they would enjoy a happiness they had never dreamed of. The people whispered that Shafey's son Rifaa was weak in the head and must be counted as mad. Some said it was because of the strange ways he was known to have, while others attributed it to his marrying a woman like Jasmine. Such discussions went on in the cafés and houses, around the barrows and in the hashish dens. Omme B'Khatirha was astounded when Rifaa whispered in her ear with his usual gentleness:

'Why don't you let me cleanse you?'

She thumped her chest and said:

'What makes you think I have an evil spirit? Is this what you think of the woman who's loved you like a son?'

'I only offer my services to people I love and respect. You do good and bring blessings, but you have a certain greed which makes you do a trade in sick people, and if you were delivered from your ruling spirit you'd give your goodness without a price.'

She couldn't help laughing as she said:

'Do you want to ruin me? God help you, Rifaa!'

Omme B'Khatirha's story was passed round amid laughter. Even Shafey laughed, though without joy, but Rifaa said to him:

'Even you need my treatment, father; it's my duty as a son to start with you.'

Shafey shook his head gloomily and hammered the nails in front of him with a fierceness that showed how upset he was.

'God give me patience!'

Rifaa tried to persuade him, but he said miserably:

'Isn't it enough for you to have made us the talk of the quarter?'

Rifaa went away into a corner of the shop, dejected. Shafey looked at him suspiciously.

'Have you really given your wife the same invitation as you've given me?'

'And she like you does not want happiness.'

Rifaa went to Shaldam's hashish den in the ruin behind the café. He found Shaldam, Hejazi, Borhoom, Ferhat, Hanoura and Zaituna round the brazier. They looked at him queerly and Shaldam said:

'Welcome, son of Shafey; has marriage convinced you of the advantages of hashish-smoking?'

Rifaa put down a packet of honey cakes on the table and said as he sat down:

'I've brought you this in honour of the company.'

Shaldam said, passing round the pipe:

'Thank you for your generosity.'

But Borhoom laughed and said unkindly:

'And next he will suggest performing an exorcism to rid us of our evil spirits.'

Zaituna shouted in his nasal voice, glaring at Rifaa with hatred:

'Your wife is possessed by an evil spirit called Bayumi; free her from him if you can.'

The men were amazed and looked embarrassed. Zaituna said, pointing to his broken nose:

'Because of him I had my nose smashed.'

Rifaa seemed not to be angry. Ferhat looked at him sadly and said:

'Your father's a good man and a skilled carpenter. But you're getting him into trouble by this behaviour of yours. The man's scarcely got over your marriage when you walk out of his shop to free people from evil spirits. May God restore you to health.'

'I'm not ill, all I want is your happiness.'

Zaituna took a short puff and held it, looking at him harshly, then blew out the smoke, saying:

'Who told you we weren't happy?'

'Our ancestor wanted something different for us.'

Ferhat said laughing:

'Never mind about our ancestor; how do you know he hasn't forgotten us?'

Zaituna gave him a long look of hatred and anger, but Hejazi kicked him and said warningly:

'You must respect the company and not be unfriendly.'

He wanted to change the atmosphere, and he shook his head and gave his friends a sign; they began singing:

> The boat comes,
> Bringing my lover.
> The sails hang,
> Over the water.

He left the place, followed by regretful looks from one or two of them, and went home broken-hearted. Jasmine met him with a peaceful smile. At first she used to abuse him for his behaviour, which had made him, and her, a joke. But she had given up in despair, and bore this life patiently, though she did not know where it would lead to. Moreover she treated him kindly and gently.

There was a knock on the door, and there stood Khonfis, the Gebelite chief. He came in without asking whether he might do so. Rifaa rose to greet him, and Khonfis seized his shoulder with a grip like that of a dog's jaws. He asked Rifaa without any preliminaries:

'What did you say about the Founder at Shaldam's hashish session?'

Jasmine went pale with fear, but Rifaa said calmly, although he was like a sparrow in the claws of an eagle:

'I said our ancestor wanted our happiness.'

He shook him violently.

'How do you know that?'

'It's one of the things he said to Gebel.'

The hand gripped his shoulder still tighter:

'He talked to Gebel about the estate.'

Rifaa was exhausted by the pain.

'The estate doesn't concern me at all. This happiness that I've so far been unable to give to anyone is not from the estate, not from drink, nor

170

from hashish. I've said that everywhere in Gebel's quarter, and every-one's heard me say it.'

He shook him again and said:

'Your father was a rebel and then thought better of it. Mind you don't follow his path, or I'll squash you like a bedbug.'

He pushed him backwards on to the divan and went. Jasmine hurried over to comfort Rifaa. He was bending his head over his shoulder in pain, and she rubbed it. He seemed almost unconscious, and muttered as though to himself:

It was my grandfather's voice that I heard.'

She looked into his face with alarm and anxiety, and wondered whether he was right out of his mind. She did not repeat to him what he had said. Fear such as she had never known gripped her.

One day he left the house, and a woman who was not a Gebelite stood in his path and said to him warmly:

'Good morning, Mr Rifaa, sir.'

He was amazed at the tone of respect in her voice and at the way she called him 'sir'. He asked her:

'What do you want?'

She said beseechingly:

'I have a son who's possessed. I hope you can cure him.'

Like all the Gebelites he looked down on the other people of the alley, and he was unwilling to put himself at her service lest his people should despise him still more. He said:

'Isn't there an exorcist down the alley?'

She said, almost crying:

'Yes, but I'm a poor woman.'

His heart softened towards her and he rejoiced at her seeking help from him, from him, who met with nothing but scorn and mockery from his own people. He looked at her, his mind made up, and said:

'I'm at your service.'

## 54

Jasmine was looking down out of the window on to the road, enjoying the new view. Boys played in front of the house, sellers of palm nuts cried their wares, while Batikha had a man by the collar and was punch-ing him in the face. The man tried to conciliate him, but in vain. Rifaa, who was sitting on the divan cutting his toenails, asked her:

'Do you like our new home?'

She turned round towards him:

'Here we have the alley below us; there we used to see only the dark passage.'

'If only the passage had remained ours! It was a blessed place, for in it Gebel won his victory over his enemies. But it was impossible to go on staying among people who mocked us at every step. Whereas the poor people here are good. And the good men, not the Gebelites, are the real lords.'

'I've hated them ever since they decided to persecute me.'

He smiled:

'In that case why do you tell the neighbours you're a Gebelite?'

She laughed, showing her fine teeth, and said proudly:

'So that they'll know I'm above them all.'

He put the scissors down on the divan and put his feet on the rush matting:

'You'll be better and finer when you conquer vanity. The Gebelites are not the best people in our alley; the best are those who do most good. I used to make the same mistake as you, and paid attention only to the Gebelites. But the people who deserve happiness are those who seek it sincerely. Look at the way the poor accept me and are cured of evil spirits.'

'But everyone here works for wages except you.'

'If it wasn't for me, the poor wouldn't have found anyone to heal them. They can be cured, but they can't pay the price. I didn't have any real friends before I knew them.'

She refused to argue and looked resentful. Rifaa said:

'If only you would submit to me as they submit . . . Then I could cure you of what spoils life's happiness.'

'Do you find me *that* annoying?'

'Some people love an evil spirit without realizing it.'

She shouted:

'How I hate this talk.'

He smiled:

'You're a Gebelite, and all of them refused to submit to my healing, even my own father.'

There was a knock at the door, announcing that a new patient had arrived. Rifaa got ready to receive him. The truth was that Rifaa had never known happier days than these. In the new quarter he was called 'Mr Rifaa, sir', which was said sincerely and lovingly. He was known as the man who delivered people from evil spirits and gave health and happiness, just for the love of God. Such a way of life had never been known before, and because of this the poor loved him as they had never loved anyone else. Naturally Batikha, chief of their new quarter, did not love him, partly because of his goodness and partly because he was not

172

able to pay any protection money; but at the same time, he could find no excuse for attacking him. Each of those who had been cured at his hands had his story to tell and re-tell: Omme Daoud had bitten her child in a fit, and today she was a model of calm and balance; Senara, whose only pleasure had been arguing and quarelling, became mild and gentle; Tolba the pickpocket repented genuinely and worked for the metal beater; Owayss gave up his old way of life and married.

Rifaa chose four of his patients, Zaki, Hussein, Ali and Kerim, to be his friends, and they became brothers. None of them had known friendship or affection before they knew him. Zaki had been a layabout and Hussein an incurable opium eater, Ali had been a hardened bully and Kerim a pimp. All changed into good-hearted men. They used to meet at Hind's Rock where there was emptiness and fresh air, and there they would hold untroubled conversations, gazing up at their healer with eyes full of loyalty. They all dreamed of a happiness that would shelter the alley with wings of mercy. One day Rifaa asked them as they sat in the twilight calm looking at the red sunset:

'Do you know why we're so happy?'

Hussein answered enthusiastically:

'It's you; you're the secret of our happiness.'

He smiled gratefully.

'No! It's because we've been freed from our evil spirits and from hatred and greed and malice.'

Ali took this up:

'Even though we're poor and weak, with no share in the estate and no power.'

Rifaa shook his head sadly.

'How people have suffered because of wanting those things! Damn the estate and power.'

Ali picked up a stone and threw it with all his might at the gebel. Rifaa spoke again:

'Ever since the story has been told that Gebelawi asked Gebel to make the houses of his quarter magnificent like the Big House, people have had their eyes fixed on Gebelawi's magnificence. They have forgotten his other virtues. That's why Gebel was unable to change people by merely winning their rights in the estate, so when he died the strong took over and the weak became full of hatred and misery came back. But I'm opening the gates of happiness without any estate or power.'

Kerim embraced him and said:

'And tomorrow, when the strong see the happiness of the weak they'll realize that their power and their stolen money are nothing.'

A song was carried on the wind from far off in the desert. A single star appeared in the sky. Rifaa looked into his friends' faces and said:

'But I can't cure the people by myself. It's time for you to do something yourselves, and to learn the secrets of freeing the sick from evil spirits.'

Their faces filled with joy, and Zaki exclaimed:

'That's what we want most.'

He smiled at them and said:

'You will be the keys of happiness in our alley.'

When they got back to their quarter they found it bright with the lights of a wedding in one of the houses. Lots of people saw Rifaa coming and met him with handshakes. Batikha was annoyed and got up from his place in the café, cursing and swearing and cuffing one or two people, then turned to Rifaa and asked rudely:

'Who do you think you are, sonny?'

Rifaa said gently:

'The friend of the poor, sir.'

Batikha shouted:

'Then go around like the poor, not like a bridegroom. Have you forgotten that you've been driven out of your quarter, or that you're Jasmine's husband and earning nothing with your exorcism?'

He spat provocatively and the people moved away and depression fell. But the women's youyous of joy at the wedding drowned everything.

## 55 ✳ ✳ ✳ ✳ ✳ ✳ ✳ ✳ ✳ ✳ ✳ ✳ ✳ ✳ ✳ ✳ ✳ ✳ ✳ ✳

Bayumi, chief of the alley, stood at the back gate of his garden which opened on the desert. It was late evening, and he was waiting and listening. A finger tapped softly on the door and he opened it, and into the garden slipped a woman, who seemed, in her black shawl and veil, like part of the darkness. He took her hand and led her along the garden paths, avoiding the house, till he came to the garden house. He pushed the door open and went in, followed by her. He lit a candle and put it on the windowsill. The garden house looked strange, with the divans arranged round the sides and a big tray in the middle, bearing a pipe and its accessories and surrounded by cushions.

The woman took off her shawl and veil, and Bayumi hugged her so fiercely that it hurt, and she begged for mercy with her eyes. At last she freed herself from him nimbly. He laughed quietly and sat down on a cushion. He began poking about with his fingers in the ashes of the brazier, until he uncovered a glowing coal. She sat down beside him and kissed his ear, then pointed to the pipe saying:

'I'd almost forgotten the smell.'

174

He covered her cheek and neck with kisses and said, tossing a bit of hashish into her lap:

'No one in the alley smokes this brand except the Trustee and yours truly.'

From the alley came the noise of a fight breaking out: insults flying, sticks banging, glass breaking, feet running off, a woman's screams, then dogs barking. The woman's eyes took on an anxious, questioning look, but Bayumi went on cutting hashish, not caring. She said:

'It is difficult for me coming here. To be safe from prying eyes I go from the alley to Gemalia, and from Gemalia to Derrasa, and from Derrasa into the desert and then to your back gate.'

Without stopping the work of his fingers he leaned over and sniffed playfully at her shoulder:

'I wouldn't mind visiting you in your house.'

She smiled.

'If you did, none of the cowards would get in your way. Even Batikha would smooth out the sand for you. Then they would take it out on me alone.'

She played with his thick moustache.

'But you slip out to the annexe for fear of your wife.'

He set down the piece of hashish, put his arm round her and drew her to him so hard that she groaned. Then she whispered:

'God preserve us from the love of chiefs!'

He let her go, tossing his head back and puffing his chest out like a turkey cock. He said:

'There's only one chief; the rest are boys.'

She played with the hair on his chest, showing through the neck of his smock.

'Chief to other people, not to me!'

He pinched her gently on the breast.

'You are the crown on the chief's head.'

He reached over behind the tray and picked up a jug.

'Marvellous booze!'

She said regretfully:

'It has a strong smell which my dear husband might notice.'

He drank his fill from the jug and began packing together the lumps of hashish. He scowled.

'What a husband! I've caught sight of him several times, wandering about like a madman; the first male exorcist this strange alley has ever seen.'

She watched him smoking:

'I owe him my life; that is why I put up with his company. And he does no harm, for nothing is easier than deceiving him.'

175

He passed her the pipe and she thrust the end into her mouth and took several greedy puffs, then breathed out the smoke with closed eyes and reeling senses. He smoked in his turn, taking short puffs and talking between them:

'Leave him . . . He is playing with you . . . like a child.'

She shrugged her shoulders scornfully.

'My husband does nothing in this world except relieve the poor of evil spirits.'

'And you – haven't you relieved him of anything?'

'Not on your life! One look at his face is enough, without anything needing to be said.'

'Not even once a month?'

'Not even once a year! People's evil spirits leave him no time for his wife.'

'Let evil spirits possess him! What does he get out of it?'

She shook her head hopelessly:

'Nothing at all. But for his father we should have starved to death. He believes it's his duty to make the poor happy and to cleanse them.'

'And who gave him this duty?'

'He says it's what the Founder wants for his children.'

Bayumi's narrow eyes looked worried. He put the pipe down in the ash bowl.

'So he said the Founder wanted it?'

'Yes.'

'And how does he know what the Founder wants?'

She felt anxious and alarmed and was afraid of spoiling the atmosphere or talking of dangerous matters. She said:

'That's how he interprets the sayings of Gebelawi which the storytellers sing.'

He pressed down some more grains of hashish.

'A bitchy alley! And Gebel's quarter is the foulest of all; that's where the worst swindlers come from. They spread strange stories about the estate and the ten conditions as though Gebelawi was only *their* ancestor. Yesterday their swindler Gebel came with some lie by which he stole the estate, and today this lunatic starts interpreting words which won't bear interpretation. Tomorrow he'll be claiming he heard them from Gebelawi himself.'

She said anxiously:

'He isn't interested in anything except freeing the poor from evil spirits.'

The chief snorted scornfully:

'How do we know? Maybe the estate has an evil spirit!' Then, in a

176

voice louder than befitted the secrecy of their meeting: 'Gebelawi is dead, or as good as dead, you dogs!'

Jasmine was alarmed. She was afraid the opportunity would be lost and the atmosphere spoilt. She put her hand to her dress and drew it slowly off. His face relaxed and lost its scowl and he gazed at her with eager eyes.

## 56 ✳ ✳ ✳ ✳ ✳ ✳ ✳ ✳ ✳ ✳ ✳ ✳ ✳ ✳ ✳ ✳ ✳ ✳ ✳

The Trustee looked small in his big cloak. There was anxiety in his round white face with its drooping eyelids and its prematurely old eyes, baggy from debauchery. Bayumi's puffy face did not betray the inward pleasure he felt at his master's anxiety – an anxiety which showed the importance of the news he had brought, and so of his service to the Trustee and the estate. He said:

'I'm sorry to have to bother you with this, but I couldn't act without referring the matter to you as it concerns the estate; and besides, this mad troublemaker is a Gebelite, and we have an agreement not to attack any of them without permission.'

Ihaab asked, his face glowering:

'Does he really claim to have been in touch with the Founder?'

'I'm certain of that from more than one source. His patients believe it, although they keep very quiet about it.'

'Perhaps he's a madman, just as Gebel was a swindler. But this filthy alley loves madmen and swindlers. What do the Gebelites want after plundering the estate? Why doesn't Gebelawi get in touch with someone else? Why doesn't he get in touch with me when I'm more closely related to him than anyone? He's confined to his room, and the gates of his house only open when his provisions are brought. No one sees him, and he sees no one except his maid. And yet it's so easy for the Gebelites to meet him or hear him!'

Bayumi said angrily:

'They won't rest until they have taken over the whole estate.'

The Trustee was livid with rage, and jumped up to give orders, but he sank back and asked:

'Did he say anything about the estate, or has he confined himself to casting out devils?'

'Like Gebel who confined himself to getting rid of snakes!' Then, sarcastically: 'What does Gebelawi have to do with devils?'

Ihaab stood up.

'I don't want to suffer the fate of Effendi.'

177

Bayumi invited Jabir, Handousa, Khalid and Batikha to his hashish den and told them they must find a cure for the madness of Rifaa, the son of Shafey. Batikha asked with annoyance:

'Have you just invited us for that, Chief?'

Bayumi nodded, and Batikha was astonished and shouted:

'What a man! The chiefs of the alley meet over a creature who's neither male nor female!'

Bayumi gave him a look of contempt:

'He's carried on his activity under your very nose, and you didn't see any danger, and of course you never heard his claims to have been in touch with the Founder.'

They exchanged glances through the smoke. Batikha said, flabbergasted:

'The son of a bitch! What does the Founder have to do with evil spirits? Is our ancestor an exorcist?'

They began to laugh but stopped in a moment at Bayumi's scowl as he said:

'You're stuffed with cocaine, Batikha. A chief may get drunk and smoke hashish, but cocaine isn't good for him.'

Batikha defended himself:

'Chief! I was at Antar's wedding and twenty men came at me with their sticks, and my face was covered with blood but I didn't let my cudgel drop from my hand.'

Handousa said hopefully:

'Let's leave the matter to him to deal with as he thinks best, or he'll lose face. Let's hope he finds a better way than attacking the madman, it would be beneath a chief's dignity to attack such a creature!'

Meanwhile the alley slept, and no one knew what was hatching in Bayumi's hashish den.

Next morning Rifaa left the house and found Batikha in his path. He greeted him:

'Good morning, Mr Batikha.'

The man gave him a look of hatred and shouted:

'A black morning to you, son of an old baggage. Back to your house, and don't leave it or I'll smash your head in.'

'What's upsetting our chief?'

He yelled:

'You're talking to Batikha now, not the Founder. Don't shilly-shally; go!'

Rifaa was about to speak, but the bully sent him staggering into the wall with a push. A woman saw what happened and let out a scream that filled the alley. Other women followed suit. Voices called loudly for help for Rifaa. In the twinkling of an eye many people were running towards

178

the spot, among others Zaki, Hussein and Kerim. Then up came Shafey, and Gewaad the storyteller feeling the way with his stick. In no time the place was crowded with Rifaa's friends, both men and women. Batikha, who had not expected any trouble, was surprised. He lifted his hand and brought it down on Rifaa's face, and Rifaa took the blow without any defence, but the bystanders let out a roar of consternation and were thoroughly roused. Some implored Batikha to leave him alone and others mentioned Rifaa's virtues. Many asked what led to the attack and there were loud protests. Batikha burst with anger and shouted:

'Have you forgotten who I am?'

Their love for Rifaa that had brought them crowding round gave them the courage to answer back to Batikha's warnings. A man standing in the front row said:

'You're our chief, our leader; we only came to ask your pardon for this good man.'

A man in the middle of the crowd took courage from the number of people and his position among them and shouted:

'You may be our chief, but what has Rifaa done?'

A third man shouted from the back, where he was safely hidden:

'Rifaa is innocent. God help any man who stretches out a hand to harm him.'

Batikha was beside himself with rage and he brandished his cudgel above his head shouting:

'You women! I'll make an example of you.'

The women screamed on every side until the scene was like a funeral. There were bloodthirsty warnings. Stones began showering down in front of Batikha to prevent him from advancing. He found himself in a nastier situation than he had ever been in, even in his worst dreams. He would rather die than ask the other chiefs for help, and the shower of stones threatened to kill him. He showed that he was still the chief by his silence, and his eyes blazed. The stones continued to fall and the people went on defying him completely. Nothing like it had ever happened to any of the chiefs.

Rifaa suddenly rushed across and stood in front of Batikha. He signalled to the people with his hands until silence fell, and shouted:

'Our chief has done nothing wrong. I'm to blame.'

There were looks of protest, but no one spoke. Rifaa said:

'Break it up before you become the objects of his anger.'

Some people understood that he wanted to save Batikha's honour as a solution to the crisis, and they dispersed. Others followed them, bewildered by the whole business, and the rest hurried off for fear of being left alone with Batikha. The quarter was deserted.

Tension rose after this event. What the Trustee feared most was that the people would feel that in solidarity lay a strength by which they could stand against the chiefs. It was therefore necessary in his view to destroy Rifaa and those who had been led to support him, and this needed the agreement of Khonfis, the Gebelite chief, to avoid causing a general battle. The Trustee said to Bayumi:

'Rifaa is not as weak as you think. Behind him he has friends who can save him in defiance of a chief. What would things come to if the whole alley was as attached to him as his quarter is? Then he would leave evil spirits and proclaim that the estate is his goal.'

Bayumi poured out his anger on Batikha. He shook him violently by the shoulders and said:

'We left it to you, and look what you've done – you've made a laughing-stock of the chiefs.'

Batikha gritted his teeth in resentment. He said:

'I'll get rid of him for you, even if it means killing him.'

Bayumi shouted:

'You'd do best to clear out from the alley for good.'

Bayumi then sent for Khonfis to meet him, but Shafey, more frightened than ever, intercepted him. He had tried to persuade Rifaa to come back to the shop and to give up the activity that was bringing such trouble upon him; but this attempt had failed and he had come back disappointed. When he learnt that Khonfis had been asked to see Bayumi, he stopped him and said:

'Mr Khonfis, take a seat. You're our chief and our protector. They want you to give Rifaa up, but don't do it. Promise them what they want, but don't give him up; order me to go and I'll leave the alley taking him with me, by force if need be. But don't give him up.'

Khonfis said cautiously:

'I know better than anyone what's in the interest of the Gebelites.'

The truth was that Khonfis had been afraid on account of Rifaa since he had heard of Batikha's trouble; he had said to himself that he was the one who must be on his guard, not the Trustee or Bayumi. He went on to the latter's house and met him in the annexe. Bayumi explained that he had sent for him in his capacity as Gebelite chief to come to an agreement over the problem of Rifaa.

'Don't underestimate him; events have proved his dangerous influence.'

Khonfis agreed with this, but he said:

'I hope he won't be attacked in front of me.'

'We are men, my dear sir; our interests are the same. We don't attack anyone in our houses. The boy will come before us now and I will question him in your presence.'

Rifaa came in looking radiant and sat down where Bayumi motioned him to, on a cushion in front of them. Bayumi studied his calm face wondering how this gentle boy had become the source of frightening disturbances. He asked him in a harsh voice:

'Why did you leave your quarter and your people?'

He said simply:

'None of them answered my call.'

'What did you want from them?'

'To deliver them from the evil spirits which spoil their happiness.'

Bayumi asked indignantly:

'Are you responsible for people's happiness?'

'Yes, as long as I am able to give it to them.'

Bayumi scowled:

'People have heard you say you despise importance and power.'

'To show them that happiness lies not in their imaginings but in what I'm doing.'

Khonfis asked angrily:

'Doesn't that mean you despise the people who have importance and power?'

Quite unruffled, he answered:

'No, sir; but it does mean that happiness is not the same as their importance and power.'

Bayumi asked him with a piercing look:

'People have heard you say too that this is what Gebelawi wants for them.'

His clear eyes grew anxious.

'They say that!'

'And what do you say?'

He hesitated for the first time.

'I can only speak according to my understanding.'

Khonfis said sinisterly:

'Disasters can come from an addled brain.'

Bayumi's eyes narrowed.

'They say you repeat to them what you've heard from Gebelawi himself.'

His eyes were confused, and he hesitated again.

'That's how I understand his words to Adham and Gebel.'

Khonfis shouted:

'His words to Gebel don't bear interpretation.'

Bayumi grew still angrier and he said to himself: 'You're all liars and Gebel was the biggest liar of you all, you thieves.' Out aloud he said:

181

'You say you've heard Gebelawi, and you say this is what Gebelawi wants; but no one can speak in the name of Gebelawi except the Trustee of his estate and his heir. If Gebelawi wanted to say anything he would say it to them. He is responsible for his estate and is the executor of its ten conditions. You idiot; how can you despise power and importance and wealth in the name of Gebelawi when he himself has those very things?'

Rifaa's open face showed signs of pain:

'I was speaking to the people of our alley, not to Gebelawi; it is they who are possessed by evil spirits, and it is they who are tormented by their desires.'

Bayumi bellowed:

'It's just that you are incapable of getting power and importance, and you curse them because of that and in order to raise your contemptible position, in the eyes of fools, above that of their masters; but once you've got them under your thumb, you'll use them to seize power and importance.'

Rifaa's eyes widened in astonishment:

'My only aim is the happiness of the people.'

Bayumi shouted:

'You cunning villain; you make people think they're sick, that we're all sick and that only you in the whole alley are well.'

'Why do you hate happiness when it's in front of you?'

'Cunning villain! A curse on any happiness that comes from anyone like you!'

Rifaa sighed:

'Why do people hate me when I've never hated anyone?'

Bayumi screamed at him:

'You won't take us in as you've taken in the fools. Stop taking people in, and understand that my orders are not to be disobeyed. Be thankful that you're in my house, or you wouldn't have got away in one piece.'

Rifaa stood up hopelessly, saluted them and left. Khonfis said:

'Leave him to me.'

But Bayumi said:

'The lunatic has lots of friends, and we don't want a blood bath.'

58 ✻ ✻ ✻ ✻ ✻ ✻ ✻ ✻ ✻ ✻ ✻ ✻ ✻ ✻ ✻ ✻ ✻ ✻ ✻ ✻

Rifaa left Bayumi's house to go home. The sky was veiled in autumn clouds and there was a mild breeze. The people of the alley were crowding round the lemon sellers' baskets as it was the pickling season. There was a hubbub of conversation and laughter, while boys were brawling, pelting each other with mud. Rifaa was greeted by many people but also by a spattering of mud. He went on home, brushing the dirt off his shoulder and his turban. He found Zaki, Ali, Hussein and Kerim waiting for him and they embraced as they always did when they met. Then he told them, and his wife who joined the company, what had passed between him and Bayumi and Khonfis. They followed with concern, and when he finished his story they looked gloomy. Jasmine wondered what this delicate situation would lead to; was there not some solution that would save the good man from destruction without threatening her happiness? Their eyes were all full of questions, but Rifaa just leaned his head against the wall, feeling tired. Jasmine said:

'You can't ignore Bayumi's orders.'

Ali said:

'Rifaa has friends. They attacked Batikha, and he has disappeared from view.'

Jasmine frowned.

'Batikha is not Bayumi. If you defy Bayumi you won't get much peace.'

Hussein turned to Rifaa:

'First let's hear our leader.'

Rifaa said, his eyes almost closed:

'Don't think of fighting. Someone who tries to bring happiness to people can't think lightly of shedding their blood.'

Jasmine's face brightened. She hated the idea of being a widow for fear that people would watch her so that she could not find a way to her terrible lover. She said:

'The best thing you can do is to spare yourselves that sort of trouble.'

Zaki said:

'We shan't give up this work; we must leave the alley.'

Jasmine's heart pounded at the thought of going far away from her lover. She said:

'We can't live as strangers, lost far away from our alley.'

They all looked at Rifaa's face and he lifted up his head slowly and said:

'I don't want to leave.'

At that point there was an impatient knocking at the door. Jasmine went to open it. Rifaa and his friends heard Shafey and Abda asking about their son. Rifaa got up and embraced his parents. Shafey and his wife sat down, breathing heavily, and their faces spoke of the bad news they bore. In no time Shafey was saying:

'My son, Khonfis has withdrawn his protection from you and your life is in danger. My friends tell me that the chiefs' followers are lurking round your house.'

Abda dried her reddened eyes and said:

'If only we hadn't come back to this alley where people are sold for nothing.'

Ali said eagerly:

'Don't be afraid, Mrs Abda; all the people in our quarter are our firm friends.'

Rifaa sighed:

'What have we done to deserve punishment?'

Shafey shouted:

'You belong to the Gebelites whom they so hate. I've been so frightened since you first mentioned Gebelawi.'

'Yesterday they fought against Gebel for wanting the estate and today they fight against me for despising it.'

Shafey made a helpless gesture with his hand:

'Say what you like about them; it won't change them at all. But realize that you're a dead man if you set foot outside your house; and I don't feel you're safe if you stay in it.'

Fear crept into Kerim's heart for the first time, but he hid it with a great effort of will and said to Rifaa:

'They are lying in wait for you outside, and if you stay here they'll come and get you, or I don't know them. Let's escape over the roofs to my house, and there we can think about what's to be done.'

Shafey shouted:

'From there you can escape from the alley by night.'

Rifaa sighed:

'And leave what I've built to be ruined?'

His mother implored him tearfully:

'Have pity on your mother and do as he says.'

His father said angrily:

'Start again on the other side of the desert if you must.'

Kerim stood up anxiously and said:

'Let's get things organized. Mr Shafey and his wife can wait a little and then go to Victory House as if they were going home from an ordinary visit. Jasmine can go off to Gemalia as if she was shopping, and when she comes back she can slip round to my place; that will be easier for her than escape over the roofs.'

Shafey liked the plan. Kerim said:

'There's not a moment to lose, I'm going up to scout round the roofs.'

He left the room. Shafey got up and took Rifaa's hand. Abda told Jasmine to collect the clothes together in a bundle, and she began gathering together their few clothes, broken-hearted, a wave of fury mounting

184

in her. Abda kissed her son and said some prayers over him, her eyes brimming with tears. Rifaa thought sadly about his predicament. He loved others with all his heart and he had striven so hard for their happiness; how could he suffer from their hatred? And would Gebelawi accept failure? Kerim came back and said to Rifaa and his friends:

'Follow me.'

Abda burst into tears.

'We'll join you, even if it is later on.'

Shafey said, fighting back his tears:

'May safety go with you, Rifaa.'

Rifaa embraced his parents, then turned to Jasmine and said:

'Wrap yourself up in your shawl and veil so that no one knows you.' Then, whispering in her ear: 'I couldn't bear any harm to be done to you.'

# 59

Jasmine left the house wrapped in black, with Abda's parting words echoing in her ears: 'Good-bye my daughter; may God preserve you and guard you. Rifaa is in your charge; I'll pray for you both, night and day.'

Darkness was gathering and the lamps in the cafés were being lit. Boys played in the light shed by the lamps of the barrows, and the cats and dogs fought over the piles of rubbish, as usually happened at that time of day. Jasmine went towards Gemalia, and passion left no room for pity in her heart. She felt no hesitation, but she was filled with fear and imagined that many eyes were fixed on her. She did not ease up until she got from Derrasa into the desert, and even then she did not relax properly until she was with Bayumi in the garden house. When she drew off the veil he examined her with concern and asked:

'Frightened?'

She was breathing hard.

'Yes.'

'But no, you're no coward. Tell me what's wrong.'

She said almost inaudibly:

'They've escaped across the roofs to Kerim's home, and they'll leave the alley at dawn.'

Bayumi muttered:

'At dawn! The sons of bitches!'

'They've persuaded him to go away; why not let him?'

He smiled scornfully:

'Gebel went away, long ago, and then he came back. These insects don't deserve to live.'

She said, lost in thought:

'He denies life; but he doesn't deserve death.'

His lips curled in disgust.

'There are enough madmen in the alley.'

She looked at him beseechingly, then dropped her gaze and whispered, as if to herself:

'He once saved my life.'

He laughed brutally.

'And here you are handing him over to destruction. Tit for tat; and the one who started it is the loser.'

She was so upset that she felt ill. She looked at him reproachfully and said:

'I've done this because you are dearer to me than my life.'

He stroked her cheek gently.

It'll be easy for us afterwards; and if things get tough for you, there is a place for you in this house.'

She recovered a little from her depression.

'If they offered me the Founder's house without you I wouldn't accept it.'

'You're a faithful girl.'

The word 'faithful' pierced her, and again she was so upset that she felt ill. She wondered whether the man was mocking her ... But there was no time for talking any further, and she got up. He stood up too, to see her off, and she slipped out by the back gate.

She found her husband and his friends waiting for her and sat down beside Rifaa, saying to him:

'Our house is being watched. Your mother was wise to leave a lamp burning behind the window. It'll be easy to escape at dawn.'

Zaki said to her, looking sadly at Rifaa:

'He's unhappy. But aren't there sick people everywhere? And don't they need to be healed too?'

Rifaa said:

'The need for healing is greatest where the sickness is worst.'

Jasmine looked at him mournfully and thought to herself it would be outrageous to kill him. She wished he had just one feature that deserved punishment. She remembered that he was the only person in this world who had been good to her; and his reward was to be death. Inwardly she cursed these thoughts and said to herself: 'Let those who find good in their lives do good.' Then she saw him returning her look and she said:

'Your life is dearer than the whole of this damned alley.'

Rifaa smiled:

186

'That's what you say, but I read sadness in your eyes.'

She trembled, and said to herself: 'I'm lost if he can read eyes as he can cast out devils.' She said to him:

'I'm not so much sad as afraid for you.'

Kerim got up, saying:

'I'll make supper.'

He came back carrying a tray and invited them to sit round it. It was a supper of bread and cheese and whey with cucumbers and radishes, and there was a jug of homebrew. Kerim filled their mugs, saying:

'Tonight we shall need warmth and courage.'

They drank. Then Rifaa said, smiling:

'Liquor wakens up evil spirits, but it gives fresh life to those who have been freed from their devils.'

He looked at Jasmine by his side, and she understood the meaning of his look and said:

'You shall free me from my evil spirit tomorrow, if we live that long.'

Rifaa beamed with pleasure and his friends congratulated one another. They went on eating. The bread was divided, and their hands met over the dishes. It seemed as though they had forgotten death which hovered round them. Rifaa said:

'The master of the estate wanted his children to be like him, but they refused to be like anything but evil spirits. They are fools, and he does not like foolishness, as he told me.'

Kerim shook his head sadly and swallowed his mouthful, then said:

'If I had some of his former strength, things would go as he wished.'

Ali said angrily:

'If . . . if . . . if . . . What's the use of it! We must act.'

Rifaa said forcefully:

'We've never fallen short. We have waged war on the devils; and whenever one of them makes room, love comes in. There's no goal beyond that.'

Zaki said with a sigh:

'If they'd leave us to our work we could fill the alley with health and love and peace.'

Ali protested:

'I'm amazed that we can think of running away when we have so many friends.'

Rifaa smiled.

'Your evil spirit still has a hold on you. Don't forget that our goal is to cure, not to kill. It's better for a man to be killed than to kill.'

Rifaa turned suddenly to Jasmine.

'You're not eating and not listening.'

Her heart contracted with fear, but she controlled her agitation and said:

'I'm amazed that you can talk so gaily, as if you were at a wedding.'

'You will get used to joy when you're set free from your devil tomorrow.' Then, looking at his brothers: 'Some of you are ashamed of being peaceful, and we are children of an alley which only respects the chiefs' ways, but true strength doesn't mean bullying; battling against the evil spirits is many times harder than attacking the weak or fighting the chiefs.'

Ali shook his head sadly:

'And the reward of doing good is the miserable position we're in.'

Rifaa said:

'The battle won't end as you imagine. We're not weak as you think. We have simply moved the fight from one battlefield to another one where we need more courage and strength.'

They went on with their supper, thinking about what they had heard. He looked to them calm and strong as well as beautiful and gentle. In the silence they heard the storyteller of the quarter relating how:

Once Adham sat dozing at midday in Watawit Alley when he was wakened by a movement and saw some boys about to make off with his barrow. He stood up threatening them and one boy noticed him and warned his friends with a whistle, pushing the barrow over to distract him from giving chase. The cucumbers spilt all over the ground while the boys bounded away like locusts. Adham was furious and poured forth a torrent of the foulest curses. Then he bent down to gather up the cucumbers which were smothered in dirt. He found no outlet for his anger and it mounted till he said with passion: 'Why did your rage burn everything up? Why did you love your pride more than your own flesh and blood? How can you be happy with your life of ease and plenty, knowing that we are trampled on like insects? Mercy and sweetness and tolerance are all lacking in your great house, you tyrant.' He took hold of the shafts of the barrow and was about to push it far away from this wretched alley when he heard a jeering voice:

'How much are those cucumbers, mister?'

He saw Idris standing with a mocking smile on his lips.

A woman shouted, drowning the storyteller's voice:

'Oyez, oyez! A child is lost. Oyez!'

The companions chatted on, and Jasmine was in torment as the hours went by. Hussein wanted to take a look at the alley, but Kerim protested that someone might see him and wonder what was up. Zaki wondered whether they had attacked Rifaa's house and Rifaa said there was nothing to be heard except the drone of the fiddle and the shouts of the boys. The life of the alley went on, and there was nothing to show that a crime was being prepared. The thoughts went round and round in Jasmine's head until she was afraid her eyes would give her away. She wished her torment would end, in any way and at any price. She wished she could fill herself with liquor and forget what was going on around her. She said to herself that she was not the first woman in Bayumi's life and would not be the last; stray dogs gather round rubbish. But let this torment end at any cost.

As time went on, silence gradually swallowed up the noises. The children's voices fell silent and the pedlars' cries stopped. Only the drone of the fiddle was left. A sudden hatred for these men came over her, simply because they were, in a way, what tormented her. Kerim said:

'Shall I get the pipe ready?'

Rifaa said firmly:

'We need to have our wits about us.'

'I thought it would help us to bear the passing of time.'

'You're more frightened than you need to be.'

Kerim denied this charge:

'There doesn't seem to be any reason to be frightened.'

Indeed, nothing had happened and Rifaa's house had not been attacked. The music stopped and the storytellers went home. There were the sounds of doors being locked, the chatter of men on their way home, coughs, laughs, then silence.

They watched and waited until the first cock crowed. Zaki got up and looked out of the window at the road:

'Silent and empty. The alley is as it was the day Idris was thrown out.'

Kerim said:

'Time for us to go.'

Jasmine was in anguish. She wondered what would become of her if Bayumi was late or had changed his mind. The men stood up, each carrying his bundle. Hussein said:

'Good-bye to you, hellish alley.'

Ali led the way. Rifaa pushed Jasmine gently in front of him and followed her with a hand on her shoulder as though afraid he might lose her in the dark. Next went Kerim, then Hussein, then Zaki. They crept out one by one through the door of Kerim's lodgings, and climbed the

189

stairs, guiding themselves by the handrail in the thick darkness. The roof seemed less dark, although there was not a star to be seen. A cloud was passing in front of the moon and scattering its light. Ali said:

'The roofs almost touch. We can help Jasmine if she needs us.'

They followed one another on to the roof. As Zaki, the last of them, came to, he sensed a movement behind him. He turned round to face the trapdoor and saw four figures. In a panic he asked:

'Who's that?'

They all stopped dead and looked round. Bayumi's voice came:

'Stand still, you bastards!'

To his right and left stood Jabir, Khalid and Handusa. Jasmine let out a cry, slipped from Rifaa' s hand, and ran towards the trapdoor. None of the chiefs stopped her, and Ali said to Rifaa:

'The woman has betrayed you.'

In a moment they were surrounded. Bayumi began scrutinizing them from close to, one by one, asking: 'Where is the exorcist?' until he recognized Rifaa and caught his shoulder in a grip of iron, asking him jeeringly:

'Where are you off to, you friend of evil spirits?'

Rifaa said:

'Our presence here annoys you; we prefer to go away.'

Bayumi gave a scornful laugh and turned to Kerim.

'And you; was it any good your hiding them in your place?'

Kerim swallowed hard and said, trembling with fear:

'I didn't know of any quarrel between you and them.'

Bayumi hit him in the face with his free hand and knocked him over, but in a moment he leapt up and ran off in a panic to the roof of the next house. Hussein and Zaki rushed after him. Handusa leapt at Ali and kicked him in the stomach. He fell to the ground letting out a deep groan. At the same time Jabir and Khalid made to catch those who had fled, but Bayumi said contemptuously:

'There's no need to be afraid of them. They won't say a word; and if they do they've had it.'

Rifaa's head was twisted over Bayumi's hand by the tight grip. He said:

'They've done nothing to deserve punishment.'

Bayumi hit him in the face and said mockingly:

'Tell me; haven't they heard Gebelawi as you did?' Then, pushing him in front of him: 'Go in front of me and keep your mouth shut.'

Rifaa moved off, surrendering to fate. He went carefully down the dark stairs, followed by their heavy footsteps. He was overwhelmed by the darkness and the hopelessness and the evil that threatened him. He hardly thought of those who had fled or betrayed him. A deep, total sadness came over him, hiding even his fears. It seemed to him that this darkness was to endure over the world. They came to the alley and passed through the quarter where, thanks to him, no one was sick. Handusa led them towards Gebel's quarter, and they passed under the locked up Victory House, so that Rifaa imagined he could hear his parents breathing. He wondered about them for a moment and thought he heard Abda weeping in the night stillness, but in no time he was reclaimed by the darkness and hopelessness and the evil that threatened. Gebel's quarter looked like the shapes of huge ruins. How dark it was, how deeply asleep! The squeaking of the executioners' shoes in the thick blackness was like the laughter of demons in the night.

Handusa led them to the desert opposite the walls of the Big House. Rifaa looked up at the house, but he saw it was as dark as the sky. A figure appeared at the end of the wall and Handusa asked:

'Mr Khonfis?'

'Yes.'

He joined them without another word. Rifaa's eyes remained on the house. Did his ancestor know of his plight? A word from him could save him from the clutches of these tyrants and frustrate their schemes. He could speak to them as he had done to him in this place. Gebel had been cornered like this and had then escaped and been victorious. But he passed the wall without hearing a thing, except the footsteps and heavy breathing of the villains. They went deep into the desert, and the sand slowed their steps. Rifaa felt lost and remembered that the woman had betrayed him and that his friends had fled. He wanted to turn towards the house, but Bayumi's hand pushed him suddenly in the back and he fell on his face. Bayumi raised his cudgel and shouted:

'Mr Khonfis?!'

The man raised his stick.

'With you all the way, Chief.'

Rifaa asked in despair:

'Why do you want to kill me?'

Bayumi cracked his cudgel down on Rifaa's head and he screamed, then shouted from deep down: 'Gebelawi!' A moment later Khonfis's cudgel caught him on the neck and the blows rained down . . .

Silence fell, broken only by his dying gasps.

They began digging hard in the dark with their hands.

The murderers left, heading for the alley. They melted away into the darkness in no time. Four figures stood up not far from the place of the crime, sobbing. One of them shouted:

'You cowards; you winded me, and so he was killed without anyone to defend him!'

Another said to him:

'If we listened to you we should all have died and still have been unable to save him.'

Ali spoke again:

'You're cowards – just cowards.'

Kerim said tearfully:

'Don't waste time talking, we have a difficult job in front of us which must be done before morning.'

Hussein looked up at the sky with his eyes full of tears and murmured:

'Daybreak is near, we must hurry.'

Zaki cried out:

'It flashed by like a bad dream, but in that short time we lost the best friend we've ever had.'

Ali started towards the place of the crime muttering: 'Cowards!' The others followed him, fanning out in a semicircle, and knelt down, feeling the ground. Kerim suddenly shouted as though he had been bitten:

'Here! This is his blood.'

At that moment Zaki yelled out:

'This soft place is his grave.'

They gathered round him, scrabbling at the soil. No one in the world was more miserable than they who had lost their friend, and let him die without being able to help him. In a moment of madness Kerim said stupidly:

'Perhaps we'll find him alive.'

Ali said contemptuously, his hands working away:

'Listen to the coward's delusions!'

Their nostrils were filled with the smell of earth and blood. From the direction of the gebel they heard dogs howling.

Ali shouted:

'Go slowly; this is his body.'

Their hearts almost stopped beating. Their hands searched gently. In anguish they felt his clothes and they wept aloud. They worked together to free the body from the sand and lifted it out carefully. From the streets and alleys came the crowing of cocks. One of them urged haste, but Ali insisted that they fill up the hole. Kerim took off his smock, spread it out on the ground and put the corpse on it. They worked together again to fill in the hole. Then Hussein took off his smock and put it over the corpse, and they carried it towards Bab el Nasr.

The darkness began to thin out over the gebel, revealing clouds; dew and tears moistened their faces. Hussein led the way to his tomb. They busied themselves silently opening it. Daylight came gradually until they could see the shrouded body and their bloodstained hands and their eyes red from crying. They carried the body down into the depths of the tomb, and stood round it humbly, fighting back their tears. Kerim whispered, sobbing:

'Your life was a brief dream, but it has filled our hearts with love and purity. We didn't imagine you'd leave us so soon, let alone that someone would kill you, someone from our ungrateful alley, which you loved and served and which wanted only to destroy the mercy and healing you brought. They've damned themselves till the end of time.'

Zaki moaned:

'Why do the good die? Why do the wicked live?'

Hussein sighed:

'But for your love remaining in us, we'd hate people for ever.'

At that Ali said:

'We shan't know any peace of mind until we make up for our cowardice.'

As they left the cemetery for the desert, dawn was tinting the horizon with rose.

62 ✳ ✳ ✳ ✳ ✳ ✳ ✳ ✳ ✳ ✳ ✳ ✳ ✳ ✳ ✳ ✳ ✳

None of the four friends showed himself again in Gebelawi Alley. Their people thought they had left the quarter with Rifaa to be safe from the attacks of the chiefs. They lived on the edge of the desert, fighting with all their might against their anguish and remorse. The loss of Rifaa was worse than death to them, and his absence was a dreadful torture. Their only hope in life was to honour his memory by reviving his mission, and to bring punishment on his murderers as Ali was resolved to do. Of course, it was not in their power to return to the alley, but they hoped to achieve their aims outside it.

One morning Victory House was awakened by Abda's screams. The neighbours hurried round to find out what had happened and she shouted hoarsely:

'My son Rifaa has been killed.'

The neighbours were dumbfounded. They looked at Shafey who was drying his eyes. He said:

'The chiefs killed him in the desert.'

Abda wailed:

'My son who never harmed anyone in his life.'

Someone asked:

'Did our Khonfis know about it?'

Shafey said angrily:

'Khonfis was one of the murderers.'

Abda sobbed:

'And Jasmine betrayed him and told Bayumi where he was.'

They looked disgusted. A voice said:

'That's why she's been living in his house since his wife left him.'

The news spread in Gebel's quarter, and Khonfis came to Shafey's house and shouted at him:

'Are you mad, man? What've you been saying about me?'

Shafey faced him fearlessly.

'You joined in his murder – *you*, his protector.'

Khonfis put on a show of resentment and shouted:

'You're mad, Shafey; you don't know what you're saying. I'll leave you, in case you force me to teach you manners.'

He stalked out fuming with rage. The news reached Rifaa's quarter, where he had stayed after leaving Gebel's, and the people were stunned. There were shouts of rage and sounds of crying. But the chiefs went out into the alley and walked up and down it, their cudgels in their hands and a cruel glint in their eyes. Then a report went round that the sand to the west of Hind's Rock had been found stained with Rifaa's blood. Shafey went with his closest friends to look for the body. They searched and dug, but found nothing. There was uproar at the news, and great confusion, and many people expected things to happen in the alley. The people of Rifaa's quarter wondered what he had done to be condemned to death. The Gebelites pointed out that, now that Rifaa was dead, Jasmine was living in Bayumi's house.

The chiefs slipped out by night to the place where Rifaa was killed. They dug up his grave by the light of a torch, but found no trace of the body. Bayumi mused:

'Has Shafey taken it?'

Khonfis answered him:

'Oh no; he found nothing, so my spies tell me.'

Bayumi stamped on the ground and shouted:

'It was his friends! We were wrong to let them escape; here they are fighting us from behind.'

As they went back Khonfis whispered in Bayumi's ear:

'Your keeping Jasmine is a source of trouble for us.'

'What you mean is you aren't in control of your quarter.'

194

Khonfis left him angrily.

Tension rose again in Gebel's quarter and Rifaa's. Again the chiefs acted against the malcontents. Terror reigned until people hated to go out unless they had to. One night, when Bayumi was at Shaldam's café, his last wife's people crept into his house to attack Jasmine. She discovered them and fled in her gown to the desert with them chasing her. She ran like a mad woman in the darkness, even after they had stopped following. She went on running till she could hardly breathe and had to stop, panting violently. She threw her head back and shut her eyes, standing like that until she got her breath back. She looked behind her and saw nothing, but she was afraid to go back to the alley by night. She looked in front of her and saw a faint light far off, coming perhaps from a hut. She walked towards it, hoping to find a refuge till the morning. She had to go a long way before she reached it.

It was, as she thought, a hut. She went up to the door, calling out to the people. Suddenly she found herself face to face with her husband's friends: Ali, Hussein, Zaki, and Kerim. She stood rooted to the spot, and her glance shifted from face to face. They seemed to her like a wall barring her way in a nightmare. They stared at her in disgust, especially Ali whose eyes were cruel. She shouted:

'I'm innocent, by the Lord of Heaven, I'm innocent. I went with you until they attacked us, and then I ran away just as you did.'

They scowled. Ali asked angrily:

'How do you know we ran away?'

She said in a trembling voice:

'If you hadn't you wouldn't have lived. But I'm innocent; all I did was run away.'

Ali gnashed his teeth.

'You ran away to your master, Bayumi.'

'Never! Let me go! I'm innocent.'

Ali shouted:

'You shall go under the ground.'

She tried to escape but he leapt at her and seized her by the shoulders. She screamed:

'Let me go, for his sake: he had no love for killing or killers.'

Ali put his hands round her neck. Kerim said wretchedly:

'Wait till we've thought about it.'

Ali shouted:

'Keep quiet you cowards.'

He tightened his grip on her throat, putting into it all his pent-up anger and hatred and suffering and remorse. She tried in vain to free herself; she seized his forearms, kicked him, shook her head – all to no avail. Her strength failed, her body was convulsed, and she was still for ever. He let her go and she fell at his feet, a corpse.

## 63 ✳ ✳ ✳ ✳ ✳ ✳ ✳ ✳ ✳ ✳ ✳ ✳ ✳ ✳ ✳ ✳ ✳ ✳ ✳

Next day Jasmine's body was found at Bayumi's gate. The news spread like a sand storm, and men and women came running to his house. There was uproar. A mass of confused explanations were offered, and people hid their real feelings. The gate of Bayumi's house opened and out he charged like a mad bull. He laid about him with his cudgel, hitting everyone he could catch. They all ran away in terror and took refuge in the houses and cafés. Bayumi stood in the empty road, cursing and swearing and uttering threats, beating the air and the walls and the ground.

That same day Shafey and his wife left the alley. It seemed as if all trace of Rifaa had vanished, but there were still things that recalled him, such as Shafey's home in Victory House, the carpentry shop, Rifaa's home in the quarter which was now called 'The Home of Healing', the place west of Hind's Rock where he had died, and above all, his faithful friends who kept in touch with his followers and taught them the secret ways by which he had cast out evil spirits to cure the sick. They were convinced that in this way they were bringing Rifaa back to life. But Ali could not rest unless he was cursing the wicked. Hussein reproached him:

'You aren't Rifaa's follower at all.'

Ali said:

'I know Rifaa better than you. He spent his short life in a violent fight against evil spirits.'

Kerim said:

'You want to go back to violence, and he hated nothing more.'

Ali shouted:

'He was a chief, the greatest of all, but his mildness deceived them.'

Each party set to work according to its views with sincere faith. The true story of Rifaa, which most people did not know, was told in the alley. It was also told that his body had remained in the desert until Gebelawi himself had carried it away, and that it lay hidden under the soil of his luxuriant garden.

Strange happenings almost stopped after that, but for the disappearance of a chief: Handusa. Then his body was found one morning in front of the house of Ihaab the Trustee. The Trustee's house was paralysed, and so was that of Bayumi, and the alley went through a terrible period of fear. Attacks were made on anyone who had any connection, or seemed to have any connection, with Rifaa or one of his friends. No head was safe from sticks, no stomach from kicks, no chest from punches, no neck from bruises. Many people shut themselves up in their houses; many others left. Those who were careless of the danger got killed in the desert. The alley resounded with shouts and howls and all seemed black and overcast. The smell of blood hung everywhere. The strange thing is that all this did not put an end to the goings-on. Khalid was killed as he was leaving Bayumi's house a little before dawn. The reign of terror reached an insane peak. Then the alley was awakened in the early hours by a great fire, which destroyed the house and family of Jabir. Bayumi shouted:

'Rifaa's madmen are spreading like bed bugs. They must be killed, by God, even if it's in their own houses.'

The rumour went round that the houses would be attacked by night. People were mad with terror. They stormed out of their houses brandishing sticks, stools, saucepan lids, knives, clogs, bricks. Bayumi decided to strike before things got any worse. Waving his cudgel, he charged out of his house with a crowd of supporters.

Ali was at the head of the rebels, together with some tough men, showing himself for the first time. As soon as he saw Bayumi coming up he ordered a volley of stones to be thrown. The stones fell like a cloud of locusts on Bayumi and his men, and the blood began to flow. Bayumi attacked, roaring like a wild beast, but a stone hit him on the head and he stopped, for all his anger and strength and pride. He staggered and fell, his head covered in blood. His men fled in no time and the angry crowd surged into his house. The sounds of rending and breaking reached the Trustee in his house. There was chaos. Retribution fell on the rest of the chiefs and their friends, and their homes were destroyed. The danger mounted and almost got out of hand. At that moment the Trustee sent for Ali.

Ali went to meet him, and his men stopped their vengeance and destruction to wait for the outcome of the meeting. Things quietened down and tempers cooled. The meeting produced a new agreement about the alley; the Rifaaites were recognized as a new quarter, with the same rights and privileges as Gebel's quarter. Ali was made trustee of their part of the estate, which meant chief over them. He would receive their share of the estate's revenues and share it out among them on a basis of perfect equality.

All those who had fled from the alley during the reign of terror came back to the new quarter, led by Shafey and his wife, and Zaki, Hussein and Kerim. Rifaa enjoyed in his death an honour and respect and love that he had never dreamed of while alive. His life became a glorious story repeated by everyone, and chanted to the music of the fiddle, especially the part about Gebelawi taking up his body and burying it in his garden. The Riafaaites all agreed about this, as they agreed on loyalty to his parents and veneration for them, but they disagreed about everything else. Kerim, Hussein and Zaki maintained that Rifaa's mission had been to heal the sick and that he despised importance and power. They and their followers continued his ways. Some of them went to extremes and shunned marriage out of a desire to imitate him and repeat his way of life.

Ali on the other hand took all that was due to him from the estate and married. He called for the renovation of Rifaa's quarter and said that Rifaa had not despised the estate for itself, but in order to show that real happiness could be gained without it, and to condemn the evils aroused by greed; if the revenues were fairly shared out and used for building and for good ends, then they were wholly good.

In any case people enjoyed a good life and their faces were glad. They said with faith and conviction that today was better than yesterday, and tomorrow would be better than today.

Why is our alley plagued with forgetfulness?

# *Kassem*

✳ ✳ ✳ ✳ ✳ ✳ ✳ ✳ ✳ ✳ ✳ ✳ ✳ ✳ ✳ ✳ ✳ ✳ ✳ ✳

Hardly anything changed. Bare feet still left their prints in the dust, and flies went on flitting between heaps of rubbish and people's eyes. Faces were still haggard and drawn, clothes still tattered. Insults were exchanged like standard greetings, and hypocrisy was rife. The Big House remained closed up behind its walls, immersed in silence and memories. To the right stood the Trustee's house, and to the left the Chief's. Next to them was Gebel's quarter and adjoining it lay Rifaa's. As for the rest of the alley, the part that ran down to Gemalia, it was the home of a mass of ill-bred people, the 'Jerboas' as they were called, who were the poorest and wretchedest of all.

At this time the Trustee was Rifaat, who was just like his predecessors. The Chief was Lehita, a short slim man whose appearance did not betray his strength, but who was transformed in battle into an enemy as swift, as sharp and as deadly as flame. He had become Chief after a series of battles that had made the blood flow in every quarter. The Gebelite chief was called Galta. His people were still self-confident, boasting that they were the most closely related to Gebelawi, that theirs was the best quarter, and that Gebel had been the first and the last whom Gebelawi had favoured and spoken to; and for this they were little loved. Haggaag was the Rifaaite chief. He did not follow Ali's example in his conduct of affairs, but behaved like Khonfis and Galta and other usurpers. He took the estate income for his own use and beat up anyone who complained, urging his people to follow Rifaa in despising power and wealth. Even the Jerboas had their chief, Sawaaris, but he of course was not trustee of part of the estate.

Things went on like this, and those who held the cudgels maintained, as did the storytellers with their fiddles, that it was a just system based on Gebelawi's ten conditions, which the Trustee and chiefs took care to carry out and safeguard.

Among the Jerboas a sweet potato vendor called Zechariah was known for his goodness. He was distinguished by a distant connection with Sawaaris, chief of the quarter. He used to push his barrow about the various quarters of the alley, crying his wares. In the middle of the barrow stood the stove from which wafted an aromatic smoke, which drew Rifaaite and Gebelite boys as well as boys from Gemalia and Otouf, from Derrasa and Kafr el Zaghari and Beit el Kadi. Zechariah had been married a long time without having any children, but his little nephew, Kassem, had come to live with them when his parents died. Zechariah did not find the child a burden, for life, especially in that part of the alley, cost little more than that of the dogs and cats and flies, which found their food amidst the rubbish. Zechariah loved him with fatherly love, and, when his wife became pregnant after the little boy had joined the family, he regarded the child as a good omen and grew still more fond of him. His love did not lessen when he was blessed with a son, Hassan.

Kassem grew up almost alone, for his uncle passed the day away from home and his aunt was busy with her house and her baby. Then, as he grew up, his world expanded and he took to playing in the courtyard and the alley, and made friends with boys his own age from Rifaa's quarter and Gebel's, as well as from his own. He went too to Hind's Rock, and got to know the desert well, and climbed the gebel. He used to gaze up with the other little boys at the Big House and feel proud of his ancestor. But he could find nothing to say when some people spoke only of Gebel and others only of Rifaa, and he could not think what to do when people insulted one another and quarrelled and fought. Often he looked at the Trustee's house in wonder and astonishment, and gazed with longing at the fruit on the trees.

Once he saw the gatekeeper dozing and slipped quietly into the garden without seeing anyone or being seen. Full of joy, he walked along the paths and picked up guavas off the grass and ate them with delight, until he found himself in front of the fountain. He gazed in delight at the column of water rising out of the basin and, throwing off his smock, he jumped in and waded about, splashing his hands in the water and pouring it on his body, completely forgetting where he was. In no time a harsh voice shouted, 'Osman, you dog, come here you blind idiot!' He turned to see where the voice came from and saw on the terrace a man wearing a red robe, pointing at him with a trembling finger, his face burning with rage. Kassem rushed to the side of the basin and swung himself out, pivoting himself on his elbows. Then he saw the gatekeeper hurrying up and ran towards the jasmine trellis beside the wall, forgetting his smock where he had left it. He raced to the door, shot out into the alley and ran off at top speed. The children saw him and followed, yelling. Dogs barked. Then Osman the gatekeeper rushed out into the alley, ran after him, caught him by the arm and stood there panting. Kassem screamed so that the whole quarter heard.

In a moment his aunt appeared, carrying her child, and Sawaaris came out from the café. His aunt was amazed at his appearance and took his hand, saying to the gatekeeper:

'For Heaven's sake, Mr Osman, you've frightened the boy. What's he done? Where's his smock?'

'His honour the Trustee saw him bathing in his fountain. The little demon needs a beating. The damned brat got in while I was asleep. Why don't you keep your devils away from us?'

'Forgive him, Mr Osman; he's an orphan. You're quite right, of course.'

She rescued the boy from his hands:

'I'll beat him for you, but please do give back his one and only smock.'

The gatekeeper waved his hand angrily, turned his back and went off, saying:

'Because of this insect I've been cursed and insulted. Devils! Alley of dogs!'

The woman went back home, carrying Hassan on her hip and pulling Kassem along by the hand. He was crying loudly.


65 ✳ ✳ ✳ ✳ ✳ ✳ ✳ ✳ ✳ ✳ ✳ ✳ ✳ ✳ ✳ ✳ ✳ ✳ ✳ ✳

Zechariah said to Kassem, looking at him admiringly:

'You aren't a child any more, Kassem; you're almost ten. It's time you had a job.'

Kassem's eyes lit up with pleasure.

'I always hoped you'd take me with you, uncle.'

Zechariah laughed.

'It was play, not work, that you were after. But now you're a sensible boy and you can help me.'

The boy rushed over to the barrow and tried to push it, but Zechariah stopped him. His aunt said:

'Mind the potatoes don't roll away, or we'll starve to death.'

Zechariah took hold of the shafts of the barrow, saying:

'Walk in front and shout "Best sweet potatoes! Roast sweet potatoes!" Notice whatever I say or do; and you can carry the potatoes up to customers on the upper floors. Keep your eyes open.'

Kassem looked sadly at the barrow:

'But I'm strong enough to push it.'

Zechariah set off pushing the barrow.

'Do as I tell you and don't be stubborn; your father was the nicest of men.'

The barrow rumbled down towards Gemalia with Kassem shouting in his squeaky voice 'Best sweet potatoes! Roast sweet potatoes!' Nothing could match his joy as he went off to strange parts and worked like the grown-ups. When the cart got to Watawit Alley, Kassem looked round and said to his uncle:

'This is where Idris got in Adham's way.'

Zechariah nodded without interest, and the boy went on, laughing:

'Adham was pushing his barrow just like you, uncle.'

The barrow followed its daily route, from El Hussein to Beit el Kadi and from Beit el Kadi to Derrasa. Kassem gazed in wonder at the passers-by and at the shops and mosques, until they came to a little square which Zechariah said was Souk Mukattam. The boy looked at it in wonder.

'Is this really Souk Mukattam? This is where Gebel ran away to, and where Rifaa was born.'

Zechariah said unenthusiastically:

'Yes. But those two have nothing to do with us.'

'But we're all children of Gebelawi: why aren't we like them?'

Zechariah laughed bitterly.

'At any rate we're all equally poor.'

He pushed his barrow towards a tin hut on the edge of the square by the desert; it was a shop selling rosaries, incense and charms, and in front, on a skin sat an old man with a white beard. Zechariah stopped the cart in front of the hut and shook the old man warmly by the hand. The man said:

'I have enough sweet potatoes today.'

Zechariah sat down beside him.

'I'd rather sit with you than make a profit.'

The old man looked at the boy with interest. Zechariah called to him:

'Come here, Kassem and kiss Mr Yehya's hand.'

He went up to the old man, took his wrinkled hand and kissed it reverently. Yehya began guessing at Kassem's story and studying his attractive face.

'Who is he, Zechariah?'

Zechariah stretched his legs out in the sun.

'My late brother's son.'

The old man made him sit down beside him on the skin.

'Do you remember your father, my boy?'

'No, sir.'

'Your father was a friend of mine. He was a good man.'

Kassem stared up at the different kinds of goods for sale. Yehya stretched out his hand, took a charm from a near-by shelf and hung it round the boy's neck.

'Take this; it will keep you from all evil.'

Zechariah told Kassem:

'Mr Yehya was from our alley – from Rifaa's quarter.'

Kassem looked at Yehya.

'Why did you leave, sir?'

'The Rifaaite chief was angry with me and I preferred exile.'

'Just like Shafey, Rifaa's father.'

Yehya laughed long, showing his toothless gums.

'So you know about that, my boy! How well the people of our alley know the old stories; what's wrong with them, that they don't learn their lesson!'

A boy brought a pot of tea from a café and put it down in front of Yehya, then went back. Yehya brought out a small package from the breast of his smock and began opening it.

'I have something precious and very powerful; the effect will last till tomorrow.'

Zechariah said eagerly:

'Let's try it.'

Yehya chuckled.

'I never heard you say no.'

'How could I say no to pleasure, Yehya?'

The two men shared the lump and began chewing it. Kassem watched them so eagerly that he made his uncle laugh. The old man sipped his tea and asked Kassem:

'Do you dream of being a chief like the other people in our alley?'

Kassem smiled.

'Yes.'

Zechariah laughed and said apologetically:

'Forgive him, Mr Yehya. As you know, in our place a man is either a chief or a target for their punches.'

Yehya sighed.

'God rest your soul, Rifaa; how did you come out of our hellish alley?'

'That's why he met his end, as you know.'

Yehya said, frowning:

'Rifaa didn't die the day he was killed; he died the day his successor turned into a chief.'

Kassem asked eagerly:

'Where was he buried, sir? The Rifaaites say Gebelawi buried him in his garden, and the Gebelites say his body was lost in the desert.'

Yehya shouted:

'Damn those hard-hearted people! They still hate him even today.'
Then changing his tone: 'Tell me, Kassem, do you like Rifaa?'

The boy looked cautiously at his uncle, but answered clearly:

'Yes, sir, I like him very much.'

'Which would you prefer; to be like him or to be a chief?'

Kassem looked up at the old man, his eyes both smiling and confused.
His lips moved but he made not a sound. Zechariah laughed.

'Be content with selling sweet potatoes, like me.'

They fell silent, At the same time a row began in the market place,
where a donkey had thrown itself down on the ground, pulling over the
cart to which it was harnessed. The women riding in it scrambled out
while the driver flogged the donkey violently.

Zechariah got up.

'We have a long walk ahead of us. Good-bye, Yehya.'

'Bring the boy with you whenever you come.'

He shook Kassem's hand and fondled his hair.

'You're a good lad.'

## 66 ✳ ✳ ✳ ✳ ✳ ✳ ✳ ✳ ✳ ✳ ✳ ✳ ✳ ✳ ✳ ✳ ✳ ✳ ✳

Hind's Rock offered the only protection in the whole desert against the
scorching sun. Kassem sat there on the ground with only the flock for
company. He was wearing a clean, blue smock – as clean as is possible
for a shepherd – and had a turban to protect him from the sun, and a
pair of old slippers worn through at the toes. Part of the time he was
sunk in himself, and part of it he watched the rams, ewes and lambs and
the goats. His staff lay beside him. From where he sat he could see Gebel
Mukattam close by, towering up, vast and threatening. It was as if he
were the only living thing under the dome of the sky who defied the
anger of the sun with stubborn determination. The desert stretched out
to the horizon, sunk in a heavy silence and stifled in hot air.

When his thoughts and dreams and passionate youthful desires wearied
him, he would turn his gaze to the sheep, watching their games and
antics, their quarrels and affections, their activity and repose, especially
those of the lambs, which he adored. He used to marvel at their eyes and
his heart would beat harder at the sight of them as though they were
speaking to him. He in his turn would speak to them and would compare
the love they found in his care with the degradation which the people of
the alley met with under the arrogant chiefs. He was not worried by the
way people looked down on shepherds, for he believed from the outset
that a shepherd was better than a crook, a layabout or a beggar. Quite

apart from that, he loved the desert and the fresh air, and knew well Gebel Mukattam and Hind's Rock and the dome of sky with its wonderful changes. Besides, being a shepherd led him constantly to visit Mr Yehya!

Yehya asked him when first he saw him as a shepherd:

'From selling sweet potatoes to watching sheep?'

'Why not, sir! It's a job that hundreds of poor wretches in my quarter envy.'

'Why've you left your uncle?'

'My cousin Hassan has grown up; he has a better right to go with my uncle on his rounds. Watching the sheep is better than begging.'

Never a day passed without his visiting his teacher. He loved him and enjoyed his conversation. He found him to be a man who knew all about the alley, past and present. He knew the tales chanted by the storytellers and knew things, too, which they did not know. Kassem used to say to Yehya: 'I watch over sheep from every quarter, sheep of Gebel's, sheep of Rifaa's, and sheep belonging to the rich men in our quarter too. The strange thing is that they graze together in a brotherhood which their hard-hearted owners don't enjoy.' He said to him as well: 'Hammam was a shepherd. And who are the people who look down on shepherds? They're beggars and down-and-outs and poor wretches. Yet at the same time they look up to the chiefs who are just shameless robbers and shedders of blood. God forgive you, people of the alley!'

One time Kassem said to Yehya playfully:

'I'm poor and content. I've never harmed any man. Even my sheep meet with nothing but love from me. Don't you think I'm like Rifaa?'

Yehya looked at him disapprovingly and said:

'Rifaa! You like Rifaa! Rifaa spent his life freeing his brothers from evil spirits to win happiness for them.' Then, laughing: 'And you're crazy about women. You lie in wait for girls in the desert when the sun goes down.'

Kassem smiled.

'Is there anything wrong in that, Mr Yehya?'

'That's your business. But don't say you're like Rifaa.'

Kassem thought about this for a while, then said:

'And Gebel, wasn't he, like Rifaa, one of the good men of our alley? Yet he fell in love and married, and won his people's rightful share of the estate and ruled them justly.'

Yehya said sharply:

'But he made the estate his goal.'

'No, rather good behaviour towards other people; and justice and order were his goals too.'

Yehya was annoyed:

'So you prefer Gebel to Rifaa?'

Kassem's dark eyes were filled with perplexity. He hesitated for a long time, then said:

'They were both good men, and there've been so few good men in our alley – Adham, Hammam, Gebel, Rifaa – that's all our share of goodness. But what a lot of chiefs there have been!'

'And Adham died of grief, and Hammam was killed, and Rifaa was killed.'

'Such were the good men of our alley: a beautiful life and a sad end!' Thus he spoke to himself as he sat in the shade of the big rock. A strong desire to be like them sprang up in his heart. And the chiefs, how foully they behaved! A deep sadness came over him. He soothed himself: 'What a lot of events and people this rock has seen: the love of Kadri and Hind; the killing of Hammam; Gebel's meeting with Gebelawi; Rifaa's conversation with his ancestor. And now what's become of all that?! But the memory remains, and is worth more than flocks and flocks of sheep and goats. This rock saw our great ancestor too, when he roamed here alone as far as the eye can see, taking possession of what he wanted and scaring off the brigands. I wonder how he is in his isolation. Is he still in his right mind or is he senile? Does he move about, or is he bed-ridden? Does he know what's going on around him, or has he lost interest in everything? Does he remember his children, or has he forgotten even himself?'

At the end of the afternoon Kassem got up and stretched and yawned. He picked up his stick and whistled a tune, then waved the stick and called the sheep, which flocked together and moved off towards inhabited parts. He began to feel hungry; he had eaten nothing all day except a sardine and some bread. But a good supper would be waiting for him in his uncle's house. He walked faster, until he caught sight of the Big House in the distance with its high wall and its shuttered windows and the tops of its trees. What could its garden look like? That garden which the storytellers sang of, and for which Adham died of grief?

When he got near to the alley he heard its noises. Walking parallel to the wall of the Big House, he reached the top of the road. Dusk was shedding its gloomy light. He pushed his way through gangs of boys who were playing and throwing mud. His ears were filled with the street sellers' cries, the women's chatter, the men's arguments, the shouts of idiots and the bell on the Trustee's carriage. His nose was filled with the penetrating smell of honeyed tobacco, the stench of rubbish, the sharp odour of garlic. He stopped at the Gebelite houses to return their sheep to them and did the same in Rifaa's quarter. He was left with just one ewe which belonged to Mrs Kamar, the only woman in the Jerboas' quarter who owned property. She lived in a two-storey house with a courtyard in the middle of which stood a palm tree and in the far corner a guava tree. Kassem drove 'Grace' into the courtyard, meeting with the housekeeper, Sekina, with her curly greying hair. They greeted one another and she smiled and asked him in her husky voice, 'How's Grace?' He told her of his admiration for the ewe, handed it over to her and was about to leave. Then in came the mistress of the house returning from the alley. A shawl was wrapped round her plump body, and her dark eyes looked out affectionately over her veil. Kassem stepped aside for her and looked at the ground. She said to him gently and politely:

'Good evening.'

'Good evening, madam.'

She stopped and studied Grace, then looked at him.

'Grace is getting fatter every day, thanks to you.'

He was affected by her tender glance even more than by her kind words.

'Thanks to God, and to your care.'

Mrs Kamar turned to Sekina.

'Bring him some supper.'

He threw up his hands to decline gratefully.

'You're too good, madam.'

He won another glance from her as he said good-bye, then off he went. He was much moved by her gentleness and affection, as he was whenever he was lucky enough to meet her. It was an affection of a kind he had never known except from what he had heard about mother-love. If his mother had lived she would have been about this woman's age, about forty. How wonderful this quality seemed in an alley that took pride in strength and violence. The only thing more wonderful was her shy beauty and the joy it breathed into him. It was not like the hot-blooded adventures in the desert with their blind, burning hunger and their sad, transient satisfaction.

He hurried towards his uncle's house, carrying his staff over his shoulder, hardly seeing what was in front of him for the strength of this emotion. He found his uncle's family waiting for him on the balcony overlooking the courtyard. He sat down with the three of them at the table. A supper of felafel, leeks and melons had been put out. Hassan was sixteen, and so tall and well built that Zechariah dreamed that he would one day become chief of the Jerboas. After supper Kassem's aunt cleared the table and Zechariah left the house. The two cousins remained on the balcony until they heard a voice calling from the courtyard:

'Kassem!'

The two boys stood up and Kassem answered:

'We're coming, Sadek.'

Sadek met them happily. He was about the same age and height as

Kassem, but thinner. He worked as assistant to the metal-beater in the last shop before Gemalia. The three friends went off to Dongol's café. As they went in they were looked at by Taza, the storyteller, who sat cross-legged on his bench at the back. Sawaaris was sitting near to Dongol at the entrance and they went over and shook hands with the chief, humbly in spite of his close relationship to Kassem and Hassan. They sat down and the boy brought them their usual orders. Kassem loved the hubble-bubble and mint tea.

Sawaaris looked contemptuously at Kassem and asked him rudely:

'What's wrong with you, boy? You look as tidy as a girl.'

Kassem blushed with shame.

'There's nothing wrong with being clean, sir.'

The chief scowled:

'It's bad manners at your age.'

There was silence in the café. Sadek gave his friend a look of sympathy for he knew how sensitive he was. Hassan hid his face behind his cup of ginger so that the chief would not see his annoyance. Taza picked up his fiddle and started playing. After saluting Rifaat the Trustee, Lehita the chief, and Sawaaris, master of the quarter, the storyteller began:

Adham imagined her heard footsteps, slow and heavy. Submerged memories flooded back – a penetrating fragrance beyond understanding. He turned his head towards the door of the hut and saw it open. Then the doorway seemed to be filled by a huge person. He gazed in astonishment and with a mixture of hope and despair. He sighed deeply and murmured:

'Father—!'

It seemed that he heard the old voice saying:

'Good evening, Adham.'

His eyes swam with tears and he tried to stand up but could not. He felt a joy he had not known for over twenty years.

67 ✳ ✳ ✳ ✳ ✳ ✳ ✳ ✳ ✳ ✳ ✳ ✳ ✳ ✳ ✳ ✳ ✳ ✳ ✳

Sekina, the housekeeper, said:

'Wait, Kassem; I have something for you.'

Kassem stood by the palm tree to which he had tethered the ewe, waiting for the servant, who had gone inside, his heart pounding. He told himself that the thing she promised could only come from the generous heart of the mistress of the house. He longed to see her glance or hear her

208

voice to cool his body which had burnt all day long in the desert. Sekina came back with a package which she gave him, saying:

'A pancake; enjoy it.'

He took it in his hands.

'Thank the generous lady for me.'

Her voice came from behind the window, saying gently:

'Thanks belongs to God, my dear child.'

He made a gesture of gratitude with his hand without looking up, and went off. He repeated her words to himself 'my dear child', intoxicated with happiness. The shepherd boy had never heard anything like it before. And who had said it? The one respected lady in his wretched quarter. He looked with affection at the alley in the gathering darkness and thought: 'In spite of our alley's misery, it is not empty of things that could bring happiness to troubled hearts.'

He was roused from his daydreams by a voice shouting: 'My money ... my money ... Robbery!' He saw a man in a turban and a flowing smock hurrying towards the top of the alley, coming from the Gemalia end. Everyone turned towards the shouting man; the children ran after him; the pedlars and the people sitting in their doorways craned their necks. Heads were poked out, and faces peered up through the windows of basements. The customers came out of the cafés, and the man was surrounded on all sides. Kassem saw a man standing near to him, scratching his back with a stick through the neck of his smock and watching the scene with languid eyes. Kassem asked him who the man was, and he answered without stopping his scratching:

'An upholsterer who was working in the Trustee's house.'

Sawaaris went up to the man, and so did Haggaag and Galta, the Rifaaite and Gebelite chiefs. They lost no time in ordering the people back, and they withdrew a few paces. A woman's voice came from a window in Rifaa's quarter:

'The man's been touched by the Evil Eye.'

And another woman's voice came from the first house in Gebel's quarter:

'She's right. There's no one who didn't envy him the money he was going to make out of upholstering the Trustee's furniture. God preserve us from the Evil Eye!'

A third woman, who was standing in a doorway delousing a boy's head, said:

'Poor fellow. He was laughing as he came out of the Trustee's house. Little did he know he'd soon be screaming and crying. Curse money and everything to do with it!'

The man yelled at the top of his voice:

'All the money I had on me: stolen! A week's wages, and more besides that was in my pocket! Money for the house and shop and the children! Twenty pounds odd! Perish the bastards!'

Galta, the Gebelite chief, shouted:

'Ssh! Quiet everyone! Quiet you goats! The good name of the alley is in the balance, and any blame will be put on the chiefs in the end.'

Haggaag, the Rifaaite chief, said:

'God! There won't be any blaming! But how do we know he lost the money in this alley?'

The upholsterer shouted hoarsely:

'It was stolen in your alley: I'll divorce my wife if I lie. I took it from the gatekeeper of his honour the Trustee, and when I felt in the breast of my smock at the other end of the alley I found no trace of it.'

There was a hubbub of voices. Haggaag shouted:

'Quiet, you cattle! Listen, man; where did you realize your money was gone?'

He pointed to the end of the Jerboas' quarter:

'In front of the metal-beater's shop, but, to tell the truth, no one was near me there.'

Sawaaris said:

'Then it was stolen before he got to our quarter.'

Haggaag said:

'I was in the café when he went past, and I didn't see anyone in Rifaa's quarter go near him.'

Galta roared:

'There are no thieves among the Gebelites; they're the lords of this alley.'

Haggaag answered angrily:

'Enough, Mr Galta; you're wrong about the lords.'

'Only a fool can deny it.'

Haggaag thundered:

'Don't rouse the devil in me. Damn you and your bad manners!'

'A thousand curses on bad manners – which are not found in our quarter.'

The upholsterer said in a tearful voice:

'Gentlemen, my money was lost in your alley. You're all lords I'm sure, but where's my money? Poor Fengari's ruined.'

Haggaag said defiantly:

'We must have a search. Let us search every pocket, every man, every woman, every child, ever corner.'

Galta said contemptuously:

'Search away; you won't disgrace any of *us.*'

Haggaag said:

'The man left the Trustee's house and passed first through Gebel's quarter, so let's begin by searching the Gebelites.'

Galta snorted:

'Across my dead body! Remember who you are, Haggaag, and who I am.'

'I have more scars on my body, Galta, than you have hairs on your head.'

'There's no room for hair on my body.'

'God, don't let the devil in me get wild!'

'Send me all the devils in the world!'

Fengari the upholsterer shouted again:

'Look here! My money, doesn't it worry you that people will say it was stolen in your alley?'

A woman shouted furiously:

'Careful, owl-face, with your insults!'

A voice asked:

'Why should the money have been stolen anywhere but in the Jerboas' quarter, where most of them are thieves and beggars?'

Sawaaris shouted:

'Our thieves don't steal in their own alley.'

'How do we know that?'

Sawaaris grew red with rage.

'We don't need any more bad manners; the search will uncover the thief, or it's good-bye to the alley.'

More than one voice shouted:

'Begin with the Jerboas.'

Sawaaris yelled:

'Anyone who changes the natural order of the search will get my cudgel in his face.'

He brandished his cudgel and his men flocked round him. Haggaag did likewise, and Galta withdrew to his quarter and did the same. The upholsterer took refuge in a doorway, crying. Night was about to fall. Everyone expected a bloody battle. Suddenly Kassem rushed to the middle of the alley and shouted at the top of his voice:

'Stop! Bloodshed won't show where the lost money is. People will say in Gemalia and Derrasa and Otouf that anyone who enters Gebelawi Alley is robbed, even if it is protected by its Trustee and its chiefs.'

A Gebelite asked:

'What does the shepherd boy want?'

'I have a plan for giving the money back to its owner without a fight.'

The upholsterer ran towards him, shouting:

'I'm so grateful.'

Kassem said, addressing the crowd:

'It will give the money back to its owner without exposing the thief.'

There was complete silence. All eyes were fixed on Kassem. He went on:

'Let us wait till it is pitch dark, which will be soon. Not a single candle shall be lit. Then we'll all walk from one end of the alley to the other, so that suspicion doesn't settle on any one quarter, and during that time the one who has the money will be able to throw it down without giving himself away. Then we'll find the money and avoid a nasty battle.'

The upholsterer seized Kassem's arm in desperate entreaty and shouted:

'A good solution; accept it for my sake.'

Someone shouted:

'A sensible solution, young man!'

Someone else shouted:

'A chance for the thief to save himself and save the alley!'

A woman youyoued with joy. The people looked from one to another of the three chiefs, half hopeful and half afraid. But each of them was too proud and haughty to be the first to announce his acceptance. The people waited and wondered whether reason would prevail or whether the cudgels would fall and the blood would flow. Then there came a voice they all knew, shouting:

'Look here!'

All heads were jerked round towards the voice. There stood Lehita, the Chief, not far from his house. Silence fell, and everyone hung on his words. He said contemptuously:

'Accept the plan, you vagabonds. If you weren't such idiots you wouldn't have to be saved by a shepherd boy.'

A murmur of relief ran through the crowd, and there were more youyous. Kassem's heart pounded. He looked at Kamar's house, feeling certain that her dark eyes were gazing at him from one of the two windows that overlooked the road. A glow of happiness filled him, and he felt the pleasure of a great triumph such as he had never known before. Everyone was waiting for the darkness, looking now towards the sky, now towards the desert. They followed its gradual deepening. The landmarks disappeared; the faces blurred; the people became shapes. The two paths into the desert on either side of the Big House were swallowed up in the darkness. The figures began to move and walked up to the Big House and then hurried down towards Gemalia. Then each man went back to his own quarter. Lehita shouted:

'Lights on!'

The first light to appear was in Kamar's house, in the Jerboas' quarter. Then the lamps were lit on the hand carts, then the lights in the cafés, and the alley came back to life. The people began searching the ground by the light of the lamps till the cry went up: 'Here's the wallet!' Fengari rushed straight over towards the light, took the wallet and counted the money, then hurried off to Gemalia, taking no notice of anything and leaving behind him a clamour of laughter and shouting. Kassem found

212

himself the focus of attention, the centre for congratulations, jokes and explanations.

When Kassem with Hassan and Sadek went to the Jerboas' café that evening, Sawaaris greeted him with a smile of welcome, and called:

'A pipe for Kassem on my account!'


68 ✳ ✳ ✳ ✳ ✳ ✳ ✳ ✳ ✳ ✳ ✳ ✳ ✳ ✳ ✳ ✳ ✳ ✳ ✳

Flushed, bright-eyed and glad-hearted, Kassem went into Kamar's courtyard to collect the ewe, calling out: 'Veils on!' He began undoing the ewe's tether at the foot of the steps when he heard the door creaking open, and her voice saying:

'Good morning!'

He said fervently:

'May God grant you a happy morning, madam!'

'You did our alley a very good turn yesterday.'

His heart pounded.

'God was my guide.'

'You've taught us that wisdom is better than force.'

'And your affection is better than wisdom,' he thought to himself. He said:

'You're very kind.'

He could hear that she was smiling as she said:

'We saw you shepherding the people as you shepherd your flocks. Good-bye and bless you!'

He set off with Grace, and, with every house he passed, he added a billy goat or a nanny goat or a ram or a ewe to his procession. Everyone welcomed him, and even the chiefs who had ignored him before, acknowledged his greetings. He passed through the gap by the garden wall of the Big House on his way to the desert, behind a long line of sheep and goats. He was met by the burning heat of the sun, which was just up over the gebel, and by warm puffs of morning wind. At the foot of the mountain could be seen some shepherds. A man in tattered clothes passed him, playing a reed pipe. In the cloudless bowl of sky kites circled. Every breath of air he took was pure and clean. He imagined the great gebel must contain hidden treasures, hopes and promises. His gaze roamed over the desert with a strange satisfaction and his heart was light with joy. He began to sing:

> My sweet, my lovely Nubian,
> Your name is tattooed on my hand.

His eyes wandered over the rock of Kadri and Hind, and the places where Hammam and Rifaa had been killed, and where Gebelawi and Gebel had met. Here were the sun and the gebel and the sands, majesty and love and death, and a heart in which love was dawning. But he wondered what all this meant, that which had passed and that which was to come. He wondered about the alley with its warring factions and its feuding chiefs and about the stories that were told in a different form in each café.

A little before noon he drove his flock to Souk Mukattam, then went to Yehya's hut and sat down. The old man asked:

'What's this they're saying you did yesterday in the alley?'

Kassem sipped his tea to hide his embarrassment. The old man went on:

'It would have been best for them to fight it out until they were all dead.'

Kassem said, without raising his eyes:

'You're only saying that.'

'Avoid your admirers for fear of provoking the chiefs.'

'Could someone like me provoke them?'

The old man sighed:

'Who could have imagined that anyone would betray Rifaa?'

Kassem was amazed.

'What do I have in common with the great Rifaa?'

When he was about to go the old man's parting words were: 'Always keep my talisman.'

In the afternoon he was sitting in the shadow which spread out behind Hind's Rock, when he heard Sekina's voice calling 'Grace!' He leapt up and went round the rock and saw Kamar's servant standing by the ewe's head, fondling its wool. He greeted her with a smile and she said in her husky voice:

'I've been on an errand to Derrasa and I took this short cut home.'

'But it's a hot way to come.'

She laughed.

'And that's why I'm going to rest a little in the shade of the rock.'

They sat down together in the shade where he had left his staff. Sekina said:

'When I saw what you did yesterday I was sure your mother must have prayed for you before she died.'

He asked smiling:

'And you, don't you pray for me?'

She suppressed a cunning glance.

'For a man like you I pray for a wife from a good family.'

He laughed.

'Whoever would be satisfied with a shepherd boy?'

'Luck works wonders. Today you are respected by the chiefs without having shed any blood.'

'I swear your words are sweet as honey.'

She looked at him with her languid eyes.

'Shall I tell you a good path to take?'

A sudden agitation overcame him.

'Please!'

With Negro simplicity she said:

'Try your luck and propose to the lady of our quarter.'

Everything looked suddenly different.

'Who do you mean, Sekina?'

'Don't pretend you don't know who I mean; there's only one lady in our quarter.'

His voice trembled.

'Her husband was an important man, and I'm just a shepherd.'

'But when fortune smiles everything smiles with it, even poverty.'

He said, almost to himself:

'Won't my proposal annoy her?'

Sekina stood up.

'No one knows when women will be pleased and when they will be annoyed; trust in God.' Then, as she was going: 'Look after yourself.'

He turned his face towards the sky and shut his eyes as though overcome by fatigue.


69 ✳ ✳ ✳ ✳ ✳ ✳ ✳ ✳ ✳ ✳ ✳ ✳ ✳ ✳ ✳ ✳ ✳ ✳ ✳

Zechariah stared into Kassem's face in amazement, and so did his wife and so did Hassan. They were resting in their living-room after supper. Zechariah said:

'Don't talk like that. I thought you were a model of sense and honour in spite of your poverty – of our poverty. What's become of your sense?'

His aunt's eyes were filled with a hungry desire for information. Kassem said:

'I had reason to feel encouraged; it was her servant who opened the door for me.'

His aunt exclaimed eagerly:

'Her servant?'

His uncle let out a short confused laugh.

'Perhaps you misunderstood her.'

Kassem spoke quietly to hide his emotion:

'No, no, uncle.'

His aunt cried out:

'I see! If the servant has said it the mistress has said it.'

Hassan said:

'Kassem is a real man, and there are not many men.'

Zechariah shook his head and muttered:

'Best sweet potatoes! Roast sweet potatoes!' Then, to Kassem: 'But you don't possess a single piastre!'

His wife said:

'He grazed her ewe, as you know very well.' Then, laughing: 'Mind you never kill a ewe, Kassem, in honour of Grace.'

Hassan said thoughtfully:

'Mr Owayss the grocer is Mrs Kamar's uncle and the richest man in our quarter. He will be our in-law, just as Sawaaris is our relative. How splendid!'

His mother said:

'Mrs Kamar has connections with Lady Amina, the Trustee's wife. Her late husband was Amina's relative.'

Kassem said uneasily:

'Will all that make things difficult?'

Zechariah said with surprising enthusiasm, realizing the status he would get from the contemplated match:

'Talk as you did on the day of that incident with the upholsterer. You are bold and sensible. We'll go along together to the lady to take up the question with her, and then we must talk to Owayss. If we began with Owayss he would send us to the mad house.'


Things went as Zechariah had planned. And so Owayss sat down in the drawing-room in Kamar's house, waiting for her to come and playing with his huge moustache to hide his confusion. Kamar came, in a modest dress, with a brown kerchief over her head. She shook hands graciously with him and sat down, with a look of calm determination in her eyes. Owayss said:

'You bewilder me, my girl! Not long ago you refused the hand of Mr Moursy my manager, on the grounds that he was not good enough for you; and now you are satisfied with a shepherd boy!'

She blushed.

'Uncle, he is indeed a poor man, but everyone in the quarter can witness to his and his family's goodness.'

Owayss said frowning:

'Yes, just as we say a servant is trustworthy or clean. Eligibility is something quite different.'

Kamar said politely:

'Show me one man in the alley who is as well behaved as him; show me just one man who doesn't boast of some act of trickery or meanness or brutality.'

The man nearly burst with rage, but he remembered that he was talking, not just to his niece but to a woman who had invested a lot of money in his business, so he said:

'Kamar, if you liked I could marry you to any chief in the alley. Lehita himself would have you, if you'd agree to share him with his other wives.'

'I don't like those bullies, nor that kind of man. My father was a good man, like you. He suffered so much from their cruelty that I inherited his hatred of them. But Kassem has a good character. He only lacks money; and he by himself is enough for me.'

Owayss sighed and looked at her for a long time, then said as a last resort:

'I have a message from Lady Amina, the Trustee's wife, She said to me: "Tell Kamar to be sensible; she's heading for a mistake that would make us the gossip of the whole alley." '

Kamar said sharply:

'I don't care about her advice. It's a pity she doesn't know who it is that gets herself talked about!'

'My dear niece, she's concerned for your reputation.'

'Don't you believe it, uncle; she doesn't care about us or even remember us. Since my husband died ten years ago, she's never given me a thought.'

The man hesitated a while in obvious embarrassment, then said resentfully:

'She also said it's foolish for a woman to marry a man beneath her, especially if for some reason he's kept on visiting her house.'

Kamar jumped up, livid with rage, and shouted:

'Cut her tongue out! I've been born and brought up and married and widowed in this alley; everyone knows me and speaks well of me.'

'Of course, my girl, of course; she's only pointing out what might be said.'

'Uncle, let's forget about her ladyship; she'll only give us a headache. I tell you as my uncle that I've agreed to marry Kassem, and it'll be with your approval and in your presence.'

Owayss was silent, deep in thought. It was impossible to stop her, and it was no light matter to anger her to the point of her withdrawing her money from his business. He just stared at the ground in misery and confusion. He opened his mouth to say something, but all that came out was an indistinct mumble. Kamar gazed at him patiently.

Zechariah gave his nephew some money – most of it borrowed – to get himself ready for the wedding.

'I'd shower you with money if only I was able to, Kassem. Your father was a kind brother; I shall never forget how generous he was on my wedding day.'

Kassem bought a smock, some underclothes, a brocaded turban, some bright yellow slippers, a cane and a box of snuff. Soon after dawn he went to the bath house and steamed himself, then plunged into the cold pool and had a massage. Then he washed and was perfumed, and finally stretched out in his cubicle sipping tea and dreaming of bliss.

Kamar undertook to provide the wedding feast. She got the roof of her house ready to receive the women guests, sent for a famous woman singer and hired the best cook in the neighbourhood. A marquee was put up in the courtyard for the men guests and the musicians. Kassem's family and friends came, and the men of the quarter led by Sawaaris. Cups of liquor were passed round, and twenty pipes, so that the smoke dimmed the lights and the air was laden with the smell of the very best hashish. Every corner echoed the youyous and the cheering and laughter.

Zechariah began boasting drunkenly:

'We're a noble family, and we go back a long way.'

Owayss hid his annoyance. He was sitting between Sawaaris and Zechariah. He said tersely:

'It's enough that you're related to Sawaaris.'

Zechariah shouted:

'A thousand greetings to Mr Sawaaris!'

The band at once played for Sawaaris who smiled complacently and waved his hand. In the past he had been annoyed by Zechariah harping on his distant relationship to him, but his feelings had begun to change when he heard that Kassem was to marry Kamar; in fact, he had already made up his mind not to exempt Kassem from paying protection money. Zechariah went on:

'Kassem is a much liked young man; who is there that doesn't like him?'

He detected a certain annoyance in Sawaaris's look and added:

'But for his wisdom on the day of the theft, the Rifaaites and Gebelites would have found no defence against the cudgel of our Sawaaris.'

Sawaaris beamed, and Owayss hastily agreed with Zechariah:

'You're right, by the God of heaven and earth!'

The musician sang: 'The time of love's delight is near.' And Kassem's confusion increased. Sadek understood at once how he felt, as usual, and got him a fresh cup of liquor which he swallowed straight down, even the dregs, still holding the pipe in his hand. Hassan had overdone the drinking, and the marquee was dancing before his eyes. Owayss saw this and said to Zechariah:

'Hassan's drinking more than's good for him at his age.'

Zechariah stood up, mug in hand, and said to his son:

'Hassan, don't drink like that.'

He replied by swallowing another mugful, spluttering with laughter. Owayss was infuriated and said to himself: 'If it wasn't for my niece's foolishness, what you've drunk tonight would have cost you all that you possess.'

In the middle of the night, Kassem was summoned to his procession and the men guests went to Dongol's café led by Sawaaris, the head of the procession and its guardian. The alley outside the house was crowded with boys and beggars and cats, drawn by the smell of the cooking. Kassem sat down between Hassan and Sadek. Dongol greeted them, and said to his waiter:

'What a happy evening! Dongol's own pipe for the young man.'

Then everyone who could afford to paid for a pipe for the company. Sadek brought out from the breast of his smock a lump of hashish the size of a marble. He turned it in his fingers under the lamp and whispered in Kassem's ear:

'Mixed with something sweet. And powerful! God!'

Kassem took it and put it in his mouth, smiling, already red-eyed from drink. Sadek went on:

'Chew it first, then suck it.'

The singers came, following the pipers and drummers. Sawaaris stood up and said in a commanding voice:

'Let the procession commence!'

Kabura led wearing only a smock, dancing barefoot and balancing a cudgel on the top of his head. Behind him went the singers and Sawaaris, then the bridegroom's party, Kassem and his two friends, flanked by torchbearers. The singer began in a sweet voice:

> First of all – ah – with my eyes.
> Next of all – ah – with my hands.
> Third of all – ah – with my feet.
> When I was snared by love, it was with these eyes.
> When I waved to my love, it was with these hands.
> When I walked to my love, it was with these feet.

There were drunken 'ohs' and 'ahs' as the procession made its way to Gemalia and Beit el Kadi and then to the Hussein mosque and Derrasa. The night passed, unnoticed by the rejoicing people, and the procession returned, as it had set out, gaily and happily. It was the first bridegroom's procession in the alley ever to pass off without an incident. Not a cudgel was raised, not a drop of blood was spilt. Zechariah's delight reached its peak and he took his stick and began dancing, twirling the stick, swaying proudly, twisting and turning now his head, now his chest, now his waist, his movements now aggressive, now erotic. When he brought his dance to an end with a final spin, there was cheering and clapping.

Then Kassem went in to the women and found Kamar sitting at the head of the two rows of women guests. He went to her, accompanied by youyous of delight, took her by the hand, and walked with her to the bridal chamber, preceded by a belly dancer. They shut the door and with it shut out the world. There was silence, except for a few whispers or light footsteps. In a glance Kassem took in the bed with its pink linen, the comfortable couch, the patterned carpet, things such as he had never imagined. Then his eyes rested on the woman, who sat taking off her jewellery. She looked beautifully plump, soft and sweet. The walls seemed to shimmer with light, and he saw everything with confused excitement and boundless happiness. He drew close to her in his silk smock, glowing with warmth and rather drunk, and stood looking down at her, while she dropped her eyes expectantly. He took her face between his hands and was about to say something, but then seemed to change his mind. He bent over till her hair stirred under his breath, and kissed her forehead, her cheeks . . .

From behind the door the smell of incense reached his nose, and he heard Sekina's voice reciting some mumbled prayer.


71 ✳ ✳ ✳ ✳ ✳ ✳ ✳ ✳ ✳ ✳ ✳ ✳ ✳ ✳ ✳ ✳ ✳ ✳ ✳ ✳

Days and nights of love and companionship, joy and peace of mind followed – and how sweet is happiness in this world! He only went out of the house because he would have been ashamed for people to say he had not left it since his wedding. His heart was drunk with every kind of pleasure and he enjoyed all the love and tenderness and care that he wished for. He liked things to be clean, and here he saw everything tidy and breathed a perfumed atmosphere and looked upon a woman who never appeared before him unadorned, her face always shining with love. One day as they were sitting side by side in the drawing-room, she said to him:

'You are as gentle as a lamb; you don't demand, you don't boss and you don't scold, though everything in the house is yours.'

He played with a lock of her henna-red hair.

'I've reached a state in which I have no demands to make.'

She squeezed his hand hard.

'My heart told me from the beginning that you were the best man in our quarter. But sometimes, with your politeness, you seem like a stranger in your own house, and that hurts me you know.'

'You're speaking to a man whose good fortune carried him from the burning sands to the paradise of this house.'

She tried to look serious, but couldn't help smiling.

Don't imagine you're going to have an easy time in my house. Sooner or later you'll take my uncle's place managing my property. Do you think you'll find it a burden?'

He laughed.

'It'll be child's play compared with minding sheep.'

So he took over the management of her property, which lay scattered about between the Jerboas' quarter and Gemalia. Handling the difficult tenants called for skill, but with his flexibility he coped with things in the best possible way. The job only took up a few days each month and the rest of his time was free, a thing he was not used to. Perhaps the greatest triumph he won in his new life was earning the confidence of Owayss, his wife's uncle. He treated the man from the beginning with respect and attention, and volunteered to help him with some of his work, until Owayss grew to like him and returned his friendship and respect. He could not help saying frankly one day:

'Some thoughts are really wrong. You know, I used to think you were one of the scoundrels of the alley, and that you were exploiting my niece's passion to get her money and would squander it on your pleasures or would use it to marry another woman. But you've proved that you're wise and trustworthy and that she chose well.'


In Dongol's café Sadek used to laugh merrily and say to Kassem:

'Order us a pipe on your account; that's what important men like you are meant to do.'

And Hassan used to say:

'Why don't you take us to the tavern?'

But he answered seriously:

'I have no money except what I earn by managing my wife's property, or by services I do for Mr Owayss.'

Sadek was amazed.

'A loving woman is a plaything in a man's hand.'

Kassem retorted angrily:

'Unless the man is also loving. You're just like everyone else, Sadek; you see love only as a means of exploitation.'

Sadek gave an embarrassed smile.

'That's how weak men think; I'm not as strong as Hassan, or even as strong as you, so I've no hope of being a chief; and in our alley it's either hit or be hit.'

Kassem softened his tone:

'What a place! You're right, Sadek; the alley makes us sad.'

Hassan smiled.

'If only it was like the idea that people outside have of it.'

Sadek agreed with him:

'They say Gebelawi Alley is the place with real chiefs.'

Kassem's face filled with sadness. He stole a glance at Sawaaris' place at the front of the café, to be sure he was out of earshot, and said:

'It's as if they had never heard of its wretchedness.'

'People worship power, even its victims.'

Kassem thought for a while, then said:

'But you must remember the power which does good, like Gebel's and Rifaa's, not the power of toughs and crooks.'

Taza, the storyteller, was reciting his tale:

> Adham yelled at him:
> 'Carry your brother!'
> Kadri groaned:
> 'I can't.'
> 'You were able to kill him . . .'
> 'I can't, father.'
> 'Don't call me father; a man who kills his brother has no father, no mother, no brothers.'
> 'I can't.'
> He tightened his grip on him and said:
> 'A murderer must bear the burden of his victim . . .'

Then the storyteller took his fiddle and began singing. At that point Sadek said to Kassem:

'Today you're living the life that Adham dreamed of.'

'But at every step I meet something to upset me and destroy my happiness. Adham dreamed of leisure and plenty only as the means to true happiness.'

They all fell silent for a while, until Hassan said:

'True happiness can never be found.'

Kassem said, with a dreamy look in his eyes:

'Until the things that lead to it are plentiful for everyone.'

He thought about the way that he enjoyed money and leisure while the wretchedness of others spoilt his happiness. Yet here he was, meekly paying his protection money to Sawaaris. And so he wanted to fill his leisure time with work, to escape from himself or from the cruel alley.

Perhaps Adham, if he had got what he longed for in such circumstances, would have been oppressed by his happiness and would have longed to work.


At that time Kamar began to show strange cravings and Sekina said they were the signs of pregnancy. Kamar could hardly believe her – her hopes for a baby had been just a dream – and she was carried away with joy. Kassem was delighted and spread the news wherever he had friends. It was known in his uncle's house and in the metal-beater's shop, in Owayss's grocery and in Yehya's hut. Kamar became excessively concerned about herself. She said to Kassem in a meaningful voice:

'I must avoid any sort of upset.'

He smiled.

'Sekina must carry all the household burdens for you and I must be very patient.'

She kissed him, and said with child-like happiness:

'I could kiss the ground I'm so grateful.'

He went off to the desert to visit Yehya, but he stopped by Hind's Rock, went round to the shade and sat down. In the distance he saw a shepherd grazing his flock. His heart filled with sympathy and he wished he could say to him: 'A man is not made happy just by being important; in fact, a man is not made happy by that at all.' But wouldn't it be better to say it to the chiefs like Lehita and Sawaaris? How he felt for the people of the alley; they dreamed of happiness and time scattered their dreams like rubbish. Why not enjoy the happiness he had been granted and shut his eyes to what surrounded him? Here was the question that had troubled Gebel and perhaps Rifaa, who could have enjoyed lifelong ease and tranquillity. What is the reason for this sorrow that torments us?

Thus he pondered as he gazed at the sky over the gebel, a pure blue sky apart from a few flecks of cloud. He lowered his head wearily and his glance fell upon something moving. It was a scorpion hurrying towards its hole. He lifted his stick quickly, brought it down on the creature and squashed it. He looked at it for a while in disgust, then got up and went on his way.


72 ✳ ✳ ✳ ✳ ✳ ✳ ✳ ✳ ✳ ✳ ✳ ✳ ✳ ✳ ✳ ✳ ✳ ✳ ✳ ✳ ✳

A new life was born into Kassem's house. The poor people of the quarter joined in the celebrations. The baby was called Ihsan after Kassem's mother whom he had never seen. With her birth the house became used to tears and messes and sleepless nights, but she also gave it more joy and satisfaction. Yet why did the baby's father sometimes seem distracted, as if oppressed by cares? Kamar was deeply disturbed, and asked him one time:

'Are you not feeling very well?'

'I'm fine.'

'But you're not your usual self.'

He lowered his eyes.

'God knows what's wrong with me.'

She hesitated before asking:

'Is there something about me you don't like?'

'No one's dearer to me than you; not even our little girl.'

She sighed.

'Perhaps it's the Evil Eye.'

He smiled.

'Perhaps.'

She said prayers over him and burnt incense for him and prayed for him in her heart. One night she was woken by Ihsan crying and did not find him beside her. At first she thought he had not yet come back from the café, but when the baby stopped crying, she noticed the deep silence which normally only fell some time after the cafés closed. She was filled with doubt, and got up to look out of the window. She saw that complete darkness covered the sleeping alley. She went back to the baby, which had started crying again, and fed it at her breast. She began wondering what could have kept him until this hour for the first time in their life together. Ihsan fell asleep and she left the bed to go to the window a second time. Not hearing a sound, she went out to the hall and woke Sekina. The maid sat up drowsily, then jumped up in alarm. Her mistress told her why she had come, and Sekina decided at once to go to Zechariah to ask him about her master. Kamar asked herself what could have kept him at his uncle's house until this time, and she answered herself, dashing her hopes. Still she did not stop Sekina from going, perhaps because she hoped for something unexpected or because she wanted at least to ask for his uncle's help in her distress. When Sekina had gone, Kamar began wondering again what had kept him; could it have anything to do with the change that had come over him? Might it be connected with the walks he used to take in the desert in the evenings?

Zechariah and Hassan woke in alarm at Sekina's calls. Hassan said Kassem had not joined him that evening. Zechariah asked when his nephew had left home, and Sekina answered that it had been early in the afternoon. The three of them then set out; Hassan went to the neighbouring house and came back with Sadek, who said anxiously:

'It will soon be dawn; where can he have gone?'

Hassan said:

Perhaps he fell asleep out at the Rock.'

Zechariah told Sekina to go back to her mistress and tell her they were going off to look for him in the most likely places. The three men made for the desert. They felt the dampness of the autumn night and wound their turbans more tightly round their heads. They walked along, lit by the thin crescent of the waning moon, which had appeared in a gap in the clouds. Hassan shouted in a piercing voice: 'Kassem ... Kassem!', and the echo came back from the cliffs of Mukattam. They hastened on till they came to Hind's Rock, and walked round it examining the area, but they found no trace of him. Zechariah asked in a thick voice:

'Where can he have gone? He isn't a rake, and he doesn't have any enemies.'

Hassan murmured:

'And there's no other reason why he should flee.'

Sadek remembered that there were robbers in the desert, and his heart sank, but he said nothing. Zechariah said without conviction:

'Could he be with Mr Yehya?'

The two young men shouted together clutching at the straw:

'Mr Yehya!'

But Zechariah mused unhappily:

'Why should he stay with him?'

They walked in silence to the edge of the desert, overcome with dark thoughts. Far away they heard a cock crow, but the sky grew no lighter because of the thick cloud. Sadek moaned, 'Where are you, Kassem?' The journey seemed useless, but they walked on until they stood in front of Yehya's hut which was sunk in sleep. Zechariah went up and banged on the door with his fist, till Yehya's voice came:

'Who's there?'

The door opened and a figure appeared, leaning on a stick. Zechariah said:

'Forgive us. We've come to ask about Kassem.'

Yehya said calmly:

'I've been expecting you.'

Their spirits revived for the first time, but at once they became anxious again. Zechariah asked:

'Have you any news about him?'

'He's inside, asleep.'

'Is he all right?'

'I hope so.' Then, trying to sound natural: 'He's all right now. But some of my neighbours, coming back from Otouf, found him at Hind's Rock, unconscious. They carried him to me and I splashed perfume on his face until he came to. But he seemed tired and I left him to rest, and soon he was fast asleep.'

Zechariah said reproachfully:

'If only you'd sent word to us.'

He said very gently:

'They came in the middle of the night; I couldn't find anyone to send to you.'

Sadek said:

'He must be ill.'

The old man said:

'He'll be better in the morning.'

Hassan said:

'Let's wake him, to be sure about him.'

But Yehya was firm:

'We must wait till he wakes up by himself.'


73 ✳ ✳ ✳ ✳ ✳ ✳ ✳ ✳ ✳ ✳ ✳ ✳ ✳ ✳ ✳ ✳ ✳ ✳ ✳

He was sitting up in bed, propping his back against the pillow, with the blanket pulled right up over his chest, and his eyes were thoughtful. Kamar was sitting at his feet, holding Ihsan in her arms. The baby was waving her arms and making strange little noises whose meaning nobody could tell. A fine thread of smoke was rising from the incense burning in the middle of the room, twirling and breaking and spreading, a fragrant secret. Kassem stretched his hand out to the bedside table and took the cup of caraway and sipped at it, then put it back, leaving only the dregs, while his wife talked to the baby and played with it. But the anxious looks she stole at her husband showed that her attention to the baby was only to disguise her feelings. At last she asked him:

'How are you now?'

He turned his head involuntarily towards the closed door, then looked back at her and said quietly:

'What I have is not an illness.'

She looked bewildered.

'I'm glad to hear that, but for God's sake tell me what it is.'

He seemed to hesitate for a while, then said:

'I don't know. No, that's not what I should say. I know the whole thing, but ... The fact is, I'm afraid the easy days have passed.'

Ihsan started crying suddenly. Kamar quickly gave her her nipple, then looked at him, searching anxiously to know more.

'Why?'

He sighed and said, pointing to his heart:

'I have a great secret here, too big for me to bear alone.'

She grew still more anxious and said:

226

'Tell me about it, Kassem.'

He sat back a little, his eyes serious and determined.

'I'll reveal it for the first time; you're the first person to hear it. But you must believe me; I'm telling nothing but the truth. Last night something extraordinary happened out there under Hind's Rock when I was alone in the desert and in the night.'

He swallowed hard. She encouraged him with a warm look. He went on:

'I was sitting looking at the crescent moon. Soon it was hidden by cloud and it went so dark that I thought of getting up when suddenly a voice said, close to me: "Good evening, Kassem!" I trembled at the shock; no noise or movement had preceeded it. I looked up and saw the shape of a man standing a step away from where I sat. I couldn't make out his face but I could see his white turban and the cloak that was wrapped round him. Hiding my confusion I said: "Good evening. Who are you?" He answered, but not something you'd expect . . .'

Kamar gave an anxious nod:

'Tell me: I can't wait to hear.'

'He said to me: "I am Kindil." I was surprised and said: "Excuse me, I . . ." but he interrupted me: "I'm Kindil, servant of Gebelawi." '

She shouted:

'What did he say?'

'He said: "I'm Kindil, servant of Gebelawi." '

She was so amazed that her nipple slipped from Ihsan's mouth. The baby's face puckered up ready to cry, but Kamar gave her back the nipple. She grew pale.

'Kindil, Gebelawi's servant! No one knows anything about Gebelawi's servants. The Trustee himself packs up the things needed at the Big House, and then his servants leave them in the garden of the Big House where one of Gebelawi's servants collects them.'

'Yes that's all the people in the alley know. But that's what he said to me.'

'And you believe him?'

'I stood up at once, partly out of politeness and partly to be ready to defend myself if need be. I asked him how I was to know he was telling the truth. He said calmly: "Follow me if you like, and watch me go into the Big House." My mind was set at rest and I said to myself: "I'll believe him so that he'll explain what he's doing." I didn't hide my delight at meeting him and I asked him how our ancestor is and what he does . . .'

'You said that!'

'Yes. For God's sake, listen. He told me our ancestor is well, but he said nothing more than that. Then I asked whether he knows what goes

227

on in the alley. He answered that he does know everything and is aware of every event, big or small, and that because of this he'd sent him to me.'

'To you!'

Kassem frowned his annoyance.

'That's what he said. It was obvious that I was astounded, but he took no notice and said: "Perhaps he chose you because of your wisdom on the day of the theft and your loyalty to your family. He informs you that all the people of the alley are equally his children, that the estate is equally their inheritance, that chiefs are an evil that must end and that the alley must become an extension of the Big House." Silence fell, and I seemed to have lost the power of speech. Looking up at him, I saw the clouds part to reveal the moon. I asked him politely: "Why does he inform me of this?" "So that you yourself can bring it about." '

'You!'

'That's what he said. I was going to ask him to explain, but he took leave of me and went off. I followed him, and I thought I saw him climb to the top of the wall overlooking the desert up a very long ladder, or something like that. I stood in amazement. Then I went back to where I had been, meaning to go to Mr Yehya's, but I fainted and only recovered my senses in his hut.'

There was silence in the room again, and Kamar did not take her astonished eyes off his face. Ihsan fell asleep as she sucked, and her head rested on her mother's arm. Kamar laid her gently on the bed, then looked again at her husband with anxious eyes and a pale face. From the alley came the raucous voice of Sawaaris insulting someone, and the cries and groans of the man who was being beaten up. Then Sawaaris's voice came again as he went off uttering warnings and threats. His victim shouted in a voice of anger and despair: 'Gebelawi!'

Kassem was upset by his wife's looks and wondered: 'What can she think of me?' And Kamar said to herself: 'He's a truthful man who's never lied to me. And why should he make up such a story? He's so honest. And he didn't want my money, although it would have been safe to get; why should he want the estate's money, which is so dangerous to get? I wonder whether the easy days have really passed?'

'Am I the first person you've told your secret to?'

He nodded. She went on:

'Kassem, our lives are one, and I care for you more than for myself. This secret of yours is dangerous, and you must see its consequences. But try hard to remember; did it really happen or was it a dream?'

He said with conviction, slightly indignant:

'It really happened. It was no dream.'

'They found you unconscious?'

'That was after the meeting.'

'Perhaps you've mixed things up.'

He groaned, suffering torment.

'I've mixed nothing up. The meeting was as plain as day.'

She hesitated a little, then asked:

'How do we know he's really Gebelawi's servant and his messenger to you? Why shouldn't he have been one of the many drunkards of our alley?'

He said stubbornly:

'I saw him climbing over the wall of the Big House.'

She sighed.

'There isn't a ladder in the alley that would reach half-way up the wall.'

'But I saw it.'

She was trapped but she refused to give in.

'Had you taken hashish?'

He looked gloomy.

'You don't believe me, Kamar. I can't make you believe me.'

She was upset.

'It's just that I'm afraid for you; you know what I mean. I'm afraid for you and our home, for our daughter and our happiness. I am wondering why he should've come to you and not to someone else, and why he can't carry out his wishes himself when he's the owner of the estate and the lord over everyone.'

He in his turn asked:

'And why did he go to Gebel and Rifaa?'

Her eyes widened, and the corners of her mouth tightened, like those of a child about to cry. She looked on in confusion. He said:

'You don't believe me, and I can't force you to believe me.'

She burst into tears and gave herself up to sobbing to escape from her thoughts. Kassem leaned over and took her hand and drew her towards him. He asked her gently:

'Why are you crying?'

She looked at him through her tears.

'Because I believe you, yes, I believe you. I'm afraid the easy days have passed.' Then, in a low, anxious voice: 'What are you going to do?'


# 74 ✳ ✳ ✳ ✳ ✳ ✳ ✳ ✳ ✳ ✳ ✳ ✳ ✳ ✳ ✳ ✳ ✳ ✳ ✳

The atmosphere in the drawing-room was charged with dismay and tension. Zechariah was frowning, deep in thought. Owayss kept fiddling with his moustache. Hassan seemed to be talking to himself. Sadek could not take his eyes off the face of his friend Kassem. Kamar was in the corner of the room praying to God to lead them all aright. The coffee cups were empty, and two flies had begun buzzing round them. Kamar called Sekina to fetch the tray, and she came and picked it up and went out, shutting the door behind her. Owayss said, puffing:

'What a nerve-racking secret!'

A dog howled in the alley, as though hit by a stone or stick. A date seller cried his wares in a loud, sing-song voice. An old woman shouted wretchedly: 'Oh God, deliver us from this life!' Zechariah turned to Owayss saying:

'Mr Owayss, you're the most important of us. Tell us what you think.'

Owayss looked from Zechariah to Kassem and said:

'Kassem's a real man, and there aren't many of them. But his story's made my head spin.'

Sadek had been bursting to speak for some time:

'He tells the truth. I bet no one can think of a lie that he's told. He's to be trusted; I swear it by my mother's grave.'

Hassan said:

'That goes for me too. He'll always find me at his side.'

Kassem smiled for the first time, gratefully, looking admiringly at his strongly built cousin. But Zechariah gave his son a critical look, and said:

'This business is no game. Think of our lives and our safety.'

Owayss nodded his head in agreement:

'You're right. No one's ever heard anything like we've heard today.'

Kassem said:

'They did. They heard that and more from Gebel and Rifaa.'

Owayss was shocked.

'Do you think you're like Gebel and Rifaa?'

Kassem looked down unhappily and Kamar gazed at him anxiously. She said:

'Uncle! Who knows how these things happen?'

Owayss fiddled with his moustache again. Zechariah said:

'What's the good of his thinking he's like Gebel and Rifaa? Rifaa died the worst of deaths, and Gebel would have been killed if his people hadn't united behind him. And who do you have, Kassem? Have you forgotten that our quarter is called the Jerboas' quarter and that most of its people are either beggars or paupers?'

Sadek said with feeling:

'Don't forget that Gebelawi has chosen *him*, and not someone from the other quarters with their chiefs. I don't suppose he'll abandon him when things are difficult.'

Zechariah said angrily:

'That's what they said about Rifaa, and Rifaa was killed a stone's throw from Gebelawi's house.'

Kamar cautioned them:

'Don't talk too loud.'

Owayss stole a glance at Kassem, thinking: 'How amazing, this shepherd that my niece has made into a lord! I admit he's truthful and trustworthy, but is that enough to make a Gebel or a Rifaa of him? Do great men come so easily? And what would happen if his dreams came true?' Out loud he said:

'It's plain that Kassem won't listen to our warnings. I wonder what the boy wants? Is he worried that our quarter alone remains without a share of the estate? Kassem, do you want to be the chief and trustee of our quarter?'

Kassem looked angry.

'He didn't tell me *that*. He just said all the people of the alley are equally his children, that the estate is equally their inheritance, and that the chiefs' ways are an evil.'

Sadek's eyes shone, as did Hassan's. Owayss was taken aback, but Zechariah said:

'Do you know what that means?'

Owayss said furiously:

'Tell him.'

'You're challenging the Trustee's power and the cudgels of Lehita, Galta, Haggaag and Sawaaris.'

Kamar went pale. Kassem said quietly:

'That's right.'

Owayss laughed, annoying Kassem, Sadek and Hassan. Zechariah took no notice, but went on:

'It'll be the death of us all. We'll be trodden on like ants. No one'll believe you. They didn't believe the man who met Gebelawi, nor the man who heard his voice and talked to him; how can they believe a man he's sent one of his servants to?'

Owayss said in a new tone:

'Never mind what the stories say. No one saw the meeting of Gebelawi and Gebel, nor Gebelawi and Rifaa. Those accounts are handed down, but there were no witnesses. And yet they brought benefits to the people concerned, and Gebel's quarter became what it is, and so did Rifaa's. Our quarter has a right to the same thing, why not? We're all descended from that man who is hidden away in his Big House. But we must handle the thing sensibly and carefully. Think of your own quarter, Kassem; stop this talk of children and equality and what's right and what's wrong. It'll be easy to get Sawaaris on our side as he's your relation. We could make an agreement with him to let us have a share of the revenue.'

Kassem scowled.

'Mr Owayss, you're in another world from us. I don't want any bargain or any share of the revenue. I've set my heart on carrying out our ancestor's wishes as I was told them.'

Zechariah groaned:

'Oh God!'

Kassem went on frowning. He remembered his times of sadness and solitude, and his conversations with his teacher Yehya. He remembered how relief had come to him through a servant he had never met before, and how new horizons had opened out; now Zechariah thought only of safety and Owayss of the revenue. Life would only be good when they faced the new horizon. He sighed and said:

'Uncle. I had to begin by consulting you all, but I'm not going to ask anything of you.'

Sadek seized his hand.

'I'm with you.'

Hassan clenched his fist.

'I'm with you too, through thick and thin.'

Zechariah said:

'Don't be deceived by the words of these children. When the cudgels are lifted the bolt-holes will be full of people like them. For whose sake are you exposing yourself to death? There are only beasts and vermin in our alley. You have the means to live in ease and luxury; be sensible and enjoy life.'

Kassem wondered what the man was saying; it was as if he were listening to some of his own thoughts: 'Your daughter . . . your wife . . . your house . . . yourself! But you've been chosen, as Gebel and Rifaa were; let your answer be like theirs.' He said:

'I thought for a long time, uncle; then I chose my path.'

Owayss struck his hands together in dismay and exclaimed:

'God Almighty! The weak will mock you and the strong will kill you.'

Kamar looked in dismay from her uncle to her husband's uncle, upset by Kassem's disappointment, and at the same time afraid for him of the consequences if he persisted in his views. She said to Owayss:

'Uncle, you're the most important man round here; you could use your influence to help him.'

But Owayss said:

'What do you want, Kamar? You have your money and your daughter and your husband; why should you care whether the estate is shared out to everyone or kept by the powerful? We reckon that a man who aims to be a chief is mad; what do you think of someone who aims to be trustee of the whole alley?'

Kassem jumped up and said:

'I am not aiming at any such thing; I only want the good that our ancestor wants.'

Owayss tried to appease him with a forced smile.

'Where is he? Let him come out, even if he has to be carried, and put into effect the conditions of his endowment as he wishes. Do you think anyone, however powerful, could look Gebelawi in the eye if he spoke, or raised a finger against him?'

Zechariah added to this:

'And if the chiefs attack us, will he move an inch to help us, or even care what happens to us?'

Kassem said miserably:

'I haven't insisted on anyone believing me or backing me up.'

Zechariah went over to him and put his hand affectionately on his shoulder.

'Kassem, you've been touched by the Evil Eye. I know these things. People have kept talking about your sense and your good luck, until the Evil Eye has got you. Fly to God from Satan. Realize that today you are one of the big men in our quarter; if you want, you can trade with some of your wife's money and enjoy great wealth. Give up your ideas and be content with the goods and pleasures God has given you.'

Kassem bowed his head in sorrow, then looked up at his uncle and said with determination:

'I wouldn't give up my ideas, even if I alone possessed the whole estate.'

## 75

'What are you going to do? How long are you going to think and wait, and what are you waiting for? As long as your relations won't believe you, who ever will believe you? What's the use of being sad? What's the point of sitting alone under Hind's Rock? The stars don't answer, nor the darkness, nor the moon. It seems you hope to meet the servant again; but what new thing do you expect from him? You wander in the dark around the spot where it is said that Gebelawi met Gebel. You stand for hours beneath the great wall in the place where he is said to have spoken to Rifaa. But you have not seen him or heard his voice, nor has his servant returned. What are you going to do? That question will pursue you, as the desert sun pursues the shepherd. All the time it will rob you of your peace of mind, of the pleasure of good things. Gebel was alone, like you, and yet he triumphed; and Rifaa knew his path and followed it until he was killed, and then he triumphed. What are you going to do?'

233

Kamar said to him reproachfully:

'You neglect your beautiful baby girl terribly. She cries and you don't comfort her; she plays and you don't play with her.'

He smiled at the little face, and it consoled him for his raging thoughts. He murmured:

'How sweet she is!'

'Even when you're sitting with us, you're far away, as though we were just anyone.'

He moved closer to her on the sofa and kissed her cheek, then kissed the child's face several times. He said:

'Don't you see that I need your sympathy?'

'You have my heart, and all the sympathy and love that are in it. But you must spare yourself.'

She handed him the baby and he hugged it and began rocking it and listening to its croonings. Suddenly he said:

'If God grants me victory, I shan't stop women from sharing the income of the estate.'

'But the estate is for men only, not women.'

He gazed into the baby's eyes'

'Our ancestors told me through his servant that the estate belongs to everyone. Half the people are women; it is amazing that the alley doesn't respect them; but it shall respect them on the day that it knows the meaning of justice and mercy.'

She felt both love and dismay and she said to herself: 'He talks of victory; how distant we are from this victory!' She longed to advise him to do what was safe and peaceful, but her courage gave way. She wondered what tomorrow held in store for them. Would she have the good fortune of Shafika, Gebel's wife, or would she suffer the fate of Abda, Rifaa's mother? She trembled, and looked away so that he would not see anything in her eyes to alarm him.

When Sadek and Hassan came to take him to the café, he proposed that they should all visit Yehya, so that he could introduce them to him. When they reached his hut they found him smoking his pipe, and smelt the rich fragrance of hashish. Kassem presented his friends to him and they all sat down in the doorway, with the full moon shining down through a window. Yehya looked in amazement at the three faces as if he were wondering, are these really the people who are going to turn the alley upside down? He began telling Kassem, as he had already done several times:

'Mind you don't let anyone know your secret before you're ready.'

The delicious pipe went round. The moonlight coming through the window fell on Kassem's head and touched Sadek's shoulder, while the charcoal glowed in the darkness. Kassem asked:

'How can I get ready?'

The old man laughed and said playfully:

'It's not right for someone chosen by Gebelawi to ask advice from an old man like me.'

Silence fell, broken only by the gurgle of the pipe. Then Yehya said:

'You have your uncle and your wife's uncle. Now your own uncle will be neither a help nor a hindrance, but you could bring the other one over to your side if you gave him something to hope for.'

'What hope can I give him?'

'Promise him the trusteeship of the Jerboas.'

Sadek said fervently:

'No one is to have any special share of the estate's revenue; it's everyone's inheritance equally, as Gebelawi said.'

Yehya laughed.

'What an amazing old man! With Gebel it was strength, with Rifaa mercy, and today it's something else.'

Kassem said:

'He's the owner of the estate; he has a right to make changes in the ten conditions.'

'But you have a hard task, my son; it involves the whole alley, not just one quarter.'

'Such is the will of Gebelawi.'

Yehya was shaken by a fit of coughing that winded him, and Hassan took over the tending of the pipe from him. Yehya stretched out his legs, wheezing loudly, then asked:

'Will you rely on force, like Gebel, or will you choose love, like Rifaa?'

Kassem ran his hand over his turban.

'Force when necessary and love always.'

Yehya nodded and smiled.

'Your only fault is your interest in the estate; it will lead to endless troubles for you.'

'How can people live without it?'

The old man said proudly:

'As Rifaa lived.'

Kassem said seriously and politely:

'He lived with the help of his father and those who loved him, and he left behind followers who were none of them able to follow his example. The fact is that our miserable alley needs honour and purity.'

'Is the estate necessary for that?'

'Oh yes, Mr Yehya; the estate and the destruction of the chiefs' power; then we'll achieve the honour that Gebel gave to his people, and the love that Rifaa called for; more than that, the happiness that Adham dreamed of.'

Yehya laughed.

'What have you left for those who come after you?'

Kassem thought for a while, then said:

'If God gives me victory, the alley won't need anyone else after me.'

The heavenly pipe went round, and the water sang in its bulb. Yehya yawned contentedly and said:

'What will be left for any of you when the revenue of the estate has been shared out equally?'

Sadek said:

'We only want the estate in order to use it, so that the alley will become an extention of the Big House.'

A passing cloud hid the moon, but in a minute the light returned. Yehya looked at Hassan's sturdy body and said:

'Will your cousin be able to defeat the chiefs?'

Kassem said:

'I'm thinking of consulting a lawyer.'

Yehya raised his voice:

'What lawyer could challenge Rifaat the Trustee and his chiefs?'

Dazed by hashish, they sank into a thoughtful silence. The three went home in something of a stupor.


Kassem suffered bitter torment in his solitary meditations. He was so anxious that Kamar one day said to him:

'We mustn't be so concerned for other people's happiness that we make ourselves miserable.'

'I must justify the faith that has been put in me.'

'What are you going to do? Why don't you draw back from the brink of this abyss, this graveyard of dreams?'

But one day he invited Sadek and Hassan round and said to them:

'It's time for us to begin.'

Their faces shone. Hassan said:

'What do you have in mind?'

'After much thought I've decided to start a sports club.'

They were tongue-tied. He smiled and went on:

'We shall have it in the courtyard of this house.'

'And what does it have to do with our task?'

'A club for things like weight-lifting! ... What does that have to do with the estate?'

Kassem's eyes shone.

'The young men will come to us because they love games of strength, and we'll be able to choose the ones who are sound and suitable.'

Their eyes opened wide. Hassan shouted:

'They'll make a team, and what a team!'
'Yes; and young men from Gebel and Rifaa will come to us.'
They were all overcome with joy, and Kassem almost danced along.

## 76 ✳ ✳ ✳ ✳ ✳ ✳ ✳ ✳ ✳ ✳ ✳ ✳ ✳ ✳ ✳ ✳ ✳ ✳ ✳

Kassem sat beside the window watching the people of the alley celebrate the festival with their usual enthusiasm. The water carriers had sprinkled the ground from their water skins, and the necks and tails of the donkeys had been decorated with paper flowers. The air was bright with the colours of the children's clothes and balloons. Little flags were fixed on the hand carts. There was a babble of shouts and cheers mingled with the music of reed pipes. The pony traps swayed along, carrying men and women dancers. The shops were shut, and the cafés and taverns and hashish dens were packed. Everywhere people were smiling and wishing each other well.

Kassem sat, wearing a new smock and holding Ihsan, who stood on his knees. She explored his features with her little fingers and clung to him. A voice sang under the window:

'When I was snared by love, it was with these eyes.'

He at once remembered his wedding and his heart melted. He loved music and song. How Adham had longed to sing in the garden! And now what was the man singing on this festival? 'When I was snared by love, it was with these eyes.' How true that was; since he had looked up at Kindil in the darkness, he had been robbed of his heart and mind and will. And now the courtyard of his house had been turned into a club for building bodies and purifying minds, and he too was lifting weights and learning to fence with sticks. Sadek added strong arm muscles to the strong leg muscles he had developed at the metal-beater's. As for Hassan, he was just a giant. The others too were very enthusiastic. Sadek one day had the excellent idea that they should invite the beggars and the jobless to the club. In no time they were taking a great interest in the games, and also in what he had to say. Of course, few of them came, but because of their zeal they were a match for many times their number.

Ihsan squeaked 'Da! Da!' and he kissed her several times. She wet the corner of his new smock. From the kitchen he could hear the pounding of mortar and pestle, the voices of Kamar and Sekina, and the miaowing of the cat. A pony trap passed under the window and the people in it were singing:

A prayer for the soldier if you please;
He took off his cap and now he's a saint.

Kassem smiled, remembering the night that Yehya had sung this song, completely drunk. 'If only things were put straight, you would have nothing to do but sing, dear alley. Tomorrow the club will be full of firm allies; tomorrow I shall challenge the Trustee and the chiefs and attack our troubles, so that there will remain only a kind father and his loyal children. Poverty, filth, begging, tyranny will be wiped out. The vermin the flies, the cudgels will disappear. All will be peaceful in the shade of lovely gardens.'

He was wakened from his dreams by Kamar's voice railing at Sekina. He listened in astonishment and called his wife. She burst in, pushing the servant in front of her and saying:

'Look at this woman. She was born in this house, like her mother before her, and yet she spies on us!'

He looked disapprovingly at Sekina. She shouted in her husky voice:

'I'm not a traitor, master, but my mistress is unkind.'

Kamar said, unable to hide her fear:

'She smiled and said to me: "The next time the feast comes, please God, Mr Kassem will be master of the whole alley, as Gebel was of Hamdaan's quarter." Ask her what she means.'

Kasem frowned anxiously.

'What do you mean, Sekina?'

'I mean what I say. I'm not an ordinary servant, here today and gone tomorrow. I've grown up in this house; it wasn't right of you to hide a secret from me.'

Kassem exchanged a quick glance with his wife and pointed at the child. She came and took her from him. He told the servant to sit down, and she sat at his feet, saying:

'Was it right for people outside to know your secret when I knew nothing?'

'What secret do you mean?'

'What Kindil said to you at Hind's Rock . . .'

Kamar gasped, but Kassem signed Sekina to go on.

'. . . just as he spoke to Gebel and Rifaa before. You're not a lesser man than them, master, you're a lord. I was the go-between who brought you two together, you remember; I ought to have known before anyone else. How can you trust strangers and not trust me, your servant? God forgive you! But I pray for your victory, yes, I pray for your victory over the Trustee and the chiefs – who would not pray for that?'

Kamar exclaimed, rocking the baby nervously:

'It wasn't right for you to spy on us. You won't live it down.'

'I didn't mean to eavesdrop, God knows, but I heard something through the door and couldn't help listening. It would have been more than anyone could do to close my ears to that. What breaks my heart,

238

mistress, is that you don't trust me. I'm not a traitor; and you're the last person I would betray. For whose sake would I betray you? God forgive you, mistress.'

Kassem studied her carefully. When she had finished, he said gently:

'You're loyal, Sekina; there's no doubt about your loyalty.'

She looked up at him and murmured:

'Long may you live, master; I am that, by God.'

He said quietly:

'I know who's loyal; treachery isn't going to grow in my house as it did in that of my brother Rifaa. Kamar, this woman's as loyal as you are; don't think badly of her. She belongs to us as we belong to her, and I'll never forget that she was the messenger of happiness to me.'

Kamar sounded somewhat appeased as she said:

'But she eavesdropped.'

'She didn't exactly eavesdrop; our voices reached her by the will of God, just as Rifaa heard our ancestor's voice without taking steps to do so. You've been blessed, Sekina.'

The servant seized his hand and covered it with kisses.

'My soul is your ransom, master. By God, you'll triumph over your enemies and our enemies and rule over the whole alley.'

'It isn't our wish to rule, Sekina.'

She stretched out her arms in prayer.

'Oh, God, grant his wishes.'

'Amen.'

He looked at her and smiled.

'You shall be my messenger when I need one, and in that way you'll take part in our work.'

Her face shone with joy, and her eyes were full of pride. He added:

'If fate allows the estate to be shared out as we wish, no woman shall be deprived of it, whether lady or maid.'

Sekina was tongue-tied. He went on:

'The Founder said the estate is for everyone, and you, Sekina, are the Founder's daughter just as much as Kamar.'

Her face was full of joy and she gazed up gratefully at her master. From the alley came the notes of a pipe. Someone shouted: 'Lehita . . . a thousand greetings!' Kassem turned towards the road and saw the chiefs in procession down the road on decked-out horses, and the people greeted them with cheers and gifts. Then they went off into the desert as usual on feast days, for racing and mock fights.

No sooner had their procession gone than Agrama appeared outside, staggering along drunk. Kassem smiled to see the boy, whom he counted one of the most honest young men in the club. He watched him come to the middle of the Jerboas' quarter, where he stood and shouted:

'I'm a fine fellow.'

A sneering voice came from the nearest house in Rifaa's quarter:

'You handsome Jerboa rat!'

Agrama raised two bloodshot eyes towards the window and yelled drunkenly:

'It's our turn, you bastards!'

A crowd of boys and drunks gathered round him amid a great noise of singing and howling and drums and pipes. A voice shouted:

'Listen . . . It's the Jerboas' turn . . . Don't you want to listen?'

Agrama yelled, swaying about:

'One ancestor for everyone . . . One estate for everyone . . . Good-bye chiefs!'

Then he disappeared in the crowd. In a moment Kassem was on his feet, grabbing his cloak. He rushed out of the room, saying:

'Damn liquor and everything to do with it!'


77 ✳ ✳ ✳ ✳ ✳ ✳ ✳ ✳ ✳ ✳ ✳ ✳ ✳ ✳ ✳ ✳ ✳ ✳ ✳ ✳

'Don't go out drunk,' said Kassem, frowning. He was sitting beneath Hind's Rock looking round the faces of his close friends from the club: Sadek and Hassan, Agrama and Shaaban, Abou Fasaada and Hamroush. Behind them towered the gebel, over which night was falling. The desert was empty, but for a shepherd leaning on his staff far away to the south. Agrama was downcast.

'I wish I'd died before that happened.'

'There are some mistakes it's no use being sorry for. I think the important thing now is to know how much your raving has affected our enemies.'

Sadek said:

'It has certainly been widely heard.'

Hassan said gloomily:

'I found that myself in Gebel's café where a Gebelite friend had invited me. I heard a man telling the story about Agrama in a loud voice and laughing scornfully. I shan't be surprised if the story makes some people suspicious, and I'm afraid it will go from mouth to mouth till one of the chiefs hears it.'

Agrama moaned:

'Don't exaggerate, Hassan.'

Sadek said:

'It is better to exaggerate than to underrate. Otherwise we'll be caught off guard.'

240

Agrama said:

'We've sworn not to fear death.'

Sadek added:

'Just as we've sworn to keep the secret.'

Kassem said:

'If we die now, all hope will be lost.'

The silence and the darkness deepened. Kassem spoke again:

'We must organize things.'

Hassan said:

'In our plans we must assume the very worst.'

Kassem said sadly:

'That means a fight.'

They exchanged glances in the dark. Above them the stars came out one by one, and a breeze blew, still containing some of the warmth of day. Hamroush said:

'We shall fight to the death.'

Kassem was annoyed.

'And things will remain as they were.'

Sadek said:

'They would finish us off so quickly.'

Abou Fassada said to Kassem:

'Luckily there are family links between you and Sawaaris, and also between your wife and the Trustee's wife; besides, Lehita was one of your father's friends in his youth.'

'That might perhaps put off the end, but it couldn't stop it from coming.'

Sadek asked hopefully:

'Do you remember you once thought of taking the matter to a lawyer?'

'And we were told no lawyer would dare challenge the Trustee and the chiefs.'

Agrama said, trying to make up for his misdeed:

'There's a lawyer at Bayt el Kadi known for his boldness.'

But Sadek backed down.

'What I'm most afraid of is letting everyone know our enmity by bringing the case. I think we're being afraid before we need be over the consequences of what Agrama's done.'

Agrama said:

'Let's consult the lawyer, and agree with him to put off bringing our case until we are forced to; then we can find someone to sponsor it for us, even if it is somebody from outside the alley.'

Kassem and the others agreed to take this precaution. They got up straight away and went to the office of Shanafri, the religious-court lawyer at Bayt el Kadi. The sheikh met them, and Kassem explained their problem and told him that they meant to put off opening the case till a later date, but that the lawyer should make a study of the question and prepare the necessary measures. Contrary to what most of them expected, the lawyer accepted the case and took part of his fee in advance, and they went off delighted. They split up, and Kassem went to Yehya while his friends went back to the alley. Kassem and Yehya sat together in the doorway of the hut, smoking and exchanging views. The old man seemed sad at what had happened and told Kassem to be on his guard. After that Kassem went home, and when Kamar opened the door to him the look in her face disturbed him. He asked what was wrong and she said:

'His honour the Trustee has sent for you.'

Kassem's heart pounded.

'When?'

'The last time was ten minutes ago.'

'The last time!'

'He's sent for you three times in an hour.'

Her eyes were full of tears. He said:

'This is not what I expect from you.'

She wailed:

'Don't go.'

He turned calmly to go.

'It's safer to go than to stay away. Don't forget that those thieves won't attack anyone in their own houses.'

Ihsan cried inside the house and Sekina hurried to her. Kamar said:

'Put off going till I've seen Lady Amina.'

He said with determination:

'That wouldn't be worthy of us. I'll go at once. There's no cause for fear; none of them knows anything about me.'

She clung to him.

'He sent for you, not Agrama; I'm afraid one of them has given you away.'

He broke away from her gently.

'I told you from the beginning the easy days have passed. We all know we must face trouble sooner or later. Don't be so upset. Look after yourself till I get back.'

242

The gatekeeper came back from the Trustee's house and said to Kassem brusquely:

'Come in.'

He led the way, and Kassem followed, trying his utmost to control his feelings. The pure scents of the garden met him but he did not notice them. They reached the entrance to the drawing-room, the gatekeeper stepped aside, and in he went, more in possession of himself than he'd ever been. He saw the Trustee in front of him, sitting on a divan at the far end of the room. Two men sat on chairs, one on each side of him, but Kassem could hardly make them out and did not try to look closely at them. He went up and stood a few feet from the Trustee's seat, raised his hand in greeting and said politely:

'Good evening, your honour.'

He glanced at the man sitting on his right, and saw Lehita, looking at the other man, he could not help staring; the shock nearly shattered him: the man was none other than Sheikh Shanafri, the lawyer. Kassem realized the gravity of the situation; his secret was out, the despicable lawyer had betrayed his trust and he was trapped. Despair mixed with rage in his heart. He realized that cunning and trickery could not save him, and so he decided to defy them. It was impossible to withdraw, so he had to advance or at least stand firm. In later days he came to think of this occasion as marking the birth of a new personality in him, whose existence he had never imagined.

The Trustee's harsh voice brought him back to his senses.

'You are Kassem?'

Kassem's voice was natural.

'Yes, sir.'

The Trustee went on without asking him to sit down.

'Are you surprised to see this gentleman?'

'Not at all, sir.'

'You are the shepherd?'

'I stopped being a shepherd more than two years ago.'

'What do you do now?'

'I'm the manager of my wife's property.'

The Trustee nodded scornfully and motioned to the lawyer to speak. He addressed Kassem:

'Perhaps you are surprised at my position, considering I'm your lawyer, but his honour the Trustee is above all such considerations. My action gives you the chance to withdraw; that will be better than getting embroiled in hostilities that would lead to your destruction. His honour the Trustee has given me leave to tell you that I have interceded with him to pardon you if you announce your withdrawal. I hope you'll appreciate my good intentions. Here is your advance fee, which I'm giving back to you.'

Kassem eyed him coldly.

'Why didn't you tell me the truth when I was in your office?'

The lawyer was taken aback by his boldness, but the Trustee came to his rescue.

'You are here to answer questions, not to ask them.'

The lawyer got up and asked leave to go. He went out adjusting his gown to hide his embarrassment. Then the Trustee examined Kassem with hard eyes and almost spat out the words:

'How did you persuade yourself to start bringing a case against me?'

He was trapped: either fight or be killed. But he did not know what to say. The Trustee said:

'Speak up; tell me what you're up to. Are you mad?'

Kassem said quietly:

'I'm sane, thank God.'

'That seems to be in doubt. How dare you embark on your foul action against me? You haven't been poor since that mad woman took you for a husband. What did you want out of your action?'

Kassem sighed as if to prevent himself from getting angry.

'I don't want anything for myself.'

The Trustee looked at Lehita, then back at Kassem, and shouted:

'Then why did you do as you have done?'

'I only wanted justice.'

The Trustee's eyes narrowed.

'Do you think your wife's connection with mine will protect you?'

Kassem looked down.

'Oh no, sir.'

'Are you capable of taking on all the chiefs in the alley?'

'Not at all, sir.'

The Trustee screamed:

'Say you're mad and have done.'

'I'm sane, thank God.'

'Who do you want justice for?'

He thought hard as he said:

'For everyone.'

The Trustee peered at him incredulously and said:

'What's that to do with you?'

Kassem replied, intoxicated with courage:

'In that way the Founder's conditions will be realized.'

The Trustee screamed:

'You rat! You talk of the Founder's conditions?'

244

'He's the ancestor of us all.'

The Trustee leapt up and struck Kassem in the face with all his might with his horsehair fly-whisk. He yelled:

'Your ancestor! None of you even knows who his own father was; yet you have the cheek to say "our ancestor". Thieves, rats, scum! You only persist because you think this household will protect you and your wife, but a dog loses its protection when it bites the hand that feeds it.'

Lehita stood up to calm the Trustee's rage. He said:

'Don't let him excite you; it's not right for you to be upset by a fly.'

Rifaat sat down, his lips trembling. He shouted:

'Even the Jerboas covet the estate and say without any shame, "our ancestor".'

Lehita sat down again, saying:

'Obviously it's true what they say about the Jerboas. Unfortunately the alley is racing towards destruction.' Then, turning to Kassem: 'Your father was one of my earliest companions; don't force me to kill you.'

The Trustee bellowed:

'His action deserves worse than death. If it wasn't for my wife, he'd die right now.'

Lehita went on with the interrogation.

'Listen to me, young man; who is behind you?'

Kassem said, still feeling the sting of the fly-whisk:

'What do you mean, sir?'

'Who made you bring the case?'

'Only myself.'

'You were a shepherd and then you had good luck; what more do you want?'

'Justice, sir.'

The Trustee ground his teeth and shouted:

'Justice? Dogs! Villains! That's your password when you are bent on stealing and plundering.' Then, to Lehita; 'Force him to confess.'

Lehita said threatening:

'Who is behind you?'

With strange defiance, Kassem said:

'Our ancestor.'

'Our ancestor?'

'Yes. Look at the conditions of his endowment; you will realize that he's the one who made me act.'

Rifaat leapt up again, shouting:

'Get him out of my sight. Throw him out.'

Lehita got up and seized Kassem by the arm and led him towards the door. Kassem bore the iron grip bravely. Then Lehita hissed in his ear:

'For your own sake, think. Don't force me to drink your blood.'

245

Kassem went home and found there Zechariah, Owayss, Hassan, Sadek, Agrama, Shaaban, Abou Fassada and Hamroush. They looked up at him, anxious and silent. When he had sat down beside his wife, Owayss said:

'Didn't I warn you?'

Kamar reproached him:

'Wait, uncle, let him rest a bit.'

But he bellowed:

'The worst troubles are the ones a man brings on himself.'

Zechariah began studying Kassem's face, then said:

'They insulted you, my child; I know you as well as I know myself. You could have done without that.'

Owayss said:

'But for Lady Amina you wouldn't have come back in one piece.'

Kassem looked round his friends' faces, and said:

'That vile lawyer betrayed us.'

Their faces hardened and they looked at one another angrily, but Owayss spoke before any of them could:

'Split up quietly now; and thank God for his escape.'

Hassan said:

'What do you say, cousin?'

Kassem thought for a while, then said:

'I won't hide it from you that death threatens us. I'll release anyone who doesn't wish to help me any more.'

Zechariah said:

'Don't let things go any further.'

'I am not going to drop the matter, whatever the consequences. I shall not be less loyal to our ancestor and to the alley than Gebel and Rifaa.'

Owayss got up in a rage and stalked out of the room, saying:

'The man's mad. God help you, my niece.'

Sadek leapt across and kissed Kassem on the forehead.

'You've revived my spirits with what you've said.'

Hassan said:

'The people here kill for the sake of a piastre or for no reason at all. Why should we be afraid of dying, when we have a real reason?'

Sawaaris's voice came from the alley, calling Zechariah, who leaned out of the window and invited him in. In a moment he had come into the room and sat down scowling grimly. He looked at Kassem and said:

'I didn't know there was another chief in our quarter besides me.'

Zechariah said anxiously:

246

'Things are not as you have heard.'

'What I heard was even worse.'

Zechariah moaned:

'Satan has tampered with the minds of our young men.'

'Lehita gave me a long lecture about your nephew. I thought he was a sensible boy, but he turns out to be the wildest of madmen. Now look here; if I'm too easy on you all, Lehita's going to come and deal with you himself. But I'm not letting any of you drag my good name in the dirt, so behave yourselves, and heaven help anyone who's obstinate.'

Sawaaris began keeping a watch on Kassem's followers and not letting any of them go near his house. In the course of doing so he humiliated Sadek and beat up Abou Fassada. He asked Zechariah to tell Kassem to stay at home until the storm had blown over. Kassem found himself prisoner in his own house, visited only by his cousin Hassan. But there was no power that could keep the news from getting about. Whispers reached Gebel's quarter and Rifaa's, telling what was stirring among the Jerboas: the case that had nearly been brought against the Trustee, allegations that had been made about the ten conditions, even the connection between Kindil, servant of Gebelawi, and Kassem. There was great excitement and plenty of scepticism and scorn.

Hassan said to Kassem one day:

'The news is being whispered around. They talk about nothing but you in all the hashish dens.'

Kassem looked up, his face, as usual of late, haggard with anxiety and thought. He said:

'We've become prisoners, and the days pass without action.'

Kamar said:

'No one is called on to do the impossible.'

Hassan said:

'Our brothers are as keen as can be.'

Kassem asked:

'Is it true that the Gebelites and Rifaaites accuse me of being a liar and a madman?'

Hassan looked down unhappily.

'Cowardice ruins men.'

Kassem nodded.

'Why do the Gebelites and Rifaaites call me a liar when among them was the man who met Gebelawi and the man he spoke to? Why do they call me a liar when they of all people should be the first to believe me and back me up?'

'Cowardice is the plague of our alley; that's why they cringe before their chiefs.'

From outside came the sound of Sawaaris bellowing curses and insults. The family looked out of the window and saw Sawaaris grabbing Shaaban by the collar and screaming at him:

'What brings you here, you bastard?'

The young man tried in vain to free himself from his grip. Sawaaris held his collar with his left hand and rained blows on his face and head with his right. Kassem was furious and left the window and hurried to the door, ignoring Kamar's pleas. In a moment he was standing in front of Sawaaris.

'Let him go, Mr Sawaaris.'

But he didn't stop punching his victim and shouted at Kassem:

'Mind yourself or I'll make your enemies cry for you.'

Kassem seized his right hand and gripped it tightly, shouting furiously:

'I won't let you kill him whatever you do.'

Sawaaris let go of Shaaban, who fell to the ground unconscious, and then snatched a basket of earth off the head of a passing woman and emptied it over Kassem. Hassan was about to spring at him, but Zechariah arrived just in time to throw an arm round him. Kassem lifted off the basket, and his head emerged, covered with earth, which went all over his clothes too. He was seized with a fit of coughing. Kamar and Sekina screamed, Owyss hurried up, men, women and children rushed out from doorways on to the scene, and there was uproar. Zechariah held on to Hassan's arm with all his strength and looked pleadingly into his large eyes. Owayss went up to Sawaaris and said:

'Forgive him for my sake, Mr Sawaaris.'

Several voices cried: 'For God's sake, chief!' and Sawaaris bawled:

'What with relatives and friends! It's as if Sawaaris was a woman and not your chief.'

Zechariah shouted:

'God forbid, Chief; you're our lord and master.'

Sawaaris went off to the café, and some men lifted up Shaaban, and Hassan began brushing the earth off Kassem's head and clothes. With Sawaaris out of the way, the crowd were able to express their grief.

80 ✳ ✳ ✳ ✳ ✳ ✳ ✳ ✳ ✳ ✳ ✳ ✳ ✳ ✳ ✳ ✳ ✳ ✳ ✳

That evening wails from one of the Jerboas' houses announced that someone had died. The cry was taken up by dozens of voices in the quarter. Kassem looked out of his window and asked Fatin, the melonseed seller, about it. The man answered: 'Long may you live! Shaaban is dead.' Kassem was horrified and left the house to go to Shaaban's which was two doors away. He found the courtyard there in darkness and packed with the people who lived in the downstairs rooms who were talking together sadly and indignantly, while from upstairs came sobs and wails. Kassem heard a woman saying bitterly:

'He didn't just die; he was murdered by Sawaaris.'

'The devil take Sawaaris.'

A third woman protested:

'It was Kassem who murdered him; he tells lies and our men get killed for them.'

Kassem was deeply distressed. He made his way through the darkness up to the first floor, where the dead man's rooms were. By the light of a lamp fixed to the wall of the passage he saw his friends, among them Hassan, Sadek, Agrama, Abou Fassada and Hamroush. Sadek came to meet him, crying, and they embraced without a word. Hassan, whose face looked ghastly in the dim light, said:

'His blood will not have been spilt in vain.'

Agrama came up to Kassem and whispered to him:

'His wife's in a dreadful state; she even accused us of killing him.'

Kassem whispered back:

'God help her.'

Hassan said:

'The murderer must be killed.'

Abou Fassada growled:

'Who is there that would give evidence against him?'

Hassan said:

'But we can kill like everyone else.'

Kassem punched him to silence him, and said:

'It'll be wisest for you all not to join in his funeral, but we'll meet in the Karafa graveyard.'

He went towards the dead man's lodgings and Sadek tried to bar his way, but he pushed him aside and went in. He called Shaaban's widow and she came out and looked at him in astonishment with her reddened eyes. Her look hardened, and she asked:

'What do you want?'

'I've come to offer you my condolences.'

'You killed him. We could so easily do without the estate, and we needed him so much.'

'May God give you strength to bear it, and may He destroy the wicked. We are your family whenever you need us. His blood isn't spilt in vain.'

She looked askance at him, then turned and retreated. When she got back inside there was an outburst of wails and moans. He left the place grief-stricken.

Next morning the people saw Sawaaris sitting in the doorway of

Dongol's café watching the passers-by with a defiant, evil look on his face. They greeted him with extra servility to hide their anger. They avoided going to the wake, skulking in their shops or by their barrows or sitting on the ground. Later in the morning the bier was carried out, followed only by the family and close relatives, and by Kassem, who ignored the chief's furious looks. The dead man's brother-in-law was angry and said to Kassem:

'You kill the man and then attend his funeral!'

He bore this in silence until someone else asked:

'Why did you come?'

'No murder was more cruel than that of my friend, God rest his soul. He was brave. You're not like him; you know who killed him but you vent your anger on me.'

Most of them fell silent. The women gathered together behind the men, hurrying along with bare feet, dressed in black, pouring dust on their heads and beating their cheeks. The funeral passed through Gemalia towards Bab el Nasr. When the burial ceremony was over the mourners all went back, except Kassem, who walked on slowly until he was separated from them and then returned to the grave and found his friends waiting for him. His eyes swam with tears and they all began to cry. Kassem rubbed his eyes and said:

'Anyone who wants to be safe had better go.'

Hamroush said:

'If we had wanted to be safe, you wouldn't have found us round about you.'

Kassem put his hand on the tombstone.

'I'm very upset to have lost him. He was brave and enthusiastic, and he's gone just when we need him most.'

Sadek said:

'He was killed by a bastard. Some of us will live to see the death of the last chief in the alley.'

Hamroush said:

'But we mustn't get caught as our friend was. We must think about tomorrow, and how we can win our victory, and how we can meet.'

Kassem said:

'Thinking about that was my only consolation in my imprisonment. I've come to a conclusion; not an easy one, but there is no way out of it.'

They clamoured to hear it. He went on:

'Leave the alley. Each of us must make his arrangements and leave. We shall move out as Gebel did long ago, and as Mr Yehya did more recently. We must set up in some safe place in the desert until we have built up our strength and our numbers.'

Sadek exclaimed:

'That's the answer.'

'We can rid the alley of chiefs only by force, and we can carry out the Founder's conditions only by force, and justice and mercy and peace can reign only by force. Our force won't be tyrannous; it will be the first just force.'

They listened eagerly and felt as though Shaaban were listening with them and giving them his blessing. Agrama said feelingly:

'Yes. The problems will be solved by force; by just, not unjust force. Shaaban was on his way to you when Sawaaris accosted him; if we'd been with him the brute would have met with a force he couldn't easily have overcome. Damn fear and division.'

Kassem gave a sigh of relief and pleasure.

'Our ancestor has put his trust in us, in the certainty that some of his children are worthy of it.'


81 ✳ ✳ ✳ ✳ ✳ ✳ ✳ ✳ ✳ ✳ ✳ ✳ ✳ ✳ ✳ ✳ ✳ ✳ ✳

Kassem did not get home till midnight, but he found Kamar awake and waiting for him. She was even more worried about him and affectionate towards him than usual. He was sad that she should have stayed awake so long. Then he saw how tired and red her eyes were.

'Have you been crying?'

She did not answer, as though preoccupied with the milk she was heating up for him. He spoke again:

'The death of Shaaban, God rest his soul, has grieved us all.'

'I was crying for Shaaban before, but then I cried at that man's hatred for you; you're the last person to deserve earth poured over his head.'

'That's nothing compared to what happened to our poor friend.'

She sat down, beside him, handing him the mug of milk, and murmured:

'And I'm upset by the things they say about you.'

He smiled, pretending to make little of it, and raised the mug to his lips. She went on indignantly:

'Galta tells the Gebelites you want the estate for yourself, and Haggaag says the same to the Rifaaites, and they tell everyone you're far below Gebel and Rifaa.'

He did not hide his grief.

'I know; and I know I wouldn't be alive today if it wasn't for you.'

She caressed his shoulder tenderly, and began for no reason thinking of bygone days of endless conversations and happiness, the luminous nights of pleasure before Ihsan was born. And now she did not possess any of him; indeed, he did not possess himself. She even concealed from him the pains of the illness that troubled her from time to time. He did not think about himself so how could she trouble him with her problems? She was afraid of adding to his burden and helping his enemies without meaning to. Who could assure her of him when life was passing just as the days of ease had passed? God forgive you, old alley. Kassem said:

'I haven't lost hope, even at this dark hour. I have so many good friends, even if I seem alone. One of them defied Sawaaris; and who would have dared do that before? The others are like him, and courage is what the alley needs most if it isn't to live for ever under tyranny. Don't advise me to play safe; the man who's been killed was on his way to my house, and you wouldn't like your husband to be a mean coward.'

Kamar smiled, taking the empty mug. She said:

'The chiefs' wives screech with joy over battles, which are evil; how could I rejoice less over what is good.'

He realized that she was more unhappy than she seemed. He stroked her cheek and said:

'You're everything in the world to me, you're the best companion for my life.'

She smiled and recovered the peace of mind she needed in order to go to sleep.


Mr Shantah the metal-beater was amazed by the disappearance of Sadek. He went to his home, but found no trace of him or his family. In the same way Abdel Fattah, the dried-fish merchant, could find no sign of his man Agrama. Abou Fassada stopped going to Hamdoun's nut stall without giving any notice. And where was Hamroush? Hassuna the baker said he had disappeared as if the flames of the oven had devoured him. Others vanished too. The news was all over the Jerboas' quarter and the echo reached the rest of the alley. The Gebelites and Rifaaites said scornfully that the Jerboas were all leaving and that Sawaaris would soon find no one to pay him protection money. Sawaaris sent for Zechariah to come to Dongol's café and said to him sinisterly:

'Your nephew would be the best person to tell us the secret of the disappearances.'

'Mr Sawaaris, don't wrong him. For days, weeks, months the man hasn't left his house.'

The chief roared:

'Child's play! But I sent for you to warn you what may happen to your nephew.'

'Kassem is your own flesh and blood. Don't do anything that will please his enemies.'

252

'He's an enemy to himself as well as to me. He thinks he's the Gebel of today, and that's the quickest way to Bab el Nasr graveyard.'

'Steady on, Mr Sawaaris; we're all under your protection.'

When Zechariah got back home he met Hassan coming back from Kassem's house, and he vented on him the fury with which Sawaaris had fillled him, but Hassan cut him short, saying:

'Control yourself, father; Kamar is ill, very ill, father.'

The whole alley heard of Kamar's illness, even the Trustee's house. Kassem stayed beside her, overcome with sorrow. He would shake his head hopelessly and say:

'All of a sudden you lie down helpless.'

Once she said in a weak voice:

'I hid my state of health from you out of pity, because of all your other troubles.'

'You should have let me share your sufferings from the beginning.'

Her pale lips parted in a faint smile:

'I shall recover my former health.'

That was what he was praying for. But what was this mist that covered her eyes? Why was her face so dry? What was this power of concealing pain? 'All this is because of you. Oh God watch over her with your mercy. Preserve her for me, and have pity on the baby's tears.'

'Because you forgive me I can't forgive myself.'

She smiled again, almost reproachfully.

Omme Salem was brought to burn incense for her, and Omme Ateya to make her some ointments, and Ibrahim the barber to cup her, but Kamar seemed to resist all remedies. Kassem said to her:

'I wish I could bear your pain for you.'

Her reply was hardly audible:

'May no harm touch you, my dearest.'

He said to himself: 'The sight of her makes all the world look dark.'

She said:

'A man like you is never at a loss for comforting words.'

Men and women came to visit her, but he could not longer bear the place and took refuge on the roof. He could hear the women's voices from the houses, and the curses and street-cries from the road. He heard crying too, and thought at first that it was Ihsan, until he saw a child rolling in the dust on the next roof. Darkness was falling slowly, and a flock of pigeons flew back to their loft. A solitary star winked on the horizon. He wondered about the meaning of the strange look in Kamar's eyes, as if she could not see, of her bouts of shivering, of the blueness of her lips, and of her depression. He stayed several hours and then went down. He met Sekina carrying Ihsan in the hall, and she whispered to him:

253

'Go in quietly so as not to wake her.'

He sat on the divan opposite the bed, in the feeble light of the lamp on the window ledge. The only sound from outside was the wail of the fiddle. Then Taza the storyteller began.

His grandfather said quietly:

'I have decided to give you a chance that has not been offered to anyone else from outside. It is that you should live in this house and marry in it and begin a new life here.'

Hammam's heart raced, drunk with joy. He said:

'Thank you for your kindness.'

'You have deserved it.'

The boy looked from his grandfather to the carpet, then asked anxiously:

'And my family?'

Gebelawi said reproachfully:

'I said quite clearly what I meant.'

Hammam implored him:

'They deserve your mercy and forgiveness.'

The sleeping woman started and woke. Kassem rushed over from the divan. He saw a new brilliance in her eyes in place of the misty look. He asked what was wrong and she shouted:

'Ihsan! Where is Ihsan?'

He hurried out and came back followed by Sekina carrying the sleeping baby. Kamar pointed at Ihsan and Sekina brought her so that she could kiss the child's cheek, while Kassem sat on the edge of the bed. She looked at him and whispered:

'I'm even worse.'

'What do you mean?'

'I have caused you much pain, but I'm worse.'

He bit his lip, then said:

'Kamar, I feel wretched being so helpless.'

'I'm afraid for you after I'm gone.'

'Don't talk about me.'

'Kassem, go and join your friends; you'll be killed if you stay.'

'We shall go together.'

'We aren't going the same way.'

'Don't you want to have pity on me as you used to?'

'Oh, that was in the past.'

She seemed to be struggling against some terrible force. She made a sign with her hand. He leaned over still closer to her. She writhed and stretched out her neck. Her chest collapsed and her breath rasped out. Sekina shouted:

'Help her to sit up! She wants to sit up!'

He put his arms round her to help her up, but she groaned feebly and her head fell forward on to her chest. Sekina hurried away with the baby, and from outside her howls rang out and broke the silence.


## 82 ✳ ✳ ✳ ✳ ✳ ✳ ✳ ✳ ✳ ✳ ✳ ✳ ✳ ✳ ✳ ✳ ✳ ✳ ✳

Next morning Kassem's house and the road in front of it were full of people offering their condolences. The alley had a deep respect for the ties of kinship, without enjoying any of their advantages. Sawaaris had to come, and in no time all the Jerboas were following him. Even Trustee Rifaat had to come, followed by Galta and Lehita and Haggaag, and soon everyone trooped along. The funeral procession was joined by huge crowds such as had never been seen before except at the funerals of chiefs. Kassem showed a philosophical fortitude. Even during the burial he wept only inwardly and not with his eyes.

The mourners went, leaving only Kassem, Zechariah, Owayss and Hassan at the grave. Zechariah patted Kassem on the arm, and said:

'Pull yourself together, my child; and God help you.'

He hunched forward a little, moaning:

'My heart has been buried too, uncle.'

Hassan's face was contorted. There was a deep silence in the graveyard. Zechariah moved a pace or two.

'Time we went.'

But Kassem stayed where he was. He said resentfully:

'Why did they come?'

Zechariah saw what he meant.

'Let's be thankful to them anyway.'

Owayss plucked up his courage and said:

'Make a fresh start with them. What they have done today requires you to make a move. Luckily what they say about you outside our quarter is not to be taken seriously.'

Kassem remained sunk in silence rather than argue with him. Then up came a party led by Sadek. It seemed that they had been waiting for the mourners to disappear. There were many of them, and not one of them a stranger. They embraced Kassem and his eyes filled with tears. Owayss looked at them angrily, but no one took any notice of him. Sadek said to Kassem:

'There's no longer anything to keep you in the alley.'

But Zechariah retorted hotly:

'His little girl and his house and his property are there.'

255

Kassem said:

'It was necessary for me to stay, and thanks to my staying your numbers have built up over the weeks.'

He looked at the faces that gazed up at him as if to reassure himself of the truth of his remark. Most of them were amongst those he had urged during his nocturnal prowls to leave and join his friends. He had crept out each night after the alley had fallen asleep and had gone to those of whose friendship and readiness to be convinced he was sure. Agrama asked him:

'Shall we have to wait long?'

'Until there are enough of you.'

Sadek leaned over and whispered:

'I'm heart-broken for you. I know better than anyone how great your misfortune is.'

Kassem whispered:

'You're right; the pain is terrible.'

'Hurry up and join us, now that you're alone.'

'All in good time.'

Owayss said loudly:

'We must get back.'

The friends embraced, and Kassem went back with his companions. He passed the days, lonely and sad, in his house, and Sekina began to be afraid of what his sorrow might lead to. But he went on with his night-time prowls with a determination that knew no weakness. The number of those who had disappeared kept on growing, and people began to wonder anxiously about them. Still more fun was made of the Jerboas and their chief in the rest of the alley; they said it would be Sawaaris' turn to run away tomorrow, if not today. Zechariah said to Kassem one day:

'This is all very alarming and may lead to worse things.'

But he had to wait. Those were days of activity and danger. Ihsan was his only cause for smiles. She was learning to stand, holding on to the edge of chairs, and she would look up at him with her innocent face and talk to him in baby-language. He used to enjoy looking at her face and would say to himself: 'She will be beautiful, but above all I hope she'll be good and loving like her mother.' The dark eyes gazing up at him out of Ihsan's round face were a lasting symbol of the bond that fate had broken. He wondered whether he would live to see her a beautiful bride, or was she fated to have only painful memories of the house she was born in?

One day there was a knock at the door and Sekina went and asked who was there. A young voice said:

'Open the door, Sekina.'

She opened the door and found a girl of twelve or so, wrapped for some reason in a woman's shawl and with a veil over her face. Sekina was surprised and asked what she wanted, but she hurried into Kassem's room and said breathlessly:

'Good evening, sir.'

She took off the veil, revealing a round, copper-coloured face with perfect features. Kassem was surprised.

'Hello! Sit down! Welcome!'

She sat down on the edge of a chair.

'I'm Badria. My brother Sadek has sent me to you.'

'Sadek!'

'Yes.'

He looked at her inquisitively.

'What makes him take such a risk?'

She said, with an anxiety that made her still more attractive:

'No one could know me in this shawl.'

He realized that she looked older than she was. He nodded and she went on, still more anxious:

'He says you must leave at once, and that Lehita and Galta and Haggaag and Sawaaris have plotted together to kill you tonight.'

He frowned uneasily. Sekina groaned. He asked:

'How does he know this?'

'Mr Yehya told him.'

'But how did Mr Yehya find out?'

'A drunken man gave the secret away in a tavern where a friend of Mr Yehya's was; that's what my brother said.'

He stared at her silently until she got up and began wrapping the shawl round her lovely body. He got up too, saying:

'Thank you, Badria. Keep well out of sight, and give my greetings to your brother. Good-bye!'

She drew the veil over her face and asked:

'What shall I say to him?'

'Tell him we'll meet before the morning.'

They shook hands, and she went.


83 ✳ ✳ ✳ ✳ ✳ ✳ ✳ ✳ ✳ ✳ ✳ ✳ ✳ ✳ ✳ ✳ ✳ ✳ ✳

Sekina was pale and her eyes were full of terror. She cried out:

'Let's leave the house without delay.'

And she jumped up to get busy. He said:

'Wrap up Ihsan and hide her under your shawl and go out as if you were on some errand. Go to Kamar's grave and wait there.'

'And you, sir?'

'I shall join you when the time comes.'

She looked worried. He said calmly:

'Hassan will take you to the place where we're going to stay.'

In a few moments she was ready to go. He kissed Ihsan several times. Sekina said as she went towards the door:

'God be with you.'

He stood by the window, watching the road, and saw her walking towards Gemalia, until she was hidden by the bend. His heart pounded as he gazed after the precious burden in her arms. He looked around the quarter and saw several of the chiefs' followers, some sitting in Dongol's café and others hanging about here and there. Their features were indistinct in the gathering darkness. They showed every sign of getting ready, but would they lie in wait till he went out on his night-time wanderings – if they had discovered about them – or would they encircle his house later in the evening? They were now beginning to break up, to prevent their secret being discovered. There they were, creeping about in the darkness like noxious insects. Would he meet the fate of Rifaa or that of Gebel? Rifaa had found himself in this position one dark night. He had hidden in his house, his heart full of good intentions, while downstairs bloodthirsty brutes crept in. When will you have had your fill of blood, unhappy alley?

Kassem paced up and down in his room till there was a knock at the door and he heard Hassan calling him. Hassan came in, big and strong. His eyes were anxious. He said:

'Something strange is going on, something suspicious . . .'

Kassem showed no outward concern at this remark.

'Has my uncle got back from his walk?'

'No. But I tell you, something suspicious is going on. Take a look through the shutters.'

'I've seen what's worrying you, and I know what's behind it. Sadek warned me in good time by sending his little sister to me. If this message is true, the chiefs are going to try and kill me tonight; so Sekina has fled with Ihsan, and they are waiting for you at Kamar's grave. Go to them and take them to where our friends are.'

'And you?'

'I'll escape in my turn and meet you.'

Hassan said with determination:

'I'm not leaving you alone.'

'Do as I say and don't hesitate. I shall use cunning, not strength, to escape, and your strength would be no use to me if I was forced to fight. But by going you will protect my daughter and you will be able to put some of our men at the end of the roads from Gemalia to the gebel,

258

where they may perhaps help me if I need them during my flight.'

Hassan gave way and shook his hand hard:

'You're so clever; the plan you've made will perhaps be the best.'

Kassem answered with a calm smile and Hassan went off with a frown on his face. Not long after, Zechariah came in panting, and Kassem was sure he had come from Yehya with the news and got in first:

'Sadek sent me the news.'

'I heard it a short time ago when I passed by Yehya's place and I was afraid it wouldn't have reached you.'

Kassem sat him down and said apologetically:

'Forgive me the trouble I've caused you.'

'I've been expecting this for a long time. I found Sawaaris was behaving differently towards me, and I began to watch carefully. Today I see the devils swarming like locusts, and here you are alone, with flight almost impossible.'

Kassem looked still more determined.

'I shall try, and if I fail there are men in the gebel who will not be defeated.'

Zechariah said angrily:

'What's the use of that compared with your life and your child?'

'I'm surprised you are not at the head of my men.'

Zechariah said, as if he hadn't heard him:

'Come with me to Sawaaris. We'll strike a bargain with him and agree to what he wants.'

Kassem gave a short laugh of scorn. Zechariah went over to the window and looked through the shutters at the alley which was dark and sinister. Kassem said:

'Why did they choose this particular night?'

'The day before yesterday a Gebelite proclaimed that your cause is for everyone's good, and the same is said of a Rifaaite. Perhaps that's what made them hurry.'

Kassem beamed.

'You see, uncle? I'm the enemy of the Trustee and the chiefs but I'm the friend of the alley, and everyone will know that soon.'

'Think now about the fate that is waiting for you.'

'I'll tell you my plan; I'll escape across the roofs to your house, leaving my lamp lit to mislead them.'

'Someone may see you.'

'I shan't start until the people have stopped sitting out on the roofs for the evening.'

And if they attack your house first?'

'It won't happen until the alley is asleep.'

'They've got more reckless than you think.'

259

He smiled.

'In that case I'll die; and who can put off the hour fixed for his death?'

Zechariah loked imploringly at him, but Kassem's face was all determination. He said in despair:

'They may search my house.'

'Luckily they don't know we've heard of their scheme, and so, by God's grace, I'll get away before they can stop me.'

They gave each other a long look, which said more than tears could have done. Then they embraced. When he was alone again, Kassem mastered his feelings and went to the window to look at the road. Life seemed to be going on as usual; children playing round the lamps on the barrows, the café full of people chatting, the fiddle wailing, the roofs noisy with women's gossip and the coughs, jokes and insults of hashish smokers. But Sawaaris stood on the doorstep of the café, and the messengers of death lurked in every corner. 'Treacherous brood! Since Idris laughed his cruel laugh, you have been inheriting wickedness and plunging the alley into darkness. Isn't it time for the caged bird to be set free?'

The time passed slowly and oppressively, but it brought the end of the evening for the gossips. The roofs fell silent and the alley was deserted by barrows and children. The cafés emptied, and for a while there were the sounds of people going home. The drunks reeled back from Gemalia, and even the hashish dens put out their braziers. Only the killers remained in the darkness. Kassem said to himself: 'Time to get busy.' He hurried to the stairs and climbed up on to the roof and went to the wall which divided his roof from that of the next house. He got over it without difficulty and was about to hasten on when a voice said 'Stop!' He realized that killers were posted on the roofs and that he was even more completely surrounded than he had thought. He turned to go back, but the man jumped after him and caught hold of him with strong arms. Kassem summoned up all his strength, which was redoubled by fear, and he gave the man a sudden blow in the stomach, broke free from his grip and kicked him, and he fell down groaning and did not get up again. There was a muffled cough from a roof three or four houses away, which made Kassem change his mind about going on. He went back to his own roof in great alarm. He stood by the stairs listening and heard footsteps coming up. Several men gathered outside his door and burst it open, almost smashing it. They rushed in and Kassem did not waste another second before hurrying down to the courtyard. He ran to the gate and saw a figure moving outside. He sprang at the man and seized him round the neck, then rammed him and kneed him in the stomach. The man fell to the ground and lay there motionless.

Kassem hurried towards Gemalia, his heart racing. By now they would have seen that the house was empty and would perhaps have gone

on to the roof and found their companion laid out. They might already
have come down after him. He passed the house his uncle lived in without stopping, and when he got to the end of the alley he started running.
But at the entrance to Gemalia a man sprang into his path and shouted,
very loud so as to warn the others: 'Stop, you bastard!' He lifted his
cudgel before Kassem could swerve out of his way, but another figure
appeared from round the corner and clubbed the man over the head so
that he fell down with a scream. Hassan said to Kassem:

'We must run for all we're worth.'

And away they ran through the darkness, not caring about stones or
holes in the road.


84 ✳ ✳ ✳ ✳ ✳ ✳ ✳ ✳ ✳ ✳ ✳ ✳ ✳ ✳ ✳ ✳ ✳ ✳ ✳

At the beginning of Watawit Alley Sadek joined them, and at the other
end of it they found Agrama, Abou Fassada and Hamroush standing
round a four-wheeled carriage. They jumped in and the horse made off
at great speed through the darkness, driven on by the driver's whip. The
sound of the carriage exploded in the silence of the night. They kept
turning to look back fearfully. Sadek said to reassure them:

'They will go to Bab el Nasr, thinking you'll hide in the wasteland
round the graveyards.'

Kassem said doubtfully:

'But they know you're not living near the graveyards.'

However, the speed of the carriage seemed decisive, and they began to
feel they were really out of danger. Kassem said:

'You organized it very well. Thank you, Sadek. But for your warning
I'd be dead by now.'

Sadek pressed his hand silently. The carriage rushed on until they made
out Souk Mukattam in the starlight. It was wrapped in darkness and
desolation, except for the lamp shining in Yehya's hut. As a precaution
they left the carriage in the middle of the square and walked to the hut.
They heard Yehya asking who was there, and, when Kassem answered,
his voice was raised again in thanksgiving. The two embraced warmly
and Kassem said:

'I owe you my life.'

The old man laughed.

'It was sheer chance, but it saved the man who most deserves to live.
Hurry now to the gebel; the mountain is your best fortress.'

Kassem pressed his hand and looked lovingly and gratefully at his face
in the lamplight. Yehya said:

'Today you are like Rifaa or Gebel. I shall go back to the alley when you are granted victory.'

They went off eastwards from the hut, making their way through the desert to the gebel. Sadek went in front as he knew the path best. A lightening of the darkness announced the approach of dawn. From far off came the crow of a cock. They reached the foot of the mountain and followed it southwards until they found the difficult path that led to their new home on the gebel. They followed Sadek up, going in single file because the path was so narrow. Sadek said to Kassem:

'We've made you a hut in between ours; Ihsan is sleeping there now.'

Agrama said:

'Our huts are built of tins and sacking.'

Hassan said gaily:

'Not much worse than our huts in the alley!'

Kassem said:

'It's enough that we don't have a trustee or a chief.'

They heard voices from above and Sadek said:

'Our new alley is awake and waiting for you.'

They looked up and saw the first light of day. Sadek shouted at the top of his voice: 'Hey there!' and men's and women's heads popped up. There were shouts and cheers, and they started singing: 'Put henna on the bird's tail and make it sing.'

Kassem was overjoyed.

'What a lot of them!'

Sadek said proudly:

'A new alley on the gebel, whose inhabitants increase in numbers as the days pass. With the guidance of Mr Yehya, all the emigrants have joined us.'

Hamoush said:

'The only trouble is that we have to make our living in far-off places for fear of meeting someone from the alley.'

When Kassem reach the top the men embraced him and the women shook his hand, and there was a hubbub of greetings and cheers and shouts of 'Thank God!' Sekina was among those who greeted him and she told him that Ihsan was asleep in the hut that had been put up for them. They all went together, cheering and singing, to the 'new alley', which was in the form of a square of huts in a level area on the side of the mountain. The horizon was filled with the rosy light of dawn. A man shouted:

'Welcome to Kassem, our chief!'

Kassem scowled and said:

'Damn all chiefs; there's no peace and no safety where they are. We shall raise our cudgels as Gebel did, but for the sake of the mercy that

262

Rifaa called for. Then we'll use the estate for the common good to realize Adham's dream; that's our task, not being chiefs.'

Hassen led him gently towards his hut saying to the crowd:

'He hasn't slept a wink all night; let him have some of the sleep he deserves.'

Kassem threw himself down on the straw-filled sack beside his daughter, and in no time he was fast asleep. He woke up in the early afternoon with a thick head and a weary body. Sekina brought Ihsan and put her in his lap, and he kissed her adoringly. She handed him a mug of water, saying:

'They fetched us this water from the public pump, just as Gebel's wife used to fetch it.'

He smiled, for he liked anything that connected him with the memory of Gebel or Rifaa. He looked at the hut and saw walls of sacking. He hugged Ihsan still more affectionately, then stood up and handed the child to Sekina and left the hut. He found Sadek and Hassan waiting for him and sat down with them after saying good morning. He took a look at the encampment and saw only women and children. Sadek explained:

'The men have gone off to Sayyida Zaynab and to Zeinhom to earn a living. They left us behind to reassure you.'

His eyes followed the women, who were at work cooking or washing in front of the huts, and the children who were playing here and there. He mused:

'I wonder if they're happy.'

Sadek said:

'They are dreaming of possessing the estate, and the good things that Lady Amina enjoys.'

He smiled broadly, then looked slowly from one to the other and asked:

'What do you two have in mind for the next step?'

Hassan shrugged his broad shoulders.

'We know just what we want.'

'But how do we get it?'

'We seize our chance to attack them when they're off their guard.'

But Sadek said:

'No. We hold out till more people have joined us from the alley, and *then* we attack. That way we'll be sure of victory and there'll be less casualties.'

Kassem cried out:

'Splendid!'

They fell dreamily silent. A voice said shyly:

'Some food?'

Kassem looked up and saw Badria holding a dish of stewed beans and a loaf, and looking at him with her dancing eyes. He could not help smiling as he said:

'Welcome to my messenger of life!'

She put the dish down in front of him, saying:

'Long life to you!'

And away she went to Sadek's hut which was next to his own. He was filled with tenderness and happiness and ate with a good appetite. He said:

'I have a fair amount of money which will come in useful.' Then, after a pause: 'We must get on so everyone we know will be ready to join us. There are plenty of poor people who long for our victory, and only fear holds them back.'

Hassan and Sadek soon went off after the other men and he found himself alone. He got up and wandered round to investigate. The children he passed took no notice of him, but the women called out their greetings. A very old woman caught his attention. Her hair was white and her eyes clouded with age, and her chin trembled. He went up to her and greeted her. She returned his greeting and he asked:

'Who are you, mother?'

Her voice crackled like dry leaves.

'Hamroush's mother.'

'Welcome, mother of us all. How could you think of leaving home?'

'Where my son is, there's a place for me; and it's good to be far away from the chiefs.' Then, taking courage from his smile: 'I saw Rifaa when I was young.'

'Really?'

'Yes, upon your life. He was gentle and handsome, but it never crossed my mind that he would give his name to a quarter, or that his story would be told to the music of the fiddle.'

He asked still more eagerly:

'Didn't you go to him like everyone else?'

'Oh no! Nobody knew us in our quarter; we hardly knew ourselves. But for you, the Jerboas would never have been talked of.'

He looked at her curiously and wondered: 'How is our ancestor today?' but he went on smiling sweetly at her, and she said several prayers for him till at length he went.

He walked on till he came to the top of the path down the side of the gebel. He looked down at the desert below and then towards the horizon. In the distance he could see the domes and roofs, merging together. He said to himself: 'Only one thing is needed, and it looks so small from here. Trustee Rifaat and the chief Lehita seem so unimportant. From here there's no difference between Rifaat and Uncle Zechariah. It would be difficult to find your way from this place back to the alley that has

264

caused so much trouble if it wasn't for the house of the founder, which seems cut off from time and place – our ancestor's house, with its amazing wall and its tall trees. But he is old, and his prestige has gone down like this setting sun. Where are you and how are you and why do you seem as though you no longer exist? Those who pervert your will are a few yards from your house, but these women and children, far away from you on the gebel, these are the closest to your heart. You will regain your proper place when the conditions of your endowment are carried out, just as the sun will rise tomorrow to its zenith. Without you we should be fatherless and homeless, with no estate and no hope.'

A sweet voice roused him:

'Coffee, Mr Kassem?'

He turned and saw Badria holding out the cup to him. He took it:

'Why the trouble?'

'It's a pleasure to take trouble for you.'

He said a prayer in his mind for Kamar's soul and began sipping the coffee gently. Between sips his eyes met hers in a smile. How good coffee tasted on the edge of the gebel, way above the desert.

'How old are you, Badria?'

'I don't know.'

'But you know what has brought us to the gebel?'

She hesitated shyly.

'You.'

'Me?'

'You want to beat the Trustee and the chiefs and get the estate for us; that's what father says.'

He smiled. Then he realized that he had emptied the cup and forgotten to give it back to her. He handed it to her.

'I wish I could thank you enough.'

She smiled and turned away blushing and went off. He murmured 'Good-bye.'


85 ✳ ✳ ✳ ✳ ✳ ✳ ✳ ✳ ✳ ✳ ✳ ✳ ✳ ✳ ✳ ✳ ✳ ✳ ✳ ✳

Late afternoon was fencing time, and the men used to practise difficult strokes with their sticks. This would begin when both men and women had come back with a little money and some plain food after a gruelling day's work. Kassem himself was the keenest fencer. He was very happy to see the enthusiasm of his men, and their eagerness for the crucial day. They were big and strong, but they felt towards him such love as the alley had never known. The sticks rose and fell and clashed together, and

265

the boys watched or copied, while the women rested or made the supper.

The row of huts grew longer as more people joined them. Sadek and Hassan and Abu Fassada proved skilful hunters. They would lie in wait in likely places for men from the alley and would not leave them till they had persuaded them to join them. Then they would leave the alley secretly, inspired by hopes they had not known before. Sadek used to say to Kassem:

'With all this movement I'm afraid our enemies may find their way to our camp.'

'The only way to reach us is that narrow path; they're doomed if they come up it.'

Ihsan was his constant happiness. When he played with her and when he rocked her and when he talked to her. But it was not the same when she reminded him of his lost wife; then loneliness would oppress him, and he would yearn for her who had been snatched from him at the beginning of the road and had left him the victim of loneliness whenever he was by himself, and sometimes of remorse, as had happened on the edge of the mountain on the day Badria brought him the coffee, or on the day she had looked at him so tenderly. One night he could not sleep and was tormented by loneliness in the dark hut. He got up and went out to walk in the space between the huts under the starlight, enjoying the fresh air of the summer night on the gebel.

A voice called him and asked:

'Where are you going at this hour of the night?'

He turned and saw Sadek approaching. He asked:

'Haven't you gone to sleep yet?'

'I caught sight of you as I was lying in front of my hut. You are dearer to me than sleep.'

They walked side by side to the edge and stood there. Kassem said:

'Loneliness is sometimes too much to bear.'

Sadek laughed:

'Damn loneliness!'

They looked towards the horizon. The world was a glowing sky above a dark earth. Sadek said:

'Most of your men are husbands or have a family; they don't feel lonely.'

Kassem tried to sound disapproving.

'Whatever do you mean?'

'A man like you can't do without a woman.'

The more he felt how right Sadek was, the more argumentative Kassem sounded.

'How could I marry again after Kamar?'

'If she could speak to you, she'd say the same as me.'

Confused emotions raged in Kassem's heart. He said as if talking to himself:

'It's like a betrayal.'

'The dead don't need our loyalty.'

Kassem thought: 'Is this true, or just what I want to hear? Truth can taste bitter. You have never faced up to yourself as frankly as you have faced up to the condition of the alley. He who fixed these things in your world is He who fixed the stars in the sky. The simple truth is that your heart beats still, just as it has always done.' He groaned audibly. Sadek said:

'You, more than anyone, need a companion.'

When he got back to his hut he found Sekina standing at the door. She looked up at him anxiously:

'I saw that you'd gone out when I thought you were fast asleep.'

Kassem was so much troubled by his thoughts that he said without any preliminaries:

'Look at the way Sadek is urging me to get married.'

She seized on this heaven-sent opportunity.

'I wish I'd been the first to say it.'

'You!'

'Yes, sir. It wounds my heart to see you sitting there so lonely and full of thoughts.'

He pointed at the sleeping huts.

'All those people are with me.'

'Yes, but you have no one with you at home. I'm an old woman with one foot in the grave.'

He felt that his hesitation was a proof that he accepted her idea. Still he did not go into his hut but said mournfully:

'I shan't find a wife like her.'

'That's true, but there are promising girls.'

They exchanged glances in the darkness. She was silent for a while, then murmured:

'Badria, what a sweet girl . . .'

His heart pounded.

'That little girl!'

Sekina suppressed a crafty smile.

'She's a ripe little thing when she brings a meal or some coffee.'

He turned away.

'You devil! A curse on your brood!'

The news was joyfully received throughout the mountain encampment. Sadek almost danced, and his mother's cries of joy could be heard in the desert below. Kassem received many congratulations. They celebrated the wedding without any professional singers or dancers. Several

267

of the women did the dancing, including Badria's mother, and Abu Fassada sang in a sweet voice: 'I was a fisherman, and fishing is fine.'

The bridegroom's procession went round the huts, lit by the lamps of heaven. Sekina moved with Ihsan to Hassan's hut, leaving Kassem's hut empty for the bridal pair.

## 86 ✳ ✳ ✳ ✳ ✳ ✳ ✳ ✳ ✳ ✳ ✳ ✳ ✳ ✳ ✳ ✳ ✳ ✳ ✳ ✳

He really enjoyed sitting on a skin in front of the hut and watching Badria kneading the dough. She was very young – there was no denying it – but what woman was more energetic or efficient? She stretched her arms and pushed the hair back from her forehead with the back of her hand. She looked most seductive. A blush showed that she could feel his eyes on her. She stopped flirtatiously, and he laughed and went over to her, took her plait and kissed her several times, then sat down again. He was happy and carefree as he usually was when not bothered with his companions and his thoughts. Not far off, Ihsan was toddling about, watched by Sekina who was resting on a stone.

There was a noise at the top of the path, and he saw Sadek and Hassan and some other friends coming towards him, clustered round a man whom he recognized as Khorda the dustman, a Rifaaite. Kassem stood up at once to meet them and the women youyoued with joy, as they did whenever a new man came to the gebel from the alley. The man embraced Kassem, saying:

'I'm with you, and I've brought my cudgel with me.'

Kassem said happily:

'Welcome Khorda. We don't make any difference between one quarter and another; it's all one alley, and the estate belongs to everyone.'

The Rifaaite laughed:

'They're wondering where your hideout is, and they expect terrible things from you, but many hearts long for your victory.' Khorda looked around at the huts and the people and said in amazement: 'All these people are with you!'

Sadek said:

'Khorda has brought important news.'

Kassem looked at him curiously and Khorda said:

'Sawaaris is marrying his fifth wife today; the bridegroom's procession will take place this evening.'

Hassan said eagerly:

'There won't be another chance like this for destroying him.'

The men were all enthusiastic and Sadek said:

'One day we shall attack the alley, and every chief we can get out of the way before then will make our battle easier and its outcome more certain.'

Kassem thought for a while, then said:

'We'll attack the procession just as they do; but remember, we are attacking to put an end to their ways.'

A little before midnight the men gathered on the edge of the gebel. They followed Kassem down one by one, gripping their cudgels. The sky was clear, and the full moon, which is called 'Badr', was at the zenith, giving a dreamy quality to the world. They reached the desert and followed the cliffs of Mukattam northwards so as not to lose the way. When they were near Hind's Rock a man came towards them. He had been sent to spy for them and he told Kassem:

'The procession will go towards Bab el Nasr.'

'But our bridegroom's processions usually go towards Gemalia.'

'Perhaps they are keeping away from the places where they think you are staying.'

Kassem thought rapidly, and said:

'Sadek will take a party to Bab el Fotouh. Agrama and another party will go to the desert beside Bab el Nasr. Hassan and I will wait with the rest outside Bab el Nasr Gate. You will attack when I give you the command.'

The men split up into three parties. Before they set off, Kassem said:

'Keep your blows for Sawaaris and his men; the rest will be your brothers tomorrow.'

The parties went their different ways, and he and Hassan and their party followed the gebel northwards; then they turned left to the cemetery road and hid behind the gate. He and his men watched the road, while Sadek lay in wait to the right and Agrama to the left. Hassan said:

'The procession will stop at the Falaki café.'

Kassem said:

'We must attack before they get to it, so as not to harm anyone who has nothing to do with us.'

They waited tensely in the dark. Hassan said suddenly:

'I remember the murder of Shaaban very vividly.'

'The chiefs have had countless victims.'

Sadek whistled and Agrama followed suit. They became still more determined. Hassan said:

'If Sawaaris is killed the people of our quarter will soon join us, and, when the rest come to destroy us, we'll kill them on the mountain path.'

These dreams were like the moonlight. Within the hour they would have won their victory; or their hopes would have been lost with their lives. Kassem seemed to see the figure of Kindil and to hear the voice of

Kamar. An age seemed to have passed since he had watched the flocks. He gripped his cudgel tighter and said to himself: 'We can't possibly be beaten.' He heard Hassan say:

'Can you hear something?'

He pricked up his ears and heard faint music.

'Get ready; the procession is coming.'

The sounds drew nearer and clearer. Then they heard the pipes and the drums and 'Ohs' and 'Ahs' and there were cheers and shouts. The procession appeared in the light of its torches, and they saw Sawaaris surrounded by a ring of dancers juggling with sticks. Hassan said:

'Shall I whistle to Agrama?'

'When the front of the procession reaches the garlic stall.'

The procession came on and the dancing and juggling grew wilder. One dancer in a frenzy began leaping in the air and rushing round in circles in front of the procession at fantastic speed with his stick spinning round his hand, which he held above his head. After each circle he moved forward a step until he passed the garlic stall. The procession followed him very slowly, till its head reached the stall. At that moment Hassan whistled three times, and Agrama and his men swept down from Atfat el Tamaain on the tail-end of the procession, brandishing their cudgels and breaking its ranks. There were howls of rage and confusion. Hassan whistled three more times and Sadek and his men fell on the middle of the procession from the Samakein before it had recovered from the first attack. At once, Kassem and his men rushed out from under the gate and attacked the front of the procession as one man.

Sawaaris and his men recovered from the shock, raised their cudgels and joined battle. It was a bitter fight and many of the peaceable people fled and took refuge in the alleyways. The cudgels fell still more savagely and the blood flowed from heads and faces. The lamps were smashed and the flowers were scattered and trampled underfoot. Screams went up from the windows round about and the cafés locked their doors. Sawaaris hit out cruelly and deftly, and his stick flew about like a mad thing, now here, now there. The violence grew, and the men were filled with hatred.

Suddenly Sawaaris found himself face to face with Sadek. With a scream of 'Bastard!' he aimed a blow at him which found its mark. Sadek trembled and staggered. Sawaaris raised his cudgel and brought it down a second time. Sadek took the blow on his stick which he held gripped with both hands, but he was forced to his knees by the strength of it. Sawaaris was about to give the third and fatal blow, but he saw Hassan rushing down on him like a wild beast to save his friend, and he turned from Sadek in a fury, yelling: 'You too, son of Zechariah, son of a bitch!' aimed a terrible blow at him, which would have killed him if he had not dodged it with a sideways leap. As he jumped he jabbed

Sawaaris in the neck with the end of his stick. The blow prevented Sawaaris for a few moments from hitting again. Hassan recovered his balance and struck Sawaaris on the forehead with terrific force. The blood spurted, and in a moment the cudgel had slipped from his hand. He staggered back a few steps and fell motionless on his back. A man shouted above the noise of the cudgels: 'Sawaaris is dead.' Agrama caught him on the nose with his cudgel and he retreated and fell over a prostrate body. Kassem's men grew still more resolute and their blows fiercer, while Sawaaris' men flagged, frightened by the number of them who had fallen. They withdrew and then fled.

Kassem's men began gathering round him, panting. Some of them were bleeding, others were carrying the wounded. They looked at the bodies lying on the ground by the light from the windows of the cafés. Some were dead, others just unconscious. Hamroush stood over Sawaaris and shouted:

'Your body can rest in peace, Shaaban.'

Kassem took him aside and said:

'The day of victory is near, the day when the other chiefs will meet their fate, when we shall become the masters of the alley and share our estate and be loyal children to Gebelawi.'

When they got back to the gebel, the women greeted them with youyous of joy, and the news of the victory flew round. Kassem went to his hut, and Badria said to him:

'You are covered with dust and blood; you must wash before you go to sleep.'

When he lay down after his wash he moaned with pain. She brought him some food and waited for him to sit up and take it, but he was in a state between sleeping and waking. He felt relief that was almost happiness, but at the same time mixed with sadness. Badria said:

'Take your food.'

He looked up at her with heavy, dreamy eyes.

'Soon you'll see my victory, Kamar.'

He realized at once that his tongue had slipped and he saw her face fall. He sat up in bed and said lovingly:

'Your food is so appetizing.'

But she frowned and did not respond. He took a bite of the felafel and said:

'It's my turn to invite you to eat.'

She turned her face away, muttering:

'She was old and she wasn't beautiful.'

He doubled up with grief.

'Don't speak ill of her. One like her deserves to be remembered with mercy.'

271

She looked quickly back at him and saw the sorrow in his face. She fell silent.

The losers of the battle went back utterly ashamed. They kept as far away as they could from the lights of Sawaaris' house which was bright with rejoicing and merry-making. Each man crept away to his home. The black news spread like fire in a forest, and the wedding feast was extinguished. There were wails of lament for Sawaaris and for those of his men who had been killed. The calamity had also involved some Rifaaites and Gebelites who had been in the procession. And who was the culprit? Kassem, the shepherd; Kassem, who would have had to stay a beggar all his life but for Kamar. One man said he had followed Kassem's party back to their hideout on the gebel. Many people wondered whether they would remain encamped on the mountain until they had destroyed all the men of the alley.

Those who were asleep woke up and went out into the road or the courtyards. A Gebelite came out and shouted:

'Kill all the Jerboa rats.'

But Galta silenced him, shouting:

'They've done nothing wrong; their chief and many of their men have been killed.'

'Set fire to Mukattam.'

'Bring Kassem's body for the dogs to eat.'

'I'll drink his blood, or divorce my wife.'

'The rat! The vermin! The coward!'

'He thinks the gebel will protect him.'

'He used to accept a millième from me and kiss the ground.'

'He used to pretend to be so nice and friendly to us; now he betrays us and kills people.'

Next day the whole alley appeared at a mass funeral. The day after that the chiefs held a meeting in the house of Rifaat, the Trustee, who was furious. He said with bitter sarcasm:

'We'd better barricade ourselves into the alley, so as to be safe from death.'

Lehita was more upset than any of them, but he wanted to play the thing down to lessen his responsibility. He said:

'It was just a battle between one chief and some men from his quarter.'

Galta protested:

'One man in our quarter was killed and three wounded.'

Haggaag said:

'And one of our men was killed.'

Rifaat said craftily to Lehita:

'It's a blow to your reputation as chief of the alley.'

His face puckered up with rage:

'A shepherd! God! You're joking!'

'A shepherd, if you like; but he's become a menace. We didn't take his ravings seriously for a while, and we closed our eyes to him out of respect for his wife. But his wickedness has got out of control. He pretended to be poor until he was powerful enough to destroy people. Now he's encamped on the gebel and his ambition will stop at nothing.'

They exchanged angry glances. The Trustee went on:

'He's luring people out; that's the tragedy; we needn't pretend not to know that. He promises the estate to the people. The estate won't be enough even for his friends, but no one will believe that; the beggars – most of the people – won't believe it. He promises to end chiefs, and the cowards – most of the people – are delighted. You always find people here on the winning side; we'll be lost if we don't move.'

Lehita shouted:

'He's surrounded by rats; it'll be easy to kill them.'

Haggaag said:

'But they are encamped on the gebel.'

Galta said:

'We must watch the mountain till we find a path to them.'

Rifaat urged them on:

'Do that. As I said, we're lost if we don't move.'

Lehita was still angrier and said to the Trustee:

'You remember how I planned to kill him while his wife was alive, and your wife objected?'

The Trustee looked at the eyes that were fixed on him.

'It's no use dwelling on our mistakes.' Then, after a brief silence: 'These bonds of kinship have been respected in our alley for a very long time.'

There was an uproar outside, seeming to indicate some fresh disaster. They were in a tense state of nerves, and the Trustee called the gatekeeper and asked him what was going on. The man said:

'They say the shepherd has joined Kassem, taking all the sheep with him.

Lehita jumped up, shouting:

'The dog – alley of dogs – curse him!'

The Trustee asked:

'What quarter does the shepherd come from?'

'The Jerboas. He's called Zakla.'

'Welcome, Zakla!'

Kassem embraced him and the shepherd said enthusiastically:

'I was never against you; my heart was always with you. If I hadn't been afraid I'd have been one of the first to join you. As soon as I heard of the death of Sawaaris, damn him, I hurried to you bringing my enemies' sheep.'

Kassem glanced at the flock in the space between the huts. The women had collected round them and there was a tumult of joy. He laughed.

'It is right for us to have them in return for the property of ours that they have grabbed.'

That day many more people than usual rallied to Kassem. Their determination grew stronger and their hopes higher. But Kassem was awakened very early the following morning by a strange commotion. He left his hut at once and saw his men hurrying towards him in confusion. Sadek said:

'The alley has come out to get its revenge, and they're gathering at the foot of the path.'

Khorda said:

'I was the first to go off to work and I saw them when I was a few steps from the desert. I hurried back and some of them chased me and caught me in the back with a stone. I called Sadek and Hassan and a lot of our people came to the top of the path, realized the danger and threw stones at the attackers until they withdrew.'

Kassem looked towards the top of the path and saw Hassan and others standing there with stones in their hands.

'We can hold them off there with ten men.'

Hamroush said:

'It would be suicide to come up under fire; let them come if they want.'

The men and women gathered round Kassem, leaving the huts empty. The men brought their cudgels, and the women baskets of stones that had been prepared for such a day. The first rays of the sun shone from a clear sky. Kassem said:

'Is there another path to the town?'

Sadek said gloomily:

'There is a path two hours journey to the south of the gebel.'

Agrama said:

'I don't think we have enough water for more than two days.'

There was a murmur of anxiety, especially among the women. Kassem said:

'They have come for revenge, not for a siege. If they besiege us we'll rely on the other path to get through the blockade.'

He began thinking, but his face, at which they were all gazing, remained calm. If they were blockaded they would have the greatest difficulty in fetching water by the southern path. And if he and his men attacked, would they be sure of victory against men led by Lehita, Galta and Haggaag? What fate lay waiting for them at the end of this day? He went back to his hut and came out clutching his cudgel, then went over to Hassan and his men at the top of the path. Hassan said to him:

'None of them dares come close.'

Kassem went to the edge and saw his enemies in a crescent formation in the desert, far out of range of any stones. He was horrified at their numbers, but he could not pick out the chiefs among them. He looked out across the waste at the Big House, the home of Gebelawi who was sunk in silence as though he did not care about the way his children were fighting because of him. How they needed his tremendous strength, to which these places had submitted in past times! Kassem would perhaps not have been anxious if it hadn't been for the memory of the death of Rifaa near to his ancestor's house.

He felt an urge to shout at the top of his voice 'Gebelawi!' as the people of the alley do in times of stress, but he heard women's voices and turned to look. He saw the men standing along the edge of the gebel looking at their enemies and the women approaching the danger spot. He shouted at them to go back, and when they hesitated he shouted still louder that they must get some food ready and carry on work as usual. He insisted till they yielded to his orders. Sadek came over saying:

'Well done! What I'm most afraid of is the effect of Lehita's name on us.'

Hassan said:

'Our only course is to strike.' He waved his cudgel. 'It would be impossible for us to go on, now that they know our hiding place. Our only course is to attack.'

Kassem turned his head and looked at the Big House.

'You're right. What do you say Sadek?'

'We wait till night comes.'

Hassan said:

'Waiting would harm us; and night would be no use to us in the battle.'

Kassem mused:

'I wonder what their plan is.'

Sadek said:

'To force us to come down to them.'

Kassem thought for a while, then said:

'If Lehita is killed, victory is ours. He looked at the two of them and added: 'If he falls, Galta and Haggaag will fight for his place.'

The sun climbed higher, pouring down its heat, and the stones burned. Hassan said:

'Tell me what's to be done.'

The question clearly referred to the siege, but while they were hesitating for an answer, there came a woman's scream from the direction of the encampment followed immediately by more screams. They heard a voice shouting:

'We've been attacked from the other side.'

The men abandoned the edge and rushed to the southern end of the encampment. Kassem told those who stayed to defend the path to be extra watchful. He ordered Khorda to get the able-bodied women to join the guard on the path. Then he ran with Hassan and Sadek towards the encampment where he stood in the midst of his men. They could all see Lehita leading a large company of men from the south of the gebel. Kassem said angrily:

'They distracted us while he made his journey round the gebel and reached us by the southern path.'

Hassan shouted, his great body bursting with eagerness:

'He's walking to his death.'

Kassem bellowed:

'We must win and we shall.'

His men spread out on either side of him. The enemy came on, cudgels at the ready, until they could be seen clearly. Sadek said:

'Neither Galta nor Haggaag is with them.'

Kassem realized that Galta and Haggaag must be leading the besiegers at the bottom of the path. He guessed they would attack whatever the cost, but he told no one his thoughts. He went a few steps forward, brandishing his cudgel, and his men gripped theirs. They heard Lehita's voice shouting:

'You shan't have a decent burial, you bastards!'

Kassem rushed in to the attack, surrounded by his men. The enemy hurled themselves forward, and the onslaught began with a great roaring and a banging of cudgels. At the same time the women defending the path pelted stones at an attack from below. But every one of Kassem's men was locked in combat with one of the enemy. Kassem and Dongol were fighting violently and cunningly. Lehita broke Hamroush's collar bone with a blow of his cudgel. Sadek struggled with Zeinhom till Hassan knocked him out with his cudgel. Lehita struck Zakla on the neck and he fell down. Kassem managed to hit Dongol on the ear and he screamed and retreated, then collapsed. Zeinhom made a violent attack on Sadek, who was too quick for him and jabbed him in the stomach twice, bringing him down. Khorda got the better of Hafnawi, but Lehita put his arm out of action before he could enjoy his victory. Hassan aimed a blow at Lehita, but he dodged it nimbly and lifted his cudgel to strike back. Before he could do so, Kassem hit at him, catching his cudgel. Abu Fassada rushed across to give him a third blow, but Lehita butted him in the face with his head, breaking his nose. He seemed almost unbeatable.

The battle grew fiercer and the cudgels banged together mercilessly and there was a stream of curses and insults. The blood flowed under the burning sun, and one man after another fell on each side. Lehita was afire with fury at this unexpectedly brave resistance, and his attacks and his cruelty became still fiercer. Kassem told Hassan and Agrama to take the chance and join him in an attack on Lehita to save the emigrants' stronghold. At that moment up came a woman who had been defending the path to scream a warning:

'They're coming up under cover of pastry boards.'

The men of the gebel were terrified. Lehita shouted:

'You shan't have a decent burial, you bastards!'

Kassem shouted to his men:

'Win your victory before the villains get to the top.'

He charged at Lehita, flanked by Hassan and Agrama. The chief struck at him, but he took the blow on his cudgel. Agrama tried to get in a quick smash, but the brute caught him on the chin and he fell flat on his face. Hassan leapt towards Lehita and exchanged a blow with him, then threw himself on him for a fight to the death. The women at the top of the path were screaming and some of them began running away. The position was critical. Kassem hastily sent Sadek with some men to the cliff's edge, then he leapt at Lehita, but Zehliffa got in his way and a fierce battle started between them. Hassan pushed Lehita with all his might, forcing him to retreat one step, then spat in his eyes, bellowing, kicked him on the knee, and charged with terrific speed, head down, and butted him in the stomach like a mad bull. The tyrant lost his balance and fell on his back. Hassan knelt on top of him and pressed his cudgel on the man's neck with all the strength of both his hands. Men came up to defend their chief, but Kassem and some of his men kept them off. Lehita's legs thrashed and his eyes bulged and his face went crimson and he began to choke. Suddenly Hassan pounced on his weakening enemy, brought his cudgel down with wild fury and smashed his skull. He shouted in a thunderous voice:

'Lehita is dead; your chief is dead; see his body!'

The unexpected death of Lehita had a powerful effect, bringing new hope to one side, desperation to the other. Hassan joined Kassem in his struggle, and every blow he struck hit its mark. The battlefield was all men crouching and springing and cudgels rising and falling. A cloud of dust was rising, and the fighters were crowned with blood. Groans, shouts, curses, screams, roars ... Every few minutes a man staggered and fell, or drew back and fled. The fallen lay strewn on the ground and blood glistened in the sun.

Kassem went aside and looked towards the top of the path where the situation worried him. He saw Sadek and his men sending down basketfuls of stones with an urgency that showed how near was the danger from below. He heard the women, among them his wife, screaming for help. He saw some of Sadek's men taking hold of their cudgels to be ready to meet those who persisted in coming up under the hail of stones. He realized how dangerous the position was and at once went over to Lehita's body, which was now some way from the fighting because the men from the alley had retreated. He began dragging it behind him towards the path. He called Hassan who hurried over and helped him to carry the body to the top of the path. They threw it over and it plunged down and then rolled to the feet of the attackers under their pastry boards. There was consternation; Haggaag's voice rang out:

'On! Up! Curse the monsters!'

Kassem shouted scornfully, with great self-control:

'Come on! That's your chief's body, and behind me are the bodies of the rest of your people. Come on! We're waiting for you.'

He gave a sign to the men and women and they rained down stones until the vanguard of the attackers halted and began to retreat slowly, in spite of the urging of Haggaag and Galta. Kassem heard a murmur of rebellion and argument and grumbling, and he shouted:

'Galta! Haggaag! Come on! Don't run away!'

Galta's voice came, full of hatred:

'Come down if you're men! Come down you women, you bastards.'

Haggaag yelled, standing still amid the wave of retreating men:

'May I die if I don't drink your blood, you filthy shepherd.'

Kassem picked up a stone and hurled it at him with all his might. The shower of stones went on, and the retreat grew faster till it was almost a rout. Then Hassan came up and said, wiping away the blood that flowed from his forehead:

'The battle is over. Those of them that are alive are running away towards the south.'

Kassem shouted:

'Call the men to pursue them.'

But Sadek said:

'Your mouth and chin are bleeding.'

He wiped his mouth with his hand, looked at it and saw that it was bright red. Hassan said sadly:

'Eight of us have been killed, and those who are still alive are so badly wounded that they won't be able to move.'

He looked down through the shower of stones and saw his enemies running at the bottom of the path. Sadek said:

'If they had finished their climb they would not have found a single man able to stand against them.' He kissed Kassem's bleeding chin. 'Your shrewdness saved us.'

Kassem ordered two men to stay on guard at the top of the path, and sent others after the fleeing enemy to obtain news. Then he went back with Sadek and Hassan, all three of them dragging their feet, towards the level ground where only the corpses of the dead remained. What a bloody sight! Eight of his men had been killed and ten of the enemy, besides Lehita. Not one of the survivors amongst his men was without a fracture or a wound. They had retired to their huts and the women had begun dressing their wounds. while the huts of the dead were filled with crying and wailing. Badria came up sadly and invited them to go to the hut so that she could bathe their wounds. Then Sekina came, carrying Ihsan who was crying loudly. The sun was pouring down its heat from the zenith, and kites and crows circled and swooped in the sky. The air was heavy with the smell of blood and dust. Ihsan could not stop crying, but no one took any notice of her. Even the gigantic Hassan was almost reeling. Sadek murmured:

'God have mercy on our dead.'

Kassem said:

'God have mercy on both the living and the dead.'

Hassan's spirits began to revive.

'We shall win our victory soon, and the alley will say good-bye to the age of blood and terror.'

Kassem said:

'To hell with terror and blood.'

89 ✳ ✳ ✳ ✳ ✳ ✳ ✳ ✳ ✳ ✳ ✳ ✳ ✳ ✳ ✳ ✳ ✳ ✳

The alley had not seen such a disaster before. The men came back silent, dazed, drained of energy, eyes downcast. They found news of the defeat had already arrived and the houses were filled with the sound of wailing and breast-beating. The story spread round the district, and the terrible reputation of the alley became the talk of malicious tongues. It became clear that all the Jerboa families had fled their quarter, fearing reprisals. Their houses and shops were empty, and no one doubted that they would join their victorious brother and add to his numbers and his strength. Grief lay over the rest, weary now of mourning, but the people still breathed hatred and longed for revenge.

Some Gebelites began talking about who should be the next chief of the alley. The same question was asked among the Rifaaites. Bad feeling spread like dust in a storm. The Trustee, Rifaat, learned what was going on in people's minds, and sent for Haggaag and Galta to meet him. They went along, each surrounded by his strongest men, so that the Trustee's drawing-room was packed. Each party occupied one half of the room, as though it was no longer safe for them to mix with their neighbours. The Trustee saw this and grew still more worried. He said:

'As you know, disaster has befallen us, but we aren't dead yet, we aren't finished yet; we still have the power to win victory, as long as we maintain our unity. Otherwise it's goodbye to us.'

One of the Gebelites said:

'We shall strike the last blow, as sure as day follows night.'

Haggaag complained:

'If they weren't encamped on the gebel they would have died to the last man.'

Someone else said:

'Lehita faced them after a long, hard journey that would have exhausted a camel.'

The Trustee asked impatiently:

'Tell me how united you are.'

Galta replied:

'We're brothers, thank God, and we shall remain so.'

'That's what you say, but your coming in such numbers shows the suspicion between you.'

Haggaag said:

'No, that's because of everyone's thirst for revenge.'

'Be honest; you have one eye on each other and one eye on Lehita's empty place. There'll be no security as long as this lasts. My greatest fear is that you'll bring your cudgels into it and all be killed, making the alley an easy prey for Kassem.'

Many voices cried out together:

'God forbid!'

The Trustee said in a loud, clear voice:

'There's now only Gebel's quarter and Rifaa's. There's no need for one chief over both. Let us agree on that and be one force against the emigrants.'

For a few moments there was an awed silence; then several voices said without enthusiasm:

'Yes! Yes!'

Galta said:

'We'll be content with that, although we've been the masters of our quarters for a long time.'

Haggaag said argumentatively:

280

'Let's accept; but there's no need for gratitude. There are neither masters nor servants here, especially since the Jerboas went away. Who denies that Rifaa was the noblest man our alley has known?'

Galta shouted furiously:

'Haggaag! I know your treacherous heart.'

One of the Rifaaites was about to speak, but the Trustee yelled:

'Tell me whether or not you're going to be men. If any news of your weakness gets around, the Jerboas will sweep down from the gebel like wolves. Tell me, can you stand united, or must I look elsewhere?'

Several men, scattered about the room, shouted:

'Quiet . . . Shame on you all . . . We have everything to lose . . .'

They looked submissively at the Trustee. He said:

'You're still growing in numbers and strength, but don't attack the gebel again.'

They looked puzzled. He went on:

'We shall besiege them. We'll keep a watch on the two paths leading up, and either they'll die of hunger or they'll be forced to come down to you and you'll destroy them.'

Galta said:

'That's the answer. That's what I told poor Lehita but he said a siege would be cowardice and refused to do anything but attack.'

Haggaag said:

'That's the answer. But we must put off doing it until our men have rested.'

The Trustee called on them to make a pact of brotherhood and co-operation and they shook hands and swore oaths.

It was plain to everyone in the following days that Galta and Haggaag were treating their followers more harshly, to cover up the effects of their defeat. They spread it around that, but for Lehita's stupidity, Kassem would have been destroyed without difficulty, and that his determination to climb the gebel had upset his men and taken away their strength and courage, so that they had met the enemy in the worst possible condition. The people believed what they were told, and anyone who showed any doubt was insulted and cursed and beaten. As for who should be chief of the alley, no one was allowed to talk about it at all, at least not openly; but many discussed in the hashish dens who would succeed Lehita after victory.

In spite of the past and the oaths, an atmosphere of hidden mistrust developed. Each chief surrounded himself with men, and neither of them would move from his headquarters without a crowd of followers. But preparations for the day of vengeance did not stop for a single moment. They agreed that Galta and his men should camp opposite the Souk Mukattam path and that Haggaag should camp with his men opposite the Citadel path. They would keep to their positions, however long it lasted. The women would do all the buying and selling and would bring them food.

The evening before they were to set out, they gathered in the various hashish dens, bringing jugs of liquor and wine, and went on smoking hashish and getting drunk until late in the night. Haggaag's men said good night to him in front of his building in Rifaa's quarter, leaving him in a high state of intoxication. He pushed open the door and staggered down the passage humming: 'First of all – ah . . .!' But he did not finish the tune. A figure leapt at him from behind, put one hand over his mouth, and plunged a knife into his heart with the other. The body shuddered between his arms and he let it down without a sound and left it lying motionless on the ground in the pitch darkness.

90 ✳ ✳ ✳ ✳ ✳ ✳ ✳ ✳ ✳ ✳ ✳ ✳ ✳ ✳ ✳ ✳ ✳ ✳ ✳

The alley was wakened very early next morning by a terrible uproar. Windows opened and heads peered out towards the house where Haggaag, the Rifaaite chief lived. There a large crowd had gathered, shouting and wailing. The entry passage of the house was packed with men and women. There was much asking of questions and giving of explanations, but the many eyes red with crying showed it was something very bad. People hurried over from every house and every hovel, and soon Galta arrived with his men. The crowd made way for them and they reached the passageway. Galta shouted:

'An utter disaster! If only I could have ransomed you, Haggaag!'

The crying and the wailing and the questions stopped, but he didn't hear a single friendly word. He spoke again:

'A foul plot! No chief would be guilty of such treachery, but Kassem, the shepherd, he's a beggar, not a chief. I shan't be happy till I have thrown his body to the dogs.'

A woman shouted angrily:

'Congratulations on becoming chief of the alley, Galta!'

He scowled. Those nearest to him were silent, but there was a murmuring from further back. He bellowed:

'The women had better keep their mouths shut on this black day.'

The woman spoke again:

'Let those who have ears hear.'

There was uproar. When it had died down Galta said:

'A cunning plot. It was done by night to cause trouble between us.'

Another woman shouted:

'Plot indeed! Kassem and the Jerboas are on the gebel, and Haggaag was murdered here in the midst of his own people and of his ambitious neighbours.'

Galta yelled:

'A mad woman! Anyone who listens to her is mad. If you go on like this we'll start killing each other as Kassem planned.'

A jug smashed at Galta's feet. He and his men retreated. He said:

'The bastard knew how to ruin relations between us.'

He went off at once to the Trustee's house. There was a still worse noise after he had gone. Two men, a Rifaaite and a Gebelite, got into a violent quarrel. Two women followed suit, and a couple of boys began fighting. Battles of words began through the windows and there was confusion until the men of both factions had gathered in their own quarters, cudgels at the ready.

The Trustee left his house, surrounded by servants, and went to a point midway through the two factions. He shouted at the top of his voice:

'Come to your senses. Rage has blinded you to your real enemy, the murderer of Haggaag.'

One of the Rifaaites shouted:

'How do you know that? Which of the Jerboas would have dared to enter the alley?'

Rifaat yelled:

'How could the Gebelites have killed Haggaag today when they most needed him?'

'Ask the culprits, don't ask us.'

'The Rifaaites will never submit to a Gebelite chief.'

'They'll pay dearly for his blood.'

The Trustee shouted again:

'Don't fit in with the plot, or you'll see Kassem descending on you like the plague.'

'Let Kassem come if he wants to, but Galta shan't be our chief.'

The Trustee was in despair.

'We're finished. We'll be destroyed.'

There were shouts of:

'Destruction is better than Galta.'

A brick was flung from Rifaa's quarter and landed among the Gebelites. The Gebelites sent one back. The Trustee retreated hastily. The stones flew in both directions. In no time the two factions were involved in a bloody battle, extending even to some of the house tops, where the women pelted each other with stones and lumps of earth and wood. The battle lasted a long time, although the Rifaaites were fighting without their chief, but many of them fell before Galta's unerring blows.

Women began shouting from the windows, but their cries were lost in the noise of the battle. However, they could be seen pointing in horror,

283

now to the east and now to the west. Some people turned to look, and saw Kassem in front of the Big House approaching with a party of his men brandishing their cudgels, and Hassan approaching from the opposite direction with another party. Shouts rang out. Events followed one another quickly. The fighting stopped. Instinctively they drew together, those who were winning and those who were losing, and divided into two parties to meet the attackers. Galta shouted furiously:

'I said it was a trick, and you didn't believe me.'

They got ready for battle in a terrible state of exhaustion and despair. But Kassem suddenly stopped his approach and so did Hassan, both acting on one plan. Kassem shouted at the top of his voice.

'We don't want to harm anyone. There is no victor and no vanquished. We are all children of one alley and one ancestor, and the estate belongs to everyone.'

Galta shouted:

'A new trick!'

Kassem said angrily:

'Don't force them to fight to defend you as chief. Defend your position by yourself if you like.'

Galta screamed:

'Attack!'

He rushed at Kassem's party, and a number of men followed him while others attacked Hassan and his men. But many hung back. The wounded and the exhausted slipped away into their houses, and the hesitant followed them. Only Galta and his gang were left. In spite of that they put up a savage fight, lashing out desperately with cudgels, fists, feet, heads. Galta concentrated his attack on Kassem with blind hatred. They exchanged fierce blows, but Kassem's men overcame Galta's gang by sheer numbers and they went down under dozens of cudgels. Hassan and Sadek leapt on Galta, who was battling with Kassem. Sadek hit his cudgel and Hassan brought his stick down on his head, once, twice, three times. Galta dropped his stick and leapt away, then fell flat on his face like a slaughtered ox. The battle was over and the sounds of cudgels and screams stopped. The victors stood panting and wiping the blood from their faces and arms; but in spite of that they were grinning at the thought of triumph and peace. There were howls from many windows. Galta's men lay scattered over the ground under the scorching sun. Sadek said to Kassem:

'You've won. God has given you victory. Our ancestor makes no mistakes about his choices. The alley will hear no howls of sorrow after today.'

Kassem smiled gently, then turned with determination and looked at the Trustee's house. All eyes were fixed on him.

Kassem led his men to the Trustee's house. They found the door and windows locked. The place was plunged in gloomy silence. Hassan knocked hard at the door and no one answered. Several men heaved at the door until it burst open. They went in, but found no trace of the gatekeeper or any servants. They hurried to the drawing-room, then went over the rooms on all three floors. It was plain that the Trustee with his family and servants had fled from the house. Kassem indeed was not sorry about this, for deep down he had not wanted to kill the Trustee, for the sake of his wife, but for whom he would have been destroyed at the outset. But Hassan and the others were furious at the escape of this man who had made people taste poverty and humiliation all his life.

Thus Kassem completed his victory and became the undisputed leader of the alley. He took over the duties of the trusteeship, for the estate had to have a trustee. The Jerboas went back to their quarter and with them came all those who had left for fear of the chiefs, led by Yehya. Forty days passed peacefully and the wounds healed up and people knew some peace of mind. Then one day Kassem stood in front of the Big House and called everyone to him, both men and women. They went to him, worried and curious, imagining all kinds of things. The place was packed with Jerboas, Rifaaites and Gebelites, all mixed up together.

Kassem looked at once smiling, modest and awe-inspiring. He pointed at the Big House and said:

'There lives Gebelawi, the ancestor of us all. No quarter is more closely related to him than any other, nor is any individual, man or woman.'

Their faces were filled with surprise and relief, especially the faces of those who had expected to hear the speech of a conqueror. Kassem went on:

'Around you is his estate. It will belong to you all equally as he promised Adham when he said to him: 'The estate will belong to your descendants.' We must use it properly so that we all get our share and live as Adham wanted to, in plenty and in peace and happiness.' The people looked at one another as if they were in a dream. 'The Trustee has gone, never to return, and the chiefs have been wiped out, and there need never be another. You won't pay protection money to a tyrant or submit to a drunkard. Your lives can be spent in love and mercy and peace. It is in your hands for things not to return to their former state. Watch your Trustee, and if he betrays you, dismiss him. If one of you is greedy for power, beat him; and if any person or any quarter claim to be lords, punish them. Only in this way will you secure your future. God be with you!'

That day some people were comforted for their dead, others for their defeat. They looked to the future as hopefully as they would watch the full moon rising on a spring night. Kassem shared the income of the estate out fairly after keeping back a sum for construction and repairs. Of course, each person got only a small share, but the feeling of justice and honour was boundless. Kassem's life was spent in building and renovation and peace. The alley had never known such unity and harmony and happiness as it enjoyed in his time. Of course, there were a few Gebelites who concealed other feelings and who whispered to one another: 'Are we, children of Gebel, to be ruled by one of the Jerboas?' and the same was true of some Rifaaites. Indeed, some of the Jerboas did become proud and haughty; but not a voice was raised to disturb the harmony while he was alive.

The Jerboas saw in him a model man such as had never been before nor would ever be again. He combined strength and gentleness, wisdom and simplicity, lordliness and humility, was an honest trustee and was both feared and loved. Moreover he was witty, friendly and correct, and it was a pleasure to smoke hashish with him. He was an affectionate companion, quite apart from having good taste and a love for songs and jokes. Nothing changed about him, except of course his further marriages. It was as if he were following the same course there as he did in his renewal and expansion of the estate. In spite of his love for Badria, he married a beautiful Gebelite woman and another from Rifaa's quarter. He also wooed and won another Jerboa woman. Some people said he was looking for something he had lost with his first wife, Kamar. His uncle, Zechariah, said he wanted to strengthen his ties with all three quarters. But the alley did not need any explanation or justification of what happened; the truth was that for every one time that they admired his character, they admired his virility and love of women many times. In our alley the capacity to love women is a thing men boast of, and it gives a man a prestige as great as or greater than that of being a chief.

Be that as it may, the people had never before felt that they were their own masters, responsible for their affairs without a trustee who robbed them or a chief who humiliated them. Never before had they known the brotherhood and love and peace they knew in his day.

Many people said, if the alley had been plagued with forgetfulness, then it was time to be rid of that plague for ever.

That is what they said.

# Arafa

No one who contemplates us now will believe those tales. Who were Gebel and Rifaa and Kassem? Where are the achievements that are talked of in the cafés? The eye sees only an alley sunk in darkness and storytellers singing of dreams. How have things come to such a pass? What happened to Kassem and his united people and the estate which was used for the good of everyone? Where did this greedy Trustee and these mad chiefs come from?

You will hear them say, as they pass round the pipe in the hashish dens amid laughter and sighs, that Sadek succeeded Kassem in the trusteeship and followed in his footsteps, but that some people thought Hassan had a better right because of his close relationship to Kassem and because he was the man who had killed the chiefs. They urged Hassan to take up his invincible cudgel, but he refused to lead them back to the age of violence. However, the alley was divided against itself, and some of the Gebelites and Rifaaites began proclaiming their feelings openly. When Sadek died the suppressed ambitions came out into the open, the cudgels came back into action and there was bloodshed within each quarter and between the quarters, until the Trustee himself was killed in a battle. There was chaos, and the people found no way out of bringing back someone from Rifaat's family to the post that various rivals were fighting over.

Thus Kadri became Trustee, and the quarters went back to their old feuds, and again a chief ruled over each quarter. There was a series of battles over who should be chief of the alley, until Saadallah was victorious. He became the Trustee's henchman and moved into the Chief's house. They shared out the estate's income fairly at first, and the programme of building and renovation went on. But soon greed got the better of the Trustee, then of the chiefs, as was to be expected, and they went back to the old system; that is to say, the Trustee took half the revenue for himself and divided the other half between the other four, who used it for themselves instead of giving it to those who had a right to it. They did not stop at that, but made their poor followers pay protection money. The building stopped, and houses were left unfinished.

Nothing seemed to have changed, except that the Jerboas' quarter was now the Kassemite quarter, with houses on either side instead of hovels and ruins. The people had become as they were in the bad old days, without honour or dignity. They were eaten up with poverty, threatened by cudgels, pushed and punched. Filth and flies and lice were everywhere, and the place swarmed with beggars and cripples and swindlers. Gebel and Rifaa and Kassem were only names, or songs sung by drugged storytellers in the cafés. Each faction was proud of its hero, of whom no trace remained, and they quarrelled and fought about them. Various phrases went around the hashish dens: 'What's the use?' or 'We're all going to die; and let's hope we die at the hand of God and not of a chief. The best you can do is get drunk or take hashish.' They would wail sad songs about treachery and poverty, or hurl lewd ones at anyone who was seeking comfort for some misfortune. At times of particular misery people would say: 'It's fate. What was the use of Gebel or Rifaa or Kassem? Our fate is to be flies in this world and dust in the next.'

It's amazing that, after all this, our alley kept its high reputation in the neighbourhood. Men from near-by parts would point it out and say respectfully: 'Gebelawi Alley!' while we would sit about in our corners, grave and silent, as though we were wrapped up in our precious memories, or listening to the murmurings of an inner voice: 'It's not impossible that what happened yesterday will happen tomorrow, and the dreams of the storytellers will come true again, and the darkness will lift from our world.'

93 ✳ ✳ ✳ ✳ ✳ ✳ ✳ ✳ ✳ ✳ ✳ ✳ ✳ ✳ ✳ ✳ ✳ ✳ ✳

Early one afternoon, a strange young man approached from the desert, followed by another who was almost a dwarf. He wore a grey smock next to the skin, with a belt, above which it bulged with things. His shoes were worn, his head bare, and his hair thick and tangled. He was brown and had lively, piercing eyes with an anxious look, but his movements were confident. He stopped for a moment in front of the Big House, then came on slowly, followed by his friend. People stared at him as if to say: 'A stranger in the alley! ... What cheek!' He read it in the eyes of the pedlars and the shopkeepers and the people sitting in the cafés or looking down from the windows, even in the eyes of the dogs and cats. He almost imagined the flies themselves would shun him. The boys looked at him, eager to pick a quarrel, and some of them came towards him while others loaded their catapults or began searching the ground for stones. He gave them a friendly smile, put his hand into his breast pocket, pulled out some peppermints, and began handing them out. They came up happily, and stood chewing the sweets and looking up at him in admiration. He said to them, still smiling:

'Is there an empty basement to let? I'll give a bag of peppermints to whoever shows me the way.'

A woman sitting on the ground in front of one of the houses said:

'A thousand curses on you! Who are you to live in our alley?'

He laughed:

'I'm Arafa; at your service. I belong to this alley as much as anyone and I'm back after a long absence.'

The woman eyed him sharply.

'Whose son are you, mother's boy?'

He roared with laughter.

'The son of Gahsha. Did you know her?'

'Gahsha? The fortune-teller?'

'The very one!'

A woman who was leaning against a wall, following the conversation as she deloused a boy's head, said:

'In those days you were a little boy running about after your mother; I remember you. But everything about you's changed except your eyes.'

The first woman said:

'Yes! And where's your mother? Dead? God rest her soul! How often I sat before her basket asking about the unseen and whispering about the future, with her casting shells and telling the answers. God rest your soul, Gahsha.'

'Long life to you! Perhaps you can tell me of an empty basement.'

The woman stared at him out of her bleary eyes and asked:

'What's brought you back after all this time?'

He said with mock wisdom:

'Every man finds his way back to his own place and his own people.'

She pointed to a house in Rifaa's quarter.

'There's a basement there for you; it's been empty since the woman who lived there died in a fire, God rest her soul. Doesn't that frighten you?'

A woman who was looking out of a window laughed and said:

'It's the demons who'll be frightened of this man.'

He looked up, his face full of laughter.

'Delightful alley! What charming, witty people! Now I know why my mother told me to come back!' Then, looking at the seated woman: 'We must all die, whether by fire or water, demons or cudgels.'

He said good-bye to her and went towards the building she had pointed out. Many pairs of eyes followed him. One man said mockingly:

'We knew his mother, but who knew his father?'

An old woman said:

'God alone knows!'

Someone else said:

'He can claim to be the son of a Gebelite man or a Rifaaite or a Kassemite, just as it suits him. God rest his mother's soul!'

Arafa's companion whispered angrily to him:

'Why did we come back to this place?'

Arafa said, still smiling:

'You'll hear this sort of talk everywhere, and anyway this is our alley. It's the only one we can live in, and we've had enough of wandering round the souks and sleeping in the desert or in ruins. Besides, these people are good, in spite of their foul tongues, and slow, in spite of their cudgels; here we can easily earn our living; remember that, Hanash.'

Hanash shrugged his narrow shoulders as if to say: 'God knows.' A drunkard stopped them and asked Arafa:

'What do we call you?'

'Arafa.'

'Arafa what?'

Arafa ibn Gahsha.'

The by-standers roared with laughter at his humiliation. The drunk said:

'We wondered a lot when your mother was pregnant who the father could be. Did she tell you?'

Arafa laughed loudly to hide his discomfort and said:

'She herself died without knowing.'

He went off, leaving them laughing. The news of his return spread fast. Before he had taken over the basement, the boy from the Rifaaite café came and said:

'Our chief, Mr Aggaag, wants to see you.'

He went to the café, which was near by. The first thing that caught his eye was the painting on the wall above the storyteller's bench. At the bottom was a picture of Aggaag mounted on his horse, above it one of the Trustee, Kadri, with his fine moustache and his splendid robe, and at the top was a picture of Gebelawi lifting Rifaa's body out of the grave to take it to his house. He looked at these with interest, then went into the café. He found Aggaag sitting on a bench on the right hand side. Around him sat his friends and supporters. Arafa went over and stood in front of him. The chief gave him a long look of contempt, as if to hypnotize him before attacking. Arafa said, raising a hand:

'Greetings to our chief, our protector and helper.'

Aggaag's narrow eyes were full of scorn.

'Pretty words, young man, but words are not enough round here.'

Arafa smiled.

'Other things will soon follow, I hope.'

'We have more beggars than we need.'

'I'm not a beggar, sir; I'm a well known magician.'

They exchanged glances. Aggaag said with a frown:

'What do you mean, you madman?'

Arafa put his hand in the breast of his smock and pulled out an exquisite little box the size of a jujube. He went up to the chief meekly and offered it to him. He took it without interest, opened it and saw a rod of some substance. He looked up questioningly. Arafa said with boundless confidence:

'A grain of that in a cup of tea two hours before making love, and afterwards either you'll be pleased with Arafa or you can chase him away with your curse.'

They all craned their necks eagerly. Even Aggaag could not hide his interest, but he asked with feigned contempt:

'Is that your magic?'

'I also have precious incenses and wonderful medicines and potions and amulets. My real power is seen when people are weak or sick or barren.'

Aggaag said threateningly:

'Well, well! We look forward to getting your protection money.'

Arafa was alarmed but his face grew still merrier as he said:

'All I possess is at your disposal, sir.'

The chief laughed suddenly and said:

'But you haven't told us who your father was.'

'Perhaps you know better than I do!'

They rocked with laughter, and there were plenty of sarcastic comments. When Arafa got away from the smoke-filled café he said to himself: 'No one knows who his father was, and nor do you, Aggaag. Sons of bitches!'

He and Hanash went over the basement happily. He began saying:

'Bigger than I expected; very suitable, Hanash. This room will be good for seeing people, and we can live in the one at the back. The other one will be the workshop.'

Hanash asked anxiously:

'Which room do you think the woman was burned to death in?'

Arafa's hearty laughter echoed round the empty rooms. He said:

'Are you afraid of demons, Hanash? We shall work with them, as Gebel worked with snakes.'

He looked round happily and said:

'We have only one window, in the room next to the alley; we shall look up at the road between iron bars. This tomb has one excellent feature, it can't be robbed.'

'It might be broken into.'

'It *might*.' Then, with a sigh: 'Everything I do is for people's good, but all my life I've only been abused.'

'Success will repay you for all the harm that's been done to you – or to your poor mother.'

94 ✳ ✳ ✳ ✳ ✳ ✳ ✳ ✳ ✳ ✳ ✳ ✳ ✳ ✳ ✳ ✳ ✳ ✳ ✳ ✳

In his spare time Arafa used to enjoy sitting on an old divan and watching what went on in the alley through the basement window. He sat resting his head against the bars of the window. His eye was at ground level and he could see the passing of feet and barrows, of dogs and cats, of insects and of children. But he could not see people's heads and shoulders except by crouching down and craning his neck. A naked boy stopped in front of him, playing with a dead mouse. An old, blind man passed with a tray of fly-covered beans, melon seeds and sweets in his left hand and a thick walking stick in his right. From another basement window came the snarls of two men quarrelling. Arafa smiled at the naked child and asked gently:

'What's your name, clever boy?'

' 'Ouna.'

'You mean Hassouna. Do you like that dead mouse, Hassouna?'

The little boy threw it at him. But for the bar it would have hit him in the face. The boy scuttled away. Arafa turned to Hanash who was dozing at his feet.

'In every inch of this alley you see the marks of the chiefs, but you find no sign of people like Gebel or Rifaa or Kassem.'

Hanash said, yawning:

'All we see is men like Saadallah and Yussef, Aggaag and Santoury, but all we hear about is Gebel, Rifaa and Kassem.'

'But they did exist, didn't they?'

Hanash pointed at the floor with his finger.

'Our house is Rifaaite; all the people in it are followers of Rifaa, and the storytellers tell every night how he lived and died for the sake of love and happiness; and yet the first thing we hear every morning is their quarrels and curses. That's what they're like, the women as well as the men.'

292

Arafa grimaced.

'But they did exist, didn't they?'

'Insults are the least of what happens among Rifaa's people. Those fights! God help us! Only yesterday a man here lost his eye.'

Arafa stood up angrily:

'What a place! God rest your soul, mother! Look at us, for example, everyone makes use of us and no one respects us.'

'They don't respect anyone.'

He ground his teeth.

'Except the chiefs.'

Hanash said with a laugh:

'At least you are the only man in the alley who has dealings with everyone, Gebelites and Rifaaites and Kassemites.'

'Curse them all.'

He was silent for a while, his eyes shining in the gloom of the basement. He said:

'Every faction boasts stupidly about its own man, though all that is left is the name, and they never try to go any further. Cowards! Sons of bitches!'

His first client had been a Rifaaite woman who had come to him during his first week in his new home and had asked in a hushed voice:

'How can a woman be got rid of without anyone knowing?'

In his alarm he had looked at her questioningly and said:

'That's not my job, madam. If you want medicine for body or mind, I'm at your service.'

'Aren't you a magician?'

'Yes, for things that do good to people. But killing, that's for other people.'

'You're afraid, perhaps? But we'll be two conspirators with one secret.'

He had said with gentle irony:

'Rifaa wasn't like that.'

She had exclaimed:

'Rifaa! Lord have mercy on him! We live in an alley where mercy is no use; if it had been any use, Rifaa himself wouldn't have died.'

She had given up hope and gone, but he was not sorry. Rifaa himself, the finest of men, had not found safety here; so however could one hope for safety if one started one's work with a crime? And his mother! What sufferings she had undergone, without having done anyone any harm. No, he must be on the best terms with everyone, as befitted any sensible tradesman. He began visiting all the cafés, always finding a client he knew. He listened to the storytellers' tales in the various quarters until they were all mixed up in his head.

His first Kassemite client had been an old man who whispered to him with a grin:

'We've heard of the present you gave to Aggaag, the Rifaaite chief.'

Arafa studied the wrinkled face, smiling. The man said:

'Let us have one; you won't be surprised if there's life in you.'

They exchanged smiles. The old man was encouraged and said:

'You're a Kassemite, aren't you? That's what our people say.'

Arafa asked him scornfully:

'Do they know my father, your people?'

'A Kassemite is known by his looks; and you're a Kassemite. It was us who raised the alley to the heights ... but oh dear, oh dear! It's an unlucky place.' Then, coming back to the point: 'Please may I have my present?'

The old man went off holding the little jar up to his bleary eye, with a new vigour and hope in his walk.

His latest visitor had been someone unexpected. Arafa was sitting on a cushion in front of an incense burner, which was giving off a delicious smoke, when in came Hanash with an old Nubian.

'Mr Yuness, his honour the Trustee's gatekeeper.'

Arafa jumped up and stretched out his arms in greeting.

'Hello! Welcome! This is a great honour. Please sit down.'

They sat down side by side. The gatekeeper said without any preliminaries:

'Her ladyship Lady Nezira, the Trustee's wife, has been having such bad dreams that she can hardly sleep.'

Arafa's eyes lit up with interest and his heart beat more strongly with hope and ambition, but he simply said:

'Just a phase! It will pass off.'

'But her ladyship is very upset and sent me to you for something suitable.'

Arafa felt important.

'It would be best for me to speak to her myself.'

'Impossible! She won't come to you, and you're not to visit her.'

Arafa overcame his disappointment and fought hard not to lose this golden chance.

'I must have her handkerchief or some personal possession of hers.'

The gatekeeper bowed his turbaned head and stood up to go. When they got to the door he hesitated for a moment, then leaned over and whispered in Arafa's ear:

'We've heard about your present to Aggaag, the Rifaaite chief.'

When the gatekeeper had gone off with his present, Arafa and Hanash had a good laugh. Hanash said:

'I wonder who he's taken the present for, himself or the Trustee or her ladyship?'

Arafa exclaimed scornfully:

'What a place for presents and cudgels!'

He went over to the window to look at the alley by night. The wall opposite was silver in the moonlight, and the crickets were chirping. From the café came the voice of the Rifaaite storyteller:

Adham said:

'When will you realize that we are no longer joined by any tie?'

Idris said:

Merciful heavens! Aren't you my brother? That's a tie that cannot be broken.'

'Idris! You've tormented me enough.'

'Grief is ugly, but we've both been hit; you've lost Hammam and Kadri, and I've lost Hind. Gebelawi's got a whoring granddaughter and a killer grandson.'

Adham roared:

'If your punishment is not as bad as your deeds, let the world turn to dust!'

Arafa turned away from the window in disgust. When would the alley stop retelling stories? When would the world turn to dust? His mother had often repeated this phrase: 'If your punishment is not as bad as your deeds, let the world turn to dust!' His poor mother, living in the desert! But what had the alley gained from these stories?

95 ✶ ✶ ✶ ✶ ✶ ✶ ✶ ✶ ✶ ✶ ✶ ✶ ✶ ✶ ✶ ✶ ✶ ✶ ✶

Arafa and Hanash were working with determination in the back room of the basement by the light of a gas lamp fixed to the wall. The room was not habitable because of its dampness and darkness and its position at the back, so Arafa made it his workshop. On the floor and in the corners were neat piles of paper talismans, earths, lime, plants and spices, dried animals and insects, mice, frogs and scorpions, pieces of glass and bottles, tins of liquids with strange, pungent smells, charcoal and a stove. Shelves were fixed to the walls and held all kinds of vessels and containers and bags. Arafa was absorbed in mixing several substances into a paste in an earthenware vessel. The sweat was dripping from his face and he wiped it on the sleeve of his smock from time to time. Hanash was stretched out nearby watching with interest, ready to follow any instructions Arafa might give. Wishing to say something helpful, he remarked:

'The hardest worker in this wretched alley doesn't take anything like this trouble, and what's the reward? A few millièmes, or at best a piastre!'

'God bless my mother! Only I know how good she was. The day she handed me over to that wonderful magician who can read all your thoughts, my life changed completely. But for her I'd have been at best a pickpocket or a beggar.'

'A few millièmes!'

'Money mounts up if you're patient; don't despair of that. Violence is not the only way to riches. Don't forget the position I enjoy; the people who come to me rely on me completely and put their happiness in my hands; that's not to be sneezed at. And don't forget the pleasure of magic itself: the pleasure of squeezing something useful out of impure substances; the pleasure of healing people when your instructions are obeyed. And then there are the secret powers which you'd love to get if you could.'

Hanash looked at the stove. Cutting abruptly across Arafa's train of thought, he said:

'I'd better put the stove in the light shaft, or we'll suffocate.'

'Light it in hell, but don't interrupt my thoughts. None of the simpletons who think themselves important in this alley could understand the importance of the things that are made in this dark, dirty room with its strange smells. They understand the usefulness of "the present", but that present isn't everything. Unimaginable wonders can come out of this room. The fools don't realize the true value of Arafa. Perhaps they will some day, and then they'll have to ask God's mercy on my mother and not insult her as they do now.'

Hanash half stood up, then squatted down again, saying resentfully:

'Some idiotic chief may ruin all these good things with his cudgel.'

'We don't harm anyone, and we pay our protection money; how can we come to harm, you alarm bell!'

Hanash laughed.

'What did Rifaa do wrong?'

Arafa glared at him.

'Why annoy me with such thoughts?'

'You're hoping to get rich, but here nobody gets rich except the chiefs. You hope to become powerful, but here nobody is allowed to be powerful except them. Work that out, brother.'

Arafa said nothing until he was sure he had mixed the substances properly. Then he glanced at Hanash and saw that he still looked anxious. He laughed.

'My mother warned me before you. Thank you, Hanash Alarm Bell! But I've come back with a plan in my head.'

'It seems nothing interests you any more except magic.'

Arafa said, quite carried away:

'Magic is a wonderful thing; no one knows where it'll stop. For someone who possesses it, even cudgels are children's toys. Learn that Hanash; don't be a fool; imagine if all the people in the alley were magicians . . .'

'If they were, they'd all starve to death!'

Arafa laughed loudly, showing his fine teeth.

'Don't be a fool, Hanash. Ask yourself what they'd be able to do. My God! The miracles would flow as plentifully as curses and insults do now.'

'Yes, provided they didn't starve to death first.'

'Yes, and they wouldn't die as long as they . . .'

But he didn't finish his sentence. He was thinking so hard that his hands stopped their work. Then he said:

'The Kassemite storyteller says Kassem wanted to use the estate so that everyone got what he needed and do away with work in order to enjoy the blissful happiness that Adham dreamed of.'

'That's what Kassem said.'

'But bliss isn't the final goal. Imagine it if life was spent in leisure and song; it's a beautiful dream, but a laughable one, Hanash. What would be really beautiful would be to do away with work in order to work miracles.'

Hanash shook his great head, which seemed to rest directly on his shoulders, to show his disagreement with talk that seemed to have no meaning. Then he spoke again in a serious, business-like tone:

'Now let me light the stove under the light shaft.'

'Do that, and throw yourself in the flames; all you deserve is to be burnt.'

Arafa left the workshop after an hour, went to the divan and sat down, looking out through the window. After the silence the bustle of life filled his ears and he heard the pedlars' cries, the women's gossip, the shouted jokes, and the choice insults which accompanied the endless coming and going. He noticed that something new had been placed against the opposite wall: a makeshift café made of a frame with an old sheet thrown over it. In it were ranged boxes of coffee beans, tea leaves and cinnamon, a stove, coffee pots, cups, mugs and spoons. An old man sat on the ground fanning the stove to boil water, while behind the tent stood a young girl calling in a warm voice: 'Lovely coffee, my dears!' The café was at the point where the Kassemite and Rifaaite quarters met. There were plenty of customers: barrow boys and poor people. Arafa took a long look at the girl from behind the bars. That brown face with the black veil, how pretty it was! That coffee-coloured dress which covered her down to the ankles, its hem brushing the ground when she went to take an order or brought back an empty cup. How modest! And that slim figure! How lovely her eyes were, except that the left eyelid was red, perhaps from sand. From their faces she and the old man were clearly father and daughter. He must have fathered her at an advanced age, as often happens in the alley. Arafa shouted to her without any bashfulness:

'Young woman! A cup of tea, please!'

She looked across at him, then quickly filled a cup from a pot half buried in the sand. She brought it across the alley to him and he smiled as he took it and said:

'Bless you. How much?'

'Two millièmes.'

'That's a lot. But no price would be too high for you.'

'In a big café it costs five, and it's no different from what you have in your hand.'

She went off without waiting for him to speak. He sipped his tea before it could get cold, not taking his eyes off her. How happy he would be to have a young girl like that! She was perfect, except for one inflamed eye, which he could easily cure. But he would need more money than he had as yet. The basement was all ready; all that was needed was for Hanash to sleep in the hall, or in the consulting room if he wanted, provided he got rid of the insects regularly.

He heard a strange murmuring and saw that the people were looking towards the top of the alley. Some of them were saying: 'Santoury ... Santoury!' He leaned forward as far as the bars of the window would let him, and saw the chief approaching, surrounded by a gang of his men. As he passed the makeshift café, he noticed the girl and asked one of his men:

'Who is she?'

'Awaatif, daughter of Shakroun.'

Santoury raised his eyebrows in interest and went on to his own quarter. Arafa felt angry and upset. He waved the empty cup and the girl came over daintily and collected it, taking the two millièmes. He jerked his head in the direction Santoury had gone.

'Aren't you worried at all?'

'I'll ask for your help when I need it; but will you help?'

He was hurt by her scorn, a scorn that saddened rather than provoked. Then he heard Hanash calling him and he jumped down from the divan and hurried inside.

Arafa acquired many clients as time went on. But none of them pleased him as much as Awaatif, the day she came to his consulting room. He forgot the dignified air he used to put on for his customers and jumped up to welcome her. He sat her down on a cushion in front of him and himself sat down tailor-wise, beside himself with joy. He looked her up and down, but his glance rested on her left eye, which was almost closed by the swollen and inflamed eyelid. He said:

'You've neglected it, my girl; it was already red the first day I saw you.'

'I thought it was enough to bathe it in warm water; busy people like me do forget.'

'It's not right for you to neglect your health, especially if it's a matter of something precious like your pretty eyes.'

She smiled, touched by the compliment, while he reached back to a shelf for a mug. From it he took a small package.

'Tie the contents in a handkerchief, steam it over boiling water, then bind it over your eye, every night until it's as beautiful as its fellow.'

She took the package and got out her purse, glancing at him inquiringly with her right eye. He laughed.

'Forget about it. We're neighbours – and friends.'

'But you pay for the tea you drink.'

'In fact, though, I'm paying your father. What a grand old man! I wish I knew him. I'm sorry he has to go on working at his age.'

'But his health is good and he refuses to stay at home. His great age makes him sad about life, for he was one of those who saw the events of Kassem's time.'

Arafa's face lit up with interest.

'Really! Was he one of his men?'

'Oh no; but he tasted the happiness of those days and still sighs for them.'

'I want to get to know him and hear him talk.'

'Don't get him on that subject; I'd rather he forgot about it, for his own safety. He was once in a tavern, drinking with some of his friends, and when he got drunk he stood up and shouted at the top of his voice that things should go back to what they were in Kassem's day. As soon as he got outside he found Santoury in front of him. The brute beat him up and left him unconscious.'

Arafa felt indignant; he looked craftily at Awaatif and said:

'There's no safety for anyone with these chiefs.'

She stole a glance at him, wondering what was behind his words. She said:

'That's true, there's no safety for anyone.'

He hesitated, biting his lips, then said:

'I saw Santoury giving you such a look.'

She looked down to hide a smile.

'The devil take him!'

'Doesn't it give a girl some pleasure to be admired by a chief like him?'

'He has four wives.'

His heart sank.

'And supposing he had nine?'

'I've hated him ever since he attacked my father, and the same goes for all those heartless brutes. They take their protection money so haughtily you'd think they were doing you a favour.'

'Splendid, Awaatif! That's what Kassem thought when he destroyed them; but they came back like a plague.'

'That's why my father sighs for the days of Kassem.'

He shook his head in sudden disillusion.

'And others sigh for the days of Rifaa and Gebel; but the past will not return.'

She said, with charming indignation:

'You say that because you didn't see Kassem like my father did.'

'Did *you* see him?'

'My father told me . . .'

'My mother told *me*. But what's the good of that? It won't deliver us from the chiefs. My mother herself was one of their victims, and look at the way they talk about her after her death.'

'Really?'

His face clouded over.

'That's why I'm afraid for you, Awaatif. They threaten goods, livelihood, love, peace . . . I tell you, since I saw that brute gaping at you I've been convinced of the need to destroy them.'

'They say it's the will of our ancestor.'

'And where is our ancestor?'

'In the Big House.'

He said quietly:

'Oh yes, your father talks about Kassem, and Kassem talked about our ancestor; that's what we hear; but all we see is Kadri and Saadallah and Aggaag and Santoury and Yussef. We need power to deliver us from the torment; what use are memories?'

He became aware that the drift of the conversation had almost spoilt the meeting for him and said in a different tone:

'The alley needs power just as I need you.'

She gazed at him unbelievingly and he smiled with a boldness that

matched his piercing eyes. He said seriously, to ward off the anger showing in her frown:

'A beautiful girl, who works so hard she forgets about her eye till it's
swollen! She comes to me thinking she needs me, and finds that in fact
I'm the one who needs her.'

She made to get up.

'It's time I went.'

'Don't be annoyed, please. Remember, I haven't said anything that's
come as a surprise; you must have noticed my admiration these past
days, for my eyes are always on your café. A bachelor like me can't live
alone for ever; his untidy house needs looking after, and his earnings are
more than he needs; someone must share them with him.'

She left the room. He stood at the end of the hall to see her off. She
seemed to be unwilling to leave him without saying anything. She murmured: 'Good-bye!'

He stayed where he was and sang quietly to himself:

> Your cheek is soft as velvet,
> Your face as radiant as the moon.
> Loveliest creature I saw yet,
> Fill my cup of joy up soon.

He walked briskly to the workshop and found Hanash engrossed in his
tasks.

'What are you doing?'

Hanash showed him a bottle.

'Full, and firmly sealed. But it must be tried out in the desert.'

Arafa took it and tested the cork.

'Yes, in the desert; otherwise we'll give ourselves away.'

Hanash said anxiously:

'We're begining to earn a living, and life has begun to smile on us.
Don't throw away the happiness God has given you.'

Hanash was beginning to value life now that it tasted sweeter. Arafa
smiled at this thought and looked at him for a while, then said:

'She was your mother as well as mine.'

'Yes, but she begged you not to think of revenge.'

'You used to think differently.'

'We'd be killed before we could get revenge.'

Arafa laughed.

'I won't hide it from you that I stopped thinking of revenge long ago.'

Hanash's face shone.

'Give me the bottle and we'll empty it, brother.'

But Arafa held it tight, saying:

'No! We'll experiment with it until it's perfect.'

Hanash frowned at this teasing. Arafa went on:

'I mean what I say, Hanash; believe me, I gave up the idea of revenge, not because of our mother's pleading, but because I was convinced that we could destroy the chiefs only by ceasing to look for revenge.'

'Because you love this girl.'

Arafa laughed heartily.

'Love for the girl, love for life; call it what you like ... Kassem was right.'

'What has Kassem to do with you! Kassem was carrying out our ancestor's wishes.'

He pulled a face.

'Who can say? The people tell their stories, but we in this room are doing something decisive and certain. What security is there in the alley? Aggaag will come tomorrow to steal our earnings. If I lift a hand to marry Awaatif, Santoury's cudgel will be in my way. It's the same with every man, even the beggars. What upsets me is what upsets the alley; what will make me safe is what will make it safe. I am not a chief nor one of Gebelawi's men, but in this room I have wonderful things which give me a power ten times that of Gebel and Rifaa and Kassem put together.'

He lifted the bottle as if to throw it, then gave it back to Hanash.

'We'll use it tonight on the gebel. Cheer up and try to get your enthusiasm back.'

He left the work room, and went to the window, and sat down on the divan, looking across at the makeshift café. Night was falling slowly, and she was crying her wares. She avoided looking at his window, which showed how much he was on her mind. A smile played faintly on her lips. Arafa smiled, his whole world smiled. He was so pleased that he swore he would comb his hair every morning. From Gemàlia came the noise of people chasing a thief. The drone of the fiddle started in the café, and the storyteller started his evening by chanting:

> First of all – ah! Hail to Kadri our Trustee!
> Next of all – ah! Hail to Saadallah our chief!
> Third of all – ah! Hail to our Santoury!

Arafa was torn mercilessly out of his dream. He said to himself wearily: 'The stories are beginning again; when will they end? What's the use of listening to them every night? The storytellers sing, and the hashish dens wake up. Miserable alley!'

A strange confusion came into Shakroun's life. Sometimes he would speak in a very loud voice, as if he were making a speech. People used to say sympathetically: 'Old age! Just old age!' He would get very angry for the slightest reason or for no reason at all; 'Old age!' they said. He would lapse into silence for long periods, until he was absolutely forced to speak; 'Old age!' they said. He would say things that were counted as heresy in the alley, and people said anxiously; 'God save us from going gaga!' Arafa used to watch him often from behind his bars, with tender concern. One day as he was studying him he said to himself: 'An impressive old man, in spite of his tattered clothes and his dirtiness!' On his gaunt face was printed the decline that had overtaken the alley since Kassem's day, for it was his bad luck to have been a contemporary of Kassem's and to have enjoyed justice and security, and received his full share of the estate's revenue and seen the new buildings go up, and then to see all this stop by order of Kadri; in short he was an unfortunate man for whom life had lasted longer than it needed to. He saw Awaatif coming, her face without blemish now that her eye was cured. He turned his attention to her and shouted:

'Tea please, miss.'

She brought him a cup and he said, before he took it, to make sure she stayed:

'Congratulations on your recovery, flower of the alley.'

'Thanks be to God – and thank you.'

He took the cup, touching her fingers with his. She went away, and her springy step showed that she welcomed this. It would be so right for him to take the decisive step now, and he did not lack courage, but Santoury would make him pay many times over. Was it Shakroun's fault for putting his daughter in Santoury's path? But he was a poor man, worn out by pushing around his barrow until he was forced to stop and open this unlucky café.

From the distance came a great noise. The people looked in the direction of Gemalia. Soon a carriage appeared, full of women singing and clapping. In the midst of them was a bride returning from the baths. The boys ran towards the carriage cheering and hung on to its sides as it made its way towards Gebel's quarter. For a while the air throbbed with youyous and shouts of congratulation and whispered obscenities. Shakroun stood up furiously and thundered:

'Hit . . . Hit . . .'

Awaatif hurried over to him and sat down, patting him on the back. Arafa wondered whether the man was dreaming, or seeing things. What a curse old age was! And if it was like this, how could Gebelawi

303

still be living? He looked at the old man and when he had calmed down asked him:

'Mr Shakroun, have you ever seen Gebelawi?'

He answered without looking at him:

'Fool! Don't you know Gebelawi's been shut up in his house since before Gebel's time?'

Awaatif smiled, and Arafa laughed and said:

'May God grant you a long life, Mr Shakroun!'

'A prayer that meant something when life meant something.'

Awaatif came to take the cup. She whispered:

'Let him be. He isn't sleeping at all at night.'

'My heart is with you, Awaatif.' Then, quickly before she could go: 'I'd like to talk to you about us.'

She raised a warning finger and went. He watched some children playing leapfrog. Suddenly Santoury appeared, coming from the Kassemite quarter. Arafa drew his head back instinctively from the bars. What had brought him? It was lucky he lived in Rifaa's quarter and had Aggaag as a protector, Aggaag who was so taken with his 'presents'. The chief came up and stopped in front of Shakroun's café. He said, examining Awaatif's face:

'One coffee without sugar.'

A woman burst out laughing at her window, and another said:

'What has brought the Kassemite chief to ask for coffee at the beggar's café?'

Santoury seemed unconcerned. Awaatif brought him the cup and Arafa's heart turned over. The chief waited for his coffee to cool, grinning lewdly at her with flashing gold teeth. Arafa promised him mentally a dreadful beating. Santoury took a sip and said:

'Bless your beautiful hands.'

She was as much afraid to smile as she was to frown. Shakroun looked at them in alarm. Santoury gave her a five piastre piece and she put her hand in her pocket for change, but he did not seem to expect anything and went back to the Kassemite café. Awaatif was unsure what to do, and Arafa said to her in a low voice:

'Don't go to him.'

'And his change?'

Shakroun got up in spite of his weakness, took the change and went to the café. A little later the old man came back to his seat and was soon laughing helplessly. His daughter went up to him and said:

'That's enough laughing.'

He got up again, faced the Big House and shouted:

'Gebelawi! Gebelawi!'

Eyes were fixed on him from windows and doorways, cafés and basements. The boys hurried towards him. Even the dogs looked at him. He shouted:

'Gebelawi! How long are you going to keep quiet while your wishes are ignored and your money's wasted? You're being robbed, just like your children, Gebelawi.'

The children cheered and many people guffawed. The old man went on yelling:

'Gebelawi can't you hear? Don't you know what's happened to us? Why did you punish Idris, who was so much better than our chiefs, Gebelawi?'

At that, Santoury came out of the café, shouting:

'Watch it, you old fool.'

Shakroun screamed at him:

'Damn you, filthy wretch!

Many people murmured anxiously: 'He's had it.' Santoury came up to him, blind with rage, and punched him on the head. He staggered and would have fallen, but Awaatif caught him. Santoury saw her and went back to his place. She said, in tears:

'Let's go home, father.'

Arafa helped her to hold him up, but the old man tried feebly to push them away, breathing heavily. The bystanders were silent. A woman said from a window:

'It's your fault, Awaatif, he should have been kept at home.'

Awaatif said, still crying:

'There was nothing I could do.'

Shakroun murmured in a weak voice:

'Gebelawi! Gebelawi!'

## 98 ✳ ✳ ✳ ✳ ✳ ✳ ✳ ✳ ✳ ✳ ✳ ✳ ✳ ✳ ✳ ✳ ✳ ✳ ✳

A little before dawn a long howl shattered the stillness. The people realized that Shakroun was dead. It was not a strange event for the alley. Santoury's cronies said: 'To hell with him; he was bad-mannered, and that was the death of him.' Arafa said to Hanash:

'Shakroun has been killed, like so many others. The murderers don't even try to hide their crimes, and no one dares to complain or bring a single witness.'

'What a disaster! Why did we ever come here?'

'It's our alley.'

'Our mother left it broken-hearted. Damn it and its people!'

'But it is ours.'

'It's as if we were making up for things we didn't do.'

'The worst thing of all is to give up.'

Hanash said despairingly:

'The experiment with the bottle failed on the gebel.'

'But it'll succeed next time.'

When Shakroun's bier was carried out, only Awaatif and Arafa followed it. Everyone was astonished at Arafa's taking part in the funeral. They whispered about his remarkable courage – that mad magician! Still more amazing, Santoury joined the funeral procession when it was in the middle of Kassem's quarter. What boldness! What shamelessness! But he did it unabashed. He said to Awaatif!'

'Long may you live, Awaatif!'

Arafa realized that this was an introduction to the coming proposition. Meanwhile an important change came over the funeral procession in the twinkling of an eye; the friends and neighbours who had hung back out of fear hurried to join in and soon filled the road. Santoury said again:

'Long may you live, Awaatif!'

She looked at him defiantly.

'You kill the man and then attend his funeral.'

Santoury said, loud enough for many to hear:

'That was once said to Kassem.'

Several voices said:

'For God's sake, woman! The hour of our death is in the hand of God!'

Awaatif shouted:

'My father was killed by a blow from your hand.'

Santoury said:

'God forgive you, Awaatif. If I'd really hit him he'd have died on the spot; but in fact I didn't hit him, I just threatened him; everyone will bear witness to that.'

People said hastily:

'He threatened him. His hand didn't touch him.'

Awaatif cried out:

'God of vengeance!'

With a forebearance that was to become proverbial, Santoury said:

'God forgive you, Awaatif!'

Arafa leaned over and half whispered to her:

'Let the funeral go off peacefully.'

Before Arafa knew what was happening, one of Santoury's men, Addaad, hit him in the face and shouted:

'What business is it of yours to intervene between her and the chief?'

Arafa turned in amazement and was hit again harder than the first time. Another man punched him; a third spat in his face; a fourth seized his collar; a fifth pushed him over so that he fell on his back. A sixth man said to him as he kicked him:

'You'll be buried at Kerafa if you go near her.'

He lay there for a while, dazed. Then he gathered his strength and stood up, in considerable pain. A crowd of children had surrounded him and they began shouting: 'The calf is down – fetch the knife.' He limped back to his basement, mad with rage. Hanash looked at him sadly and said:

'I told you not to go.'

He screamed furiously:

'Shut up! Curse them!'

Hanash said with gentle determination:

'Take your eyes off this girl, or it's good-bye to us.'

Arafa thought for a while, staring at the ground, then looked up with a determined expression and said:

'You'll see me married to her sooner than you think.'

'That's sheer madness.'

'And Aggaag will be at the head of the wedding procession.'

'You might as well soak your clothes in alcohol and jump in the fire.'

'I'm going to repeat the experiment with the bottle tonight in the desert.'

He stayed at home for several days and didn't leave it, but he kept in touch with Awaatif by way of the barred window. Then he met her secretly, after the period of mourning was over, in the entry passage of her house. He said:

'We'd better get married straight away.'

She was not surprised at his proposal, but she said sadly:

'If I say yes to you, it will cause dreadful trouble.'

'Aggaag has agreed to take charge of the ceremony, and you can see what that means.'

Preparations were made with great secrecy till everything was ready. The alley learned without any warning that Awaatif, daughter of Shakroun, had married the magician and moved to his home, and that Aggaag had witnessed the marriage. Many people were astounded, and others wondered how it had come about; how had Arafa dared to do it, and how had he persuaded Aggaag to give it his blessing? But the old and wise said: 'There'll be trouble.'

Santoury and his men gathered in the Kassemite café, and Aggaag heard
of this and met his men in the Rifaaite café. The rest of the alley knew
about the two gatherings, and in no time the area between the two
quarters was empty of pedlars and beggars and children, and the shops
and windows were shut. Santoury led his men out, and Aggaag did
likewise. There was an ugly atmosphere and conflagration was imminent.
One good man shouted from a housetop:

'What are people getting angry about? Think, before any blood is
spilt.'

Aggaag shouted in the awed silence:

'We aren't angry; who's getting angry?'

Santoury said gruffly:

'You've acted as no colleague should, and no chief can approve of
what you have done.'

'And what have I done?'

'You protected a man who was defying me.'

'The man only married a lonely girl after her father's death, and I
attend the marriage of every Rifaaite.'

'He's not a Rifaaite, and no one knows who his father was; not even he
does. Perhaps you are his father, or maybe I am – or any beggar in the
alley.'

'But now he's living in my quarter.'

'Only because he found a basement.'

'Well?'

Santoury screamed:

'You know you've acted as no colleague should.'

Aggaag shouted:

'Stop screaming. It's not worth a cock fight.'

'Perhaps it's worth just that.'

'God give me patience!'

'Aggaag, watch out for yourself.'

'You damned weakling!'

'You damned bastard!'

The cudgels would have been raised but for a voice that bellowed:

'Shame on you, men!'

They turned to see who it was, and there was Saadallah making his
way through the Rifaaites till he stood midway between the two quarters. He said:

'Put down your cudgels.'

Down went the cudgels. Saadallah looked first at Santoury, then at
Aggaag, and said:

'I don't want to hear anyone speak. Go away quietly. A blood bath because of a woman? How childish!'

The men broke up in silence. Saadallah went back to his house. Arafa and Awaatif in their basement could not belive that the night would pass peacefully. They watched what went on outside with pounding hearts and dry mouths. When they heard Saadallah's commanding voice, Awaatif sighed deeply, and said:

'What a cruel life!'

He wanted to reassure her a little, and said, tapping his head:

'I work with this, like Gebel, and like Kassem, the crafty schemer.'

She swallowed hard.

'Do you think there can be any lasting safety?'

He hugged her, making a show of cheerfulness.

'If only every couple was as happy as we are.'

She buried her head in his shoulder, breathing hard, and whispered:

'Can the thing stop there?'

'No chief is ever safe.'

She raised her head.

'I know that, but I have a wound that won't heal till I see him dead.'

He knew who she meant and he looked thoughtfully into her eyes and said:

'In a case like yours, revenge is essential, but it won't be final. Our safety is threatened not because Santoury wants to be violent towards us, but because the whole alley is at the mercy of the chiefs. If we overcome Santoury, who can say that Aggaag won't start a quarrel with us tomorrow, or Yussef the day after that? Either everyone is safe or no one is.'

She smiled faintly.

'Do you want to be like Gebel or Rifaa or Kassem?'

He kissed her hair, savouring its scent of cloves, and made no answer. She spoke again:

'They were given their task by our ancestor the Founder.'

'Our ancestor the Founder! Everyone who's in trouble shouts 'Gebelawi!' just as your poor father did. But did you ever hear of people like us, never seeing their ancestor although they live round his locked house? And have you ever heard of the founder of a trust letting people play havoc with it and not making any move at all?'

'It's old age.'

He said suspiciously:

'I've never heard of anyone living as long as this.'

'They say there's a man over a hundred and fifty in Souk Mukattam.'

'God is all-powerful!' Then, after a silence, he murmured: 'It's the same with magic; it's all-powerful.'

She laughed at his delusion, pressing her fingers into his chest.

'Your magic is able to heal someone's eye.'

'And to do countless other things.'

She sighed.

'How easily we get carried away! We enjoy talking as though nothing threatened us.'

He took no notice of her interruption but went on:

'Magic may one day be able to put an end to the chiefs and build houses and bring abundant food for all the people of the alley.'

'Can that happen before the end of the world?'

His eyes swam dreamily.

'Oh, if only we were all magicians!'

'If! Kassem didn't take long to achieve justice without your magic.'

'And a long time that lasted! But with magic, the effect is lasting. Don't look down on magic, my darling, it's no less important than our love; like it, it can create a new life. But it can only work properly if more of us are magicians.'

She asked playfully:

'And how will that come about?'

He thought for a long time before answering:

'When justice is achieved, when the Founder's conditions are put into effect, and when most of us are freed from toil and rely on magic.'

'Do you want it to be an alley of magicians?' She laughed sweetly, and went on: 'What is the way to carry out the ten conditions if our ancestor is bedridden, and seems to be no longer able to give the job to one of his children?'

He looked at her strangely.

'Why don't we go and see him?'

She laughed again.

'Could you get into the Trustee's house?'

'Never! But maybe I can get into the Big House.'

She tapped his hand and said:

'That's enough joking till we're sure of our lives.'

He smiled mysteriously.

'If I was a joker I wouldn't have come back to the alley.'

Something in his tone alarmed her. She stared at him in amazement and exclaimed:

'You mean what you say!'

He gazed at her without a word. She went on:

'Imagine if they caught you in the Big House.'

'What's so strange about a man being in his grandfather's house!'

'Say you're joking. God! Why are you looking at me so seriously? Unbelievable! Why do you want to go and see him?'

310

'Isn't a meeting with him worth the risk?'

'Those were only words; how have they become real?'

He stroked her hand soothingly.

'Since I came back I've been thinking to myself about things that haven't occurred to anyone.'

'Why can't we live as we are?'

'If only we could! They won't let us live as we are; and a human being has to be secure in his life.'

'Then let's run away.'

'I shan't run away while I have my magic.'

He drew her gently to him and began stroking her shoulder, whispering in her ear:

'We'll have plenty of opportunities to talk, but now just set your mind at rest.'

100 ✳ ✳ ✳ ✳ ✳ ✳ ✳ ✳ ✳ ✳ ✳ ✳ ✳ ✳ ✳ ✳ ✳

Was the man mad or deluded? That's what Awaatif began wondering as she watched Arafa working and thinking. From her point of view the only thing that spoilt the tranquility of those days was her desire for revenge on Santoury, her father's murderer. Revenge was a time-honoured tradition in the alley; but she could forget it, though reluctantly, for the sake of the happiness marriage had given her. However, Arafa believed revenge on Santoury was only part of a great task that he had sworn to perform – or so it seemed. She did not understand him. Did he think he was one of the men the storytellers sang of? But Gebelawi had not charged him to do anything, and he clearly did not have much confidence in Gebelawi or in the tales of the storytellers. One certain fact was that he gave far, far more of his time and energy to magic than he needed to do to earn his living. When he thought, his ideas went beyond himself and his household to general problems that no one was interested in, like violence and the trusteeship, the estate and its revenue. He dreamed about a magic future, although he was the one man who did not take hashish because his work in the back room needed wakefulness and attention.

But all this was nothing beside his mad desire to get into the Big House.

'Why, my husband?'

'To ask his advice about the way things should be.'

'But you know the way things should be, we all know; so what need is there to risk death?'

I want to know the ten conditions of the endowment.'

'The important thing is not knowledge but action; and what can you do?'

'The truth is I want to look at the book that was the cause of Adham's being thrown out, if the stories are true.'

'What interests you in that book?'

'I don't know what makes me believe it's a book of magic. Gebelawi's exploits can only be explained if he used magic, not his muscles and a cudgel as they imagine.'

'What need is there for these risks when you're happy and you're earning plenty?'

'Don't imagine Santoury has forgotten us. Whenever I go out I'm almost knocked down by the nasty looks of his men.'

'Your magic is quite enough; leave the Big House alone.'

'There is the book, the greatest book of magic, the secret of Gebelawi's power, which he kept even from his son.'

'Maybe it won't be anything like what you imagine.'

'And maybe it will be worth all the risk.'

Then one time he took the final step in his explanation and said to her:

'That's how I am, Awaatif, what's to be done? I'm just the lowly son of a wretched woman and an unknown father; everyone knows that and jokes about it. But the one thing that still interests me in the world is the Big House; it's not strange for a bastard to look with all his being towards his ancestor. My backroom has taught me not to believe in anything till I've seen it with my own eyes and tested it with my own hands. There's no escape from getting into the Big House. I may find the power I am seeking for and I may find nothing at all, but I'll reach some certainty, which will be better than my present confusion. I'm not the first man to choose hardship. Gebel could have stayed in his job with the Trustee; Rifaa could have become the alley's carpenter; Kassem could have been content with Kamar and her property and could have lived as an important man. But they chose the other path.

Hanash said sadly:

'What a lot of people rush to be destroyed!'

Arafa said:

'And how few of them have had good reasons!'

But Hanash did not give up helping his brother. Late one night they set off together to the desert. When Awaatif had given up hope of preventing Arafa, she had clasped her hands in prayer for him. It was a dark night; the new moon had set soon after the sun. The two brothers followed the walls of the Big House round to the back where they met the desert. Hanash whispered:

312

'Rifaa was standing in this very place when he heard Gebelawi's voice.'

Arafa said, looking round carefully:

'That's what the story says. Soon I shall know the truth about everything.'

Hanash pointed towards the desert and said with awe:

'And in this desert he himself spoke to Gebel, and here he sent his servant to Kassem.'

'And here too Rifaa was killed, and our mother was raped and beaten – and our ancestor didn't do a thing.'

Hanash put down a basket of tools on the ground, and the two began to dig at the foot of the wall, lifting the soil out in the basket. They worked hard and with determination till their lungs were full of dust. Hanash was plainly no less excited than Arafa, as if he were driven on by the same longing, although he was very much afraid. Arafa's head was only an inch or two above the ground when he said:

'That'll do for tonight.' Then, after hoisting himself up on to the surface: 'We must cover the mouth of the hole with planks and put earth over them so that the thing isn't discovered.'

Then they hurried back, pursued by the dawn. He was thinking of tomorrow, that wonderful day when he would walk in the unknown Big House. And who could tell? He might meet Gebelawi, might talk to him, might ask him to explain events past and present, and the conditions of the endowment and the secret of the book, that dream which had only come true for the hashish-smokers. Who could tell? He might find that he had gone senile and lost his memory, or died long ago, unknown to anyone except the Trustee. Only their hazardous undertaking would decide these questions.

In the basement he found Awaatif still awake, waiting for him. She gave him a tired look of reproach and muttered:

'It's as if you were coming back from the grave.'

He hid his anxiety, saying cheerfully:

'How sweet you are.'

He threw himself down beside her. She said:

'If I was anything to you, you wouldn't ignore my views.'

'You'll change your views when you see what happens tomorrow.'

'I have one chance in a thousand of being happy and not being destroyed.'

Arafa laughed.

'If you'd seen the looks I get, you'd realize that the peace we're enjoying is an illusion.'

The early morning silence was shattered by a piercing cry followed by a howl. Awaatif frowned and murmured:

'A bad omen.'

He shrugged his shoulders.

'Don't blame me, Awaatif; you're partly the reason for my position.'

'Me?'

'I came back to the alley driven by a secret longing to avenge my mother. When your father was attacked, the desire to take this revenge on the chiefs took root in me, but my love for you has added a new idea, which has almost destroyed the old one: I want to put an end to them not for vengeance but for people to enjoy life. I've only decided to go to the Big House to find out the secret of his power.'

She gave him a long look, and in it he could see by the light of the candle her fear of losing him as she had lost her father. He smiled at her affectionately. The wailing outside was becoming unbearable.

## 101 ✳ ✳ ✳ ✳ ✳ ✳ ✳ ✳ ✳ ✳ ✳ ✳ ✳ ✳ ✳ ✳

Hanash gave a farewell squeeze to the hand of Arafa who stood at the bottom of the hole. Then Arafa got down and crawled through the tunnel, which was heavy with the smell of earth, until his head came up in the garden of the Big House. A wonderful fragrance met his nose, like the very essence of roses and jasmine and henna distilled in the moist night air. The scent intoxicated him, in spite of his deep feeling of danger. Here he was, smelling the garden for which Adham had died of grief. Nothing could be seen of it, only a deep darkness under the stars. Over it lay a terrible silence, disturbed now and then by the whisper of the leaves in the breeze. He found the ground was soft and damp, and he decided he must take his shoes off when he slipped into the house, so as not to leave tracks on the floor. Now, where could the gatekeeper and the gardener and the other servants sleep?

He began to creep along on all fours, taking great care not to make any noise that might reach the house, whose huge square form was beginning to emerge from the darkness. As he made his way towards it, he experienced worse fear than he had ever known before, although he had been used to going through darkness and spending nights in the desert or in ruins. He crawled along the line of the wall till his hand touched the bottom of the steps which, if the storytellers spoke the truth, led up to the terrace. Here Gebelawi had pushed Idris out of the house. That had been his fate for defying his father's orders. What then might Gebelawi do to someone who broke into his house to steal the secret of his power? But steady on! No one could expect that a thief would get into this house which had been safe all these years, protected by Gebelawi's terrible reputation.

He crept round the ballustrade and began climbing the steps on his hands and knees. He got to the terrace and took off his shoes and put them under his arm. Then he crept towards the side door which, according to the storytellers, led to the bedroom.

Suddenly he heard a cough, coming from the garden. He froze at the doorstep and looked in its direction. He saw a figure approaching the terrace. He held his breath, imagining that his very heartbeats would be audible. The figure came on and began walking up the steps. Perhaps it was Gebelawi himself. Perhaps he would catch him in the act just as he had once caught Adham at about the same time of the morning. The figure reached the terrace only a couple of yards from his hiding place, but it went to the other end and lay down, seemingly on a bed. The tension eased, leaving exhaustion in its train. The figure was probably just a servant who had gone out to relieve himself and then come back to bed. Now it was snoring! Arafa got back some of his courage and raised his hand to feel for the handle. He turned it carefully and began pushing the door open gently, until there was room for him to slip through. He closed the door behind him and found himself in complete darkness. He groped about with his hand until he found the first step of the stairs, and began climbing them, light as a cat. He came out on a long gallery lit by a lamp in an alcove. To the right it bent round towards the interior, to the left it ran the breadth of the house, and in the middle stood the closed door of the bedroom. At that bend Omayma had stood, and from where he was Adham had set off; and here was he setting off after the very same thing.

Fear filled his heart and attacked his will and his courage. But it would be contemptible to go back now. The servant might appear at any moment. He might be roused from his madness by a hand on his shoulder. He had better hurry. He tiptoed towards the door and turned the shiny handle. He pushed it gently open and slipped in, closing it behind him. He leaned his back against the door, unable to make out anything in the darkness. He was breathing carefully and sparingly, trying in vain to see. After a little while he smelt a pure scent of incense, which filled his heart with a strange unease and sadness. He no longer doubted that he was in Gebelawi's bedroom. When would he get used to the darkness? How could he gather his scattered wits? Who had stood in this place before? Why did he feel that all was lost unless he took hold of all his strength and determination and courage? He was in danger of destruction if he did not calculate every movement precisely. He thought of clouds scudding along and changing into strange shapes – now a gebel, now a tomb.

He felt the wall with his finger and followed it, on all fours, until his

315

shoulder touched a chair. A sudden movement in the far corner of the room made his flesh creep. He stopped behind the chair, straining his eyes towards the door by which he had come in. He heard the pad of feet and the rustle of clothes and expected that the room would be flooded with light and that he would see Gebelawi standing in front of him. He would throw himself down at his feet and plead for mercy; he would say: 'I am your descendant. I have no father. I only meant to do good. Do what you like to me.' In spite of the darkness he saw a figure going towards the door, which opened gently, and the light from the corridor outside filtering in. The person left the door ajar and went out, turning to the right. By the light of the lamp outside he made out an old Negress with a thin, shrivelled face; an unforgettable sight. Could she be a servant? Could this room be in the servants' quarters? He looked at the place from behind the chair, picking out by the faint light from the door the outlines of the chairs and the divan. At the back he could see the shape of a large four poster bed with a mosquito net. At the foot of this bed was a small one, perhaps the one the old woman had left. This big bed could belong to none other than Gebelawi. He was sleeping there now, unaware of Arafa's crime. How he longed to take a look at him, even if it was from a distance. But the open door warned him that the woman was going to come back. He looked to the left and saw the door of the little room closed on its terrible secret. This was how Adham had looked at it long ago, God rest his soul. He crept round behind the chairs, forgetting even Gebelawi, till he reached the foot of the little door.

He could not resist the temptation. He stretched his hand up, put his finger on the latch, pressed it down and pulled the door. It opened. He closed it again hastily, his heart fluttering with excitement and feelings of triumph. Then the light disappeared and the room was plunged in darkness again. Again he heard the pad of feet. Then the bed creaked as the old woman lay down and there was silence. He waited patiently for her to go to sleep, and tried hard to see the big bed, but could not. He convinced himself that it would be madness to try and make contact with the old man, for the woman would wake up before he could do so and would fill the air with screams, and that would be the end of that. Anyway, the book would be enough for him, with the conditions of the endowment and the magic spells by which Gebelawi had brought the desert and the people under his control in his young days. No one before him had imagined that the book was a book of magic, because no one before him had practised the art.

He stretched his hand up again and put his finger on the latch and pulled the door open. He crept in and closed the door behind him. He stood up cautiously and breathed deeply to soothe his nerves. Why had

316

Gebelawi withheld the secret of the book from his children, even Adham, the one dearest to his heart? There was a secret, certainly, and in a few seconds he would discover it, when he had lit his candle. Adham had lit his long ago, and here was he now, the illegitimate boy, lighting one again in the very same place. The storytellers would sing of this for ever.

He lit the candle and saw a pair of eyes looking at him. In spite of his confusion he saw that the eyes belonged to an old Negro, who was lying on a bed behind the door, and that the old man was struggling to rouse himself. He had been wakened perhaps by the sound of the match. Without thinking, Arafa leapt at him and put his right hand on his throat, pressing with all his might. The old man moved violently and caught hold of his hand, but he kicked him and increased the pressure on his throat. The candle fell from his left hand and went out. The old man made a last struggle in the darkness and then lay still, Like a madman Arafa went on squeezing till his fingers ached. Then he drew back, panting, till his back touched the door.

The seconds passed and he was in a hell of silent torment. He felt his strength ebbing. Time felt heavier than his crime. He would fall down on the ground or on his victim's corpse if he could not master this weakness. Flight called him almost irresistibly. He would not be able to step over the body to get to the ancient book, the accursed book. He had no courage to light the candle again; he would rather go blind. He felt a pain in his arms, perhaps where the man had scratched him in his desperate struggle. He trembled to think that, while Adham's crime had been disobedience, his own was murder. He had killed a man he did not know, and whom he had no reason to kill. He had come in quest of power to use against evildoers, and now he had turned unawares into an evildoer.

He turned in the darkness towards the corner where he thought the book was fastened, then pushed the door open and slipped out, closing it behind him. He crept along by the wall to the door, hesitating behind the last chair. There were only servants to be seen in this house; where was the master? This crime would come between him and Awaatif for ever. He felt disappointment and failure, to the very depths of his soul. He opened the door gently. The light dazzled him, seeming almost to attack him. He shut the door, tiptoed away, descended the stairs in pitch darkness, and crossed the terrace to the garden. Because of his exhaustion and unhappiness he was less cautious. The man on the terrace woke up and asked: 'Who's there?' Arafa crouched against the wall at the end of the terrace, his strength renewed by fear. The voice called out again and a cat answered with a miaow. Arafa stayed in his hiding place, terrified of being driven to a fresh crime. When all was quiet again he crept through the garden to the wall. He felt for the hole until he found it and crept away as he had come. When he had almost got to the end of the tunnel he bumped into a foot. The foot kicked him on the head before he knew what was happening.

## 102 ✳ ✳ ✳ ✳ ✳ ✳ ✳ ✳ ✳ ✳ ✳ ✳ ✳ ✳ ✳ ✳ ✳ ✳

Arafa leapt on the owner of the foot and for a short time they struggled. Then the other man let out a cry of rage that told Arafa who it was. He shouted in amazement:

'Hanash!'

They helped each other to climb out on to the ground. Hanash said:

'You were away so long. I went in to nose about for news.'

Arafa said, breathing hard:

'Wrong as usual; but let's go.'

They went back to the sleeping alley. When she saw him, Awaatif shouted:

'Get washed ... Oh God! What's this blood on your hand and your neck?'

He trembled, but did not answer. He went to wash himself, but in a moment he had fainted. He recovered after a while and sat down, with the help of Awaatif and Hanash, on the divan between them. He felt as if sleep was further away from him than Gebelawi was. He could no longer bear his burden alone, and told them what had happened to him on his strange expedition. When he finished they were staring at him, their eyes full of terror and despair. Awaatif whispered:

'I was against the idea from the beginning.'

But Hanash tried to lighten the blow.

'This sort of crime can't possibly be avoided.'

Arafa said:

'But it's worse than the crimes of Santoury and the other chiefs.'

Hanash said:

'Mind you don't call suspicion on yourself.'

'But I've killed an old man who'd done no wrong. Who knows, perhaps he was the servant Gebelawi sent to Kassem.'

For a while they were gloomily silent. Then Awaatif said:

'We'd better all go to sleep.'

'You two sleep. I shan't sleep tonight.'

They fell silent again. Then Hanash asked:

'Didn't you get a glimpse of Gebelawi or hear his voice?'

He shook his head sadly.

'Not at all.'

'But you saw his bed?'

'Just as we see his house.'

Hanash sighed.

'I thought your long absence meant you were talking to him.'

'It's so easy to imagine things outside the house.'

Awaatif said anxiously:

'You seem feverish. You'd better sleep.'

'How can I sleep?'

But he felt the truth of her words in his hot and dazed state. Hanash spoke again:

'You were an arm's length from the will and you didn't look at it!'

His face screwed up with pain. Hanash went on:

'What a disastrous journey!'

'Yes!' Then, in a new tone of determination: 'But it's taught me we must rely on nothing apart from the magic we now have. Haven't I risked a mad expedition in search of something that is probably quite different from my idea?'

'Yes! No one except you said the famous book was a book of magic.'

Arafa said, fighting even more than before against the confusion in his mind:

'The experiment with the bottle will succeed sooner than you imagine and it'll be very useful when we have to defend ourselves.'

The dreadful silence fell again. Hanash said:

'If only you'd known some magic that would have enabled you to get to the Big House and its master without that escapade.'

Arafa said eagerly:

'Magic has no limits. All I have now is a few cures and a plan for a bottle that could be used in defence or attack. As for what might be, it's unimaginable.'

Awaatif said angrily:

'You should never have thought of that crazy plan at all. Our ancestor belongs to one world and we belong to another. You couldn't have got anything out of talking to him even if you'd managed to. He's probably forgotten about the estate and the Trustee and the chiefs and the alley and his children.'

Arafa was angry for no apparent reason, though his unusual state excused any strange behaviour. He said:

'This stupid alley! What do they know? Nothing. All they have is stories and fiddles, but they would never do the things they hear about. They think their alley is the centre of the world, but it's just the refuge of good-for-nothings and beggars. In the beginning it was a desolate breeding ground of insects, until the most terrible bandit of all settled there – your ancestor the Founder.'

319

Hanash started, while Awaatif moistened a rag and tried to put it to his forehead, but he pushed her hand away roughly and said:

'I have something no one else has, not even Gebelawi: I have magic, which can bring things that Gebel, Rifaa and Kassem put together couldn't have achieved.'

Awaatif implored him:

'When are you going to sleep?'

'When the fire stops burning in my head.'

Hanash murmured:

'It will soon be morning.'

Arafa bellowed:

'Let morning come; it won't really come until magic has put an end to chiefs and rid people of demons and brought far more wealth than the estate could ever bring. Magic will become the music that Adham dreamed of.

He heaved a deep sigh and leaned his head against the wall from exhaustion. Awaatif hoped sleep would follow. Suddenly a dreadful voice rang out in the stillness. It was followed by screams and wails. Arafa leapt up in a panic:

'The servant's body has been found.'

Awaatif's mouth was dry as she said:

'How do you know the voices come from the Big House?'

Arafa ran out and they followed him. They stood in front of their home, looking towards the Big House. The darkness was fading and giving way to morning. Windows opened and heads poked out, all looking towards the Big House. A man came from the end of the alley, hurrying towards Gemalia. When he passed them Arafa asked him:

'What's happened?'

He answered without stopping:

'God's will be done! After his long life Gebelawi is dead.'

103 ✳ ✳ ✳ ✳ ✳ ✳ ✳ ✳ ✳ ✳ ✳ ✳ ✳ ✳ ✳ ✳ ✳

The three of them turned to go to the basement. Arafa's feet would hardly carry him. He sank down on the divan, saying:

'The man I killed was a poor Negro servant. He was sleeping in the secret chamber.'

Neither of them said a word. They looked hard at the floor to avoid his darting eyes. He said:

'I can see you don't believe me. I swear I didn't go near his bed.'

Hanash hesitated a while, then said, feeling that it was in any case better to speak than to leave him to silence:

'Perhaps you couldn't see his face clearly because of the shock.'

He shouted:

'Never! You're not on my side.'

Awaatif whispered:

'Talk quietly.'

He left them and hurried away to the back room where he sat in the dark, trembling. What madness had led him into that damnable exploit? The earth itself seemed to tremble. He had no hope left save this wonderful room.

At the first rays of sunlight the people all gathered in the alley outside the Big House. The news spread fast, especially after the Trustee had paid a short visit to the house and then returned to his own. The word was passed around that burglars had broken into the Big House through a tunnel they had dug under the wall at the back. They had killed a faithful servant and when Gebelawi learnt the news he had been more upset than his frail heart and great age could stand and he had died. People were too furious to cry or scream. When he heard the news from his wife and Hanash, Arafa shouted:

'There you are! The reports bear me out.'

Then he remembered that in any case he had been the cause of his death and he retreated into a silence of shame and grief. Awaatif could think of nothing to say. She murmured:

'God rest his soul!'

Hanash said:

'He had a long life.'

Arafa moaned:

'But I was the cause of his death; I, of all his children; I, and not one of the wicked ones.'

Awaatif wept.

'You went without any malice.'

Hanash said anxiously:

'Isn't it possible they may find out about us?'

Awaatif cried out:

'Let's run away.'

Arafa waved the idea aside impatiently.

'And give them the clearest proof of our guilt!'

From the crowded alley came a babble of voices:

'The culprit must be killed before we bury Gebelawi.'

'Accursed generation! Even the wickedest men respected this house all through the past, even Idris. We're cursed till the Day of Judgement.'

'The murderers can't be from our alley; who could imagine that?'

321

'Everything will soon be known.'

'The curse will rest on us till the Day of Judgement.'

The weeping and wailing grew louder till Hanash lost his nerve and said:

'How can we stay after today?'

The Gebelites proposed that Gebelawi be buried in Gebel's tomb, partly because of their conviction that they were more closely related to him than anyone else, and partly because they would hate him to be buried in the tomb that contained the mortal remains of Idris as well as of other members of the Founder's family. The Rifaaites demanded that he be buried in the grave he had dug for Rifaa with his own hands. The Kassemites said Kassem was the best of the Founder's children and that his tomb was the one most suitable for the body of their glorious ancestor. It almost came to blows, but Trustee Kadri proclaimed that Gebelawi would be buried in the little mosque in the old estate office of the Big House. This solution met remarkably with general approval, although people were sorry they would be denied the sight of his funeral, just as in his lifetime they had been denied the sight of the man. The Rifaaites whispered to one another that Gebelawi would be buried in the grave in which he had buried Rifaa with his own hands; but no one else believed that old story and they were jeered at until Aggaag, their chief, was furious and almost got into a fight with Santoury. At that point Saadallah shouted for all to hear:

'I'll break the head of any stuck-up fool who spoils the solemnity of this sad day.'

Only Gebelawi's trusted servants witnessed the washing of the body. They wound it in its pall and laid it on the bier and carried it through the drawing-room that had seen the family's most important events: the giving of the trusteeship to Adham and the rebellion of Idris. Then the Trustee and the notables of the three quarters were summoned to the funeral prayers. After that the body was laid to rest as the sun went down.

In the evening all the people went to the marquee that had been set up. Arafa and Hanash went along with the Rifaaites. Arafa's face was like a dead man's, for he had not slept. The conversation was all in praise of Gebelawi, conqueror of the desert, master of men, symbol of strength and courage, owner of the estate and the alley, father of so many generations. Arafa looked miserable, but no one thought of the things that were going round his head. Here he was, the man who had broken into the house, not caring about its reputation, who had not been sure of his ancestor's existence until his death, who had set himself apart from everyone and soiled his hands for all time. He wondered how he could atone for his misdeed: the glorious feats of Gebel, Rifaa and Kassem together would not be enough; destroying the Trustee and the chiefs and freeing the alley from their wickedness would not be enough; exposing himself to every danger would not be enough; teaching everyone magic with all its benefits would not be enough. One thing alone would be enough: to reach such a degree of magic that he would be able to restore Gebelawi to life, Gebelawi whom it had been easier to kill than to see. Let time give him the power to mend his broken heart. And these chiefs with their crocodile tears . . . But – oh God! – none of them had sinned as he had. They were sitting there in silence, overcome with shame and humiliation. People would say in the neighbourhood that Gebelawi was killed in his house while round about it the mighty chiefs were taking hashish. Their eyes threatened vengeance and death.

When Arafa came back to the basement late that night he drew Awaatif to him and asked her helplessly:

'Awaatif, do you think I'm a criminal?'

'You're a good man, the best I've met, but the unluckiest.'

He looked down.

'No one before me has tasted such pain.'

'I know.'

She kissed him with cold lips and whispered:

'I'm afraid the curse will rest on us.'

He turned his face away from her. Hanash said:

'I don't feel safe. They'll discover about us today or tomorrow. I don't imagine they can know everything about Gebelawi, his origin, his estate, his dealings with his sons, his contacts with Gebel and Rifaa and Kassem, and be ignorant about his death alone.'

Arafa sighed deeply.

'Have you any solution, apart from running away?'

Hanash said nothing. Arafa went on:

'I have a plan, but I want to be at peace with myself before putting it into action; I can't do it if I'm a criminal.'

Hanash said without conviction:

'You're innocent.'

'I'll do it, Hanash. Don't be afraid for us; the alley will be distracted from the great crime by other events. Extraordinary things will happen and the most extraordinary of all will be that Gebelawi will come back to life.'

Awaatif gasped, and Hanash said, scowling:

'Are you mad?'

He said in a feverish voice:

'A word from our ancestor used to cause the best of his children to act for him until death. His death is more powerful than his words; it makes it necessary for the good son to do everything, to take his place, to be him. Do you understand?'

Arafa got ready to leave the basement when the last sounds had subsided outside. Awaatif went with him as far as the porch, her eyes red from crying. She said with complete resignation:

'May Providence watch over you.'

Hanash said quite sincerely:

'Why shouldn't I come with you?'

Arafa said:

'It's easier for one person to get away than for two.'

Hanash patted him on the back and advised him:

'Don't use the bottle unless you're desperate.'

He nodded and went. He threw a glance at the alley, enveloped in darkness, then went towards Gemalia. He made a wide circle, through Watawit Alley, Derrasa and the desert beyond the Big House, and reached the north wall of Saadallah's house, overlooking the desert. He went to a point half-way along the wall and felt the ground till he found a boulder which he pushed aside. Then he got down into the tunnel that he and Hanash had been digging night after night and crawled through. He pulled aside the screen that closed the other end and emerged into the garden of the Chief's house. He hid beside the wall and took a look at the place. In the house he saw a faint light from one shuttered window. The garden was asleep and in darkness except for a light in the window of the garden house. From time to time he heard the ribaldry and coarse laughs of the men inside it. He drew a dagger from his breast and waited, ready to spring, more oppressed by time than by anxieties.

The hashish party ended half an hour after his arrival. The door opened and the men followed one another out through the garden gate into the alley. The gatekeeper came up, lamp in hand, closed the gate and went back, lighting Saadallah's way to the terrace. Arafa picked up a stone in his left hand and moved stealthily across, bending low, with the dagger in his right hand. He hid behind a palm tree until Saadallah was about to climb the steps. Then he leapt at him and plunged the dagger into his back. The man collapsed with a scream. The gatekeeper panicked and turned to run but the stone hit the lantern and smashed it. Then Arafa sped away to the wall where he had come in. In no time there was a rush of footsteps and a confuison of voices from the house and from the far end of the garden. Arafa stumbled over something upright, perhaps a tree stump, and fell flat on his face. He felt a stabbing pain in his leg and his elbow, but he overcame it and crawled the rest of the way to the tunnel. The cries and footsteps grew louder. He flung himself into the tunnel and crawled quickly through to the desert. He stood up, groaning, then hurried off eastwards.

Before he got round the wall of the Big House he turned and saw figures rushing towards him. He heard a voice shout: Who's there?' He ran off still faster, in spite of the pain, and reached the end of the back wall of the Big House. As he crossed the space between the Big House and the Trustee's house he saw torches and heard a great noise. He made off into the desert, heading for Souk Mukattam. He felt that the pain would get the better of him sooner or later, and that the pursuers were drawing closer as they shouted in the stillness: Get him! Catch him!' He drew the bottle out of his cloak – the bottle that he had spent months testing – stopped running and faced the approaching men. He strained his eyes until he could make out their shapes; then he flung the bottle at them. A second later an explosion took place such as no ears had heard before. It was followed by screams and groans.

Arafa ran on, no longer pursued. At the edge of the desert he threw himself down on the ground, panting and moaning. He lay there alone under the stars with his pain and weakness. He looked behind him, but there was only darkness and silence. He began wiping away the blood that was flowing from his leg and then stanched it with sand. He felt he must go on, whatever the cost, and he levered himself up and made his way slowly onwards. On the edge of Derrasa he saw a shape approaching. He looked at it anxiously, but it passed him without turning towards him. He sighed with relief and went back by the same roundabout way he had come. When he got near to Gebelawi Alley he heard uproar, voices snarling, weeping and screaming angrily. He hung back a while, then went forward keeping close to the walls. He peeped with one eye round the corner at the end of the alley and saw a huge crowd at the other end, between the houses of the Trustee and Saadallah. At the same time, Kassem's quarter looked deserted and dark. He crept along beside the walls till he reached cover in the basement.

He threw himself down between Awaatif and Hanash, then uncovered his bloody leg. Awaatif was alarmed and hurried away to fetch a pan of water. She washed the wound and he had to clench his teeth to prevent himself from crying out. Hanash helped her, saying anxiously:

'There's a blaze of fury out there.'

Arafa asked, screwing up his face:

'What did they say about the explosion?'

'The men who were chasing you described what happened, and no one believed them. But people were astounded by the injuries on their faces and necks, and the story of the explosion almost made them forget the murder of Saadallah.'

Arafa said:

'The chief of the alley is dead; tomorrow the others will begin to fight for his position.' Then, looking tenderly at his wife who was engrossed in binding up his wounds: The age of the chiefs is about to end, and the first to go will be your father's murderer.'

But she did not answer. Hanash's eyes continued to rove round uneasily. Arafa buried his head in his hands because of the pain.

105 ✳ ✳ ✳ ✳ ✳ ✳ ✳ ✳ ✳ ✳ ✳ ✳ ✳ ✳ ✳ ✳ ✳ ✳

Early next morning there was a knock at the door of the basement. When Awaatif opened it, she saw in front of her Amme Yuness, the gatekeeper of the Trustee's house. She gave him a friendly greeting and invited him in, but he stayed where he was and said:

'His honour the Trustee wants Mr Arafa to meet him for urgent consultations.'

Awaatif went to tell Arafa, feeling anything but the pleasure that would have been natural in any other circumstances. After a little while Arafa came out, putting on his best clothes – a white smock, a spotted turban, clean shoes – but he was leaning on a stick because of an unexpected limp, which he could not hide. He raised his hand in greeting and said: 'At your service.' He set out, following the gatekeeper. The alley was buzzing from end to end with last night's story, and people's anxious eyes seemed to be asking: 'What disasters will tomorrow bring?' The chiefs and their followers were meeting in the cafés, while in Saadallah's house there was constant wailing. Arafa followed the gatekeeper into the Trustee's house and they walked up the path under its canopy of jasmine to the terrace. He considered the points of resemblance between this house and the Big House, and there were so many that he decided the only difference was in the steps. He said to himself angrily: 'You imitate him when it suits you, not when it suits the people.'

The gatekeeper went in ahead of him to ask if he might enter, then came back and motioned him in. He went into the great drawing-room, where he found Kadri the Trustee sitting at the far end, waiting for him. He stopped a few yards away from him and bowed respectfully. He noticed at once his great height and powerful build and his red, fleshy face; but, when he smiled in acknowledgment of Arafa's greeting, he revealed dirty yellow teeth that did not correspond with the grandeur of his outward appearance. He motioned Arafa to sit beside him on the divan, but Arafa went over to the nearest chair saying:

'Excuse me, your honour!'

But the Trustee insisted that he should sit on the divan and said both gently and firmly:

'Here . . . sit here!'

326

Arafa could find no way to avoid sitting beside him. He sat down on the very end of the divan, saying to himself: 'It must be something very secret.' He became sure of this when he saw that the gatekeeper locked the door. He waited quietly and meekly. The Trustee studied him calmly then said in a conspiratorial tone:

'Arafa, why did you kill Saadallah?'

Gaze froze on gaze. His joints were weak. Everything spun round. Future became past. He saw the man's confident eyes fixed on him and did not doubt that he knew everything. The Trustee gave him no time to think, but went on rather briskly:

'Don't be afraid! Why do you kill if you are so afraid? Control yourself and answer me: just tell me why you killed Saadallah?'

Arafa could not bear the silence. He said, not knowing what he was saying:

'Sir . . . Me?'

'You son of a bitch, do you think I'm raving? Do you think I'm talking without proof? Answer me: why did you kill him?'

Utterly desperate, Arafa let his eyes wander pointlessly over the room. The Trustee said in a voice as cold as death:

'There's no escape Arafa. There are people outside who would tear you to pieces and drink your blood if they knew about you.'

The wailing in the Chief's house grew louder. All hope was lost. He opened his mouth without saying anything. The Trustee said harshly:

'Silence seems an easy escape, but I shall throw you to the wild animals outside and say to them: "Here is Saadallah's murderer." If you like, I'll say: "Here is Gebelawi's murderer."'

'Gebelawi!'

'You dig tunnels under back walls; you got away the first time but slipped up the second. Why do you kill, though, Arafa?'

He said hopelessly, without purpose or meaning:

'Innocent, your honour . . . I'm innocent.'

'If the charge against you became known, no one would ask me for proof: in our alley rumour is truth, truth is sentence and sentence is execution. But tell me what made you break into the Big House?'

The man knew everything. Arafa had no idea how; but he knew everything. Otherwise how could he alone in the whole alley pour out these charges?'

'Did you intend to steal?'

Arafa looked down in despair and said nothing. The Trustee shouted:

'Talk, you viper!'

'Sir . . .!'

'Why do you try to steal, when you're better off than most people?'

'Man is full of wicked urges.'

The Trustee laughed triumphantly. Arafa wondered confusedly why the man had put off killing him till now; in fact, why hadn't he told his secret to one of the chiefs instead of sending for him in this strange way? The Trustee was silent, as if to torment him, then said:

'You're a dangerous man.'

'I'm a poor man.'

'Can a man be called poor when he has a weapon like yours which makes nonsense of cudgels?'

This man was the true magician. The Trustee enjoyed his despair for a while, then said:

'One of my servants joined your pursuers. He lagged behind and was not caught by your weapon. Then he followed you stealthily by himself and didn't let you notice. At Derrasa he recognized you, only he didn't attack for fear of your surprises, but he hurried to me and told me.'

'Isn't it possible he told someone else?'

'He is a trustworthy servant.' Then in a meaningful tone: 'And now let's talk about your weapon.'

Arafa began to see; the man wanted something more precious than his life. But his despair was complete; what escape was there? He said in a low voice:

'It's simpler than people imagine.'

The Trustee frowned.

'I could easily search your house now, but I don't want to draw attention to you. Do you understand?' Then, after a pause: 'You won't die as long as you obey me.'

He looked threateningly at Arafa as he spoke. Arafa said in despair:

'You'll find me obedient to your will.'

'You've begun to understand me, my magician. If it had been my intention to kill you, the dogs would already have eaten you.' Then, after clearing his throat: 'Let's forget about Gebelawi and Saadallah. Tell me about your weapon; what is it?'

He replied cunningly:

'A magic bottle.'

The Trustee looked at him suspiciously.

'Explain.'

Arafa said, regaining some confidence for the first time:

'Only magicians know the language of magic.'

'Won't you explain, even if I promise you safety?'

Arafa laughed inwardly, but said, outwardly serious:

'What I have said is the truth.'

The man gazed at the floor for a while, then looked up and asked:

'Do you have many of them?'

'I have none at the moment.'

328

The Trustee shouted:

'Viper!'

'Search my house and see for yourself.'

'Could you make some more?'

'Certainly.'

The Trustee folded his arms, greatly excited.

'I want lots of them.'

'You shall have as many as you want.'

They exchanged understanding looks. Arafa said boldly:

'You want to be independent of those damned chiefs, sir?'

'Tell me what made you break into the Big House.'

'Only curiosity. I didn't mean to kill that faithful servant.'

The Trustee stared at him suspiciously.

'You caused the death of the great man.'

'I was heartbroken over that.'

The Trustee shrugged his shoulders and said:

'If only we could live like him.'

'You wicked hypocrite. You're only interested in the estate,' thought Arafa, but he said:

'May God grant you a long life.'

'You really went just out of curiosity?'

'Yes.'

'And why did you kill Saadallah?'

'Because, like you, I want to put an end to all the chiefs.'

The Trustee smiled.

'They're a great evil.'

'But you only hate them because of the money they take from the estate, not because of their wickedness,' thought Arafa.

'You're quite right, sir.'

'You'll become richer than you ever dreamed.'

Arafa said craftily:

'That's all that I wanted.'

'You needn't bother to work for millièmes; you'll have your time free to work magic for my defence, and you'll have everything you desire.'


106 ✳ ✳ ✳ ✳ ✳ ✳ ✳ ✳ ✳ ✳ ✳ ✳ ✳ ✳ ✳ ✳ ✳

The three of them sat on the divan, Arafa describing what had happened to him, and Awaatif and Hanash following his words anxiously. Arafa finished by saying:

'We have no choice. Saadallah's funeral hasn't begun yet. We must either accept or be destroyed.'

Awaatif said:

'Or run away.'

'There's no escape from his spies who're all around us.'

'We shan't be safe under his protection.'

He ignored her words, and would have liked to ignore her point. He turned to Hanash and said:

'Why don't you say something?'

Hanash said sadly:

'When we came back to this alley we came with simple hopes. You alone are to blame for the change that came about later, for the high hopes we came to have. I was against you at first, but I didn't hesitate to help you. I began to be convinced by your views, little by little, until my only hope was to set free the alley. Now you surprise us with a new plan by which we shall become a dreadful tool for oppression, a tool that can neither be resisted nor destroyed, whereas a chief can be fought or killed.'

Awaatif said:

'And after that there'll be no safety for us; he may get all he wants from you and then get rid of you by a trick, as he is now arranging to do with the chiefs.'

Deep down Arafa could not help being convinced but he said, as if trying to persuade himself:

'I shall make him need my magic always.'

Awaatif said:

'The best you can hope for is to become his new chief.'

Hanash backed her up:

'Yes, one whose weapon is a bottle, not a cudgel. And remember his feelings towards the chiefs if you want to know how he'll feel towards you.'

Arafa became angry.

'As God wills. It's as if I was the greedy one and you were both reasonable. But I only spent my nights awake in the back room and risked death twice for the good of the alley. If you are going to refuse to accept what has been forced on me, tell me what ought to be done.'

He gave them a look of angry defiance. Neither of them spoke. The world looked to him like a nightmare. He was overcome by a strange feeling that his suffering was a punishment for his attack on his ancestor. His pain and grief grew stronger. Awaatif whispered imploringly:

'Let's run away.'

He asked angrily:

'How?'

'I don't know, but it can't be harder for you than getting into Gebelawi's house.'

'The Trustee is on the look out for us, and his spies are all around; how can we possibly escape?'

There was silence, like the silence of Gebelawi's tomb. Arafa said reproachfully:

'I don't want to bear the defeat alone.'

Hanash said:

'We have no choice,' Then, eagerly: 'The future may bring an opportunity to escape.'

Arafa was far away. He said:

'Who knows!'

He went to the back room, followed by Hanash. They began packing glass and sand and other things into bottles. Arafa said:

'We must devise symbols for the secrets of our work and write them in a book so that our efforts aren't wasted and so that my death will not mean the end of these experiments. Besides, I hope you'll be ready to learn magic as we have no idea what fate has in store for us.'

They went on working with great care. Arafa happened to turn to his companion and saw that he was scowling. He knew why, but he said as if there were nothing unusual:

'These bottles will finish off the chiefs.'

Hanash said, almost in a whisper:

'Not to our advantage, or that of the alley.'

Arafa went on with his work, saying:

'What has the storyteller's fiddle told you? In the past there were men like Gebel and Rifaa and Kassem; why shouldn't such men come in the future?'

Hanash sighed.

'I almost thought sometimes that you were one of them.'

Arafa laughed a short, dry laugh.

'Has my failure made you change your mind about that?'

Hanash said nothing. Arafa went on:

'I shall never be like them from one point of view at least: they used to have a following, but as for me, no one understands me.' He laughed. 'Kassem could win a staunch follower by a single kind word, but it will take me years and years to train one man in my work and make him into my follower.'

He finished filling a bottle, put the cork in and held it up to the lamp admiringly. Then he said:

'Today these just frighten people and cut their faces; tomorrow they will kill. I tell you, magic has no limits.'

'Who is to be chief?' People began to wonder as soon as Saadallah had been laid in his grave. Each faction recommended its own leader. The Gebelites said Yussef was the most powerful and the one most certainly related to Gebelawi. The Rifaaites said they were the followers of the finest person the alley had ever known, the one Gebelawi had buried with his own hands. The Kassemites said they were the ones who had used victory not just for the benefit of their own quarter, but for the benefit of everyone, and that the alley had been united in the days of their hero and ruled by justice and brotherhood. As usual, the differences began as whisperings over the hashish, which spread and grew till people were preparing for the worst. The chiefs stopped going about alone, and if they stayed up late in a café or a hashish den they were surrounded by supporters armed with cudgels. Each storyteller prayed for the chief of his quarter to the sound of his fiddle. The shopkeepers and pedlars scowled and looked gloomy. The people were so worried and afraid that they forgot about the death of Gebelawi and the murder of Saadallah. Omme Nebawia the bean seller expressed the general feeling when she cried out at the top of her voice:

'Damn this life! Those who die are lucky.'

One evening a voice shouted from a roof in Gebel's quarter:

'Listen, you people, and let reason judge between us and you: Gebel's quarter is the oldest and Gebel was the first of our heroes, so it will disgrace no one if you accept Yussef as chief.'

Shouts of derision rang our from the Rifaaites and Kassemites, mixed with obscene insults and curses. In no time children had gathered chanting:

> Yussef, Yussef, louse-faced rat!
> Who told you to do like that?

People's hearts became still harder and their mood blacker. The only thing that put off the disaster was that three factions were involved, so long as two did not unite or one withdraw from the competition of its own accord.

Incidents happened far away. Two pedlars met at Beyt el Kadi, one a Gebelite and the other a Kassemite. They had a fight and the Kassemite lost his teeth while the Gebelite lost an eye. At Hammam el Sultan there was a battle between women from all three factions, naked in the baths. They scratched and bit each other and tore at each other's hair. The air was thick with flying jugs, pumice stones, luffas and pieces of soap. Two women fainted and one had a miscarriage. Later the same day, after the amazons had trooped back to the alley, they resumed battle on the rooftops hurling stones and filthy insults. Along came a messenger from the Trustee, making his way secretly to Yussef, the Gebelite chief. He asked him to go and see the Trustee without letting anyone know.

The Trustee received him graciously and asked him to do something to calm people down in his quarter, especially as it was the one next to the Trustee's house. When he shook his hand to say good-bye, the Trustee said he hoped that, the next time they met, Yussef would be chief. The man left intoxicated by the thought of this support and believing power was in his grasp. Soon he had organized his people, and they whispered to one another about what tomorrow held in store for them. The news got out to the rest of the alley, and feelings ran high. A few days later Aggaag and Santoury met and agreed to join forces to destroy Yussef, and then after victory to draw lots to become chief.

Next day at dawn the men of Kassem and Rifaa gathered and attacked Gebel's quarter. There was a fierce battle and Yussef and many of his men were killed. The Gebelites submitted in despair to superior strength. The afternoon was chosen for the drawing of lots that had been agreed on, and at the appointed time the Kassemites and Rifaaites, both men and women, hurried to the top of the alley, filling the area between the Trustee's house and the Chief's house, which would belong to the winner of the lottery. Santoury and Aggaag arrived, each with his gang, and exchanged friendly and peaceful greetings. They embraced in front of everyone, and Aggaag said in a voice that all could hear:

'You and I are brothers, and whatever happens we shall remain brothers.'

Santoury said eagerly:

'For ever.'

The two factions stood opposite one another, separated by a space in front of the entrance of the Big House. Two men came forward, one from each side, with a basket full of paper bags. They put it down in the space and then retreated, each to his own people. It was proclaimed that the hammer was Aggaag's symbol and the cleaver Santoury's, and that half the bags contained each. A young man, blindfolded, was brought to the basket to take out a paper bag. He dipped in his hand in the tense silence and drew out a paper bag. Still blindfolded, he opened it, took out its content and held it up. The Kassemites shouted:

'The cleaver! The cleaver!'

Santoury stretched his hand out to Aggaag who took and squeezed it, grinning. There were excited shouts of:

'Long live Santoury, chief of the alley.'

From the ranks of the Rifaaites a man came towards Santoury, his arms wide open. Santoury opened his arms to embrace him, but the man stabbed him in the heart with incredible speed and strength. Santoury fell forward, dead. There was a moment of stunned silence, then an explosion of furious shouts and threats. The two factions met in a fierce and bloody battle. But none of the Kassemites could stand against Aggaag. Soon they lost their spirit. Some fell and others fled, and by the evening Aggaag was firmly established as chief. In Kassem's quarter, the howls rang out, while Rifaa's was filled with shouts of joy. Aggaag's people danced round him in the alley.

Suddenly a voice shouted above the cheers:

'Quiet! Listen! Listen you goats!'

They looked round in amazement and there was Yuness, the Trustee's gatekeeper, coming up, followed by the Trustee himself, surrounded by servants. Aggaag went towards the party, saying:

'Aggaag, chief of the alley, at your service.'

The Trustee glared at him scornfully. In the terrible silence that fell, he said:

'Aggaag, I don't want any chiefs and I don't want their ways.'

The Rifaaites were amazed, and the triumphant smiles died on their lips. Aggaag asked:

'What does your honour mean?'

'We don't want any chiefs and we don't want their ways. Let the alley live in peace.'

'Peace?'

The Trustee looked at him coldly but Aggaag asked provocatively:

'And who will protect you?'

The bottles flew from the hands of the servants and exploded over Aggaag and his men. The walls shook, and splinters of glass and pellets of gravel flew into them. Blood flowed, and terror seized them. Bewildered and helpless, Aggaag and his men went down, and the servants finished them off. There were howls of misery from the Rifaaites, and of spiteful joy from the Kassemites. Yuness walked to the middle of the alley and called for silence, then proclaimed:

'Happiness and peace have been granted to you, by grace of his honour the Trustee. Long may he live! From today there are no chiefs to humiliate you and steal your money.'

The air rang with cheers.


108 ✳ ✳ ✳ ✳ ✳ ✳ ✳ ✳ ✳ ✳ ✳ ✳ ✳ ✳ ✳ ✳ ✳

Arafa and his family moved by night from their basement in the Rifaaite quarter to the Chief's house on the left of the Big House. It was the Trustee's order, and no one could resist his orders. They found themselves in a dream-like place. They wandered about the luxuriant garden, the delightful garden house, the terrace, the drawing-room, the bedrooms, the boudoirs, the upstairs dining-room and the roof with all its hen coops, rabbit hutches and dove-cotes. They put on fine clothes for the first time, and breathed the clean air with its delicate scents. Arafa said:

'A little replica of the Big House, but without the secrets.'

Hanash said:

'Your magic . . . doesn't that count as a secret?'

Awaatif's eyes were full of astonishment.

'No one could dream of anything like this.'

The three of them were transformed – new colours, new scents. But they had hardly settled down when a group of men and women came to them. One said he was the gatekeeper, another the cook, a third the gardener, a fourth the poultry keeper, and the rest said they were housemaids. Arafa asked:

'Who sent you?'

The gatekeeper spoke for them:

'His honour the Trustee.'

Soon after, Arafa was summoned by the Trustee and went straight away. They sat down side by side on a divan in the drawing-room and Kadri said:

'We shall meet often, Arafa; don't let it disturb you when I send for you.'

In fact he was worried both by the place and by the man, but he said with a smile:

'I hope you are well, sir.'

'Your magic is the origin of all that is good. How do you like the house?'

'It is beyond the dreams of poor people like us. And today all sorts of servants came to us.'

The Trustee studied his face as he said:

'They are people of mine whom I sent over to serve and protect you.'

'Protect me!?'

Kadri laughed.

'Yes! Didn't you know that in the alley they're talking about nothing but your move. They are saying to each other: "So, *he* makes the bottles." The chiefs' families haven't disappeared, you know, and the other people are very jealous. So you're in grave danger. My advice is not to trust anyone or walk alone or go far from your house.'

Arafa frowned; he was just a prisoner surrounded by anger and hatred. Kadri went on:

'But don't be afraid. My men are around you. Enjoy life as you please in your house and in mine. What will you lose? There's nothing else except the desert and ruins. Don't forget that the people are saying: "Saadallah's killer used the same weapon as Aggaag's, and the way the murderer got into Saadallah's house is the same as the way the Big House was broken into; so one man killed Aggaag and Saadallah and Gebelawi: Arafa the magician." '

Arafa shouted, trembling violently:

'This is a sword over my head.'

'There's no need to be afraid as long as you're under my protection and surrounded by my servants.'

Arafa thought:

'You wretch; you've made me your prisoner. I wanted to use magic to destroy you, not to serve you. Now those I love and wish to free hate me, and I may be killed by one of them.' He said hopefully out loud:

'Share out the chiefs' portion between the people; they will be pleased with you and with us.'

Kadri laughed scornfully.

'Why get rid of the chiefs then?' he examined him coldly: 'So you're looking for a way to please them! Give that up and get used to their hatred as I have done. And don't forget that your security lies in pleasing me.'

Arafa said in despair:

'I've always been at your service.'

The Trustee looked up at the ceiling, as though studying its decorations, then looked back at Arafa and said:

'I hope the pleasures of your new life won't distract you from your magic.' Arafa nodded. 'And that you'll make as many of the magic bottles as possible.'

'We don't need any more than we already have.'

Kadri smiled to hide his annoyance.

'Wouldn't it be wise to store up a good number of them?'

Arafa did not answer. He was overcome with despair; was it his turn already? He asked suddenly:

'Your honour, if my staying is a nuisance to you, let me go away for good.'

Kadri looked alarmed.

'What did you say, young man?'

'I know my life depends on how much you need me . . ,'

Kadri laughed mirthlessly.

'Don't get the idea I underrate your intelligence. I can see what you are thinking; but why do you imagine my need for you is limited to the bottles? Doesn't your magic have the power to work other wonders?'

But Arafa went on with his first line of thought.

336

'It was your men who spread the secret of my services to you; I'm sure of that. But you must remember too that your life depends on me.'

The Trustee frowned but Arafa went on:

'Today you have no chiefs; your only power comes from my bottles, and the few that you have don't make you independent at all. If I died today, you would follow me tomorrow.'

The Trustee suddenly turned on him like a wild beast, seized him by the throat and squeezed till his body trembled. But he quickly relaxed his grip, removed his hands and said, smiling evilly:

'See what your blabbering tongue has made me do, when there's no reason why we should quarrel, and when we can enjoy the fruits of victory in peace.'

Arafa breathed deeply to get his wind back. Kadri went on:

'Don't be afraid; your life is in no danger from me. Enjoy it and don't forget your magic, whose fruits we gather. As you know, if one of us betrays the other, he betrays himself.'

Awaatif and Hanash looked gloomy when he repeated this conversation to them in the new house. All three of them felt ill at ease in their new life. But they forgot their worries at supper round a table adorned with all kinds of delicious food and wine. For the first time Arafa and Hanash roared with laughter.


The two of them lived as circumstances dictated. They worked in a room behind the drawing room, which they fitted out for magic. Arafa took great trouble over putting down the symbols he had devised in a book that only the two of them knew about. Hanash said to him one time while they were working:

'What prisoners we are!'

'Talk quietly; the walls have ears.'

Hanash looked resentfully towards the door, then went on, almost whispering:

'Couldn't you make a new weapon with which we could destroy him by surprise?'

'We wouldn't get a chance to test it secretly with all these servants around; there's nothing about us he doesn't know. And if we destroyed him, then before we could defend ourselves we'd be destroyed by the people who want revenge.'

'Then why work so hard?'

Arafa sighed:

'Because work is the only thing I have left.'

In the evening Arafa used to go to the Trustee's house to sit and drink with him. At night he would come home and find that Hanash had prepared a little hashish session in the garden or the attic, and they would smoke together. Arafa had not taken hashish before, but he was swept along by circumstances, and even Awaatif learnt these habits. They had to forget their boredom and fear and guilt and hopelessness, just as they had to forget the high hopes of the past. Still, the two men had work to do but Awaatif had none. She used to eat till she got indigestion and sleep till she was tired of sleeping, and she would spend hours in the garden enjoying its beautiful colours. She remembered that she was living the life Adham had yearned for; what a tedious life it was! How could anyone want it badly enough to pine away? Perhaps it would have been as bad even if it had not been a prison, surrounded by enmity and hatred. But a prison it would remain, and the only escape was hashish.

One night Arafa was late back from the Trustee's house, and she decided to wait for him in the garden. The moon rose and the night advanced, and she sat listening to the music of the branches and the croaking of the frogs. She heard the gate open and got ready to meet the homecomer, but a rustle of clothes from the direction of the basement caught her ear and in the moonlight she saw a maid hurry towards the gate, not noticing her. Arafa came forward, staggering a little, the maid went over to the wall by the terrace, and he joined her. Then Awaatif saw them kiss, shaded from the moon by the wall.


## 109 ✳ ✳ ✳ ✳ ✳ ✳ ✳ ✳ ✳ ✳ ✳ ✳ ✳ ✳ ✳ ✳ ✳

Awaatif exploded, as befitted a woman of Gebelawi Alley. She leapt on the kissing couple like a lioness and beat Arafa's head with her fists till he staggered back, lost his balance and fell. She clawed at the maid's neck and hit her about the head till her screams pierced the evening stillness. Arafa got up, but he did not dare go near the fighting pair. Hanash hurried up, followed by a number of the servants. When he saw what had happened he sent the servants away and tactfully intervened between the two women until he was able to take Awaatif, who was pouring out a stream of curses and insults, to the house. Arafa made his way unsteadily up to the attic overlooking the desert and threw himself down on the cushions, alone in the hashish room. He stretched out his legs, propped his head against the wall and lay there half conscious. Hanash joined him after some time and without a word sat down facing him across the brazier. He gave him a quick glance, then looked back at the floor and finally broke the silence:

'The scandal had to come.'

Arafa looked up, his eyes full of shame and hastily changed the subject:

'Light up!'

He stayed in the attic till early next morning. The maid went and another took her place. The atmosphere seemed to Awaatif to lead Arafa into one affair after another, and she began interpreting his every move to fit in with her suspicions. Life became hell and she lost the one comfort that had sustained her in her fearful prison. The house did not belong to her nor did her husband. Where was the Arafa she had loved, the Arafa who had defied Santoury to marry her, who had risked death several times for the sake of the alley, until she had begun to think he was one of the storytellers' heroes? Now he was just a scoundrel like Kadri or Saadallah, and life at his side was a burning torment, one long nightmare.

Arafa came back from the Trustee's house one evening and found no trace of Awaatif. The gatekeeper said he had seen her leave the house at nightfall and not come back. Arafa asked, his breath reeking of wine:

'Where can she have gone?'

Hanash said anxiously:

'If she's in the alley she'll be with her old neighbour, Omme Zonfol, the woman who sells lemon sweets.'

Arafa said angrily:

'You can't catch a woman by kindness, as they say. I'll ignore her till she comes back humiliated.'

But she did not come back. Ten days passed. Arafa decided to go by night to Omme Zonfol, intending no one to know that he had gone. At the chosen hour he slipped out of the house followed by Hanash. They had not gone more than a few paces when they heard footsteps following them. They turned and saw two servants from the house following them. Arafa said:

'Go back to the house.'

'We're guarding you by order of his honour the Trustee.'

He was furious, but did not try to insist. They all went to an old house in Kassem's quarter and climbed to the top floor where Omme Zonfol had her rooms. Arafa knocked at the door and Awaatif herself opened it, looking very sleepy. When she saw who it was, by the light of the small lamp in her hand, she drew back, frowning. He followed her, closing the door behind him. In the corner of the room Omme Zonfol woke up and stared at Arafa in astonishment. Awaatif said:

'What brings you? What do you want? Go back to your blessed house.'

Omme Zonfol whispered uneasily:

'Arafa the magician!'

Arafa said to his wife, taking no notice of the other woman's alarm:

'Be sensible and come with me.'

She said with great feeling:

'I'll never come back to your prison. I shan't destroy the peace of mind that I've found in this room.'

'But you're my wife.'

She shouted:

'Your wives are there in good health.'

Omme Zonfol protested:

'Let her sleep. Come back in the morning.'

He glared at her coldly without a word, then looked back at his wife and said:

'Every man makes mistakes.'

She yelled:

'You're just one big mistake.'

He edged towards her and said very gently:

'Awaatif, I can't live without you.'

'But I can live without you.'

'Are you giving me up because I once slipped up when I was drunk?'

She quivered with rage.

'Don't make an excuse of being drunk; your whole life is nothing but wrongdoing. You would need dozens of excuses for all your misdeeds, and all I should ever get out of them is trouble.'

'Anyway it'd be better than life in this room.'

'Who knows! Tell me why your jailers let you come to me.'

'Awaatif!'

'I'm not coming back to a house where I have nothing to do except yawn and watch the love affairs of my husband, the great magician.'

He tried in vain to make her change her mind. She countered his gentleness with stubbornness, his anger with anger, and his abuse with abuse. He gave up in despair and left the place, followed by his companion and the two servants. Hanash asked:

'What are you going to do?'

'The same as every day.'

Kadri the Trustee asked him:

'Any news of your wife?'

Arafa answered as he sat down beside him:

'Stubborn as a mule.'

'Don't bother with the woman; you have better ones.' Then after studying Arafa anxiously: 'Does your wife know any of the secrets of your work?'

Arafa gave him a queer look.

'Only a magician knows magic.'

'I'm afraid . . .'

'Don't be afraid of something that doesn't exist.'

There was silence for several moments. Then Arafa said with feeling:

'You shan't lift a finger against her as long as I'm alive.'

The Trustee suppressed his anger and smiled, indicating two full glasses.

'Who said anyone would lift a finger against her?'

110 ✳ ✳ ✳ ✳ ✳ ✳ ✳ ✳ ✳ ✳ ✳ ✳ ✳ ✳ ✳ ✳ ✳ ✳

When Kadri's friendship with Arafa had grown firm, he began inviting him to his special parties, which usually began at midnight. Arafa attended a strange one in the drawing-room. There was every kind of food and drink, and beautiful women danced naked. Arafa was nearly mad with the drink and the spectacle. He saw the Trustee acting with complete abandon, like a wild beast. He invited Arafa to another party in the garden, in a clump of shrubs encircled by a stream that flashed in the moonlight. Beside them they had fruit and wine, and in front of them were two lovely girls, one to tend the brazier, the other to look after the pipe. The night breeze stirred, wafting to them the perfume of the flowers and the music of a lute. Voices were singing:

> Carnation scents and mint
> And lute's refrain unleash
> A moonlight spell to bind
> The smokers of hashish.

The full moon was shining. Its whole disc appeared whenever the breeze swayed the leafy mulberry bough, and as the bough moved back points of light shone through the mass of twigs and leaves. The pipe in the girl's hand made Arafa's head spin. He said:

'God have mercy on Adham.'

The Trustee smiled:

'God have mercy on Idris! What makes you think of him?'

'Sitting here.'

'Adham loved dreams but he only knew the ones that Gebelawi put in his head.' He laughed. 'Gebelawi whom you relieved from the torment of old age.'

Arafa was seized with grief and his intoxication vanished. He murmured:

'I never in my life killed anyone except a wicked chief.'

'And Gebelawi's servant?'

341

'I didn't mean to kill him.'

'You're a coward, Arafa.'

He gazed at the moon through the branches, leaving the hashish party and the sounds of the lute, then stole glances at the girl's hand as she packed down the hashish. The Trustee bellowed:

'Where are your thoughts wandering?'

Arafa turned to him and said, smiling:

'Do you stay up like this alone, sir?'

'No one here is fit to join me.'

'Even I have only Hanash to drink with.'

'When you're drunk beyond a certain point it doesn't worry you to be alone.'

Arafa hesitated a little, then said:

'We're prisoners aren't we, your honour.'

'What do you expect as long as we are surrounded by people who hate us?'

He remembered Awaatif's words, and the way she had preferred Omme Zonfol's lodgings to his house. He said with a sigh:

'What a curse!'

'Be careful, or you'll spoil our enjoyment.'

Arafa picked up the pipe.

'May life be always enjoyable.'

Kadri laughed:

'Always! It would be enough if we could keep some of the spirit of youth all our lives by magic.'

Arafa filled his lungs with the night air of the garden, whose fragrance was enhanced by the dew.

'Luckily Arafa is not without his uses.'

The Trustee let the girl take back the pipe and puffed out a thick cloud of smoke, which shone silver in the moonlight. He said sadly:

'Why does old age overtake us? We eat the tastiest food, we drink the finest wines, and we enjoy the best possible life, but age creeps over us when the time comes, and nothing can turn it back any more than the sun or the moon.'

'But Arafa's pills will turn the coldness of old age into warmth.'

'Is there anything that makes you helpless?'

'What would it be sir?'

The Trustee looked sad in the moonlight.

'What do you hate most?'

Perhaps it was the prison in which he had been placed, or perhaps it was the hatred all round him, or else it was the goal he had given up; but he said:

'Losing my youth.'

342

'No, no; you're not afraid of that.'

'How can I not be when my wife has gone off?'

'Women will always find one reason or another to be upset.'

There was a gust of wind, which made the branches rustle and the charcoal glow. Kadri said:

'Why do we die, Arafa?'

Arafa stared at him gloomily but said nothing. Kadri went on:

'Even Gebelawi died.'

It was as if a needle pierced his heart, but he said:

'May your life be long, sir.'

'Long or short, the end is that pit of worms.'

'Don't let thoughts spoil your tranquility.'

'They won't leave me. Death ... death ... always death. It comes at any time and for the slightest reason, or for no reason at all. Where is Gebelawi? Where are the storytellers' heroes? There should be no death.'

Arafa glanced at him and saw his pale face and his troubled eyes. There was a complete contradiction between his state of mind and his surroundings. Arafa was uneasy and said:

'The important thing is life.'

Kadri waved his hand angrily and said with such feeling that all tranquility vanished:

'Life is fine; it has everything. Even youth can be brought back by your pills. But what use is all that when death follows like a shadow? How can I forget, when it comes back into my mind every hour?'

He enjoyed Kadri's suffering, but soon he despised his own feelings. He followed the girl's hand with intense longing, and wondered: 'Who can guarantee that I'll see the moon again?' Then he said:

'Perhaps we need more wine.'

'Its effects would be gone in the morning.'

Arafa felt contempt for him. He thought this was a good opportunity and he took it, saying:

'If it wasn't for the envy of those around us who are deprived, the taste of life would change in our mouths.'

The Trustee laughed scornfully.

'Talk of the impossible! Suppose we could raise the life of the people to our level, would death stop hunting us?'

Arafa nodded and waited for Kadri's scorn to subside, then said:

'Death breeds where there's poverty and misery and bad conditions.'

'*And* where there are none of those things, you fool.'

Arafa smiled.

'Yes, because it's contagious.'

The Trustee laughed.

'That's a strange argument to hide your helplessness.'

Arafa took courage from his laughter.

'We don't know anything about it; it may be like that. As people's conditions improve life grows in value. Every happy man has felt the urge to struggle to bring others to happiness.'

'And that's not an atom of use.'

'Oh, but it is. The magicians will join forces to resist death. Everyone who is able will work with magic. And so death will be threatened with death.'

The Trustee laughed loudly, then closed his eyes and was lost in dreams. Arafa took the pipe and drew a long puff till it glowed. After an interval the lute sounded again and the sweet voice sang: 'Be long oh night.'

'You're a hashish addict, Arafa, not a magician.'

'That's how we kill death.'

The Trustee listened to the music unenthusiastically for a while, then said:

'Oh, if only you could succeed, Arafa! What would you do if you succeeded?'

The words seemed to burst out:

'I'd bring Gebelawi back to life.'

Kadri grimaced.

'That's you business, you are his murderer.'

Arafa frowned and muttered inaudibly:

'Oh, if only you could succeed, Arafa!'


# 111 ✳ ✳ ✳ ✳ ✳ ✳ ✳ ✳ ✳ ✳ ✳ ✳ ✳ ✳ ✳ ✳ ✳

Arafa left the Trustee's house at dawn. He walked in a drugged man's enchanted world, full of blurred sounds and sights. His feet would hardly carry him. He went towards his house across the sleeping alley bathed in moonlight. Half-way across, in front of the gate of the Big House a phantom looked up and whispered to him:

'Good morning, Mr Arafa.'

He was terrified, perhaps out of shock, but his two guards leapt on the figure and caught hold of it. He peered at it and saw, in spite of his blurred vision, that it was a Negress dressed in a black gown from shoulder to foot. He ordered his servants to let her go, then asked her:

'What do you want, woman?'

'I want to speak to you alone.'

'Why?'

'I'm an unhappy woman with a plea to make.'

344

He said with annoyance, making as if to go:

'May God be gracious to you!'

She implored him.

'By the life of our dear ancestor, please won't you let me?'

He gave her an angry look, but his eyes did not leave her; where and when had he seen that face before? His heart pounded and his intoxication vanished. This was the face he had seen in the doorway of Gebelawi's room as he hid behind the chair on the fateful night. This was Gebelawi's servant who had shared his room. His limbs went weak with fear and he gaped at her. One of his servants asked:

'Shall we chase her off?'

'Go to the gate of my house and wait for me.'

He waited till they had gone and he was alone with her in front of the Big House. He studied her thin, Negro face with the high, narrow forehead, the pointed chin and the wrinkles round the mouth and brows. He felt certain that she had not seen him that night; but where had she been since Gebelawi's death, and what brought her now? He said:

'Yes, my good woman?'

'I have no plea; I wanted to be alone with you to carry out someone's will.'

'What will?'

She leaned towards him a little and said:

'I was Gebelawi's servant and I was with him when he died.'

'You?'

'Yes! Believe me.'

He needed no proof. He asked her in a confused voice:

'How did the old man die?'

'He was grief-stricken when his servant's body was found, and all of a sudden there he was at death's door. I hurried over to support his trembling back – that great man who had subdued the desert!'

Arafa sighed deeply. His head was bowed in sorrow. The woman went back to her first line of thought.

'I have come to carry out his will.'

He looked up at her, trembling.

'What do you mean? Talk!'

She said in a voice as gentle as the moonlight:

'Before he gave up the ghost, he said: "Go to Arafa the magician and tell him for me that his grandfather died pleased with him." '

'Liar! What's your scheme?'

'Sir! Please!'

'Tell me what game you're playing.'

'Nothing but what I've said, so help me God!'

He asked her suspiciously:

'What do you know about the murderer?'

'I don't know anything, sir. Since my master died I've been bed-ridden. The first thing I've done since getting better is come and see you.'

'What did he say to you?'

' "Go to Arafa the magician and tell him for me that his grandfather died pleased with him." '

'Liar! You know, you cunning creature, that I . . .' Then, changing his tone: 'How did you know where I was?'

'I asked about you as soon as I came, and they said you were at the Trustee's so I waited.'

'Didn't they tell you I killed Gebelawi?'

She said in horror:

'No one killed Gebelawi; no one *could* have killed him.'

'You're wrong. The man who killed his servant killed him.'

She shouted angrily:

'Lies and fairy tales! He died in my arms.'

Arafa wanted to cry, but no tears came. He gazed at the woman with half-closed eyes. She said simply:

'Good-bye, then.'

He asked her in a heavy voice:

'Do you swear that you've told the truth?'

'I swear by God; let Him be my witness.'

She left as dawn began to tint the horizon. He followed her with his eyes until she disappeared, then he went. In his bedroom he fainted. After a few minutes he came to and realized that he was dead with fatigue, but he only slept an hour or two before his inner turmoil woke him again. He called Hanash and told him the story of the woman. Hanash stared at him in alarm and, when he had finished, he laughed and said:

'You had a good dose yesterday!'

Arafa was furious.

'What I saw wasn't a hallucination; it was real and there's no doubting it.'

'Sleep. You need to sleep properly.'

'Don't you believe me?'

'Of course I don't. When you've had a good sleep you won't come back to this story.'

'Why don't you believe me?'

Hanash laughed.

'I was at the window as you left the Trustee's house and I saw you cross the road to our house. You stopped for a while in front of the Big House gate; then you went on, followed by your two servants.'

Arafa jumped up and said triumphantly:

'Bring me the two servants.'

Hanash made a gesture of warning.

'No, or they'll doubt your sanity.'

He said with determination:

'I'm going to ask for their evidence in your presence.'

Hanish implored him:

'We have only a little respect now from the servants; don't throw it away.'

Arafa's eyes had a crazed look.

'I'm not mad. It wasn't a hallucination. Gebelawi died pleased with me.'

Hanash said tenderly:

'All right. But don't call any of the servants.'

'If anything terrible happens it will hit you first.'

Hanash said patiently:

'God forbid! Let's call the woman to talk to us herself. Where does she live?'

Arafa frowned as he tried to remember.

'I forgot to ask where she lived.'

'If what you saw had really happened, you wouldn't have let her go.'

Arafa shouted:

'It *did* happen. I'm not mad. Gebelawi died pleased with me.'

Hanash said kindly:

'Don't strain yourself; you need rest.'

He went over to him, stroked his head and gently led him to the bed. He did not leave him until he had lain down. Arafa closed his eyes and soon was fast asleep.

112 ✳ ✳ ✳ ✳ ✳ ✳ ✳ ✳ ✳ ✳ ✳ ✳ ✳ ✳ ✳ ✳

Calmly and firmly Arafa said:

'I've decided to run away.'

Hanash was so astonished that he stopped his work. He looked round cautiously and was frightened, although the door of the workshop was closed. Arafa took no notice of his astonishment and went on working. He said:

'This prison no longer gives me anything but thoughts of death. The pleasure and wine and dancing girls are just the music of death. I seem to smell the grave in every pot of flowers.'

'But death is surely waiting for us in the alley.'

'We'll escape far away from it.' Then, looking into Hanash's eyes: 'And one day we shall come back victorious.'

'If we're able to run away!'

'The villains feel sure of us now. Escape won't be impossible for us.'

They went on with their work silently for a while, then Arafa said:

'Isn't that what you wanted?'

Hanash muttered in embarrassment:

'I'd almost forgotten. But tell me what's made you decide this today?'

Arafa smiled.

'Our ancestor made it known that he was pleased with me. Although I broke into his house and killed his servant.'

Hanash looked astonished again.

'Are you risking your life because of a hallucination?'

'Call it what you like; I'm certain that he died pleased with me. He wasn't angry either at the breaking in or at the murder, but if he could see my present life, the world wouldn't be wide enough for his anger.' Then, in a soft voice: 'And that's why he told me he was pleased.'

Hanash shook his head in amazement.

'You used not to talk about him with respect.'

'That was earlier, when I had many doubts, but now that he's dead . . . The dead have a right to be respected.'

'God have mercy on him.'

'And how can I ever forget that I caused his death, and that because of that I must bring him back to life if I can? If I succeed, we shan't know death.'

Hanash looked at him sadly.

'All that magic has given you so far is pep pills and deadly bottles.'

'We know where magic begins, but we can't imagine where it will end.' Then, looking round the room: 'We shall destroy everything except the book, Hanash; it's the treasure chest of secrets. I shall put it next to my heart. We shan't find escape as hard as you think.'

In the evening Arafa went as usual to the Trustee's house. A little before dawn he returned home. He found Hanash awake and waiting for him. They stayed in the bedroom an hour, until they were sure the servants were asleep. The two of them then crept stealthily to the terrace. The snores of the servant on the terrace came regularly. They went down the steps and towards the gate. Hanash went over to the gatekeeper's bed and clubbed it with a stick, but it struck a cotton dummy and made an alarming noise in the stillness of the night. They were afraid it would wake someone and waited at the gate with pounding hearts. Arafa drew the bolt gently, opened the gate and went out, followed by Hanash. They closed the gate and set off through the darkness and silence, making for Omme Zonfol's house and keeping close to the walls. Half-way down the

348

alley lay a dog. It stood up curiously and ran towards them sniffing. It followed them for a few yards, then stopped and yawned. When they reached the entrance of the house, Arafa whispered:

'Wait for me here. If anything alarms you, whistle to me and escape to Souk Mukattam.'

Arafa went down the entry passage to the stairs and climbed up to Omme Zonfol's room. He tapped on the door till he heard his wife's voice asking who it was. He said eagerly:

'It's Arafa; open up, Awaatif.'

She opened the door and by the light of the lamp in her hand he saw her looking up at him, her face pale and sleepy. He came straight to the point.

'Come with me; we shall run away together.'

She stood looking at him, stupefied. Over her shoulder he saw Omme Zonfol appear. He said:

'We shall run away and live as we used to. Hurry!'

She hesitated, then said, not without annoyance:

'What made you remember me?'

'Leave talking for the proper time. Every minute is precious now.'

There came a whistle from Hanash followed by uproar. Arafa shouted in a panic:

'The dogs! We've lost our chance, Awaatif.'

He rushed to the top of the stairs and saw lights and people in the courtyard below. He went back in despair. Awaatif said:

'Come in here.'

Omme Zonfol said harshly, in self defence:

'No, don't come in.'

What was the use of going in? He pointed to the little window in the entrance to the lodgings and asked his wife hurriedly:

'What does it look on to?'

'The light-shaft.'

Taking the book from his breast he rushed to the window, pushing Omme Zonfol aside, and threw it out. Then he hurried out through the door, which closed behind him, bounded up the few steps to the roof and looked over the parapet into the alley. It was swarming with figures and torches. He heard the noise of men coming up to get him and ran to the wall dividing the roof from that of the next house in the Gemalia direction. He saw a group, led by a torchbearer, forestalling him. He went back the other way to the wall of the first roof in the Rifaaite quarter. Through the door to that roof he saw torches approaching. He was choking with despair. He thought he heard Omme Zonfol scream. Could they have broken into her lodgings? Had they taken Awaatif? A voice at the door to the roof shouted:

'Give yourself up, Arafa.'

He stood there without a word, ready to surrender. No one came towards him, but a voice said:

'If you throw a bottle, dozens will be thrown back at you.'

'I have nothing.'

They closed in and surrounded him. Among them he saw Yuness, the Trustee's gatekeeper, who came up to him and shouted:

'Criminal! Ungrateful bastard!'

In the alley he saw two men pushing Awaatif along in front of them. He shouted imploringly:

'Let her go! She has nothing to do with me.'

But a blow caught him on the temple and silenced him.


113 ✳ ✳ ✳ ✳ ✳ ✳ ✳ ✳ ✳ ✳ ✳ ✳ ✳ ✳ ✳ ✳ ✳

In front of the enraged Trustee stood Arafa and Awaatif, their hands tied behind their backs. The Trustee beat Arafa in the face. He shouted:

'You sat with me while you were plotting to betray me, you bastard!'

Awaatif said with tears in her eyes:

'He only came to me to make it up with me.'

The Trustee spat in her face and shouted:

'Shut up, you criminal!'

Arafa said:

'She's innocent. She had no hand in anything.'

'Not at all; she was your accomplice in the murder of Gebelawi and all your other crimes.' He roared: 'You wanted to escape; I'll help you to escape from this world altogether.'

He called his men and they brought two sacks. They pushed Awaatif over and quickly bound her feet together, put her into a sack and tied its neck securely. Arafa shouted with almost insane excitement:

'Kill us however you like. Tomorrow your enemies will kill you.'

The Trustee laughed harshly.

'I have enough bottles to protect me for ever.'

Arafa yelled:

'Hanash got away. He escaped with all the secrets. He'll come back one day with irresistible power and he'll rid the alley of your wickedness.'

Kadri kicked him and he fell down writhing. The men leapt at him and dealt with him as they had dealt with his wife, and set off with the two sacks to the desert. Awaatif soon fainted in her sack, but Arafa went on suffering torment. Where were they taking them and what death had they prepared? Would they club them to death? Stone them? Burn them? Or would they throw them down from the top of the gebel? How terrible was the pain that filled these last minutes of life! Even magic offered no escape from this choking, rending pain. His head, which was throbbing from the Trustee's blow, was at the bottom of the sack, and he was almost suffocating. Death was his only hope of release. He would die and with him would die hope; and that man with his harsh laugh might well live long. Those whose deliverance he had longed for would rejoice at his death. Who could tell what Hanash would do? The men who were carrying them to their death were silent; not one of them said a word. There was nothing but darkness, and beyond darkness, death. For fear of death he had put himself under the Trustee's protection and lost everything; and yet death had come – death, which destroyed life with fear even before it struck. If he could have lived again, he would have shouted to everyone: 'Don't be afraid; fear doesn't ward off death, but it wards off life. You people of our alley, you are not alive; life will never be granted to you as long as you fear death.'

One of the killers said:

'Here?'

Another protested:

'The ground is moist here.'

His heart fluttered, although he did not understand what they meant, but in any case it was the language of death. The agony of suspense grew still more intense till he almost shouted: 'Kill me!' Suddenly the sack fell to the ground and Arafa groaned as his head struck the ground and pain shot through his neck and spine. From moment to moment he expected the cudgels to descend or worse to happen. He cursed the whole of life because of evil, the ally of death. He heard Yuness say:

'Dig fast so that we can get back before morning.'

'Why were they digging the grave before killing them? He felt as if Gebel Mukattam were resting on his chest. He heard a moaning which he soon recognized as that of Awaatif, and his trussed body heaved violently. Then the sound of the digging filled his ears. He marvelled at the hardness of men's hearts. Yuness announced that they were to be buried alive. Awaatif screamed and he shouted meaninglessly. Strong hands lifted them into the pit and shovelled the earth back. A cloud of dust rose in the darkness.

The news about Arafa spread through the alley. No one knew the real reasons for his death, but they guessed that he had annoyed his master and that the latter had brought him to his inevitable fate. At some time it got around that he had been killed by the same magical weapon as he had used to kill Saadallah and Gebelawi. The people took pleasure in his death, despite their hatred for the Trustee, and the relatives and friends of the chiefs rejoiced. They were pleased at the killing of the man who had killed their blessed ancestor and given their tyrannical Trustee a dreadful weapon with which to keep them for ever in servitude. The future looked black, blacker than it had ever been, now that power was concentrated in the hands of one cruel man. There was no longer the hope that a quarrel might break out between the two men and lead to both of them being weakened and one of them siding with the people. It seemed that nothing was left for them but subjection and that they must regard the estate and its conditions and the words of Gebel and Rifaa and Kassem as forlorn dreams, fit only for the storytellers' songs and not for putting into practice.

One day a man accosted Omme Zonfol as she was going to Derrasa.

'Good evening, Omme Zonfol.'

She looked closely at him and in a moment exclaimed:

'Hanash!'

He came nearer to her and smiled.

'Did the dead man leave anything at your place the night he was caught?'

Anxious to avoid trouble, she replied:

'He didn't leave anything. I saw him throw his papers into the light-shaft. I went the next day and found a worthless book amongst the rubbish, no use at all, so I left it.'

Hanash's eyes shone strangely.

'Help me to find the book.'

The old woman started with fright and shouted:

'Go away! But for God's grace you would have died too that night.'

He pressed a coin into her hand and she calmed down. He arranged to meet her in the small hours, when everyone would be asleep. At the appointed time she led him to the bottom of the light-shaft and he lit a candle and crouched by the heaps of rubbish looking for Arafa's book. He sifted them paper by paper and rag by rag, poking his fingers into sand and dust, shreds of tobacco and fragments of rotting food. But he did not find what he was looking for. He went back to Omme Zonfol and said resentfully in his despair:

'I didn't find anything.'

She retorted angrily:

'You are nothing to do with me. When you come disasters follow.'

'Patience, mother!'

'Time has taken away our patience. Tell me why that book interests you.'

Hanash hesitated, then said:

'It's Arafa's book.'

'Arafa! God forgive him! He killed Gebelawi, then gave the Trustee his magic and went.'

'He was one of the best people that ever lived, but luck was against him. He wanted the things that Gebel and Rifaa and Kassem wanted for you, and more.'

She looked at him suspiciously, then said, to get rid of him:

'Perhaps the dustman took the rubbish with the book in it. Look for it by the incinerators at Salihia.'

Hanash went to the incinerators and found the dustman of Gebelawi Alley. He asked him about the rubbish. The man said:

'You're looking for something you lost? What is it?'

'A book.'

The man looked suspicious but pointed to a corner next to the bath house.

'Try your luck. Either you find it there or it's been burnt.'

Hanash began searching through the rubbish patiently and hopefully. The book was the only hope he had left in the world; it was his hope and the hope of the alley. The unfortunate Arafa had died defeated, leaving behind him only evil and a foul reputation. This book could make good his mistakes and destroy his enemies and reawaken hope. The dustman asked:

'Haven't you found what you're looking for?'

'Please, give me time.'

The man scratched his armpits.

'What's so important about the book?'

'It has our accounts in it; you shall see for yourself.'

He went on with his search with mounting fears, until he heard a voice he knew saying:

'Where's the bean pot, Metwalli?'

Hanash was horrified to hear the voice of Amme Shankal, the man who sold stewed beans in the alley. He did not turn round, but he wondered anxiously whether the man could have seen him and whether it would be best to run away now. His hands burrowed away still faster.

Amme Shankal went back to the alley to tell everyone he met that he had seen Hanash, Arafa's friend, at the Salihia incinerators busily hunting through the rubbish for a book, so the dustman had told him. No sooner had the news reached the Trustee's house than a party of servants set out for the incinerators, but they found no trace of Hanash. When the dustman was asked, he said he had gone to see about something, and when he had come back Hanash had already gone, so he did not know whether he had found what he was looking for.

Nobody knows how people first began whispering it around that the book Hanash had taken was none other than the book of magic in which Arafa had set down the secrets of his art and of his weapons. The rumour spread from one hashish den to another that Hanash would finish what Arafa had begun and would take a terrible revenge on the Trustee. The Trustee added force to these rumours by promising a huge reward to anyone who brought Hanash alive or dead, as his men proclaimed in the cafés and in the hashish dens. No one doubted any longer the part that Hanash was expected to play in their lives. A wave of joy and optimism swept away their despair and servility, and people were filled with love for Hanash in his unknown refuge; moreover their love extended to the memory of Arafa himself. They longed to help Hanash in his stand against the Trustee, to make his victory their own and secure a life of justice and peace. They were ready to help him in any way they could, seeing in him, the only path to deliverance; for it seemed that the magical power possessed by the Trustee could only be defeated by a similar power such as Hanash was perhaps making ready.

The Trustee heard of what people were whispering and instructed the storyteller in the cafés to sing the story of Gebelawi, emphasizing how he had died at the hand of Arafa, and how the Trustee had been forced to make a truce with the killer and be friendly with him for fear of his magic, until he was able to kill him in revenge for their mighty ancestor. The remarkable thing was that the people met the storytellers' lies with indifference and mockery. They grew so stubborn in their resistance that they said: 'The past is nothing to us. Our only hope is Arafa's magic. If we had to choose between Gebelawi and magic, we would choose magic.'

Day by day the truth about Arafa was revealed to people. It may have originated with Omme Zonfol, for she knew a great deal about him from Awaatif, or it may have come from Hanash himself when he happened to meet people far away. The point was that people knew about the man and about the good things he had wanted for them. They were astonished by the truth and they venerated his memory and exalted his name even above those of Gebel, Rifaa and Kassem. Some people said he could not possibly have been the killer of Gebelawi as was supposed, and others said he was the most important man the alley had known, even if he had killed Gebelawi. Each quarter claimed him for its own.

354

Then young men began disappearing, one by one. It was said in explanation that they had found their way to Hanash and had joined him, and that he was teaching them magic in preparation for the promised day of deliverance. Fear gripped the Trustee and his men, and they sent spies into every corner and searched every house and every shop. They fixed the harshest punishments for the slightest offences and lashed out for a glance or a joke or a laugh, so that the alley lived in a terrible atmosphere of fear and hatred and intimidation. But people bore the oppression bravely and took refuge in patience and hope. Whenever they suffered injustice they said: 'Oppression must cease as night yields to day. We shall see the end of tyranny and the dawn of miracles.'